DAUGHTER OF DESIRE . . .

Majella stood at the fountain, trembling, sick with sudden longing. Desire for Joaquín rose like creeping fire in her body. *Oh, Mother of God, help me.* She stared down into the slow-moving water, striving against it, but even as she did she could almost feel the touch of Joaquín's hands, his seeking lips.

Carefully, in case anyone was watching, she turned from the fountain and walked to a bench in the shade, her body aching for Joaquín. Forget him. Blot him out. She would never see him again. He would go his dangerous way and meet his terrible end. . . .

"Joaquín," she whispered, "I want to go with you. *I* want to." She was admitting it clearly and openly for the first time, and to them both, that she was no longer his unwilling captive, that to feel whole she must be with him. And of her own volition, her own desire. "I love you—I think of you constantly. You are my love and it will be forever."

The old dream from her childhood came and went in her mind: That dark night. Her mother walking silently beside the tired man who was her father and whose face she never saw. She knew now that her mother would have walked to the end of the world beside that man. Looking at Joaquín, she felt it was happening all over again.

This was the man she would walk to the end of the earth with. There was no other way for her. It did not matter that their love had been born in violence and conflict. The love had been born. It lived now. . . .

Also by Virginia Myers:

Californio!
This Land I Hold

Ramona's Daughter

Virginia Myers

PINNACLE BOOKS   NEW YORK

RAMONA'S DAUGHTER

Copyright © 1981 by Virginia Myers

An original Pinnacle Books edition, published for the first time anywhere.

First printing, September 1981

ISBN: 0-523-40964-8

Cover illustration by John Solie

Printed in the United States of America

PINNACLE BOOKS, INC.
1430 Broadway
New York, New York 10018

A Letter
From the Author
To the Reader

Dear Reader:

As you open this book do you have a question in mind? Do you wonder how a modern novelist can have the sheer nerve to attempt a sequel to the old and beloved classic *Ramona*, by Helen Hunt Jackson? The thought occurred to me, too, when the project idea was first presented by Gaye Tardy, the imaginative editor with whom I had worked on a previous book.

My initial, astonished *I-wouldn't-dare* reaction almost immediately was countered by the instinctive reaction of the storyteller. The storyteller thought that it would be fascinating to know the story—never told—of that beautiful child of Ramona and her beloved, the Indian Alessandro: What became of her? How did she live out her life? I would certainly like to read that story if someone wrote it.

Ramona, you will recall, was the half-Scottish, half-Indian ward of a prominent California Mexican family. Her guardian, Señora Gonzaga Moreno, a cold, strong, manipulating woman, despised the girl. Señora Moreno's son, Felipe, however, was a kind and gentle man who loved Ramona. But Ramona, following her heart, eloped with an Indian ranch worker, Alessandro

v

Assis. This act so infuriated Señora Moreno that she disowned Ramona, and withheld from her information about her birth and her inheritance of some jewels.

The love of Ramona and Alessandro was doomed from the start. Alessandro, like many early California Indians, suffered deep griefs and privations, such as the loss of land and village, and loss of loved ones. His growing uncertainty and distrust grew despite his efforts and personal courage, and he was unable to cope successfully with the flood of American settlers coming into California.

Ramona's and Alessandro's life together was a series of innocent strivings and bitter defeats, each more hurtful than the last. With deepening anguish, Ramona not only must experience the death of her first daughter, but also must watch the slow disintegration of the once strong and wise Alessandro, her always beloved husband, until at last—when even his fine mind is gone—she sees his tragic death.

Shattered and crushed by this ultimate of defeats, Ramona is finally discovered by her old friend, Felipe Moreno. She is sick and destitute in a poverty-stricken Indian village. Señora Moreno, Felipe's bitter implacable mother, has died. Felipe takes Ramona and her surviving infant daughter home to the rancho with him.

Eventually, he decides to return to Mexico and Ramona consents to marry him. Although both of them know that her love still belongs to the dead Alessandro, Ramona does attain, if never happiness now, at least a measure of peace. She and Felipe have other children, but her first daughter—Alessandro's daughter, with her shadowed beginnings—remains their cherished favorite.

In each of my previous novels I had always worked alone—my idea; my characters; my story beginning, middle, ending; my complete concept. Was it even possible for me to build a story on foundations left by someone else? Intimidating, yes—but so intriguing that the idea would not go away. Meanwhile, the storyteller was hard at work tossing up all sorts of thoughts, questions, and musings, so that the back-and-forth confusion between *I wouldn't dare* and *I must* became . . . *I can try*!

There is, of course, never just one reason why something comes about; it is always a collection of reasons. In thinking about it now, I can see some of the many small reasons why Gaye Tardy's idea held such fascination for me personally. First, I grew up a Californian, spending my early years in San Fernando, one of the original California Mission towns. I remember the year my mother decided that I might have as my birthday party a picnic in the old Mission gardens, among the lawns and flowers and that statue of Father Junípero Serra and the Indian boy. There, forgetting for a time my picnic-party, I wandered around in the Mission, which is one of the best preserved in the Mission chain. Always a book-reading, daydreaming child, I believe it may have been there that I fell in love with the past.

Part of the past was to be the book *Ramona*, which I would read and reread, the film *Ramona*, and the play *Ramona*, both to be seen and seen again whenever I had the chance. How much this one work by Helen Hunt Jackson influenced my own writing later I can only guess. But when I did start to write in the novel form, I began with early California. I was so *Californian*, so immersed in the past and present of that golden land that it did not occur to me to start with anything else.

Then there was the manner in which Helen Hunt Jackson ended her book *Ramona*. Some of the final words on the last page are: ". . . but the most beautiful of them all and, it was said, the most beloved by both father and mother, was the eldest one . . . stepdaughter to the Señor . . . daughter of Alessandro, the Indian . . ." Millions of readers have read the ending with satisfaction and laid the book aside. Others also may have thought about that beautiful, "most beloved" daughter and wondered about her. She had been given both her mother's Spanish name of Ramona and her mother's Indian name, "Majella," a derivative of "Majel" or "Wood Dove." So it would seem, then, that she was not intended to lose her Indian heritage.

What would the daughter of Ramona and Alessandro make of her life? How would she fare? Would she have the same capacity for undying love and limitless courage that her mother Ramona had had? Would Majella know the soul-shattering defeats her father, Alessandro, had known? The fascinating storyteller words of *What if*—must have occurred to many readers of *Ramona*. Gaye Tardy also thought 'What if—' and further wondered if another writer now could write this story of the most beloved daughter of Ramona. I shall be forever pleased that she knew my work and thought I could do it.

For my first California novel, *Californio!,*° I had buried myself in the lotus-land of the 1830's and 40's, the era of the building of the great ranchos under Spain and Mexico. In my second novel, *This Land I Hold,*°° I became lost for two years in California of the 1850's and 60's. It was the turbulent time during which California became part of the United States, whereupon the subdivision of the big estates, emerged—the impact again of one culture upon another.

Now, for *Ramona's Daughter*, I would plunge into the 1870's and 80's and into the lives of those lost people, the California Indians—wanderers adrift in the new alien culture, their very identity fragmented and

° *Californio!* (Los Angeles: Pinnacle Books, 1979).
°° *This Land I Hold* (Los Angeles: Pinnacle Books, 1980).

lost. In a tragic, almost self-destructive drive, they adopted whatever shreds they could of the white man's ways, further blurring their own distinctive image and losing—indeed, almost discarding—whole segments of their history. As a result, sometimes no record will exist of that ceremony, or this custom, or the original name of a tribe. They imitated Spaniards, Mexicans, Americans, forgetting if at all possible that they were Indians because—and there was no way for them to escape it—*they were considered of no value.* Dispersed, despised, invisible—existence was so grim and so bleak that ever increasing numbers of them began to accept the idea that it was better not to exist at all. Self-induced abortion became widely practiced among the women and their people gradually diminished to a remnant of their former numbers. It was a giving up, a letting go, a hopeless surrender. And it was this sorrowful heritage that would be Majella's true heritage, the legacy from her real father, Alessandro.

I started my think-work on *Ramona's Daughter* by a careful rereading of the original *Ramona*—not as an eager reader now, but as another writer reading analytically, searchingly. This cherished story, my old favorite, became my textbook. To my great satisfaction, I found that Helen Hunt Jackson's primary characters had been developed so well and were so fully realized that they provided a great variety of foundation stones upon which some later author, following in her footsteps, could build. Since I had agreed that another story indeed could be told, I found that reading the book was like a treasure hunt. Idea after idea now sprang from the pages to my mind.

If Majella had been the "most beloved" of the children, how would her half siblings feel about this?

If Majella is living in Mexico as the beautiful and privileged daughter of Felipe Moreno, how would she ever experience her real California Indian heritage?

Did Majella even know that she was more Indian than white? If she did not know, what would she do if she found out?

And what other legacies did Majella receive from other forebears? Here I found a splendid foundation stone: Her unknown Scottish grandfather, Angus Phail, was very fully characterized. He was a man of force and inner violence, willing to gamble with everything he had for what he wanted. Could there be an imprint from him in Majella? What then of Ramona's father, Angus Phail?

As an example, the book *Ramona* says, of the tragic Angus, that he had been "well born in Scotland" and "owner of one of the richest line of ships that traded along the coast." His temperament was such that when he loved he could not accept rejection, becoming unbalanced. " . . . until one of the commonest sights to be seen in Santa Barbara was Angus Phail reeling about, tipsy, coarse, loud, profane, dangerous." Then Angus, after dissipating his fortune, dropped from sight, "and after a time news came up from Los Angeles that he was there, had gone out to the San Gabriel Mission, and was living with the Indians. Some years later came . . . the news that he had married a squaw . . . with several Indian children . . ."

So this Indian woman with several children had become Ramona's mother and Majella's unknown grandmother. This yielded another fine stone. Somewhere, unknown to herself, Majella could have kinsmen among the Indians, people who had been half-brothers and half-sisters to her mother, Ramona. It also seemed to say that Majella might have a "streak of madness" where her loved ones were concerned, that she might have the capacity to throw everything away, make any sacrifice, for the sake of her love.

Then there were the Ortegna jewels, a gem collection that had left a trail of sorrow through two generations. In the book *Ramona* these jewels are destined finally to come to Ramona's daughter, Majella. Ramona says to Felipe of the jewels, "I have thought it all over about those jewels. I believe it will be all right for my daughter to have them. Can some kind of paper be written . . ." So the jewels are there—somewhere—waiting for Majella. How would she receive them? What impact would they have on her life?

Helen Hunt Jackson did not live a long life, but she was a prolific writer. One could not have seen her 'retiring' from writing. The book *Ramona* was published a year before her death; as I found one thing after another that seemed to lead naturally into another story, I could not help but wonder: Did she intend perhaps to write this book herself? One never will know for sure, but it seems likely, does it not? The beginnings were there, all laid out and waiting. Why had they had to wait so long? I was convinced now that Majella's story was certainly worth writing and I wanted, most fervently, to be the one to write it.

This, in turn, raised the question of style: How to tell the story? I accepted at the outset that I should not—possibly could not—imitate the leisurely narrative style of another era. As Helen Hunt Jackson had written *Ramona* in the style of her time, I knew I must write *Ramona's Daughter* in the style of ours.

I set to work on the story with deep pleasure, with some sorrow, with excitement at times, with anger and joy—and always with love. I hand it to you now as the story of Majella, and I hope you find her worthy to be Ramona's daughter. Let me know?

Faithfully,
Virginia Myers

This book is dedicated to the memory of

Helen Hunt Jackson

She was born Helen Maria Fiske on October 15, 1831, in Amherst, Massachusetts, and died on August 12, 1885, in San Francisco. Between those two dates and places she lived her life as a valiant human being and a great woman. She was a poet, novelist, essayist, humanitarian, wife, mother, widow—and her nation's relentless conscience regarding the then deplorable conditions of the Native Americans.

Upon the tragic deaths of her husband, Captain Edward Hunt, and her two sons, she rose above personal grief and concentrated on her writing and the other tasks she had assigned to herself. Nor did she cease these labors when she became a wife again by marrying William Jackson in 1875. One has to pause and ponder that in her lifetime it was a rare woman who sought more than those worthwhile roles of wife and mother. That she found she must seek more, and managed somehow to carry it off, is evidenced by her achievements.

Her continuing efforts on behalf of the American Indians resulted in her stern indictment of the government's Indian policy in several articles published in *Century Magazine*, and culminated in *A Century of Dishonor*, published in 1881. She was subsequently appointed to a federal commission investigating the Indian situation. The mass of materials she gathered in her work on this commission gave her the rich background for *Ramona*, published in 1884, a year before her death.

One does wish that somehow she could have known that her final labor of love for the American Indians would become the classic Indian story, and would live on to touch the hearts and minds of millions of readers yet unborn. One does wish that.

Ramona's Daughter

Chapter One

They said she must sign a receipt for the jewels, and for the letter, and this seemed somehow to make all three men uneasy. Señor Aguilar, who had always handled the family's business affairs, did not meet her eyes. Miguel, her rock during their bereavement, drummed his fingers lightly on the surface of the polished table as if impatient—and Miguel was never impatient. Hernán, her other brother, said, stammering slightly:

"Don't forget, you must use Mama's name, Majella. Your—your—your Christian name is the same as hers was." Hernán was glib, clever, smooth. Hernán never stammered. He did not avoid her eyes, but he looked as if he wanted to cry. How strange all this was. Senseless. The way a dream is senseless but goes on anyway. Hiding any sign of increasing disquiet, as Mama had always taught them, Majella extended her hand in a graceful gesture.

"By all means," she said, smiling at them, feel-

1

ing greater disquiet when no one returned her smile. "Is Cecilia to sign also? Perhaps we should call her. I think she's out in the garden with Eduardo." She took the paper and, without reading it, wrote her legal name, Ramona Moreno, in graceful script where Señor Aguilar's finger indicated. She was not surprised to notice that Señor Aguilar's finger quivered just slightly. He took the paper and folded it quickly.

Miguel said, "You will not share these jewels with Cecilia, Majella. They are to be yours—a special legacy left to you by Mama. They were hers and it seems her wish was that they be yours. She—never wore them," he ended.

"Cecilia doesn't know of it yet," Hernán said, but then stopped, although he clearly had intended to add something else.

"Well, then," Majella said pleasantly, rising from the table, "let us have some chocolate—now that our business is done. Cecilia and Eduardo will be coming in soon. Hernán, would you ring the bell? You are closest."

Señor Aguilar was restless. "Forgive me, my dear. I must deny myself the pleasure of visiting with you at the moment." He had nervously folded the receipt into smaller and smaller squares until it was a ridiculous size. Majella held back a smile. He poked it down into an inside jacket pocket where it made a small lump. "But I shall return to dine, as Miguel was good enough to suggest this morning."

"Then I shall forgive you for rushing away," Majella said, offering her hand and knowing somehow that his would be damp when it touched hers.

An Indian maid, in anticipation of what was wanted, entered with a loaded tray. She hastily concealed a look of astonishment that the guest was leaving so quickly. At Majella's gesture she placed the tray on the low table amid a cluster of chairs near the balcony windows. They were open, for the front of the house was shady in the afternoon. The warm Mexican sun would now be over the kitchen garden and stable. There was a lazy breeze and the flame-red bougainvillea vine moved indolently now and then. Little patches of shadow and light played back and forth across the tiled floor. The scent from the orange blossoms in the garden below was heady.

"I think I shall have to share those jewels with Cecilia," Majella said, picking up the chocolate pot to pour. She was long accustomed to placating her younger sister. How odd that Miguel had sent the maid away with a dismissive gesture. Well, it didn't matter. She was really quite able to pour chocolate into the cups and hand them to her brothers. One lived such an idle life as it was.

"When are we to be finished with all the estate business?" she asked, half laughing to hide her feeling of exasperation.

Miguel put down his cup without tasting of it. "Legal matters take forever," he said. "And Papa's estate is extensive." His eyes were resting morosely on the leather jewel casket still on the other table. "It has been a year and a half and still things come to light—one never knows what will turn up next. Thank God Señor Aguilar is so thorough—he will unearth it all."

Majella sipped her chocolate, observing her two younger brothers, so similar and so different.

3

Both, though somewhat darker, had Papa's handsome features, but there the resemblance between the two brothers ended. Miguel was the quiet one, the steady one. How fortunate, in a way, that he was the elder son who had inherited and would eventually manage the Felipe Moreno holdings. Responsible, thoughtful, always mature beyond his years. Born to take care of others. And Hernán— her eyes softened as she looked at him and a smile touched her lips: Hernán, the youngest of the four of them, born full of laughter, born to enjoy life and in so doing enrich the lives of all around him. Hernán was one of God's vivid people.

"I suppose those jewels are quite old," Majella said, putting down the delicate china cup. Why did she feel so uneasy about this? "But I suppose Luis will be pleased." She laughed lightly. "If I have suddenly inherited a box of jewels he won't have to buy me any. So I shan't be so expensive a wife." Why, then, was she so reluctant even to open the box? She was exasperated with herself.

Miguel cleared his throat and Hernán got up, rather suddenly, and went to stand at the windows, his back to them.

"The letter was written by Papa, Majella. I read it. There was a brief note to me, instructing me to read it first. As the heir, and as your brother and guardian—"

"Of course, Miguel," she agreed, eager to set his mind at rest. "You must read everything like that."

"Well, I think we should get on with it," Miguel said, sounding as if the last thing he wanted to do was get on with it.

4

Hernán turned from the window. "Perhaps Majella would like to read the letter in private."

"I thought the jewels were from Mama," Majella said. She fixed Miguel with a polite, level stare. It was an old signal from their childhood. Majella's eyes were a much darker brown than those of her brothers, and they could become opaque and expressionless when she was becoming displeased. It seemed an inner retreating, a closing away of her personality that was almost Indian-like in its silent withdrawal. It always totally unnerved Miguel.

"Yes, of course," he said too briskly. He made several halting beginnings. "It is not really good news, Majella, which is why it is so difficult—the jewels are from Mama, true, but she never wore them because—the letter, of course, is from Papa because—"

Majella sighed gently. Another old signal.

"Oh, Majella, I am sorry." He sounded miserable. "We all love you so—so dearly." For a moment he sounded very young.

"I'll read the letter, Miguel. Now." Majella got up and brushed a reassuring caress on her brother's head as she passed him.

Being three years older had always given her a slight advantage over Miguel; despite the fact that she was a girl, she was the first-born. Then after three years, Mama had borne four more children in yearly succession—Miguel, Cecilia, Hernán, and Francisca. Only the infant Francisca had never quickened into life, and Mama had been ill—sick unto death—for a long time. She had recovered, but there had been no more brothers and sisters.

5

Beautiful, gentle, serene Ramona Moreno emerged again from the sickroom to be with her family, but the sense of her inner fragility had increased. Sometimes—and this was fanciful, of course—Mama's deep blue eyes had held a pensive look of waiting. Sometimes there was just a hint of absent-mindedness in her conduct. As if she were gently and politely going through all the motions of living because they all needed her. As if she was with them all, but not really of them. As if she were just passing among them on her way to another place or another time.

Majella picked up the thick letter. The old papers crackled faintly in her hands. She felt a wave of love, shadowed by sorrow, at the sight of her father's handwriting. *Oh, most beloved Papa.* She stood by the jewel box and started to read.

My Dearest Daughter Majella, Should this letter ever come into your hands, it will be because your mother and I are no longer there to shield you and protect you with our love. You are the child of my heart, and I would spare you all sadness if I could. It grieves me more than you shall ever know that you are not the child of my body also.

Majella sat down suddenly.

This collection of jewels comes to you from your mother, who received them from her foster mother, Ramona Gonzaga Ortegna. You do not know this name, for it has never been spoken in your hearing. She was a woman heavy-laden with sorrow and your mother, as a child, was her only joy. Señora Ortegna had received the jewels from your grandfather, a man named Angus Phail.

6

Upon Señora Ortegna's death, your mother passed into the custody of my mother, who cared for her faithfully but, alas, without love. This was because your mother was the child of Angus Phail and his Indian wife. My mother—may God rest her soul— carried a burden of strange bitterness, and did not give your mother the jewels in a time when she could have used them. She hid them secretly away . . .

Majella dropped the letter to the table.

"Miguel!" she cried in distraction, disbelief.

Her brother was beside her in an instant. "I should have told you myself," he said, reaching for the letter.

"No. Don't. I—must finish it. He says—Papa says he isn't my father! How could this be so? He says Mama is—Mama was—part Indian. Miguel! I can't believe that!" She was remembering that she was her father's favorite. She was remembering the clear, bright gaze from her mother's steel-blue eyes. Majella picked up the letter again.

. . . she hid them secretly away. Your mother was so happy and carefree in those days, so filled with sunlight. I wish you could have known her then, before it was all shadowed with her sorrow. You see, your mother fell in love with, and married, a worker on our ranch. This was Alessandro Assis, an Indian. Majella, my dearest, despite his race he was a man to respect, and I could call him friend. He was very kind to me. . . .

No, she thought desperately. I cannot believe this!

Upon your father's death, your mother returned to me with you in her arms. In time, her grief was covered over and she did me the honor to become

7

*my wife. I must tell you also of the tragic life of
Angus Phail, your grandfather. . . .*

Majella stopped reading. At some point she had
put the letter back down on the table again and
clasped her hands in her lap. A voice echoed in
her mind, her own voice, speaking out of childhood.

"Mama, why am I called 'Majella'? What is it?
What does it mean?" And her mother, in her gentle, tranquil voice, replying,

"It is really 'Majel.' It is an Indian word, meaning 'Wood Dove.' Isn't that a lovely name? Not
every little girl can have such a lovely name."

"Miguel, I—feel a little faint." And she thought
how ridiculous that was, for she was always in the
best of health.

"I'll ring for—"

"No, wait." She reached up and caught his arm,
leaning against his strong body for a moment.
"Oh, Miguel," she whispered into the dark fabric
of his jacket. "What am I to do? What am I to tell
him?" And they both knew that she meant Luis,
whose wife she was to become within a few
weeks.

Hernán came over from his place by the windows, walking slowly and with a kind of insolence,
a little strut he sometimes assumed.

"Why must we tell him anything at all? He can
count himself lucky to marry Majella Moreno."

"I'm not Majella Moreno," she said dully. "That
is the point, Hernán. I cannot go to him without—
I must—I could not in honesty—"

"All right," Hernán said airily. "Just tell him!
Say to him, 'Luis, my dear, I hope all your grand

8

Chavero ancestors don't object, but my mother was half Indian, you see, so it must follow that my brothers and sister are also in lesser degree.'"

"Hernán," Miguel spoke in annoyance.

Hernán smoothed the folds of his black silk sash, ignoring his brother. "And as luck would have it, Luis, I'm not who you thought I was either. A little detail no one mentioned before, but Felipe Moreno was not my father. My real father was—"

"Hernán!"

"All right! But can't you just see how he will take it? I don't condemn Luis. I like Luis. But you must admit that he carries on his back a load of family pride too big for any man. He must *not* be told. He could *never* accept it. And I don't want Majella—to be hurt." He stopped because his voice quavered. He turned away in embarrassment.

A false calmness settled over Majella. She picked up the letter and folded it. She could not possibly read any more at this time.

"There is no need for me to tell him about Mother," she said carefully. "The only need is to tell him that *my father* was an Indian. That would give him a fair choice. If he wishes to end the betrothal, then we shall, but he must be able to decide."

Miguel's face had colored. "We are the family, Majella. We stand together in all things."

"Not all," she answered softly, reaching up to touch his cheek. "You are Felipe Moreno's son. I am not his daughter." She thought her heart might break as she said it. "If Mama had wanted the world to know that she was half Indian, she would have spoken. She did not. She was the wife of Felipe Moreno, and bore his children, and graced his house. Never in her life would she do anything to embarrass him."

"But Majella—"

"You have no choice that I can see, Miguel." She placed her fingers over his lips. "Without ever saying a word about it, Mama decided for you. You must accept that." Looking confused and troubled, Miguel sat down slowly on the other side of the table, holding onto her hand, almost clinging to it.

"Well," Hernán said, coming back. "Cecilia will have to be told, of course. It is her affair, too."

"And Eduardo. He's her husband. A husband has a right—" Miguel said, still deeply troubled.

"Eduardo won't care. Not that much." Hernán snapped his fingers. "He is so besotted with Cecilia you wouldn't think they had been married almost six months. He'll always be besotted with her. Some men are born to be besotted. Cecilia could be part burro and he wouldn't care. Sometimes I think she may be."

"Hernán. Don't speak of your sister like that," Majella reprimanded, making her voice like their mother's and causing them to laugh, although somewhat faintly. There was a sudden feeling of closeness, of coming together, and she closed her eyes for a moment. Then she rose. There was an inward shivering.

"Miguel, will you do one favor for me? I would rather you talk to Cecilia. I think I'll go to my room for a while before dinner."

"Of course." He was on his feet. "Anything, Majella."

10

"Oh, dear, Señor Aguilar is coming to dinner."

"No, he won't," Hernán said. "I know my godfather for the man he is—a man of great tact. I'll bet you both that he will send a little note saying he is indisposed. He will know we want just family tonight."

"Of course," Miguel said, relieved. "Go on up, Majella. I will talk with Cecilia and Eduardo."

"Thank you," she said. The sense of inward shivering increased. She must take the box with her. She looked at it with fascination. The box of heavy, hateful jewelry that had smashed into her life. *Oh, Mother, why? Why didn't you hide them, bury them?*

"Leave those. I'll bring them up," Miguel said in quick understanding.

"No. I'll take them." She made herself say it. She made herself lift the jewel case and walk out of the room with it, walking with dignity and grace, the way Mama had walked.

An Indian maid was watering potted plants on her balcony.

"Sofia, will you do that later, please? I have a headache. I'm going to lie down until dinner." She spoke carefully, still holding the jewel case, and watched in fascination as the Indian girl obediently put down the watering can. *I am an Indian girl*, she thought. Pausing at the door, the girl turned with a murmur of sympathy and asked if she wanted anything else. Some cold water? A wet cloth for her head?

"Nothing, thank you."

Then she was alone, standing by the bed. Somehow the jewel box was on the floor. The lid had snapped back and the lovely, hateful jewels were

11

all spilled about, some on the gleaming floor surface and the rest on the bedside carpet. Rubies, pearls. Many unset stones. Some in old-fashioned mountings. Diamonds of yellow and white, with a look of not having been cleaned in a long time. An amethyst. Emeralds in a bracelet. Hating them, she turned away.

They had not been just dreams and fancies, then, as Mama had told her. They had been memories. The recurring dream-memory of the strange, cramped little house and of herself as a very small child. Mama singing. Not seen, but singing somewhere, lightly, liltingly, with unquenchable joy—not like Mama at all. Then another, darker, image—herself being carried endlessly through an endless dark night by the tired, tired man who kept walking and walking and walking. Mama—again not seen, but there walking with him, by his side, and all of them so tired.

She must pick up the jewels some time. She must not leave them on the floor. Eventually this shivering would cease and she would be calm. Two things struggled in her mind. There was the image of the Indian girl who had just left, quiet, docile, totally subservient, and something else. What else?

Oh, yes, Luis. What a shock this would be to Luis, what a burden to learn that his future wife was really more Indian than white. I am sorry, Luis, she thought. I didn't ask for your love. You offered it. Do you remember how long it took me to decide? Perhaps the half-realized, half-hidden memories had held her back, made her put off marriage until, finally, at the unreasonable age of three and twenty, she must agree to it. And if she

12

must finally agree, it must be Luis—so dear, so faithful, so steadfast.

What a blow this would be to Luis' family, his proud aunts, his sick and dying father. Could they accept it? They who knew the history of every relative to the tenth and twelfth degree. They whose crest hung over the mantel, beside the antique sword that had been used—one grew weary of hearing—in the famous battle of Lepanto. They whose memorabilia included a precious trinket referred to as "the Duchess' pearl pendant," and some cherished and yellowing letters from long-dead kings, in acknowledgment of brave deeds and faithful services from Chavero ancestors.

Then it was all shattered when Cecilia came into the room in a swish of yellow silken skirts and a hint of sweet perfume—Cecilia, darkly beautiful, with shining black hair and mother's steel-blue eyes, a little breathless now, a little imperious always.

"Majella! Are you all right?"

"Yes. Of course."

"I just talked with Miguel and—good heavens! What have you done! Oh, yes, the infamous jewels." Her eyes narrowed, and her lips tightened. She was deeply and thoroughly angry, but trying valiantly to hide it. "Majella, are you sure you feel all right? This is—terrible news. I just can't—"

"No, Cecilia," Majella said a little wryly, sitting down on the side of her bed. "I didn't mean I felt all right. I feel terrible."

"I'll pick these up for you," Cecilia said, not moving. Then she crossed herself quickly. "Thank God—Jesus—Mary—that you had the sense to make the boys keep quiet about this. Eduardo doesn't care, of course. But there is no need for everyone else to know—about the rest of us. If you *insist* on telling Luis about yourself, well, then, that is your affair. But we need not all—not all—"

"Of course not," Majella agreed soothingly.

"Oh, Majella, really what—*really* what are you going to do about Luis?" And Cecilia started to cry.

Comforting Cecilia somehow made Majella feel better. Comforting her younger sister was an old and familiar habit. Together they picked up the scattered jewelry and put it back into the box.

"Cecilia, we can share these—choose whatever you like," Majella said, her own aversion to the gems so intense that she knew she would never wear a single one.

Cecilia, composed now, stood before the dresser and looked down into the jewel chest. She picked up a sapphire brooch and pondered it, her blue eyes narrowed slightly. Then, slowly, she put it back.

"No, Majella. Thank you, but no. Eduardo has some things from jewelry inherited from his mother and he has bought me some things. I—really don't want any of this." She came over to stand beside Majella at the balcony windows.

"You are determined to tell Luis, I suppose?"

"Yes."

Cecilia sighed. "You will actually offer to release him?" Her voice sounded tentative, like a little girl's. Majella knew the tone and felt herself becoming wary.

"Yes."

"I think you are taking a risk. With all respect

14

for Luis, I don't think he will want to marry you. Not Luis Chavero."

"Then we shall not marry."

"I don't think you are as calm as you sound, Majella. Or else you simply aren't thinking. Well, think! If he decides to withdraw from the betrothal, do you think for one moment that a choice bit of scandal like that can be kept quiet? Don't you realize, Majella, that all of Mexico City will hear of it! Can't you just see the women tittering behind their fans? Can't you hear the men making guesses among themselves as to *why*?"

"Cecilia, don't. Please. I have decided and I have a headache. I don't want to argue."

"I'm sorry that your head aches, but you must listen and really *hear* me. In some ways you are so *simple*!" She was exasperated and showed it.

"Like an Indian, perhaps?"

"Oh, Majella! No! Of course not. For heaven's sake. But men are worse gossips than women. The first thing they will think is that—that you are *not chaste*. Then it will have to come out why the engagement is broken. Just to protect your reputation. Don't you see that?"

"Cecilia, I really don't—"

"Well, it's true. You must know that. Then the real reason, that your—" She had difficulty saying it. "That your real father was an Indian, is going to be worse in its way. That one fact simply rules out marriage with any of the *good* families. Can't you see that, Majella?"

Majella turned to face her younger sister. "Cecilia, I do want to be alone for a while. I'm sorry. I know you only want to help me. I'm not ungrateful. But will you help me now by leaving me alone? Please? We can talk another time."

"But Luis will call after dinner. He always does. He never fails to come after dinner."

"Cecilia, please!"

"Oh, all right! But I shall not let it rest. I'm going down now to discuss it with Eduardo and the boys. Somebody has to take care of you if you haven't the sense to take care of yourself!"

When she had gone, silence descended thick and heavy in the room. I will pray, Majella thought, and she took out her rosary of amber beads linked with gold that Papa had given her for confirmation. Then she realized that she could not and found this mildly astonishing. She couldn't even pray. How odd.

Later, she dressed carefully for dinner in the rose-colored silk gown that had been Papa's favorite. She had scarcely worn it because it had been new when they had gone into mourning clothes. When, after a year, Cecilia had insisted in putting off the mourning and entering into her postponed marriage to Eduardo, Majella had unpacked it again. She loved this dress. Now, as before, she went onto her balcony to snip off two heavy-headed pink roses to place before the comb that held her mantilla.

Somehow, she got through dinner with the family. Señor Aguilar, with unfailing kindness, had found he could not come. Eduardo, with the help of Hernán, dominated the conversation. He was a large and usually quiet man, at least a decade older than Cecilia. Majella was silently grateful to him for his efforts. She, still numbed with shock, could contribute almost nothing and Miguel, when concerned, was prone to abstracted silence. But anyone listening to the dinner-table talk would have gotten the impression of an untroubled family dining together on a summer night. There was even laughter from time to time as Eduardo spoke of life on his California rancho, to which he would soon be returning with Cecilia, and of amusing incidents from their voyage along the coast when they traveled to Mexico for Majella's wedding. Devoted as he was to Cecilia, and it was in every glance he offered her, he was held within unbreakable bonds now to her family and his every instinct was to help them any way he could. Silently, Majella blessed him.

The night was so warm that they were all in the garden when Luis Chavero arrived. They must present the image of a lovely family group, utterly carefree—she in the rose silk, Cecilia like a snow princess in ice-blue satin, the men in their dark short jackets with gleaming white ruffled shirts and black silk sashes.

Again, Eduardo guided a pleasant flow of talk until Luis asked Majella if they could stroll about for a while. Majella rose at once. She bowed her head slightly so that her mantilla would hide her face. She could not suppress a wry smile, because both Miguel and Eduardo had silently reached out to touch Cecilia. The gesture said firmly, *stay here.* So Cecilia had talked to them and lost the argument. The men had decided to let her do as she wished about telling Luis.

"Let's go along a little farther," Majella murmured as they passed the orange trees. The heavy sweetness was almost too intense, making her want to escape it.

17

"Not too far," Luis answered, a smile sounding in his voice. "I don't want your brothers pursuing me."

They stopped by the mellow old wall. She observed his face in the moonlight, the fine aristocratic features, the look of elegance and breeding. The Chaveros were an ancient line. She would not speak just yet. In a moment.

His head was tilted. He was listening.

"No one is coming," he said softly. Smiling, he took her in his arms.

Majella, normally reserved, melted against him. In fondness, in wistful longing, in regret at what she would tell him. She felt his sense of surprise and the instant tightening of his embrace. For the first time in their courtship she became completely pliant against him, letting him part her lips, sliding her arms about his neck to cling closer to him, loving and yielding, pleasing him, exciting him. It was the least she could do. A small gift. Perhaps a small parting gift.

"Oh, Majella," he moaned. "Oh, my love." He crushed her closer, his mouth seeking hers again. Still, she did not stop him and one kiss blended into the next.

Finally, gently, she pushed against him.

"Oh, God," he whispered thickly, but he acquiesced, releasing her slowly, having to force himself to do it.

"We—have to talk together a moment," Majella said, breathing quickly.

"What is it?" He would not release her hands, not wanting to let her go completely. "Anything, my love."

"It is about our betrothal. Luis, I heard—I

18

learned something today about my background that may compel you to think again about our marriage plans."

A sudden look of amused astonishment touched his face.

"Well, what is it?" He slid his hands up her bare arms, clearly longing to hold her again, not letting himself until she should permit it.

"You know they are still settling father's estate and—things keep coming up."

He shrugged slightly, the smile lingering. "Is my love penniless? I think I can manage."

"Luis, it was revealed that—my mother was a widow when she married my—when she married Papa."

"Really? And they kept it secret all this time?" His tone seemed to say "What difference does it make?"

"Yes. And Luis, it seems that I am not Papa's own daughter. I am just half-sister to Miguel and the others."

He was silent a moment, gazing at her. "Does this distress you?" he asked gently. "What of your own father?" He was remembering back to childhood. "Your family came here from California, didn't they? Was your father a Californian? How sad for him never to have known you as a child." Then, finally, "What was his name? Do I know the family?"

Her mouth had gone suddenly dry.

"You would not recognize the name, Luis. He— was a worker on the Moreno rancho. He was an Indian."

For a long moment it was as if he had not heard her. Then, because he couldn't help it, he recoiled from the knowledge. He dropped her hands and stepped back, his jacket touching the wall.

"No!" he said. "I don't believe it!"

"You must." For the first time during the long evening she felt tired, a feeling almost of exhaustion. She wanted to lie down and put her head in her mother's lap. No. She could not do that. Mother was gone.

"But, *Majella*!" It was pure anguish.

There was an interminably long silence. She watched the play of expression on his naked, revealing face—the struggle against belief, the final acceptance, the silent despair. She turned her gaze away from him and waited for him to speak. When he did not, she spoke again.

"You must discuss this with your family, Luis."

"You do not look Indian," he said, his voice sounding labored. "I cannot believe this, Majella."

But she knew that he did believe it. She turned so that the moonlight struck her full in the face. She had always been darker than her sister and brothers. And she had spent long hours that afternoon studying her face in the glass. An image never before noted had emerged. Something about the broad cheekbones, the darkness of the eyes, the tightness of the eyelids, the curve of the mouth. Small, subtle things that had gone unnoticed in the face of Felipe Moreno's eldest child, but that were clearly visible if one thought to really look. Without flinching, she waited as Luis stared at her in the pale light.

"Oh, God," he was saying softly. "Oh, God, what shall I do?" Gradually his face had lost color until it was like dead ashes.

"You must think about it," Majella said, trying

20

to be fair but feeling merciless. "We can talk again tomorrow. Or," she added in kindness, "you may send me a note by a servant if you wish."

After a long, silent time she spoke again. "Luis, we must go back. The scent of the orange blossoms is making me sick."

"All right. Yes. Of course," he said slowly, not moving.

"Would you like to go out by the side gate? I'll tell my family. They will understand."

"No. Oh, no," he said, rousing himself, straightening up, pulling at his jacket sleeves. "Oh, no. I must bid them good night. It—would be inexcusable if I—" He stopped, forgetting to finish his thought.

She swallowed. Her throat ached with pity. A Chavero would never—could never—do anything inexcusable. For centuries, Chaveros, now and then with their lifeblood running out of them, had made all the correct gestures, had spoken all the correct words. His heart might be breaking, but he would do what was expected of him.

In a kind of sorrowful disbelief she observed him as he followed the old patterns, the old customs. Without flaw he went through it all. She would never know what it cost him, but he escorted her back to the others. He sat again on the stone bench. He talked courteously and pleasantly with Eduardo. He and Eduardo carried the situation now because the Morenos had all lapsed into dismayed silence at the unhappiness in Majella's eyes. Eventually—*Oh, please, Luis, go away*—he got up, made his careful farewells, and left them in the silent scented garden.

When they had gone into the house Majella did

not excuse herself as she wished to do. The family had wandered soberly into the main sitting room, at the end of which was Papa's writing table. Majella seated herself there and took a sheet of Papa's letter paper. She began to write.

"Well, why don't you tell us what he said," Cecilia finally said, in a tone of exasperation.

Eduardo lifted his hand in a silencing gesture.

Hernán said sharply, "Let her alone, Cecilia!"

Miguel murmured something Majella did not hear. She finished writing.

"I said, I wonder what Luis' reaction was," Miguel said again. "What about your marriage plans?"

"The marriage will not take place," Majella said quietly.

"Why not?" Hernán's face flamed.

"Majella! I told you so!" Cecilia said angrily. "I told you! You wouldn't listen!"

"Cecilia," Eduardo admonished gently. "Let Majella tell us in her own way. Do you care to tell us?" he added to Majella.

"Did he break the engagement?" Miguel asked in disbelief.

"No, Miguel. I have just written him a note. I am breaking it. I decided before we came in. It is for me to do it. His—situation being as it is, he cannot possibly marry me. I will not put him to the humiliation of telling me so."

"I'll kill him if he does," Hernán muttered, pacing about the room.

"No. No one will die of this, Hernán," Majella said gently. "But this is the way it must be. Please believe me."

Miguel looked at her in troubled confusion. "He

won't let you. I know he won't. He didn't say anything at all about it in the garden. He didn't look at all upset."

Majella wanted to cry and would not let herself. "Miguel, if Luis were dying he wouldn't appear upset, for fear it would embarrass the company. Please trust me. I know Luis. He will want his freedom. He deserves to have it."

"He deserves to be shot," Hernán's voice was choked. Eduardo got up, walked over to the younger man, and placed an arm about his shoulders.

Sounding strangely cool and calculating, Cecilia spoke.

"For weeks all of Mexico City has talked of nothing but the marriage of Luis Chavero and Majella Moreno. The announcement that it has been broken off will cause the greatest excitement the gossips have had for years. What will all that do to you, Majella?"

"Yes! What can we do?" Miguel got up, looking distractedly about the familiar room. "I—won't have Majella humiliated."

"Majella must come back to California with Eduardo and me."

"That would be a good solution," Eduardo agreed quietly. "And I need not say that you all are more than welcome—you know that, of course. All of you, certainly. Why don't you all come for a time, until the talk dies down. A visit of several months—or a year—would not be amiss." He smiled. "Ten years. California rancheros are usually so isolated that we seize every opportunity for guests." He appeared not to notice that no one smiled in response.

"I don't know," Miguel said uneasily. "There are the business matters. I really should not leave."

"I—will stay and help you, Miguel," Hernán said. "I can't leave everything to you."

"Is it settled then?" Cecilia asked directly of Majella.

They all turned to Majella now, waiting. Majella was staring at the note in her hand.

"Majella! You aren't even listening! Will you come home with Eduardo and me? You cannot stay on here and face all the gossip!"

"Cecilia," Eduardo murmured again, and obediently Cecilia closed her lips against whatever else she wanted to say.

"It is very kind of you," Majella said, almost formally. Rather suddenly none of it mattered. Nothing was right. She had lost Papa. And her mother, because of the old secret, had somehow slipped away into the distance. "I am tired. I think I'll go to my room. The rest of you can decide. I'll do whatever you think best."

They would, she thought, send her to California, the place from which had sprung her dark half-memories that lurked in her dreams and sometimes tinged the brightest day with melancholy for no reason she could understand. She had never fainted in her life, and she wondered somewhat remotely if she would now. Holding herself very straight, she left them.

In her bedroom she shut the door and leaned against it for a moment. She had done it. She had gotten to her room despite this feeling of sickness, of faintness. Was this the way it felt to die? No, not likely. She was too healthy. She would survive it, whether she wanted to or not. The eternal endurance of the Indian, possibly.

She began to take off the mantilla and the rose-colored dress. With the dress half off, trailing in silken folds on the floor, she strove to recall her father's face. Her real father. That faceless Indian worker on the Moreno ranch. There was a gust—almost a surge—of pure anger at her mother. *An Indian.* What madness had possessed her mother? Was it because Mother herself had been half-Indian?

I don't want to remember his face, she thought in slow rage. *I don't know him.*

Yes. Yes, she must get away from here. Must get to California. She must escape. Must escape from being an Indian. No one must ever know. No one.

Chapter Two

The two Indians ran on steadily over the spreading California countryside. Mile after mile in the moonlight. Soon they would reach the village. They were of the same people, the same clan, and near-brothers since boyhood. At the same moment they began to slacken their pace. In a few miles they would slacken it even more, each knowing from long, close friendship what the other wished to do. They entered the village, walking in an easy stride.

The village was asleep. The younger one, Joaquín, knew a pervading sense of security as he felt, rather than saw, the surrounding houses scattered in a rough semicircle. A few were traditionally built, with conical earth-packed roofs that loomed like round shadows about him in the moonlight. Some were little shacks constructed of any trash that was available.

He fell a pace or two behind the other, Leon.

Although he had lived in Leon's house since he had been orphaned as a child, it was still Leon's house first, so he fell back. Because the grandfather would be sleeping they entered quietly, lowering their heads, for both were taller than the door opening. They went down into the house proper, for it was excavated in the old way, about two feet below ground level. There was a rustling of small creatures in the tulle thatch above their heads that supported the round earthen roof. Moonlight showed dimly through the smokehole in the higher center of the dwelling. Various shadowy things were hung upon the roof-support poles.

Grandfather, his last wife long dead, lived alone except when Leon and Joaquín were there. The old one slept now, so thin that he scarcely lifted his blanket from the earth floor, and snored gently.

"The inside of my belly is twisting," Leon murmured.

"Mine, too."

They had not eaten for almost two days. They had been all the way to Los Angeles because of the rumor that an American man there was hiring Indians. It had not been a false rumor, but the man had needed only a few Indians.

The grandfather slept lightly, as the ancient sometimes do. He heard them and awoke.

"You are hungry." It was not a question. Nor did he inquire about the work in Los Angeles. They were back. No need to embarrass them. They would speak of it in good time. "Eat if you want to. There is meat."

"Meat," Joaquín moaned, clutching his stomach in exaggeration of his hunger, knowing it would please the old one. The old man got up and wrapped his blanket around his skeletal, naked body. He was cackling softly to himself. He would scold them for not being able to eat off the land the way the people had in ages past. Well, he was giving the food; let him have his fun.

It was good food: Two whole rabbits that had been roasted over the common hearth in the center of the village. Even cold it was irresistable. They sat down cross-legged on the ground and ate ravenously. From time to time they gave small grunts of satisfaction so the old one would know they appreciated his bounty. The grandfather kept up a running commentary, accusing them, without animosity of being improvident and helpless. Telling them how in ages past they would not have suffered hunger at all on so short a journey. They laughed good-naturedly and did not dispute him, though things were different now than in ages past. He had his older wisdom, but in these new times they had new and sudden knowledge in ways he could not know.

The old man was the closest thing to a Headman that the village had these days. He had been the village chief in years past. Then he had handed it on to his son, Leon's father, who was now long dead. After his death, no new Headman had assumed the duties—Leon had been far too young at the time. Outwardly the old man deplored this, complaining that the old ways had fallen away, and that the old customs had become lost and forgotten. Actually, he didn't mind, for it meant that most of the village people came to him for counsel, and he enjoyed the giving of his wisdom, which he considered great.

The grandfather thought about this a good deal. Some day Leon must be Headman of the village— when he was older, more gentled in his ways. And if not Leon, then Joaquín, who was not of their family by blood, but by love. He knew that the young men were aware of this duty that lay ahead. They had talked of it in the nighttimes while they thought him sleeping—he who almost never slept.

"But some day you must," Joaquín had said so many times. "It is your inheritance to guide the people of this village and advise them, and plan the work and speak in their behalf to the Americans and to the Mexicans. How can you escape what is in your stars?"

"But these are different days, Joaquín, than the days of olden times, the days of order when each could follow the path laid out for him. I—" he paused somberly at this, and always came back to the same conclusion. "The breaker will come for me long before then, Joaquín. I tempt him so greatly, and that I cannot help doing—it is the wildness inside that I cannot conquer."

Then Joaquín, the steadier, more logical one: "Then who will be the Headman? Who will help the people? Someday the grandfather will die."

Leon, his voice on the edge of laughter at the seriousness of the other, would say, "I give it to you, Joaquín, if I die first. You are my little brother in all but blood—would you do it?"

"Yes, I would do it," Joaquín had said slowly.

So it was decided by the young men, privately,

as things often are, and they never consulted him. Privately, he forgave them.

Replete, glutted, Leon and Joaquín didn't bother to get up. They simply lay back flat, hands beneath heads, feet toward the opening as was the custom. It was actually time for sleep, but sleep was far away. And, of course, the old man was often wakeful at night. They would all probably talk until daylight. A pleasant idea, since there was no tobacco, no wine, no money, no women. How long had it been since there had been a woman?

"They could at least pick up the bones," the grandfather complained to the air, picking them up and putting them in the jar for later grinding.

"Too weak, Grandfather," Leon commented, teasing him. "No strength left in the young people." He stretched out his strong, superbly muscled body.

"I know. What I don't know is what will happen to you when I have died."

"We will perish," Joaquín answered agreeably. He was as big a man as Leon and they both thought that some day he might beat him wrestling. He knew why he hadn't yet. Leon could make his mind cold. He could think and fight at the same time. He himself could not do that yet. Nor could he kill another man without a small earthquake of the mind. Leon could.

"Grandfather," Leon said, rolling over. "The American didn't need any more Indians when we got there."

"You found him and talked to him? You asked?"

"We found him, and asked him. That is, Joaquín asked him. The man did not know Spanish and Joaquín talked to him in the American tongue." Some of Joaquín's various periods of employment had been for Americans, and he was quick to learn. Different ways of talking interested him.

"So. You will take out the raiding party again," the old man commented after a time.

"We tried to work," Leon said, spreading his broad hands. "We have no money—we have to beg food from our grandfather."

"It takes no money to kill a rabbit or grow a squash. But you must go and steal something. So you can buy wine and get drunk, and buy a woman to spread her legs."

"That's as it may be, Grandfather," Leon agreed, lying back again.

Both younger men prepared now to listen to the old one's discourse on good and bad. They had heard it many times, with great patience. Some of it they believed. Some they did not. But they never told the old man this.

Stealing was bad. One way or another it brought on the punishers. If you became too evil the breaker would come. And he would kill you. This was known from ancient times. That stealing was bad was one of the old man's absolutes, never to be disputed. He had pieced this together because in the long ago, in the half-forgotten teachings of the people, in their original sayings, it was bad.

Then it was proved again much later during the generations of the Christian mission fathers. Then even later, when the Americans came; they also said it was bad. If the Indian old ones knew it, and the Spanish Christian fathers knew it, and the new Americans knew it, then who could sensibly

31

dispute it? He began to explain this to them again.

"This Feliciano Troncoso will talk after he is dead," Leon commented comfortably.

The grandfather's child-name had indeed been "Talkative Child." Later, of course, he had been given his virile name, but had not used it for many years. For convenience in living with the Mexicans, and later the Americans, he used his Spanish name of Feliciano Troncoso. Troncoso was a family name acquired by his ancestors some time ago while they labored for the fathers at Mission San Luis Rey de Francia.

In like manner, Joaquín's recent ancestors had used the Spanish name of Salazar and he had, in due course, become Joaquín Salazar. It was so written down some place in San Bernardino where Americans wrote down such things. This was because his family, along with the Troncosos, had been made Christian by the fathers, who had also written things.

Joaquín himself had started to learn reading and writing while working for some Americans. These arts held great allure for him, as his mind was lively, and he could not get enough of them. There had been such a magic in the idea that the markings on paper told the thoughts of his mind, and it filled him with wonder. He half-listened again to the drone of the grandfather's voice.

Most had now more or less forgotten the teaching of the Christians, as they had more or less forgotten the teaching of their own people. So it was left for the old men like Feliciano Troncoso to carry on the wisdom and impart it as needed.

As he listened, Joaquín reached over and picked up the old man's curved rabbit-killer. He liked the smooth feel of the wood, polished by the old man's hands all the years he had used it: Speaking to it, throwing it with silent skill, watching it sail through the air to kill the rabbit, and then come sailing back to his hand. He himself was good, but not as good as the old man. He was better at stealing and fighting. The times were changing.

Something the old man said against stealing made him smile now, but he turned his head so the old man would not see. He had happened to glance up and see again the familiar crucifix on the wall, which he knew that the grandfather had stolen. Now and then, when he could not explain how something was his, he would say, "It came into my hand." Which was, more or less, true after all. And you could not dispute that it was good to have the Christian crucifix on the wall. For one thing, if Mexicans, angry or otherwise, came to your house, they thought better of you if they saw the crucifix on the wall. That is, you were safer.

When the old one began to talk about Jehovah-God and Jesus-Son-of-Mary, Joaquín only half-listened. Actually, he knew more than the old one did about Jesus, the Son of Mary. There had been Mr. and Mrs. Austin, Americans, in Los Angeles. He had worked for Mr. Austin in the livery stable, cleaning up, and later, when Mr. Austin found out he could learn quickly, he cared for the horses. Mr. Austin had paid him fairly and never once whipped him, although in the beginning he had made some mistakes. It had been a good place. It was the only time he had felt safe outside the village. There had been plenty to eat and he had slept comfortably in the straw in the loft above

33

the horses. He had been very young then, without much wisdom, and so thought it would last forever. Mrs. Austin, a woman of great piety, had talked to him many times about Jesus. The Austins had both been very kind to him.

It had been she who had taught him about reading, and then about writing, guiding him ever so gently all the while, with her pale, thin bird-hands. Those little old hands, in delicate butterfly motions, had taken from him the tattered magazine he had found with such joy behind the cantina. "It is not worthy to read this and put those things into your thoughts," she told him. Regretfully, and only because of her gentle wisdom, he had given it up. Instead, he had obediently taken her Bible and found that parts of it were more exciting than the magazine.

Then with the writing—which was more difficult—again, ever so gently, the fragile white hands were laid upon his strong brown ones. "No, Joaquín, we dip the point just a little in the ink. And wait until it all falls off, leaving only a little on the point. No, carefully now, into the inkwell, Joaquín. Now, easily, lightly, we hold the pen. And we make the letters just so. Ah, Joaquín, you are a clever boy."

Then Mrs. Austin's niece had come to live with them and they were advised that it would not do to have their niece so close to an Indian. Mr. Austin had paid him and sent him away. Never in all his life would he forget the crushing sense of defeat, the sickness that had engulfed him. Speak of the punisher!

Silently, not letting them see how he felt, he fin-

34

ished cleaning the stable and then watered down one more time the dust on the road by the door. It had been a hot August day. When he was away from the town and lonely on the road, he let the tears come for whatever easing of his heart they allowed. For a long time they coursed, uncomforting, down his face, making tracks in the dust there, while dust rose in small clouds about his bare ankles. Even now it grieved him to have had so much and then have had it all snatched away.

Several times he had come back to the village from periods of working. Sometimes alone. Sometimes with Leon. It was a harsh and punishing world to live in. It was hard to find work and when found it was ill-paid and sometimes not paid at all. And what Indian would dare question? Better to be cheated and survive than to fight back openly, or try to.

One could always come home to the village. This was the sanctuary. He ran his hand over the smooth dirt floor of the grandfather's house. The village was his home place. When there was no place else to go he could always come back here. Should there be a time when he could not come to the village—well, such a thing could never happen. And some day when Leon chose to put his mind to it, it might again be one of the prosperous villages, with good houses, and growing things and men working and many children being born.

He and Leon had not started their intermittent raiding parties until that ranchero, for whom they worked for a while, had Leon whipped. There had been nothing he could do to stop it. Even now he wondered to himself, how had he been able to stand silently among the other Indians and watch? *Leon will die of this,* he had thought in anguish and horror. *He cannot stand any more.*

Then, after the whipping was finished they took Leon down from the post and dragged him away. They left him in one of the worksheds to recover and go back to work, or die.

After dark he had broken the lock on the shed door. He had carried Leon out of the shed, out of the compound. Alternately resting and carrying, he started back toward the village. Halfway there, more tired than he had known he could be and still live, he had seen, through a haze of sweat, a runaway horse. He could not believe it. He was dreaming. The reins were dragging loose and the owner was nowhere in sight. He let Leon slide gently back down to the ground and walked quite calmly over to steal the horse, knowing he could be hanged for it. It was his first big theft.

He and Leon had laughed about it later as Leon was getting well from the whipping. Safe in the grandfather's house, the story would be told again and again.

"Tell again how you stole the American horse, Joaquín."

"Well, I knew he was an American horse, of course, by the saddle. I was so tired I didn't know how I was going to reach the village that day—you are as heavy as stone, Leon—and I looked up and—there he was. I couldn't believe it—Leon, don't laugh, you'll break open the cuts—"

"I can't help it. Suddenly the thing you most need in life is standing there in front of you. It is too much—"

"Look, you're bleeding again. Here, let me—" He blotted at Leon's seeping blood.

"Be careful, or I'll knock your head off."

"I am careful. Be still. Don't move around."

"And he didn't even move when you went up to him?"

"Not a muscle. Just stood there and let me pick up the reins."

"I said be careful!"

Together they had laughed and argued. Leon still liked to hear the old story now and then. And whenever they stole a new horse, he always mentioned it.

"Well, it isn't as good as our first horse—but it will do."

They had gone back later to retrieve the American saddle where Joaquín had hidden it, and this they had given to Trinidad Méndez to sell. Trinidad was a short, heavy young man of their people, with crooked eyes. You could never tell which way he was looking. Perhaps this helped him in the selling of things. Also, he was clever about pretending to be stupid, which was not always easy to do. Most people in the village came to Trinidad now when they had something they wanted to sell. He could get the best price possible to an Indian—possibly one-tenth of the value. So it was that Leon and Joaquín took him the saddle, and later the horse. In the course of time the three of them, along with Pablo Gutierrez, formed the regular raiding party. Pablo was somewhat younger than the others, but always dependable. If you needed Pablo quickly, Pablo was there. The four of them had always gone together except for that first time when Leon and Joaquín had gone alone.

Leon had been staring up somberly at the smoke-hole, his mouth flattened with that deep and everlasting secret anger. Sometimes the anger became very demanding. The cuts on his back were healed. Some scars remained on the broad bronzed surface. He hated that, for he was comely and it pleased him.

"I mean to kill that man, you know," he murmured after a time. They were alone in the house.

"You cannot shut it away from you? Forget it?"

"No."

"Have you tried?"

"No. I don't want to forget it. I thought of it all the while he was cutting the whip into my back. All the time until the spirit left my body. Then, later, when I was locked in the shed and my spirit came back now and then, it was the first thing in my thoughts. All the time. And ever since."

Joaquín was quiet in thought a while, weighing it. There was little point in trying to change Leon's mind once it was made up. He knew that he himself was similar sometimes. At some point, he supposed, he and Leon might come into dispute. He did not want to think what might happen. But for now, he looked over to his friend, staring gravely upward; they could agree on this. There was this much about it—the man with the whip was an Indian. Indians given authority by the rancheros were unfailingly merciless to their own kind. Joaquín never could understand it. This one was widely feared. All he had to do when you worked was look at you to make sweat come onto your skin. But, when this man was killed, being Indian, there would be less anger among the Americans and the Mexicans. In the first place, it might not even be known that he had been killed by other Indians.

"You need not come with me," Leon said.

"I will come with you," Joaquín answered. "I'll lend you my knife. It is better than yours."

"Thank you. I don't need it. A dull knife has its uses, and I will use my hands. I would need nothing else."

That was possible, Joaquín thought. Without the whip and the others around him, and without Leon being tied to a post, the man would be a child against him, however Leon decided to do it.

So that had been their first killing. The man had been glad to die. In the end, Joaquín had done the actual killing after all, sticking his knife into the man's faltering heart.

"Why did you do that?" Leon, crouched, his broad face streaked with sweat, had glanced up in surprise.

"It was time for him to die," Joaquín had said, his stomach churning.

After a moment Leon had shrugged and looked at the dead man, his own rage spent now. He stood up slowly.

"See if he has any money."

He did have, and a pocket watch, and a ring, and a gold crucifix. Together they had buried him, and so far as they knew, no one had ever known what had happened to him. He simply disappeared.

In killing that man, and in the forming of the raiding party, and in the several later killings that needed to be done, they had crossed over the line into constant risk and danger, forever tempting the patience of the breaker. All four of them knew this without even talking about it. Escaping briefly now and then from the dull, endless poverty of life, they could gamble with their lives, which was all they had to gamble with. Since life was really without hope anyway, one could only live in the hour and make no plans for the next one. And yet, somehow, if one could believe the grandfather and the daydreams, Leon might rescue the village and somehow salvage the people. And if the breaker decided that Leon would not do this, perhaps he, Joaquín, would be the one.

So he listened to the old man's droning, hearing some of it, but letting his mind roam free during much of it. Since they were not sleeping tonight, they would probably sleep most of tomorrow. Then, Leon would seek out the others and they would go get the stolen horses from where they were hidden. These were the horses they did not dare ride any time but when they were raiding and their lives were at risk anyhow. If they were lucky, then there would be an interval in the caves. There would be time for plenty of wine to get drunk on and a woman or two for pleasure. He moved in faint restlessness, remembering when he had last had a woman, smiling to himself. That was something he was good at. Better than most, he thought. As good as Leon.

He rolled over and looked at his friend. Leon had taught him all he knew about riding, fighting, using a knife (or a gun when there were bullets), everything about pleasing himself with a woman. His blood started to sing.

Tomorrow, then.

Chapter Three

Majella read again the letter from her father—the letter that had crashed into her life and shattered it, No. Not father. Stepfather. That remained difficult to accept. How careful he had been to lay it all out, and how kindly. She had read it many times on the voyage up the coast, sitting up late in her tiny cabin. It was a long and detailed letter, giving faithfully all of her background that he had known.

Sighing, she refolded it and placed it on top of the things packed in her trunk. It was almost full daylight. Time to leave again. There had seemed to be a hundred people at the harbor to greet Eduardo Obregón and his ladies when he returned to California. Really, it was almost like home in many ways, except for the many Americans. She had to remind herself that she was in a foreign country now, no longer part of Mexico.

They had visited leisurely in one house and

then another for several weeks. Now the visits were over. They would start out this morning for the Obregón ranch, one of the few ranches remaining under Mexican ownership. Or was it? Eduardo was himself now legally American. How strange that seemed.

At last there would be an interval of privacy in which to think, to determine what might lay ahead. She would not let herself think of Luis. That was finished. She stood up and smoothed the delicate woolen cloth of her traveling dress. It was a light golden brown, trimmed in black braid and jet buttons. Cecilia, she felt sure, would be wearing silvery gray, which became her fair skin.

"I was thinking about you," she smiled, as Cecilia came into the room. Perhaps alone, in the isolation of the large Obregón ranch, she would not need to smile so much. Being the visiting sister-in-law of Eduardo Obregón had been a time of almost ceaseless smiling into strange faces. He had so many friends in the town, mostly Mexican but some American, too. And they all seemed overjoyed that he had returned to California.

"Haven't you got your trunk shut yet?" Cecilia said. "The men are almost ready to leave." She hurried over to the bell-pull and gave it a firm jerk. "I must say, Majella," she added, her voice softening. "You have done wonderfully well. I know a lot of times you must have wished—well, you've been a dear."

Majella smiled again. "You've been dear yourself," she said somewhat wryly. She knew how carefully Cecilia had spread the word that her sister was not well—that she needed a long rest away from the social whirl of Mexico City, building up

42

a careful tissue of half-truths to protect her. They had had their differences growing up, but both had been carefully schooled to keep them safely beneath the surface of their lives. Despite the differences, though, a deeply ingrained family loyalty existed among all of Ramona's children.

"I have packed a few necessary things in the saddle bags, and some of the men have extra packs behind them on their horses, in case we have to stop for the night some place," Cecilia was explaining. "Then the others will bring the trunks along by cart. It will take a day or two. Are you sure there is nothing you want from this trunk?"

"No, nothing," Majella said. Let them take the letter in the trunk. She knew it by heart now anyway.

"It's a terrible ride, Majella. I thought I would die the first time I made it. We thought we were such wonderful horsewomen in Mexico. We never had to cover a tenth of the distance at home that we do here. You're going to become awfully tired."

"It doesn't matter. I can rest when we reach the ranch," Majella answered. She linked her arm into Cecilia's and they strolled out to where the men were waiting.

It was a huge riding party. There was much laughter and talk as the two ladies were mounted on their horses. In addition to several friends who planned to ride a few miles with them, an armed escort of men had arrived from the Obregón rancho to accompany their master and his ladies home.

Eduardo's friends rode with them until midday. *Oh, these Californians, so persistently friendly and gracious.* Would she ever be rid of them? Then they must all have a picnic lunch by a small stream overhung with sparse willow growth. She was glad to stop, not because she was hungry but because she longed to get down and stretch her stiff, sore muscles. After the delicious lunch, thoughtfully provided in hampers by their last hostess, they lay or sat about on the men's serapes spread on the ground near the stream bank. It was time for the siesta, but few napped. Californians preferred to talk a final hour to prolong the visit. Finally, the Californians regretfully departed.

The Obregón party seemed small and depleted when they once again set out across the rolling California hills and valleys in what seemed like a near deserted land, so few were the dwellings and settlements. And they were now just the three family members and the four armed men from the Obregón rancho who were escorting them.

They alternated walking the horses and riding in short fast gallops. How fortunate that Papa himself had been a Californian and had taught them all to ride well.

There seemed a kind of formation to their grouping—she and Cecilia somewhat in the center of the men, a protective measure, she thought with mild regret, as one breathed more dust this way.

A single rider was far enough ahead of them so that the dust from his horse did not bother them. The men were a rough-looking lot, with heavy pistols, sheathed knives, and large sweat-stained hats that they had filled with damp leaves at the stream. It was hot. Majella longed for a cool drink.

Suddenly, there was a shout ahead of them and

the man turned his horse so abruptly that it reared on its hind legs. Then just as suddenly he was flung—plucked—from his saddle and was crashed to the ground. At that same moment they heard the gunshot. He seemed to grovel or crawl about convulsively for a moment before collapsing into an awkward, inert huddle in the dust.

"My God! Bandits!" Eduardo gasped and issued rapid orders to his remaining men. Two of them grouped themselves with him in front of the women. The other one dug his spurs into his horse and it leaped forward. At that moment several shouting, screaming horsemen topped the rise and pounded toward the small group.

Majella got swift impressions of Cecilia's ashen face and of Eduardo's grim, methodical firing of his pistol at the oncoming men, at the same time keeping in front of Cecilia. She knew that one of their escort, also firing, was praying softly as he did it and that she felt an uprush of unholy exultation as one—then two—of the oncoming men were hit. One fell to the ground and his horse still came on for a few paces. Then it veered off sharply and ran away. The other man clutched his stomach and crouched over in his saddle. She could see blood welling over his hands.

All of a sudden, it was over. The bandits turned as one man and pounded away in retreat, having decided that the marksmanship of Eduardo and his men was too big a price to pay for whatever gold they could have gotten. Majella was aware of a feeling of shock that they would ride off without their comrade, not even stopping to see if he were dead or alive. A heavy, thick silence seemed to well up and surround them. Impossible. There

45

were too many sounds. There was the gentle sound of horses pawing in the dust, the creak of leather, a restless whinny or two. She crushed down an impulse to start screaming and never stop, and struggled for composure.

"Señor?" It was a gentle question. The man in front of her spoke to Eduardo. He had his hands clasped over his chest. He had been hit. And, oddly, he seemed rather apologetic about it. Or possibly confused. With infinite, terrible slowness he began to slide sidewise from his saddle.

"Oh, no," Eduardo was off his horse and beside his man. "Oh, no. Pedro, no." He sounded as if he were coaxing, pleading. Carefully, he eased the man to the ground. "Listen, Pedro," he said quickly, kneeling, but the man was already dead and Eduardo fell silent, still kneeling there, looking down into the man's face.

He looked up at Cecilia, despair in his eyes. "Are you all right, my dear?"

Cecilia's face was bone-white. Little shudders rippled through her and she gripped the reins with fear-frozen hands. "I—don't want to throw up," she said tightly, with a tinge of desperation. "I just must not do that."

Majella slid down from her horse and went to her sister. "Cecilia, dismount. Quickly, dear. We must help Eduardo. Hurry now." The gentle admonition steadied the other girl and she, too, dismounted.

"I'm sorry," she muttered, tugging at the strap on the saddle bag. "Take the reins, Majella. Hold him. I'll get some handkerchiefs. We can use them for bandages. We can—"

Majella put out a restraining hand. "It is no use, Cecilia."

"Enrique," Eduardo spoke to one of the mounted men. "Ride up over that rise and see if you can see them."

Instantly, the man Enrique was pounding away from them. Eduardo rose slowly. "Majella, are you all right, too?"

"Yes, Eduardo. What may we do to help?"

"Nothing, my dears. I—the men and I must—" He stopped, hopelessness in his face. He was clearly grieved at the deaths of these two men. He waited silently for the other man to come back.

"Gone, Señor. Nowhere in sight—Manuel is dead."

"Well, then, how far back is it to that stream? We'll need some willow branches to make litters. We'll have to take them home to their families. They must be properly—"

"But, Señor," the man said diffidently, removing his hat, "it will take forever, Señor. It will be dark soon."

"I won't take these men home to their families after they've been carried head-down over the back of a horse! Or do you want to leave them for the vultures and the wild dogs!" His tone was grim. "I'm sorry," he added quickly to the women.

"No, Señor," the man said, perhaps sighing. Majella could not be sure. "I could get the branches, Señor. And Fernando could stay with you."

"All right. Go. Be careful."

"Yes, Señor."

There was a long, hot interval of waiting as the sun sank lower and lower. Eduardo and the man,

47

Fernando, went to bring back the first dead man and laid him out on the ground beside the second. They covered them with a serape and stood there silently a moment, both crossing themselves. Majella wondered dully about the dead men's families. Small shivers of shock kept running through her. Cecilia went to stand beside her husband, sliding her arm through his. She began speaking to him gently. Majella heard snatches of what she said in attempting to comfort him. She was planning how she herself would talk to this person or that person who was bereaved. She planned how they could be godparents to someone else's unborn child and provide for it. They would, of course, purchase many masses. Despite Cecilia's sometimes irritating qualities, she was being a good wife to Eduardo. Majella felt proud of her at this moment.

"Mother of Christ!" Eduardo jerked his head up, his voice tight with quick rage that mingled with panic. In one gesture he dropped his pistol and thrust Cecilia behind him. "Don't move, Majella!"

Majella, seated on an outcropping rock, remained motionless, feeling suddenly cold in the hot sunlight. Had the bandits come back? Slowly, she turned her head, hearing the thud as Fernando also dropped his pistol to the ground and very slowly raised his hands above his head.

On the rise not far away were three—no!—four Indians, mounted bareback on quiet horses. Dirty rags covered the lower portions of their faces just below the eyes. Two of them wore battered felt hats. How long they had been there she had no way of knowing. There had been no sound of their approach, so they must have been walking the horses slowly.

One of them had a rifle trained on her. Stark, raw fear danced through Majella's mind and, not knowing why, she stood up.

"What do you want!" Eduardo shouted. "I warn you. I have more men. They will be coming. Do not touch the Señorita!" Taking a desperate chance Eduardo tried to pick up the pistol he had dropped. The pistol leapt off the ground as if alive and splattered dirt up into Eduardo's face. The Indians started coming slowly down the slope.

"Don't, Señor." It was the Indian who had fired the shot, cantering his horse slowly forward. Swooping down from his horse he picked up the pistol and thrust it into the piece of rope that served him as a sash or belt.

The first one, who seemed to be the leader, kept his rifle trained on Majella and spoke briefly in an alien dialect. In apparent obedience to this, one of them cantered his horse toward Eduardo. He was dark, squat, and heavily muscled. He spoke in an oddly soft voice.

"He says money, Señor."

In white-faced silence Eduardo took his soft leather purse from his pocket and tossed it to the man, who caught it neatly in mid-air. "Jewelry, Señor."

"I warn you—my men will—"

"Your watch, Señor." Still soft-voiced, he deliberately lifted his rifle and brought it down swiftly like a club upon Eduardo's head, knocking him sprawling in the dust.

"Eduardo!" Cecilia whirled about and bent over

49

him, shielding him. Eduardo, dazed, was trying to struggle up.

"Your watch, Señor. Everything." He leaned over and prodded Cecilia with his rifle. "Your rings, Señora."

Fernando stepped forward. "Do not touch the ladies!"

Another rifle blast shattered the air and Fernando froze where he was, not daring to move again. Tight-lipped, Cecilia was removing her rings.

"The cross, Lady," prompted the Indian, and Cecilia removed her gold crucifix.

"Give them your jewelry, Majella," she said tightly.

Silently, Majella removed her rings and her garnet necklace. The fourth Indian, one of those wearing a hat, slowly walked his horse down the slope. He removed the hat and held it out to Majella. She dropped the jewelry into it. Then, with incredible slowness, as if he had all the time in the world, he walked his horse completely around Majella. All about them lay the hot, vacant, silent California countryside. One of the horses shivered, knocking off flies, and snorted loudly.

"Now the guns," said the first Indian. And he gestured to the ammunition that studded Fernando's and Eduardo's belts.

"Wait! My God, you aren't going to leave us without horses!" Eduardo had struggled up and was standing, half bent-over, one hand clutching the side of his head. Blood seeped persistently between his fingers. The other Indian had gone to where the saddled horses were tethered. The horses were restless and jumpy from the shooting.

50

They milled about nervously, making it difficult.

Nobody replied.

The first Indian now went to Fernando.

"Jewelry, Señor." And grimly Fernando removed a ring, a pocket watch, and the crucifix from under his jacket.

The Indian near Majella jerked his head up sharply, as if he heard something, and spoke sharply in the Indian dialect. Suddenly all the Indians moved. They wheeled their horses quickly and galloped off, trailing the stolen horses behind them.

Then one separated from the group. Wheeling his horse, he came back and, never slowing his animal's pace, he leaned far over and caught Majella up from where she stood.

"No! Stop!" she screamed, twisting and struggling against his iron grip. In trying to hold and lift her at the same time, she got partly free and he dropped her. She fell painfully to the ground, tumbling head over heels in the dust. There was a crazy montage of images—of Eduardo, Fernando, Cecilia, all running toward her. But before they even got near, the Indian had circled around and come back. Another Indian at some distance had stopped, shouting a command, admonition, or warning. She was dragged a moment and then lifted up and flung over the front of his horse. It knocked the breath from her lungs. The horse sprang forward. Then, insanely, she was simply holding on, gripping the Indian's strong thigh, trying to keep from falling beneath the thundering hooves. The breath pounded from her lungs, dust roiled into her face, and there was an interval of insanity. At some point she lost consciousness and then regained it. They were going up hill and then down. They were among leafy branch growth—not trees, but something. Switches stung her face, snatched at her hair, jerked at her skirts. Now they were going up again, and up and up. The horse labored, striving and shuddering under the climb and the double weight. Then she lost consciousness again.

She awoke in the back of—what? A cave? Oh, surely not. It was semidark, but there was some daylight outside. Inside the cave was a flickering kerosene lantern and a fire glowing dimly in a pit. Some dead rabbits hung from an iron hook driven into the stone overhead. On a ledge were several bottles of wine. On the earth or stone floor was a helter-skelter pile of vegetables—ears of corn, squash, something root-like. Someone had detoured for provisions, or else had laid in a food supply. Oh, dear God—Cecilia—Eduardo—were they alive? Dead? *Mary, help us . . . help us!*

She was hurting. Her chest hurt. Her head throbbed. Her throat ached from thirst. Her arm quivered and collapsed when she tried to brace herself and sit up. Ahead of her, near the mouth of the cave, was movement, busyness; men piling things, pushing things, talking, sometimes laughing. Now and then Spanish phrases, but mostly their Indian dialect. She tried to sit up again. Her arm felt steadier. Not broken, after all. Mother of God, if she only had some water.

She was—had been—lying on a pile of saddles. She recognized the design in the silver mounting of one. Eduardo's saddle. Shaking, weaving a little, she sat straighter, pushing back her tangled hair. Her hands were dirty. Confusedly, she looked at her dirty hands. Then she became aware that one of the Indians had come away from the group and stood before her. She looked up at him. This one was the leader.

Big. Heavily muscled shoulders. A broad face. Small agate-hard eyes. "Joaquín," he said in Spanish, "the woman is awake."

He squatted down before her. Grasping her skirt he jerked it up roughly. At the same time he grasped her undergarments, tearing them off.

"*No!*" She kicked out, struck, trying to fend him off, struggling against him, sliding against the pile of loosely stacked saddles and saddle bags. "Get away! Stop!" Her words were cut off when he hit her a resounding blow on the side of the head. She had been half up and was slammed back into the saddles.

He stood up. He was laughing. "Joaquín. You caught us a wildcat."

She groveled away from him but there was no place to go. She huddled against the wall of the cave. The Indian who had kidnapped her now stood beside the other one. The other two came up to complete the circle. All stood looking down at her, laughing, except for the one called Joaquín, who did not even smile.

"Stay away from me! My brothers will kill you! My brother-in-law is Eduardo—" The words were cut off again by the youngest one. He kicked her, pushing her again against the rock wall.

"No, Pablo. Don't." The man Joaquín spoke, gesturing the others back. The men seemed surprised.

Then the leader laughed again. "No. We have other things in mind than kicking. Get up,

53

woman." He bent over and dragged her up. "I say this, Joaquín. Even a wildcat looks good to me." He stuck a finger beneath the top button of her bodice and ripped it open, popping off the little jet buttons without effort.

"No. Please," she gasped, trying to cover herself, half-fainting from terror. *Oh, Mary, Mother of God, please*.

"Leon," Joaquín stepped forward and placed his hand on the other man's arm. "I will take her in the back now."

"*You* will take her?" The man Leon seemed to forget her for a moment, his face blank with astonishment. "I am always first. Then you. Then Trinidad. Then Pablo. That is the way it always is when there is only one woman."

"Not this time," the man Joaquín said stubbornly. "*I* took this woman. She is mine."

Leon simply dropped her, completely forgotten. She fell awkwardly onto the ground and lay huddled there, not knowing whether to move or not. Her mind, mired in shock and hysteria, held only a single idea.

Run. Escape. Get out.

"You have lost your wits!" It was the dark stocky one who spoke. "Joaquín, you know that Leon is always first with a woman."

"Trinidad is right, Joaquín," the youngest one spoke. "That is the way of it."

"Not this time. We were going to leave them. I went back. I took her," Joaquín persisted stubbornly.

"Which was a stupid thing," Leon said. "You were never stupid before." There was the beginning of anger in his tone, which heretofore had

54

held only surprise and laughter. "We don't steal our women when there is money. Trini would have brought us a whore. Now you did this and have you thought what we will do after we have finished with her? Have you? Set her free? Return her to her people? Have you thought about that?" He was frowning down at her. There was a long pause. Then he shrugged. "Well, it is done now." He stooped over and caught her arm, dragging her up. "I hope she is worth the trouble."

"No, Leon. I am sorry." Joaquín had made no other sound, but his knife was in his hand. "Let her go. I will fight you if you make me."

"*Fight* me? Fight *me*!" For a moment he clearly didn't believe it. Then his face suffused with anger, almost rage. He pushed her from him. She staggered back, watching in terror as the two men circled one another, knives switching from hand to hand so the opponent would not know from which direction the thrust would come when it came.

Run.

She scrambled up and dashed for the mouth of the cave. The youth, Pablo, thrust out a foot and tripped her. She went sprawling, knocking down the spit they had erected over the fire hole. In a moment she struggled up but the man Trinidad had caught her and held her roughly, shaking her, his fingers digging agonizingly into her flesh. She got a hazy image of his broad, placid-looking face, now dark with anger.

"Joaquín! Leon! Stop." He shouted at the fighters. "We cannot fight each other! You said so. Leon, you said—"

But the two men had crashed together, and

moved about locked in a hideous kind of dance, each striving to avoid the other's knife and somehow drive his own home. Each seemed to be straining to the limit of his strength. Then, suddenly, they broke apart and instantly the younger one, Joaquín, lunged forward and sank his knife into the leader. Leon, with a kind of grunting gasp, went down on his knees and Joaquín jerked back. There was a long moment of ugly, stark silence in the cave.

"*Joaquín—*" Leon himself broke the silence. His voice was a mixture of astonishment, anger, and disbelief.

Joaquín flung aside his knife. He was clearly appalled at what he had done now. "I didn't mean it—" His violent flash of anger was over. He seemed stunned at what had happened.

Leon, on his knees, grimaced and gripped his left hand over his right shoulder. "Well, too bad your knife did not know that. If you have cut the muscles, I'll kill you—*well, look at it*! See how bad it is!" He was in command again. Joaquín sprang forward, pulling aside the cloth to examine the cut.

"It's the woman," muttered Trinidad. "She is bad luck. She will bring us nothing but evil."

"Here. Use this cloth." The youth, Pablo, picked up a piece of Majella's torn petticoat and extended it to Joaquín, who was intent on the wound. Carefully, he ripped up the cloth and bound the wound. Some blood seeped through the cloth, but both men appeared satisfied with it. They seemed to communicate without words—low murmurs, a sigh, a glance. When the bandage was

56

firm, Leon sat back on his heels and looked up at Joaquín.

"What now?"

The others intervened quickly, uneasy about the fight.

"She is bad luck," Trinidad said, still holding Majella firmly. He pushed her forward. "We must get rid of her."

"Leon always has the woman first," Pablo said stubbornly. "It is always so."

"Joaquín?" Leon prodded.

"No," Joaquín said. "No one. She is mine." He spoke slowly, rather painfully. "I am sorry."

Majella, too, stared at the leader, knowing instinctively that his prestige hung in the balance.

"She can be my share," Joaquín bargained. "I will take her. You three can divide everything else."

Leon got up slowly, grimacing slightly with pain.

"Why don't we gamble for her?" he asked. "We gamble for everything else." His eyes locked with Joaquín's for a moment. Joaquín had been about to refuse, but then quickly agreed. He turned.

"Where are the counters, Pablo?" Joaquín asked.

The boy dived toward the back of the cave and disappeared from view. Majella knew suddenly that there were other caves behind this one.

He was back in a moment with a lopsided basket. He dumped the contents on the floor in the lantern light. There were little pegs, or bits of bone, some with markings, some plain. The game commenced, the men squatting opposite one another on the dusty floor of the cave. It was getting darker outside. They played in the flicker of the oil lantern, which cast leaping shadows about them as the flame moved. One man would pick up a counter, concealing which one it was, and hold up his fist. Then the other would do the same. Plain or marked? The second man must match the first to score. Most of the pegs were used now. There were desultory comments. Majella watched them in fascinated horror.

Once the youth Pablo said, "Someone should skin the rabbits. We need to eat sometime."

Leon said, not looking up, "Don't trust the woman to do it. She'll try to run again."

Joaquín glanced up. "Trini, let her go a while." He jerked his head toward the back of the cave. "Go back." He spoke to Majella. Trinidad released her and she stumbled back—to where? Where did he mean to go? The pile of saddles? Was that where he meant? Dazed, she tried to rub some of the numbness from her arms that Trinidad's merciless grip had inflicted.

"She is bad luck." Trinidad watched her sullenly as she paused by the saddles and sank to the ground.

"She is more than that," Leon murmured, glancing up. He shot her a fleeting look of pure hatred. "Her rich relatives will scour the countryside for her."

She went sick with the sudden intensity of fear of this man, knowing instinctively that he would kill her without a moment's hesitation. He wanted her as dead as the rabbits that hung so limply from the ceiling, their fur clotted with blood.

Then the game was over.

"You win," Leon said. "Go enjoy your woman." He leaned back against the side of the cave, closing his eyes.

Joaquín stood up, pausing uncertainly, looking down at Leon.

Leon opened his eyes. "What are you waiting for?"

Pablo stepped forward, placatingly. "Go, Joaquín. Take the woman. When you come back Trini and I will have the food cooked." The fight between Leon and Joaquín had made him uneasy and he was too young to hide it. "Here, take a drink of wine first. Get the dust out of your throat."

Still uncertain, Joaquín took the bottle. It had been opened and the cork put back in crookedly. He turned to Majella and started toward her, gesturing toward the opening.

"Take the lantern, Joaquín," Leon said. "It will be black as tar back there soon. We have the firehole. Joaquín!"

Joaquín stopped and turned back.

"Leave your knife here, you fool. She might get her hands on it. She's a fox."

A half-smile touched Joaquín's mouth. "I thought you said she was a wildcat." But he tossed his knife down at Leon's feet. Leon smiled, with his eyes still shut, grimacing slightly.

Majella stayed where she was, frozen, unable to move.

"Go, woman." There was a hint of impatience in Joaquín's tone. He jerked his head toward the back. When she still couldn't move, he transferred the bottle to the hand that held the lantern. Then he reached down and took her arm, pulling her up and starting toward the opening in the back. She stumbled and fell. He didn't even stop, but went on, tightening his grip and pulling her along on the dirty floor.

"Wait," she gasped. "Let me up. Please—" But he ignored her, dragging her through the next cave and another one before he released her. She lay inertly, feeling the coldness of the stone beneath the dust. *Oh, sweet Mother of God, protect me now and at the hour of my death.* She waited, and nothing happened.

After a time, she struggled up and sat bracing herself against the wall. The man Joaquín had set the lantern on an outcropping of rock. He opened the bottle and sat staring at her morosely.

She must talk to him, bargain with him somehow. What should she say? Her exhausted and stunned mind refused to function.

"Leon is right. It was stupid to steal you." The man spoke almost as if to himself, his tone sullen and angry. "Trinidad is right. You are bad luck. For you I cut my knife into Leon. He is like my brother." He stared down at the bottle for a long, somber time.

"You—speak very well," she said with an effort.

He appeared not to hear. Then, after a while he sighed. "Are you thirsty?"

Thirsty. Oh, dear God, if she could only have something to drink. "Water," she said desperately. "Is there any water?"

"Not back here," he answered. Then he clamped his strong white teeth about the cork and pulled it from the bottle. He held it out to her. "Drink some." A half-smile played about his mouth.

60

She didn't want wine. She wanted water. But she took it quickly and drank a swallow right from the bottle. Two. Three. In quick succession, so intense was her thirst. She drank it as one would drink water. Then she realized it was tart and strong. She strangled, gasping for breath and holding out the bottle blindly. He took it back and put it to his own lips.

"Leon would kill me if he knew I let you drink our wine," he said, still with the half-smile.

So that was what had amused him. She wished she could have refused but her thirst had been too great. She leaned against the wall; the harsh, cheap wine was like liquid fire in her throat and stomach. She wondered, vaguely, if she would vomit. What should she do now? Oh, yes, she must try to talk to this Indian, reason with him.

"Thank you for the wine," she said carefully.

He did not reply, but tipped up the bottle to take another few swallows.

"My brother-in-law will be searching for me," she said. "He is Eduardo Obregón. He is a ranchero. He will pay you to take me home."

The Indian was staring at her somberly as he corked the bottle and set it carefully on the ground. Slowly he stood up. He towered over her. Tall, strongly built, heavily muscled.

She shrank back against the wall. "He will pay you well. My brother-in-law—"

"Your brother-in-law will see me hanged, woman." He grasped her arms and pulled her up against him. "He will kill us all."

"No. Please." She gasped, struggling against him. "I promise he will—"

He half-carried, half-dragged her to the dark at

61

the back and dropped her, coming down beside her on the floor, clasping her loosely, pulling aside what was left of her bodice.

"Stop. . . . No. . . . Please. . . ." She knew in confused terror that her writhing and resisting only incited him, but she could not stop struggling.

He pushed her back roughly onto the hard stone floor.

"Lie back! You stupid bad-luck woman! I will take you. I'm going to die for it anyway." He was over her, on top of her, pinning her down.

She struggled insanely beneath him. Her mind seemed to explode. She started screaming with terror. With rage. Then she screamed with pain. Then there was nothing but blackness.

A long time later there was a lesser blackness, and a drifting in and out of it. There was a small pool of light somewhere. There was the faint smell of roasting meat. There was the murmur of voices. Not an argument exactly, but someone trying to persuade someone to do something. Some of it she could understand, some was in that other language again. She drifted slowly in and out of her blackness, making no effort to do either. She did not regret moving into the blackness. She did not regret emerging from it again, to hear the slow, persistent, almost coaxing sounds of the voice of the persuader and of the one he spoke with.

". . . bad mistake. I should not have done it. I know this . . . I am sorry . . ."

". . . not speak of sorry, my friend. It is too late. But we must . . . I will do it. You need not even know how or when. All you need is to put it behind you . . ."

"I need to keep the woman . . ."

". . . cannot. There is no way. Where . . . how safe would . . ."

"I must keep the woman . . ."

". . . other women. No need . . . dangerous . . ."

"I would keep her inside the house until she is gentled. She could help the grandfather. He is old . . ."

"I myself will do it for you. I will not even hurt her. It will be quick . . . like killing a squirrel . . ."

"No, I will keep the woman . . . keep the woman with me. I will not let her go. That is the end of it . . ."

There was movement of the little pool of light until it wavered directly over her. The man Leon stood there, looking down at her. Joaquín came and stood just behind him.

"Let her be, Leon." Joaquín's voice was deadly cold.

As cold as the ancient cold from the masses of stone she lay on. Majella felt it seeping through her body. Leon wanted her dead. The light played up in his broad face above her. She thought she could see her death in his small black eyes. She should welcome death, but realized she could not. Sick fear crawled in her stomach. *Mary, save me. Don't let him kill me.* Then *Mary* became *Joaquín* in her mind. *Joaquín, don't let him kill me.*

"Tell me when you change your mind," Leon said, sighing. He handed the lantern to Joaquín and went soundlessly toward the opening into the outer caves.

63

"I will not change my mind about the woman," Joaquín said, his voice still cold and rock-hard. Now the light flickered over his still face, broad, strong, like a stone image above her. He squatted down beside her. *He had won her a little more time.*

"You are awake? You heard?"

"Some." She found she could barely whisper.

He extended one hand and placed it on her naked chest below her breasts, caressing her flesh absent-mindedly as he might caress a child, or a dog. His thoughts were elsewhere, his eyes somber. "I will take you with me to my village. Do you understand that?"

Yes, she understood it, but now could not speak at all. She only knew she was lost to her own world because this man had made her his possession, his slave. Convulsively, without knowing, she caught at his hand and held it.

Chapter Four

Cecilia realized she had stopped praying some time ago and stared blankly at the carved wooden altar in the Obregón chapel. Since day before yesterday, her mind seemed distracted and inclined to lapse into periods of blankness. Her knees ached. Without getting up, she eased herself back against the bench.

"Come away, little one. You have prayed long enough."

She turned and saw Eduardo seated on one of the benches toward the back. They were alone in the chapel. She had not heard him come in. He had probably come through the outside door.

She got up now, feeling stiff and sick, and went to sit beside him, trying not to look at the purple smear of bruise on his face, with the smashed flesh healing darkly. *Oh, please, Mary—Don't let him be scarred*. Perhaps he would not be. It had only been two days since they had been rescued by a party of Americans on their way to the Mormon community in San Bernardino.

"Thank God for them," Eduardo had said later. Being simple and good people, they had been horrified at the tragedy and helped as a matter of course, the women in their ugly cotton bonnets tending to Cecilia and bandaging Eduardo's head. Somehow, without a common language, they had all managed to communicate. The men in the plain clothing had carefully placed the dead men in one of their wagons and, although it took them far out of their way, simply assumed they must see the Obregón party safely to their home.

This accomplished, being Americans they were anxious to be on their way. They declined with thanks Eduardo's and Cecilia's repeated invitations to stay on for a few weeks. They stayed the night and insisted on leaving at dawn the next day after a scanty meal. They did accept a gift of dried beef and some fresh fruit that Cecilia had thought to offer.

"It is best this way, my love," Eduardo said as they stood waving their guests out of sight.

"They could have stayed a few days," Cecilia murmured. It had been a godsend of a distraction, pushing to the back of her mind for the moment what had happened to her sister.

"Their ways are different from our ways. If our own people had been the ones to help us, the whole countryside would be alive with gossip within a week. This way the news of the tragedy goes with them to their new place. It gives us time to think."

They turned and walked back into the house. It had been such a happy house a few months ago when Cecilia had come here as Eduardo's bride. Now the servants seemed to skulk about, uneasy, fearful, angry at the deaths of their friends and at what had happened to the ranchero. If the master, who had seemed so invincible, could be struck down—was anyone safe? Beads were much in evidence, sliding through brown fingers. And here and there, to reinforce the beads, various charms against evil and danger began to appear.

The sun was quite high that first morning after their arrival when Eduardo had held a belated service in the small Obregón chapel, which was packed with even those people who sometimes forgot to come. Cecilia tried to imitate her husband's composure and sat sedately on the bench, fighting the dammed up tears. Eduardo had barely slept at all in what had been left of the night, and his head and face must have been painful in the extreme. But doggedly he read from the book, led the prayers, and only when they were alone again did he show his terrible fatigue. He had sat down beside her rather suddenly after the chapel was empty again, a ragged sigh escaping him.

He had put his arm around her shoulders and she leaned against him. Only when he pressed his linen handkerchief into her hand did she realize she was crying. The tears had finally escaped, and coursed silently down her face.

"If only I hadn't been so jealous," she whispered. "I was. Always. I pretended I wasn't. It was a lie." With great difficulty the broken words were wrenched out. "Always. Since we were little. Mama and Papa—they loved her best. Best of us all."

"Oh, no, my dear." Eduardo caressed her shoulder, his hand gentle and loving.

"Always. Since the beginning. She—was their best beloved. I knew it. And—she knew it. I don't know about the boys. Maybe they didn't know. Maybe they didn't mind if they did know. *I* knew. *I* minded."

"Cecilia, don't. You must not torment yourself. It is too late. Your sister—may God have mercy on her soul—is gone—" He struggled on, his voice cracking. "She loved you dearly. She would not want you to—" He could scarcely continue. All his poise, his maturity, seemed to disintegrate. He bent over, his head almost in Cecilia's lap.

It broke her heart and she gripped him close.

"Eduardo. My darling. Please."

When he had regained his composure he straightened up, his battered face twisting in a grimace.

"I am the one who has failed Majella. You don't realize it yet, but I did."

"How! What could you have done that you didn't do? Or try to do. You were helpless. There was nothing—"

"Yes. There was one thing. There is always danger of something like this happening and I should have prepared myself, but I was sick with fear—that it might be you. I couldn't think straight. I could only think of protecting you. I know that Pedro always carries a derringer in his sleeve. He is never without it. When he fell from his horse and I helped him, I could have taken it. I was within inches of that gun. I could have taken it."

"But a derringer is so small. What good would

it have been against four Indians with rifles. I don't see—"

"I could have given it to *her*, to Majella." The words, bleak and ugly, fell between them and there was silence for a time. Sunlight streamed in from the open doorway, bathing the hard-packed earth of the floor, touching the polished wood of the altar. A small white butterfly came in, hovered by the opening a moment, and then fluttered out.

"She could have used it—for herself. I couldn't stop them. I couldn't get to her then. But—when she fell from that horse, there was a moment there when I could have thrown it. She might have got it. It could have saved her from—from what she must have gone through."

"*Oh, my God.*" The strangled scream tore itself from Cecilia's throat. She really faced this thought for the first time and was sickened, stunned, horrified. She got up and stumbled to the altar. She fell to her knees and started to pray intensely, feverishly, not realizing for a long time that she was praying for Majella's soul as if she were certain that Majella was dead.

Since that time she had spent much time in the chapel. Now, she got up at Eduardo's bidding and went to him. "You have sent word to Miguel and Hernán?" She had mentioned this before.

"Yes. And word to the authorities in Los Angeles. I am offering a reward for the Indians' capture. And I have put out word among our workers repeatedly offering money for information."

"Do you think it will do any good?" She slid her arm through his. These days she felt constant need to hold to him, touch him, cling to him.

69

"The Indians often know things they don't mention to us," he said grimly. "Money loosens tongues."

"You—want those men captured?"

"I want them dead. I won't rest until they are." The usually kindly voice was suddenly chilling. "I want—God help me—I want to know the worst about Majella."

"I want my sister *back*." Cecilia spoke in a flat, unemotional voice, sounding almost childlike.

"But Cecilia—" He stared at her in astonishment, down into her beautiful upturned face with the vivid steel-blue eyes, the smooth black hair that came down to a widow's peak on her brow, the creamy skin of her forehead.

"I want my sister back," she repeated stubbornly. "It doesn't matter what—has happened to her. I want to—make it up to her. I'll take care of her. I'll—"

"Cecilia, you must accept the fact that Majella cannot possibly be alive now. If she is, she will wish herself dead. Anyhow, she must be. Those renegades would have gotten rid of her as soon as—they could," he finished awkwardly.

"I want her *back. Here.*"

He observed his young wife thoughtfully, sadly. She turned from him, intent on her own thoughts. He had to find Majella—somehow, any way at all. No matter what it cost, Miguel and Hernán would come and help. They would pay. Anything. It hadn't done Majella any good to be the favorite child, to be best beloved, if she ended like this. And that didn't matter now. She must not let it matter now.

"Eduardo," she said, after a moment, "do you

70

suppose that—being so much Indian—that it might have been easier for her?"

"Don't think about it, Cecilia. Don't torment yourself."

"But she was. Majella was three-quarters Indian. Perhaps—" she paused, considering, a frown pulling down the smooth brows.

"What about him—her white grandfather? Did you read that letter, Eduardo?"

"Yes. Miguel insisted, and Majella permitted it."

"What was he like, that man? How did it happen?"

"He was a ship's captain, Angus Phail. That is, at first he owned several ships. Quite wealthy, it seems. He had come from Scotland. None of this really matters now, Cecilia."

"It does. Tell me."

"Well, he was hurt—disappointed in love. The woman he wanted married another. A man named Ortegna. Phail seems to have become deranged to some degree. Anyway, he gave up everything, or managed to lose it all. Your father tried to be tactful in the letter, but it seemed clear that he engaged in all sorts of excesses in his—grief, I suppose. Drinking, gambling, fighting. Eventually, it was learned that he had gone to live among the Indians at San Gabriel. He lived with, or married, an Indian woman. They had a child, your mother. For some reason, he took your mother as an infant and gave her to the woman who had rejected him. It seems she had none of her own and had much sorrow in her life. Apparently, the squaw, his Indian wife, had several children from a previous husband and didn't mind giving up her infant. It is a strange story."

71

"How did Mama get to live in Papa's house?"

"Your father's mother was Señora Ortegna's sister. When Señora Ortegna died, your mother was taken into the Moreno household. With her came the box of Señora Ortegna's jewels, which had been given to her by Angus Phail. Felipe's mother, your grandmother, became her guardian and brought her up as a daughter. She was very distressed when your mother ran away, very angry."

"And she married Majella's father—who was he?"

"An Indian who worked on the Moreno ranch. They ran off together."

"Mama! I cannot imagine it." Cecilia said wonderingly. "It seems so—unlike Mama. She was devoted to Papa. She loved him very much."

"I'm sure she came to in time. The Indian—I can't think of his name—died. I think they had a difficult time. They had lost one child before your sister was born. Anyhow, your mother came back to the Moreno ranch with Majella. That is about all. Her grief finally spent itself. Eventually, she married your father. He raised Majella as his own daughter."

"I cannot imagine Mama having such a life before us, before our family."

Eduardo turned toward the chapel door, squinting against the sun. "Yes?"

One of the workers came forward, uncertainly. He was holding his battered hat, shifting it from one hand to the other.

"Yes, Fidel. What is it?"

"Señor, I have heard in the orchard that you seek to know of those who attacked you and stole the horses. That—" He ended with a shrug.

72

"Yes." Eduardo's hand went immediately to the pocket of his jacket. He withdrew a soft leather purse. "I will reward anyone who gives me information."

Again the shrug, deprecating, as if the information was of no consequence. "It is only that Manuela Esparza's cousin who works on the Acevedo rancho is of the Luiseño people. He is a good man. He goes to the chapel. He works hard. But in the village from which he came there are those—" Again the shrug, this time with an expressive gesture.

A generous amount of money changed hands. Bit by bit the scanty information was forthcoming. There was an established renegade band from this Luiseño village. But then one knew that many existed. These might not be the right ones. Then again, they might. This was a group of four men who rode together on raids. It was said that one had a cast in one eye, and was short and heavily built.

In the end there was enough information to convince Eduardo to follow through. Taking a considerable supply of money and a group of eleven well-armed men, he started out.

Cecilia watched them until they were specks in the distance. Majella must be alive. And they must find her. They must. They must bring her back. It would be all right. Everything would be all right again.

Sisters love one another. Now, tell me that. Say you love your sister. How many times had Mama said that, so softly, so gently, so relentlessly. Cecilia wanted to cry and smile at the same time. *It's*

73

all right, Mama. I'll help her. I'll take care of her now. I promise it. I'll say it. I love my sister.

She turned, a faint smile lingering on her lips. *Mama, not sister, really. Half sister.*

Chapter Five

Some daylight from the far opening crept into the back cave, so it must be daylight somewhere. There was total silence. Majella shut her eyes again, nausea rocking her. Her head was pounding. She lay perfectly still, knowing if she moved even slightly the pounding would increase to sharp pain. Everything was so quiet. Where was he now? The Indian, Joaquín?

When she opened her eyes again the Indian Leon stood before her. He must have come into the back cave as soundlessly as a shadow. The silence was intense. She watched him for a long moment, feeling a vague fear, but oddly detached from her surroundings. *Joaquín wouldn't let him kill her.* The man Leon's faded worn shirt was stiff with blackened blood from Joaquín's knife. The shirt was draped over his shoulders. In one hand he carried a battered metal bucket.

"Get up," he said in Spanish. "I have to get some water. I can't leave you here."

At first she had thought that she could not move, but the idea of water made her try. Dizzily, she sat up. After a moment she struggled to her feet, staggering, catching the wall for support. She hit her head against the low curved ceiling of the cave and gasped sharply at the sudden intensity of the pain.

"Water," she managed to whisper.

"We will get some water. Come." He started out and she followed after him. She was aware that he watched her closely as they went to the outer cave. "Don't be stupid and try to run," he said as they went outside.

She had to shut her eyes a moment against the glare. Then, with the light somewhat blurred by the protective tears that sprang up, she stumbled along after him.

They were surrounded by what seemed to be an endless towering of cliffs and rounded stone formations. He went slowly, adjusting his pace to her faltering progress. They went over stones and through craggy groups of rocks that afforded narrow passage. Always downward. The earth on which they walked was sandy, and what growth there was seemed scanty and dry, mostly weeds and brittle grasses. It was late afternoon.

"Where is the water?" She gasped once, clinging to a rough towering stone.

"Soon." He paused and waited for her, letting her rest a moment. His black eyes and his bronze face were completely without expression. There was a slight movement by her hand against the stone and a small stone-colored lizard darted away. She snatched back her hand from the rock and they continued their way downward. There could not be any water in this vacant, arid place. It was hopeless.

Yet there was. She knew there was when she saw little patches of green somewhere below. And now and then, small tufts of bright orange poppies fluttered from beneath a stone. Then, around a rock mass and downward again, and it spread before her. Water, clear and sparkling, dashing itself wastefully down the rocks to splash into the shallow spreading pool and wander on. There was even a small clump of trees—she did not know what kind. Slim with patches of dark on pale trunks. Paradise. The pool, clear, moving this way and that over sand and smooth stones, lay before her. She pushed past the Indian, stumbling, clutching at rocks and tree trunks. Then she was beside it. She went down on her knees, half in the water, drenching her torn and dirty dress. She cupped her hands and drank greedily. Not enough. Not nearly enough. She stopped, gasping for breath. Water fell through her fingers. She lay down flat and drank directly from the flowing stream. It got in her nose, strangled her. It drenched her hair.

Finally, she could lift her head and sit up, water running off her face, down her neck. She looked around for the Indian. He was seated on a rock by the stream. The front of his shirt was slightly wet, so he had drunk too.

He took the blood-stained shirt from around his shoulders, leaving them bare. The bandage over his cut was darkly crusted. He moved his shoulder carefully, and then tossed the shirt toward her.

"Wash it."

For a moment she didn't grasp what he meant. The shirt landed on a bush a little distance from her and hung there in the hot motionless air.

But she wasn't thinking about the shirt. She still had not seen Joaquín. Where was he?

"Where—are the others?" she asked carefully. She was alone with this man. The others were nowhere—nowhere in sight, in or out of the caves. And this was the one who wanted her dead.

"Pablo is getting some game. Trinidad and Joaquín took the horses." He spoke casually, no expression in his face.

"Took them where?" She tried to crush down the panic, but she had heard him last night. He would kill her quickly, like a squirrel. Had he finally persuaded Joaquín?

"To a man we know who buys horses. He buys any horses that Trinidad brings him. He doesn't ask anything. They will be back before dark. Wash the shirt. We have to go back."

Numbly, she got up. Joaquín was coming back. Relief made her giddy for a moment. This Leon wasn't going to do anything but sit there on the stone and wait for his shirt. She walked over and got it, her wet skirts dragging about her ankles. Suddenly she turned. "Where are the saddles?"

He glanced up at her sudden frantic tone. "In the cave."

Another wave of relief.

"Why, woman?"

"In my—my saddle bag. I have some things. There is a comb." It seemed vital to comb her hair. *Had Cecilia put in a change of dress?* That, too, seemed vital. She must clean herself, wash up, comb her hair, get rid of this torn and dirty traveling dress. Somehow, some way, she must gather together the shreds of her dignity. It was not fitting for Majella Moreno to—

Holding the shirt, her legs collapsed and she went down again by the stream. What dignity? She tried to shut out the searing memory of the man Joaquín, tried to shut out the memory of the night, of the back cave. *Wash the shirt*. She bent over the rushing water and started to wash the worn and bloodstained cloth. She could hardly see what she was doing because the tears had started to flow. She kept her face turned from the Indian, hoping he would not see.

"That is enough."

She lifted wet frightened eyes and knew that Leon stood beside her. Obediently, with hands numb from the cold water, she attempted to wring out the shirt.

He squatted down beside her and reached for it. With a faint sound of disgust he took the dripping cloth and twisted it in his own strong hands, wincing slightly because of the shoulder wound. Then he stood up, shaking it out in the bright sunlight that would soon dry it.

"Fill the bucket."

She got up, every aching bone and muscle in her body protesting, and went to get the bucket. After she had filled it, she set it on the ground beside him and stood waiting.

He had examined the shirt and seemed satisfied. It was still too wet to put on. He held it in a loose bundle in his good hand.

"Bring the water." He motioned to the path they had come down and started. After a moment

79

she picked up the full bucket and started after him. There was no point in trying to run. She had no idea where they were. She had no doubt but that he could catch her and overpower her, wounded or not. She had no sense of place or direction yet. All she had been able to see from the high places were the endless tortured formations of rocks and cliffs. If she could, by some miracle, escape from him, she would die before anyone found her. And if someone did—who might it be? Those bandits who had shot Pedro and the other man? More renegade Indians? Stumbling, holding onto rocks, she trudged along behind him.

"You are spilling it," he said once, turning to glance at her. There was anger in his tone. Desperately, she tried to hold it more carefully. Going back was all uphill, a gentle, relentless incline. When they finally reached the caves again she was staggering, and sweat dripped over her eyes. Her breath came raggedly.

"Put it down."

It was a long moment before she could; her fingers seemed rigidly fixed about the handle. Finally she did, then straightened up stiffly. She had to do something. What was it she meant to do? They were standing at the mouth of the outer cave. Oh, the comb. The dress.

"May I have some water, please?"

"Why? You drank." He seemed mildly surprised.

"I—want to wash."

Again he made the faint sound of disgust or contempt and reached around inside the cave, plucking a gourd from the rock shelf. "Use this.

Don't foul the water in the bucket." He handed the gourd to her.

Carefully, she dipped it into the bucket and then carried it back through the outer caves to the back one. She set it down, balancing it with some stones. Then she went back to the pile of saddles and moved them slightly. They were very heavy. She found the one she had used. Beneath it was the saddle bag. *Her comb.* A wave of thankfulness washed over her. Fresh, clean garments. *Oh, Cecilia, thank you.*

She used a handkerchief for a cloth and washed as well as she could in the semi-darkness of the back cave. When she finished there wasn't much water left in the gourd. The fresh dress was of soft, reddish-brown challis. The traveling dress with the torn bodice was in a heap on the floor. She was reaching for the challis dress when she became aware that she was no longer alone. Clutching the dress in front of her, she turned slowly around.

It was Joaquín. He had come back! Just as Leon had said. Then she saw the quick leap of desire in his eyes as he came toward her.

"Oh, no. No!" She backed away, backed up against the wall, still clutching the dress. He reached over, plucked it out of her hands, and tossed it aside.

"Come here."

She was suddenly crazed. It had seemed to her shocked and stunned mind that the degradation was finished. That it was not, filled her now with insane rage. She lashed out like an animal, her hands like claws. She would kill him. Kill. A red haze filled the cave. She would *not* submit to him again!

Then he struck her. She slammed back against the wall and slid down to the floor, no breath left in her body.

"Foolish woman."

She sat there, staring up vacantly into the broad, strong face; black, gleaming eyes: sensual mouth.

"Did you think you could fight against *me*?" His voice was somewhat quiet, with an undercurrent of amusement. "You cannot do that." He squatted down and reached over, placing one hand at the side of her neck, moving his fingers slowly, shaking his head. "Foolish little woman. Now, listen to me, foolish one. I take my pleasure with you when I want to. If you fight me I shall beat you first. Then I take my pleasure. Even without sense you should decide it is better not to fight."

"But you—last night—" she whispered. "I thought—"

"I take you when I need you." His fingers tightened on her neck.

"But I—my—you see—"

"I need you now." His tone was still quiet, oddly polite, totally relentless.

In growing dread, fear, and strange, dark fascination, she gazed up at him.

"Now," he said, standing up and pulling her up with him.

Hopeless, she did not resist him again. She did owe him her life.

* * *

Majella settled into a dull continuing nightmare. Some of the time she did not believe it was happening. She contrived to withdraw into herself to escape it, retreating into long intervals of vacancy when she thought of nothing, realized nothing, was nothing. Thus it could be morning and then, somehow, without her marking the passage of the hours, be dusk again. She did not know that she sat silently against the wall staring vacantly into space during these times, nor did she care. Gradually, she became aware of various circumstances. These small vignettes emerged clearly.

Joaquín would not permit her to starve. She realized this when she fainted the second day of her captivity. They had offered her what remained of their cooked meat and corn, and she had turned away from it, retching painfully from the emptiness inside her. Then later, she wasn't sure when, Joaquín came to her with an orange. From somewhere there was now a row of oranges on the rock shelf. He sat before her on the floor, peeling the orange, separating the sections.

"Here. Eat." He held out a section. Accustomed to obeying him now, she opened her lips. He put the bit in her mouth.

There was a deep sigh from Leon, and he said something in a mixture of Spanish and his own tongue. She got the sense of it. The woman was as helpless as a newborn infant. Then she tasted the unbelievable sweetness of the orange and the juice dribbled onto her chin. She wiped it off, reaching out a shaking hand for the rest. Smiling, Joaquín gave it to her. When he smiled it showed in his eyes. One would not think to see him smile that he was a renegade. That was the day she started to eat again.

Then there was the day that Joaquín started teaching her to cook the food.

"Let the woman do it!" Leon spoke in exasperation to young Pablo, who did most of the cooking and was about to skin some rabbits. "She's tamed enough to use the knife now. Joaquín, tell her to come and skin the rabbits for Pablo."

Joaquín jerked his head and she got up and went to the opening of the outer cave. Outside, the dead rabbits lay sprawled on the ground where Pablo had dropped them. Joaquín picked up the knife and handed it to her, watching her speculatively. When she made no move toward the dead animals, a smile twitched at his mouth. Laughter gleamed a moment in his eyes.

"Do you know how to clean rabbits for cooking?"

She shook her head.

There were groans of astonishment mingled with disbelieving laughter from the others, as they sauntered toward the front of the cave to watch.

"I will teach you," Joaquín said. "Don't laugh at her. She can't help it. No one ever taught her anything."

She learned. She learned how to keep from vomiting from the odor of a freshly cut-open animal. She learned to carry the offal far enough away from the entrance to keep out the flies. She learned to remove the pelt without tearing it too badly. She learned how to secure the meat to the wooden sticks they used as spits. She learned to roast them over the coals so that neither the meat nor the spits caught fire. She learned not to burn herself in the process. Joaquín was a careful teacher, with endless patience, laughing off the ridicule of his friends. He treated her kindly now, but she was not deceived. Beneath the kindness lay that iron determination. She belonged to him, and she must not forget it.

Her duties were to prepare the food, keep everything orderly in the caves, and wash the men's shirts. She found herself sometimes wondering anxiously if she had done everything, and done it well—wondering if she had pleased Joaquín.

Then, sometime during the sojourn in the caves, she learned that she owned nothing, that nothing at all belonged to her. The sense of the mingled Spanish and Indian languages was that Joaquín had paid for her comb and the extra clothing by taking a lesser share as they divided the stolen things.

They were satisfied with the money Trinidad had received for the stolen horses. In a day or so he, Pablo, and Joaquín took the saddles and saddle bags to sell. The money was accumulating in a broken pottery jar in the second cave. It was mounting up. The contents of the saddle bags were strewn in orderly piles on the floor. By this time, she could sit and stare impassively at Cecilia's prayer book with the gold clasp, at her own garnet necklace, at Eduardo's fine linen handkerchiefs and extra tobacco pouch, at little stacks of their clothing. Everything was carefully accounted for. Some things they decided to sell, others they kept among themselves.

Joaquín himself had taken a fancy to her garnet necklace and wore it twisted around his wrist. He only took it off when he had to leave the cave, and he put it on as soon as he came back. Often, she found herself gazing at his wrist, smooth, brown, strongly muscled, as he moved his hands—cleaning a rifle, tossing down the pegs in a game, eating with the other men. The round, dark-red beads seemed a deeper, richer color when strung so about his wrist.

They took their time, never hurrying, discussing everything leisurely. It was as if they were totally safe and secure in this impregnable fortress of stone cliffs and twisted masses of rock. Indeed, no one ever came to the caves. She saw no one but her captors.

While the business was being transacted, she was often alone with Leon. She understood that it was better for a wounded Indian not to go into settlements. It might arouse questions. Leon rarely spoke to her except to issue a command. He never hurt her. He was indisputably the master of the group, for they all obeyed him, and he made the final decisions. But Joaquín had taken one stand against him about her, and he had let it pass. Apparently Joaquín's friendship was worth more to him than any woman.

She knew, though, that he was her implacable enemy. She handed him a wine bottle once when they were alone and it slipped from her grasp, smashing the bottle and wasting the wine. There was a brief flare of anger in his eyes, quickly hidden. He had raised a hand to strike her but the blow did not fall.

She had cowered back instinctively. "I didn't mean to!"

"Get another bottle." His tone had held quiet hate.

86

She hurried to obey and when she had opened it and handed it to him, he said, still quietly, his voice the more deadly because of this:

"Don't shake like that. Some day I will kill you, woman. But not today."

She lived with this idea, and it did not seem strange in her strange new world. Often at night she watched his rough-hewn face in the light from the firehole. There was an odd sense of security in the broad strength of it. Some day Leon would kill her. But not today.

Because Joaquín didn't want him to. Joaquín was her protector against them all. He was her world.

The disposal of the stolen items took longer than they had anticipated. There was much talk, much idleness, many games with the little pegs or with a greasy pack of cards one of them had. They would go home the next day. Then the next. She became more aware of the stocky man, Trinidad. Sometimes when no one was looking he touched her, tried secretly to fondle her. She endeavored to stay clear of him. When Joaquín was gone she waited anxiously for his return. Eventually, even the youngest of them, Pablo, began to stare at her and loiter as close as he could, sometimes touching her.

Leon was aware of this and it amused him. He held them off, but just barely.

"Let her go, Trinidad," he said, half-laughing, after Trinidad had mauled her about for some time one afternoon. She was struggling grimly against him, breathlessly trying to get away from him. "Let her go!" Leon said again, unmistakable authority in his tone now. With an angry oath Trinidad released her, glaring at her.

"You don't want Joaquín's knife in you. He is crazy for this woman. Go on outside awhile. We will soon be going back to the village and you have your woman there." So it was that she knew Leon would grudgingly protect her, as long as Joaquín wanted her protected. She needed Joaquín.

Both Leon and Joaquín were outside the caves when the boy Pablo lost control and attacked her. She was in the back cave and suddenly he leaped upon her, causing them both to fall to the floor. At the sound of her smothered scream, Joaquín was there in an instant. Pablo was torn away, pushed, kicked, and beaten toward the opening. Crouched on the floor and shaking with fear, her stomach jerking with nausea, Majella heard the brutal beating Joaquín gave him, the blows, the cries.

Leon stopped it. She heard the exchange.

"Stop. *Stop it.* Joaquín! Don't kill for her."

"I killed for you," Joaquín's voice was thick with rage.

"That was different." Leon became quietly placating. "I am your friend. Pablo has been your friend since he was a child. He made a mistake. You must understand, Joaquín. He is young. His manhood is demanding. He cannot control it. You are the only one of us who has a woman. We are going back to the village soon, but in the meantime . . ."

For the remaining days in the caves they stayed sullenly clear of her. Joaquín had slashed their leader, his greatest friend, because of her. Joaquín

88

had turned on Pablo and would have killed him. So they left her alone. Joaquín had established his absolute ownership. She was Joaquín's possession.

She never again attempted to resist Joaquín. When he desired her, which was often, she submitted without murmur. He no longer hurt her, nor had he struck her again. She began to learn his ways, to know when he wanted her, from only a quick glance or a tensing of his body across the cave. Then she herself would become taut, her pulse quickening, knowing that he would make love to her—soon—any moment now.

She despised herself for this alien response within her body. She was wanton, evil. Sometimes she paced back and forth across the back cave hating herself, filled with shame. What kind of woman was she! Then she was filled with silent, rebellious self-defense. She had lost everything—had her whole world stripped from her, leaving her nothing! What was wrong, then, in losing herself for a moment in his kiss? Warming at the touch of his hands. God knew it was all she had—a few stolen moments when her flesh seemed to burn and her very bones to melt within her.

It never lasted long—she didn't let it. She struggled against her feelings, repelled by her wickedness, willing herself to be remote, detached, passive, and unresponsive in his arms.

In these days in the caves, the other men came to consider the back cave as hers and Joaquín's, seldom entering it. When she wanted to escape the endless gambling, the endless talking, she retreated to this place and no one followed. Except Joaquín when he chose to.

Nor did he confine his attentions to that place.

No matter what he was doing he remained intensely aware of her. She took a dark satisfaction in her ability to entice him. She told herself this was because she knew it filled her enemy Leon with secret rage. She needed Joaquín's protection, she told herself—as long as he remained obsessed with her Leon would not kill her sometime, quickly, like killing a squirrel.

So it was she lay with him in their dim private cave and she lay with him in the blinding sunlight beside the stream. And against a sloping rock when there was not room to lie down. It made no difference. He could not get enough of her.

He tried, she knew, to make her respond to him, and she fought a desperate silent battle within herself.

"You are like a stone," he said once, his voice shaking.

"Yes," she said. "Yes, a stone."

She became immersed in her present state, filling her mind with concentration on the smallest details. It seemed sometimes that she had never had any other life at all. It seemed that she had always been Joaquín's possession. Sometimes she was appalled that she had survived, that she wanted to survive. Appalled at the things she had endured. Her whole life shattered and smashed and then—when nothing was left—to find within herself this dark rotten little core of evil passion. She must quell that, kill it, blot it out. She was his slave, nothing more.

She schooled herself never to think of her family—of Cecilia and Eduardo, deserted in the middle of a vacant wasteland without weapons or horses or food. Of her brothers in Mexico. They would have heard by now, she supposed, of her abduction and of the probable deaths of Cecilia and Eduardo. They would think her dead also— well, it was better so. Could Cecilia and Eduardo possibly have survived? In this lawless land? Hopeless. And Luis, back in Mexico. What of Luis? She spent a solitary vacant morning that day in the rear cave, trying to remember the color of Luis' eyes and could not.

Then came the night that she and Joaquín started talking to one another. She had not wanted this, had guarded against it, never letting herself emerge from her isolated detachment from him.

"You are thinking of your people, aren't you?" he asked. They were alone in the back cave, preparing to lie down for the night. "I can tell when you dream of your people. You must stop it. It is bad."

"I will always wonder if they got home safely." There was a touch of sullenness in her tone.

"They did. They must have." He answered her in quick surprise.

"How could you know!" A wild hope clutched at her heart.

"Because I heard wagons coming. That was why we ran away so quickly. I hear better than the others. When I say something is coming, they know it is so."

"What wagons?" She dropped the garment she was holding and darted to him, looking up at him beseechingly. "What wagons! Who was coming?"

He shrugged his bare muscled shoulders. "Some wagons. Two. With Americans. We had passed them before. We didn't stop them because there were too many of them and they had so little for us to take."

"Would—would they have helped my sister and Eduardo?" In a desperate surge of hope she clasped his forearm.

"Yes."

She stood radiant for a moment of utter and unbelievable joy. "Thank you," she gasped. "Oh, thank you!" Her eyes were shining.

With a quick intake of breath he reached out and caught her close, kissing her, caressing her, his need for her clamoring once again. She clung to him, dizzy with relief, gripping him, not realizing for a moment that she was, or when she did realize it, not knowing why. Again she knew a welling-up of the yearning she had forbidden herself, a pounding excitement, a need to respond to him, to hold onto him. A little stunned at the force of her own arousal, she was this time powerless to stem it, lost in the flood of it, until the final shattering explosion of ecstasy.

When it was finished she lay spent and exhausted in his arms. He had not bothered to put out the lantern and she watched his face in the faint and flickering light, gazing at him in bemused astonishment. This could not happen to Majella Moreno. It could not, but it had. Her careful defenses had crashed down. Joaquín had won.

He raised up on one elbow and smiled at her; she was more astonished at his beauty. She had never really looked at him before, had not let herself. The gleaming black eyes, slumberous now, the smooth bronze tints of his skin, the curve of his seductive mouth. The way the muscles of his body moved.

He touched her loose and flowing hair, gently, caressingly. The light glimmered on the rich red tones of the beads around his wrist.

"I thought I would never awaken you to me," he murmured.

She could not answer, only clasping his hand between hers. She belonged to him utterly. She was his possession and for these hours in the cave she reveled in it, and could think—wanted to think—no further ahead than that.

"What is your name? I have not asked you before," he said after a while.

"Majella," she answered. How deceiving he was. So simple and uncomplicated on the surface, but filled with dark surging needs and secret subtleties no one ever knew. Why had he never asked her name before? For some hidden reason of his own.

"Majella," he repeated softly. "A Spanish name? I know Spanish. I have not heard it."

"Not really Spanish. It has been given a Spanish sound. It is really 'Majel.'"

His interest quickened. "Why? That is in the Luiseño tongue. 'Wood Dove.' Why?"

"Because I am an Indian." She spoke calmly, for the first time without shame because of it. Quietly, she began to talk to him, telling him of her life in Mexico, her love for her father, the terrible blow of learning he was not her real father, the sense of loss, of abandonment, the escape with Cecilia and Eduardo to California. They talked together until dawn, letting long silences fall, and again resuming. There was no hurry. In time all would be revealed between them. And he talked to her. She felt the anguish he had felt, the few

93

triumphs. He spoke of his love for Leon, his friend. He told her of the grandfather at home in the village. The refuge he had found in Leon's house in the village after his parents' deaths. They could think of nothing beyond this hour, this night.

She drowsed the next day, while preparing the food, and was slow to know that Leon was watching her intently. They were alone again. His wound was healing well, but he still remained at the caves when the others left.

"I see you got the red necklace," he said in his quiet voice.

Her hands went to her throat. Joaquín had given it to her this morning. She didn't answer, waiting to see what Leon would say or do. He simply shook his head.

But that night he started to press Joaquín about what they could do with the woman. They argued about it late over the embers, and after all the embers had died. She could hear only maddening snatches of the endless words from Leon. Joaquín kept his voice so low that she heard nothing at all of his responses. She only knew from Leon's continued persuasion that Joaquín withstood him. Leon was clever and he knew his friend; he never let anger show in his voice, keeping it placating, reasonable, convincing, using Spanish or Luiseño, whichever language expressed his thoughts better.

No, regardless of what the woman said, she could not be Indian. One had only to look at the clothing, the rest of her family. No, it was not possible to take her to the village and live there in peace. The village was too old, too well established, too many people knew of it. Often people came to the village—Indians, Mexicans, Americans—or they wandered there. Or they passed through and stopped. It was too big a risk. If she didn't run away, she would be seen by someone, recognized. The danger was too great to the village. Hadn't they been careful to get rid of everything that could be identified with her people? Did it make sense to take the woman herself along with them? When would he tire of her? They had all been very patient. It had been days, many days. There was no way Joaquín could keep the woman without endangering them all. He must give her up. On and on and on.

When he finally let Joaquín go, Joaquín came to her with his head bowed, his shoulders slumped. She and León were in silent battle, and Joaquín was torn between them. He took her that night with a heartbreaking urgency and didn't sleep well afterward, as he usually did. He twisted and turned and murmured and moaned. She woke him out of his strange torment.

"Joaquín, what is it? Joaquín?"

"It is nothing. A dream only. I dreamed of Mr. Austin. It is nothing. Go to sleep, Majella."

She could not. She lay awake long after he slept again, twisting and muttering beside her. *She must not die.* In spite of everything, she wanted to live, to survive, in any way at all. She was Joaquín's possession; he must protect her. He must! But what could she do to make him protect her? Now, at the very last, was she powerless against his lifelong loyalty to the determined, implacable, relentless Leon?

She made a futile attempt to come between the two men again. Joaquín had turned on Leon once because of her. Let him do it again. Deliberately, she distracted Joaquín from a card game, passing close to him several times as she went about clearing away the remains of the night meal. She knew the instant that she had his attention, although he was not looking at her and continued to play in the game. In a few minutes he tossed down his hand and left the game, following her into the back cave. Her surge of triumph was soon snuffed out.

"Majella, don't do that," he said soberly. "I knew what you were trying to do. So did Leon. He sees everything." But he did not go back to the game. Once there with her he did not want to leave her. This troubled him, too. It angered him.

She awoke to find the lantern burning and Joaquín staring at her somberly. She could feel the depth of his emotion as he watched her. What was it? Many things. Longing. Anger. Melancholy. Fear? Yes, fear. A look of entrapment. And underlying all, supporting all, part of all, was an old despair. Something he had lived with perhaps all his life.

She sat up, pushing back her hair, cold dread welling up inside her. Leon would win their deadly battle to kill her. She was sick with fear.

"Joaquín, you must help me. You must. There is—no one else. I have no place to go. I cannot—cannot ever go back to my people now. Not after what has happened to me. I want them to think I am dead. You must understand that. Joaquín, are you listening to me?"

She pushed off the blanket and crawled over to him.

96

"Joaquín, listen to me."

He put his arms around her and buried his face in her hair, rocking her back and forth. After a moment she knew that he was crying.

Chapter Six

In the morning there was in the front cave the sense of pending activity, a sense of anticipation and excitement. They were going home to the village. They took down the broken crockery pot and divided out the money among themselves, being meticulously fair according to some plan that apparently had long been in effect. Majella watched them after she had completed her chores. Her fear of this time had receded, leaving her feeling remote and detached. Joaquín would fail her, or he would not, and there was nothing she could do about it now. Only Joaquín had the power. She sat Indian-fashion on the floor against the wall and waited.

Leon expected another confrontation because he sent both Trinidad and Pablo to the hiding place for the horses, when either could have handled the errand alone. He agreed with them on a time for meeting down beside the stream. When both had left the now strangely empty caves, he turned to Joaquín.

"Well, my friend? We must now speak again of the woman. What will you do? Will you defy me again? Is our friendship so worthless?"

"Leon, you know it is not worthless," Joaquín said, his voice sounding flat and expressionless, which told Majella more about his inner conflict than if he had sounded angry. He could not look at Leon, but gazed instead at some point over his head. Although the cave was cool, sweat gleamed now on his face and neck. "I will not give up the woman. If that is defiance, then I defy you—though I never thought I would," he added, his voice suddenly unsteady.

"She will be the death of us," Leon said, sounding tired.

"I will not go with you to the village, Leon. I do not ask that," Joaquín said, and he spoke as if it cost him dearly to say it.

Majella let out a soundless sigh. Did he so love the village and his place in it that it cost him this dearly to give it up?

"Not come back to the village?" There was astonishment, disbelief, in Leon's tone. Then, "You must." He went to Joaquín and grasped his muscular forearm for a moment, shaking his head. "How could you say this? Those times when you were away from the village you were sick with longing to be back. You have said so. The village is your home place."

"I know that," Joaquín said steadily. "I am sorry to leave the village, but, as you say, it would be a risk to take the woman there. If I wish to take

99

the risk, it must be my own risk only. I have thought about it."

"Joaquín," Leon interrupted. *"Where?* Where will you go?"

"I thought I would go to Los Angeles first. I know some men there. I will try to find work again, a place to live. I have this money now. I will—"

Leon was shaking his head, his eyes never leaving the younger man's face. "It will not happen that way, Joaquín." This man who regarded her with quiet, deadly hatred, who waited in patient exasperation until he could kill her, spoke to his friend with kindness and deep regard. He said again, a half-smile on his heavy mouth, still shaking his head, "It will not happen that way, Joaquín. You might live away from the village if you got work on one of the ranchos far out, away from the town. But not in the pueblo. Never. If you take her to the town and try to live with her there, you will die. Soon I think, both of you. Look at your woman. Think how jealous you are. You stuck your knife into me—into *me*—because I wanted her. And you beat little Pablo. Even Trinidad was tempted. Do you think you can keep her hidden from the Angelenos? She is safe in Los Angeles only if she is dressed in fine garments and rides with someone like the ranchero, the rich Mexican Obregón. Only then. With you, could she be safe? Never. Walking behind you in the street of the pueblo she is only an Indian woman. Any man who wants her can make trouble for you—"

Joaquín shook his head and turned away. "Stop, Leon. It is no use. My mind is fixed."

"I doubt they would even ask your permission,"

Leon persisted. He shrugged. "Someone might give you some money afterward, if he felt like it. Listen to me, Joaquín. What would you do then? Would you stick your knife into some Mexican? Or worse yet, into some rough American? You would not even get as far as the gallows. It would be some tree by the road. Have sense. Then when you were swinging dead from a tree, or lying in the street shot, what would become of your woman? How long would she last?"

"Well, you said I should not come to the village." There was rage and anguish in his tone. "What do you want me to do! I will not let her go!"

Leon sighed and sat down suddenly on a stone. For a moment he looked older than he was. Absently, he stroked the still-bandaged shoulder.

"All right," he said finally. "All right. Come back with us to the village. Bring your woman with you." He was giving in, accepting another defeat because of her, and Majella wondered in odd sympathy if it humiliated him. She kept her gaze steadily on the stone floor of the cave in case he looked at her and their eyes should meet. He must not see the relief and triumph there. She could spare him that because he was Joaquín's friend, brother almost.

If Pablo and Trinidad were surprised that she was still with them they had enough respect for Leon not to show it. They were, however, impatient to leave. Now that they were finally leaving the caves, their attention was on the village, on home, and they wanted to get there as soon as they could. By the stream, Joaquín mounted the horse given to him and handed her the bundle of things he was keeping. Each man had such a pack of things from the raid. Then, without a word, Joaquín swung down and plucked her, bundle and all, from the ground and seated her in front of himself. All were riding without saddles, as they had considered them simply as some of the things to be sold. Majella felt herself going limp against Joaquín's body, and his arm tightened about her waist.

The long struggle was over. She was still alive, at least for a time. He would not let her die. She rested against him as they started away from the broad shallow stream, away from the hidden caves among the rock cliffs. She did not think beyond this time, or wonder where she was going or how she would be treated there. She concentrated only on the bundle of belongings she was holding. Joaquín had taken less money so she could have some of these things. Her other dress, now washed; her comb; the garnet necklace; Cecilia's prayer book. Some day she would pray again.

They rode for about three hours, she thought, before they came within sight of habitation. In the distance there was a collection of ramshackle wooden buildings.

"We can wait here. You go with them, Joaquín," Leon said, dismounting. They had stopped in a clump of oak trees that were spread over an area of sloping ground. There was a small lazy stream.

Joaquín slid down from their horse and helped Majella down. He gave her a slight smile of reassurance. "We leave the horses there," he said to her. His bothering to explain to her caused a faint look of surprise to cross Leon's face, but he said nothing. They watched the others walk all the horses across to the buildings. It looked as if there were a house and several outbuildings. Some dogs came out barking, and chickens scratched about.

She and Leon drank from the small stream and waited silently together for a time. This man was Joaquín's friend, his mentor. Somehow or other she must reach an understanding with him. She would be—and it gave her a cold feeling to think of it—she would be with this man as long as she was with Joaquín. She could not escape him. She cleared her throat gently. Speak to him. Talk to him. Could she ever talk with this man as she had finally done with Joaquín?

"Leon, why are the horses left here? That is not your village, is it?"

He looked at her, surprise again touching his face. It took him a while to answer. "No. That is not our village. A Mexican lives there. He—lets us leave our horses there with his horses. People seeing them think they are his, so they are hidden."

"He is your friend then?"

There was a brief derisive smile. "No. He is not our friend."

"But still he lets you leave the horses there?" Majella smiled a little. Perhaps she might eventually win this man's friendship.

"We pay him."

"Oh, I see."

"Do you always talk so much, woman?" There was an edge of impatience to his quiet voice. "You can put the bundle down. They will not be back for some time. The Mexican always gives them a glass of wine after he takes the money. It is his custom."

She ventured another question. "Why are we waiting here? Wouldn't you like a glass of wine? Is it still because of your shoulder?"

"No. The Mexican would not ask any questions about this." He touched his shoulder and fixed his level gaze on her. "He would ask many questions if we brought a Mexican woman with us. You are not as stupid as you pretend, woman. I know this. It is what I have tried to tell Joaquín. This is only the beginning—hiding here in the trees to keep you from being seen."

"I would have waited. I would not have run away," she said simply, hoping he would believe her.

"I am not stupid, either," he said, his mouth twisting in quick contempt.

"You don't understand," she persisted. "I have no place to go. I cannot go back to my people now. They would not want me. It is better they think me dead." Despite her effort, her voice was suddenly unsteady.

"They would not take you back because you have been Joaquín's woman?" Leon asked after a moment.

"Not because I have been Joaquín's woman. It is because—" She groped for a word to explain.

"It is forbidden by your people to be known by any man," he supplied the explanation himself. "You will not run away from Joaquín, then?"

She shook her head and silence fell between them, with only the murmuring water audible. Leon stared at her somberly. She had no idea

104

what he was thinking, but it was clear that he wished to talk no more, so she remained quiet.

They arrived in the village at dusk, having walked the last several miles from the Mexican's house. It was strange going into the village, with Majella carrying the bundle and walking slightly behind them. The return was greeted with a veritable explosion of joyful excitement. Men, women, and two or three children trooped out to meet them. Each man had bargained for and retained his few items from what they had stolen from the Obregón party. Majella watched without any expression in her face as Trinidad handed over Cecilia's small ivory fan to a young woman. So that was Trinidad's woman. She watched her through lowered lashes. The girl was young, almost childlike. She was entranced with the fan and played with it as with a toy. Pablo gave Eduardo's extra tobacco pouch to an old man who embraced him with pleasure.

The people were noticing Majella. Some were shy about it, pretending not to look at her. Others, bolder, came up to look at her closely, to reach out and touch her challis dress. She stood unmoving behind Joaquín. At a word from Joaquín—she didn't know what it was—the bolder ones stood back from her. Joaquín smiled faintly at her. One of the men asked Joaquín a question, obviously referring to her, and Joaquín answered him shortly. There was a sense of retreating among the people.

"Take her to the house, Joaquín," Leon said, which was apparently what Joaquín had waited for. He led her through the village. She got an impression of a straggle of houses, a few rounded according to what seemed a traditional plan. Most were simply shacks that had been put together out of bits and pieces of wood and other materials. A few chickens and turkeys scattered before them, and a mangy dog or two skulked out of their path.

She had to step downward into the house, and paused a moment, accustoming her eyes to the dimness.

"Grandfather?" It was said with a faint question in it. "I want to show you my woman." Joaquín gently pushed her forward.

There was an old man seated cross-legged on the ground by the firehole. He looked incredibly old and thin, but the black eyes that looked at her were keen and sharp. He lifted a withered hand and beckoned. She felt Joaquín's hand at her back again, pushing her forward.

"Sit," the old man said, and she sank to the ground before him. He glanced up at Joaquín. "You did not say you would bring back a woman for yourself."

"I did not know it, Grandfather."

The old man reached out and plucked at her skirt, the reddish brown somewhat dirty now from the journey. Slowly he shook his head.

"You stole her," he said finally.

Joaquín came down easily on his knees before the old man to be on a closer level. He now seemed diffident and a little uneasy. The old man spoke again.

"What did Leon think of this? Why did he let you do it?"

"He told me not to do it, Grandfather. I did it anyway. I would not give her up."

"Bad," the old man said. "You should not have done it."

"That's as may be, Grandfather. But it is done now."

"What if her people come and find her in the village?"

"She says they will not want her back."

"And that's as may be, my son, but if they *do* come—what then? You should have listened to Leon."

"That isn't all, Grandfather."

"Not all? What worse thing have you done?"

"I fought with Leon about her. I cut my knife into him."

"Leon!" Astonishment washed over the ancient wrinkled face. "You cut Leon!"

"Yes."

The old one shook his head in wonder. "And he did not kill you for it."

"No. And he did not take my woman."

"You are lucky."

An unhurried silence fell. The old man let go of her skirt and spoke again, sighing a little. "Did he tell you to come here to this house?"

"Yes. He told me to bring my woman here. Will you permit that, Grandfather?"

"I? I permit? I am a useless old man with no teeth and scarcely any wits left. Who am I to say? It is for Leon to say."

Joaquín smiled. He reached over and took one of the gnarled, bony hands. "Thank you, Grandfather. She learns well. She will cook and wash the clothes. You will be glad she came. You will see. She will be here to listen to your talk when Leon and I are gone. That will please you. She is very quiet."

A reluctant toothless grin appeared for a moment on the old man's face. Then in a moment he lifted his hand in a gesture to someone behind her, and Majella turned to see that Leon had entered the house.

"He lies, Grandfather," Leon said drily to the old man. "She is not quiet. And she is not stupid." There was just a hint of warning in it that the old man did not miss, and that Joaquín chose to ignore.

Both Leon and Joaquín gave a portion of their money to the old man, who accepted it with evident pleasure. "Did you bring any tobacco?" he asked with the pleased greediness of a child. "Any wine?"

"Both, Grandfather. And much more money. We did well this time," Leon answered.

"Then you need not leave again for a while," the old man said in a pleased tone.

"Not for a while," Leon agreed. He sat down on the ground and leaned back against one of the posts that supported the conical roof, and shut his eyes. His strong body seemed limp, heavy with fatigue. "Joaquín?"

"Yes."

"It would be good to have some wine. There is some in my pack. Tell the woman to get it."

Without waiting for Joaquín's instruction, Majella rose and opened Leon's pack. She saw Joaquín gesture to the gourds hanging from one of the posts, and took these for drinking cups. She poured out three and handed them around. Leon took his without opening his eyes and started sipping it slowly. Joaquín took long-stemmed pipes hanging from the wall and filled them with tobacco. Ignoring her now, the men began to smoke and drink and talk.

They told the old man about the raid and the sojourn in the caves, and he told them about the happenings in the village during their absence. During the evening other men came to the house. Pablo and Trinidad came. Everyone wanted to hear all that had happened. They talked and listened and laughed and smoked until late in the night. Majella finally fell asleep over near the wall.

The next day at dawn she began her life in the village. She went to fetch water in a large jug. There was a central well, which the grandfather had pointed out to her. As a newcomer she decided to wait until the last to get water. The other women who were there lingered to watch her curiously. Filled, the jug was heavy and would have slipped from her grasp had not one of them reached forward quickly and caught it for her, smiling slightly as she did so.

"Thank you," Majella said fervently, and the woman ducked her head and hurried away. If she had not understood the words she had understood the gratitude in them.

Bit by bit in the several days that followed, the women became friendly. Some of them spoke a little Spanish and there were sketchy conversations. They started accepting her as one of them, the younger women first, the older ones later. Her garments, her dark red beads, intimidated them less. They only half believed that she was an Indian as she told them. She sat with them some-

times in the afternoons when she was not busy.
She saw inside their houses and played with the
one or two of the smaller children, but she was
careful about this. There were few children; many
women had none at all and looked on them with
hungry eyes.

She started to pick up some phrases in their language, but did not mention this in the house. In
the house she made an attempt to be quieter to
avoid irritating Leon.

She did not return to her attitude of living from
hour to hour as she had in the caves. She felt more
secure here. Joaquín would not give her up, and
Leon and the grandfather had both agreed that
she should stay with them in their house.

Taking the outer husks of the corn she was
going to roast, she grimaced. Living in Leon's
house was the most difficult. There was a vacant
shack on the outskirts of the village. She wondered if it were possible that Joaquín would consider living there, apart from the others? At least
at the caves there had been a private place for
their lovemaking. The fact that Joaquín had his
woman in the same room in which they all slept
did not seem to matter at all to Leon and the
grandfather. She thought perhaps the old man
didn't even notice. They slept on the other side of
the house, against the wall. But always she knew
that Leon was aware of her and at night, breathless in Joaquín's arms, she knew that Leon, across
the room in the still darkness, was aware. It worried her, almost frightened her. In Joaquín's arms
she tried to blot it out, surrendering wildly to the
rush of passion Joaquín now aroused in her,

110

trying not to gasp, trying not to moan, because even in the frenzy of her response she could not forget that Leon was there, silent and grim, brooding in the darkness.

She broached the subject to Joaquín on a rare occasion when they were alone, suggesting the shack.

"I looked in it today," she said. "I could clean it up. Clear it out." She stopped at his look of astonishment.

"Why? We live here. With Leon and Grandfather."

She bit back the comment she wanted to make and began to explain as tactfully as she could. Her arguments met with a blank wall, although he did hear her out.

"No," he said when she finished. "It is better to live here."

"But, Joaquín—"

"No."

"I think that Leon might like it better if—" She changed tactics.

"No." There was deadly finality in his tone now, and the blank brows came down over suddenly savage eyes. "Forget Leon. Leon does not even know that you are alive."

They both knew this was not true, but she had no course but to accept it. She got a grim satisfaction that evening when Leon himself proved her correct. The men had been talking in their usual manner, a mingling of Spanish and their own tongue, whichever served their meaning best. She was understanding some of the phrases.

"Joaquín," Leon said, taking his pipe from his

111

mouth, "we must take care what we speak. Your woman understands much of it now." He had known without seeming to even look at her.

"Is that true?" Joaquín was startled.

"Yes, it is true," Majella answered him in his own dialect. "Leon has much wisdom of me to have known this," she added, hoping she wasn't making any mistakes. Apparently she did not, for they understood her perfectly. And Joaquín, knowing what she meant, had the grace to smile in chagrin.

Both he and the old man were delighted, especially the grandfather. When Leon and Joaquín were out of the house he took it upon himself to teach her more, taking great pains to explain things when she faltered. She realized, with a tightening in her throat, that this old man was her friend.

The next day Eduardo Obregón, and several armed men, rode into the village looking for her.

Chapter Seven

They rode in boldly at midmorning, their guns not even in their hands, so confident were they. Chickens and dogs scattered before them. They knew exactly which house they wanted—their well-paid informant had been accurate. They halted, animals milling and snorting restlessly. Majella was filling the jug at the well. She stood there, stunned, gripping the jug. *Eduardo*.

So carefully had she shut out her past life that she simply stood there frozen, watching the men who had not seen her yet.

"Leon Troncoso! Come out!" It was Eduardo's voice, with none of the well-bred gentle tones—instead, harsh, arrogant, commanding, a man who knew he must be obeyed.

Several women near the well sidled away and disappeared into their houses, leaving their jars. Majella stood like a wooden image, not knowing what to do. Still the men did not see her. They knew—must have known—that the village only appeared empty, that the people were cowering inside the houses and shacks in fear.

She watched, trance-like, and saw Leon slowly emerge from the round-roofed house. Behind him was Joaquín, still half-naked, as he had been sitting there talking with the grandfather and was slow in dressing. The sun gleamed on his splendid body.

"Are these the ones?" one of the men asked Eduardo as both Leon and Joaquín stood before the opening. Neither was armed, although Majella knew there were guns and rifles inside the house.

"I think so," Eduardo said through his teeth. "They had their faces covered. But yes, I think so."

"Then let's kill them and be done with it," the other man said grimly.

"The woman? You!" Eduardo commanded, indicating Leon. "Speak! What did you do with the woman you took?"

"We don't understand what you mean," Leon said stolidly. "We took no woman. What do you mean, Señor? We do not make any trouble. We are peaceful men."

"Go and leave us in peace, ranchero," Joaquín added. "We have nothing of yours."

For reply, Eduardo took out his gun and pointed it at Leon. The shot blasted through the morning air. But at the same instant, Joaquín, anticipating it, had pushed Leon so that they both fell to the ground.

"What have you done with the woman! Did you kill her? Is she still alive? Speak up—I'll kill you both if you don't! *Where is she?*"

114

Leon got up, half turning his back on the armed ranchero and his men in a kind of defiant, studied insolence. Taking his time, he helped Joaquín up. Joaquín stood beside him, looking blankly into the middle distance, not even looking down as blood welled out of the ragged wound on his thigh and ran down the side of his long strong leg.

Majella at the well took a sudden step forward. *Joaquín hurt.* At her sudden movement, one of the riders saw the quick motion, not realizing what it was, and wheeled his horse around, raising his revolver. But he got no chance to fire. Joaquín, hurt as he was, leaped into the air and grabbed his arm, deflecting his aim. The bullet smashed into a stray dog, causing it to jump twisting and screaming into the air. At the same moment, the mounted men realized who the woman must be.

"*Majella.*" It was Eduardo's voice, in anguish, in disbelief, in rejection. Total rejection that she was indeed alive. His wife's sister—very obviously—the squaw of a renegade Indian. This knowledge rendered him speechless now and he could only stare at her. Better, far better, that she be honorably and chastely dead. Not like this. Not standing alive before him.

Majella took a few faltering steps toward him and then stopped, not knowing what to do. She twisted her hands together in a washing motion, clasping and unclasping them.

"I'm sorry," she whispered humbly through stiff lips. "I'm sorry." Sorry that he had found her. Sorry to burden him. Sorry, really, that she wasn't dead. She should have been brave enough to die.

115

"I'm sorry," she whispered again, not knowing what else to say.

There was an odd wordless moment when they all did nothing but watch the crying, dying dog drag itself behind the house. There was the creak of leather, and Eduardo dismounted and walked slowly toward her, tentatively, regretting bitterly that he had not managed to hide his emotions, sick with pity for her.

"My dear," he said gently. "My dear." He didn't know what else to say.

Another man dismounted and came to them. "Señor, is this—" he began uncertainly.

"This is Señorita Majella Moreno, my wife's sister," Eduardo was saying politely, falling back into the safety of the old pattern of courtesy. "Majella, allow me to present Enrique Vásquez—he is my right hand at the rancho."

Oh, Eduardo. Majella's throat ached. *I'm so sorry I couldn't be dead.* She observed remotely as the men adjusted to this reality, looking at her carefully, seeing everything—the limp faded dress, the work-roughened hands, the hair loose and flowing down her back.

"What will you do, Señor?" Vásquez asked in a moment.

Eduardo passed his tongue over his lips. "I shall take my sister-in-law home," he said. "Come, Majella. You understand you are safe now. You must come with me."

She nodded, unable to speak, engulfed in shame for herself, pity for him, dread of facing Cecilia in her present state, anguish because Joaquín stood silent and bleeding in front of the doorway to the house. Why did it have to happen this way?

116

"And these men? These Indians?" Enrique Vásquez pursued.

Eduardo turned slowly to look at the two Indians. In a moment he would lift his revolver and shoot them where they stood. Then it would all be over.

"Do not move, Señor." It was the thin, reedy voice of the grandfather. His thin, spindly form stood now in the doorway, almost overbalanced by the heavy shotgun. It was aimed directly at Eduardo. "Do not shoot. You can kill us all, but if you do I take you with us. I am the Headman. I speak for this village, these people." Despite his age and frailty, the large gun held steady.

The Mexicans were nonplussed.

"I intend to take my kinswoman with me," Eduardo said stonily.

"Take her, then. But go in peace." The old man's thin voice was implacable. He would shoot and they all knew it.

Joaquín, ashen now from loss of blood, leaned against the doorpost. Leon stepped forward.

"Is that all?" he asked with his old soft-spoken insolence. "You offer us nothing? We found the woman, lost, wandering, out of her head. We saved her. What thanks do you give us for this? You come to our village with guns to shoot us all. You should thank us. You should pay us something for our trouble."

Majella was appalled.

Eduardo turned to her. "Majella?" he asked uncertainly.

Majella's gaze locked with Leon's. He was offering her—offering them all—a way out. If they stayed, honor-bound to fight it out, many, perhaps

117

all, would die. Eduardo at least would be blasted where he stood by the old man's unwavering aim. All she had to do was lie, and they could all remain alive. Joaquín would remain alive.

"That—is true," she said carefully. "I was wandering, dazed. They found me. Eduardo—please, let us go. Someone—someone should bind up that wound. He—he is bleeding."

"What are you going to do, ranchero?" Leon prodded relentlessly. "Nothing for us? You should give us some money, at least."

"All right!" Eduardo slammed his gun back in its holster, took out his purse, and flung it down on the dirt at Leon's feet.

Leon did not thank him. He did not even pick it up. He stood looking at them with no expression at all in his face.

With a faint grunting sound that was partly a moan of pain, Joaquín went to pick up the purse. His face was like stone. He handed it to Leon. All the days of her life Majella would wonder what it had cost him to do that.

"Wait, Señor?" Joaquín spoke. Limping, almost dragging his wounded leg, he went down into the house. Grimly, Eduardo lifted Majella up onto his horse and mounted behind her. There seemed nothing to do now but go.

The nightmare was finished, or perhaps it was just beginning, she wasn't sure which. Her mind was a jumble of ideas. The only thing that seemed to emerge clearly was that she had left the half-filled jug by the well, and that it was really too heavy for the old man to carry.

Joaquín came slowly out of the house, carrying something wrapped in cloth.

118

"The Señorita's things," he said dully, his eyes glazing. He lifted up the bundle toward her. There was blood on his hand, blood on the cloth. She took it from him, and tried to thank him but could not. Eduardo turned his horse and they were riding away, out of the village. She could not believe it. There was no way she could look back to see, but she knew that Joaquín must have fallen to the ground. *Leon, help him.*

The endless journey to the Obregón rancho was a series of vague impressions. Riding double with Eduardo miles and miles and miles across the limitless California countryside. Stopping to eat. The men hesitant, diffident, treating her with great courtesy and gentleness. Eduardo exhibiting unimaginable kindness. And sleep. Much sleep. Strange deep sleep. Sleep while riding cradled like an infant in Eduardo's arms when they walked the horses. Sleep in the night near a fire, curled up on someone's serape and covered by someone else's serape. Images, many images. Firelight on the quiet face of whichever man did not sleep but stayed awake to watch. Eduardo touching her gently at dawn to awaken her, pretending he didn't hear her when she said, "Joaquín?" and reached out to him. Low voices in the glimmering firelight, Eduardo swearing the men to secrecy about where and how they had found her, protecting her, protecting Cecilia, too, from the humiliation of having anyone know of her sister's shame.

She tried to shut it out and turned away from the flame to stare into the darkness and then to fall asleep again. She did not want to face what was coming. How would they all meet this thing that had crashed into their lives? Could it possibly be kept secret? In the eyes of the women she had known she would be a pariah—she had been violated, therefore was now defiled, unclean. Nevermore could she be received in any house where before she had been welcomed. Respectable women would pretend they didn't know her—would look the other way, or cross the street to avoid her. Why had she not died? Wouldn't it have been better so?

It was in this dull gray haze of disgrace and misery that she faced her sister when they reached the Obregón ranch. But Cecilia, pale and shaken at what had happened to her, with a bright, frantic glitter in her blue eyes, tried to cover up, pretend it did not exist. She made a valiant effort.

"Majella, my dearest Majella." She embraced her, patted her cheek, plucked at her dress, stroked her tangled hair. "My dearest. Oh, come with me. Let me help you. Come. I'll take you to your room. It looks out onto the patio. You must rest. We must throw away these awful rags. Oh, my dearest, come with me."

And Majella, shrinking from these ministrations, bore them silently, letting herself be washed, letting Cecilia brush her hair dry, letting Cecilia tuck her between gleaming white lace-trimmed sheets, and listening to her determined chatter as servants came and went at her bidding. She watched the ruffle on the table cover near the window flutter in the evening breeze, she looked at the whitewashed adobe of the wide window ledge, she observed the tiny tucks in the bodice of her fine lawn nightgown, she gazed at her hands that Cecilia had rubbed with scented oil—anything to keep

120

from looking into her sister's eyes. And Cecilia, who could be so inquisitive, so persistent, asked her nothing, pressed her for no details of her captivity.

But she was not to escape so easily, for her room was next to that of Cecilia and Eduardo, and she heard her sister's stormy weeping in the night. She caught fragments of conversation.

. . . Eduardo, she is so dull, so witless . . . what did they do to her? . . .

And Eduardo, soothing, reassuring: *. . . exhaustion . . . give her time . . . great hardship . . . must have worked her like a slave. . . .*

And Cecilia, gulping back strangling sobs, on the edge of hysteria: *. . . the scandal if it is found out . . . hold up our heads . . . we've got to protect her. . . .*

Majella tried to bury her head in the pillow to shut out the sound of the havoc she was causing.

Morning was different. Sunlight streamed into the room, splashing across the polished floor, on the mellow wood of the massive pieces of carved furniture, on the silken folds of the coverlet trailing down the side of the bed. Cecilia's bustling into the room had awakened her: Cecilia, bright and determinedly cheerful, dressed in immaculate fine blue cotton touched with white lace, all ironed to perfection with little white ruffles cascading down her bosom to her tiny waist.

Cautiously, moment by moment, Majella went into the day with her sister, trying to fit back into the safety of the comfortable pattern of formality and courtesy and graceful, genteel things.

Cecilia's careful mask did not slip until mid-

morning. They were both seated in a small sitting room Cecilia reserved for her own use in the large house, Cecilia in her fine blue cotton and Majella in pale pink, similar in design. Both held embroidery in their hands but seldom took a stitch. They tried to talk, but odd little silences fell between them. Majella kept up a constant inner struggle to accept all this around her now as real, accept this luxurious room, this apparent quiet serenity of two ladies at their sewing. Try as she would she could not make any of it seem real.

Cecilia's hands dropped to her lap for the hundredth time, causing the crisp fabric of her dress to whisper faintly.

"I—can't stand this, Majella," she said. There was a slight jerking movement in her slim body. "What—did they—do to you? What happened? I—must know. I am going crazy."

Now she must face it. Majella's sewing also dropped to her lap. She made herself look at Cecilia, feeling far removed from her, feeling a thousand years older. Poor little Cecilia. Trying to be kind, trying to help, trying to understand—when there was no possibility that she could ever understand—and hating every moment of it.

"They took me to their hiding place. I—had to—to—" Her voice, steady at first, faltered.

"They violated you." Cecilia said, white-lipped.

"Not they. Only one. He kept me from the others. He—protected me. I was considered his woman."

Cecilia closed her eyes and rested her head against the high back of the chair. "You cannot ever marry now," she said dully after a moment.

"No man of family could consider—you must—" Her voice trailed off.

"Cecilia, my dear." Eduardo spoke from the doorway.

They both glanced up, Majella with relief, Cecilia with childlike guilt. He came into the room and shut the door behind him. "I was not going to broach this subject until you both felt like talking about it. It seems you both do." There was just a hint of reproach that they had not come to him first. He sat down, moving his holster slightly, his silver spurs sounding softly.

"Majella—God help her—has been defiled and degraded. How she survived such wretchedness I do not understand, but I do not question the will of God in these matters. I have thought of nothing but this for hours. I think all we can do now is to keep her safe until her brothers arrive."

"You have been in touch with Miguel?" Majella's voice sounded faint and her hands were suddenly damp. What would Miguel say—Miguel who had adored, almost idolized her, his older sister? It was one more thing to be faced.

"Yes. They will both come, of course. It will be for them to decide. I naturally will agree with whatever they decide, and help them in any way they wish. I bear a heavy responsibility for this—this tragedy."

"It wasn't your fault." Both sisters spoke at once.

Eduardo lifted a hand to silence them.

"Fortunately, the rancho is remote—we have visitors about once a year, if we are lucky. I have done everything I can to keep this quiet—anyone who speaks of it will pay dearly for his rashness. I have impressed this upon them all. There is one thing that I must ask you, Majella." He turned to her, a look of speculation in his eyes. "It wasn't true, was it, that they found you wandering about and saved you? The things in that little bundle were the things they stole from us. They were the men who robbed us, weren't they? The ones who killed my men? Why did you lie?"

Cecilia gave a sharp intake of breath.

"I felt I must," Majella said with an effort. "You would have tried to kill them and the grandfather would have killed you."

"That old man in the doorway?"

"Yes. He would have. You and your men might have killed them all but—you would have died too."

"That is the only reason?"

Lie again. "Yes," she said steadily. "That is the only reason." She could feel heat stealing into her face. "I didn't want anyone else to die. I wanted it to be—finished. I wanted to get away." She was trembling now.

"All right. I am sorry. I should not have questioned you about it. And we must not dwell on it. You two must not dwell on it, either." There was a hint of sternness in his tone. "We cannot decide anything yet. We must wait for Miguel and Hernán to arrive. It is for them to say what is to be done. You, both of you beloved ladies, put it out of your minds. Obey, now." He was smiling fondly as he said it, but he meant it. He got up, touching Cecilia's smooth hair a moment, and turned to leave the room.

124

"You lied to my husband," Cecilia said as soon as the door was shut.

"I saved your husband's life," Majella said steadily. "If I had not lied he would be dead now." That much was true. She must get out of here. She could not stay in this room a moment longer. She rose and placed her embroidery on the chair and went toward the door.

"Where are you going?"

"I am going out onto the patio."

"I'll come with you," Cecilia said sullenly, rising from her chair.

Majella turned. "I want to be by myself."

Cecilia paused, uncertain. "I am sorry I spoke sharply. I shouldn't have. Not after all that you have endured. I am sorry." Like a child in quick contrition for wrongdoing she darted forward and kissed Majella. "Go out. It is lovely on the patio. There are orange trees, just like at home. And gardenias."

Majella escaped into the sun-dappled patio with its hard-packed earthen surface, its ornamental pots and jars with masses of flowering plants, its round fountain in the center with water rippling gently down over old stones. She put her hands to her cheeks. They felt hot to the touch. What was she going to do? What would her brothers do? Would Miguel turn away in disgust, sorry that she was alive? Oh, dear God, no. Not Miguel.

Leon had helped Joaquín, would help him until his leg healed. He would lay down his life for Joaquín, as would Joaquín for him. *What made her think of that?* She buried her now flaming face in her hands. *Hide.* But there was no place to hide.

125

She stood at the fountain, trembling, sick with sudden longing. Desire for Joaquín rose like creeping fire in her body. *Oh, Mother of God, help me.* She stared down into the slow-moving water in the round bowl, striving against it, but even as she did she could almost feel the touch of Joaquín's hands, his seeking lips.

Carefully, in case anyone was watching, she turned from the fountain and walked to a bench in the shade, her body aching for Joaquín. Forget him. Blot him out. She would never see him again. He would go his dangerous way and meet his terrible end, by gunshot or hanging or some other way, and she would never know about it. That quick strong body would be inert, lifeless. She would think of him years from now and never even know that the breaker already had come and gone and Joaquín was long, long dead.

Leon would help him, her stubborn mind persisted. She could depend on Leon for that. Desperately, she tried to crush the smoldering passion that tormented her still. *Wicked. Evil. Wanton.*

Cecilia came out to the patio and hesitantly stood before her. "Majella, I'm sorry. I know you want to be alone, but—"

"But what?" Majella asked, trying to make her voice calm and ordinary, trying to push down the vivid image of Joaquín's gleaming eyes, the curve of his mouth.

"Majella, you have to come inside. Luis is here."

"Luis?" Majella looked at her blankly, not really knowing for the moment who she meant. Luis who? Who was she talking about?

"*Luis!* Luis Chavero. For God's sake, Majella! You must remember. All the way from Mexico! He is here. He has come to see you. You—have to come inside! You have to! *He doesn't know what has happened.* Majella, come inside. *Come in and receive Luis."*

Chapter Eight

Majella stood up slowly. "Where is Eduardo?"

"I don't know. He went out. I'll send someone to find him," she added quickly, clapping her hands for a servant.

In a few moments the sisters left the patio and entered the main sitting room of the house. Luis Chavero rose quickly from his chair. He seemed leaner, his fine features thinner, more sharply drawn. Or perhaps it only seemed so as he was dressed all in black.

"Majella," he said softly. "You are radiant! As always." He sprang forward to take her hand and kiss it, while she stared at him, bemused and faintly disbelieving.

Mistaking her expression, an embarrassed flush slowly stained his face. "It was unforgivable for me to come like this without invitation. But I could not help myself. Much has happened. I had to talk with you." His tone was pleading.

"Please, Luis," Cecilia cut in smoothly. "Let us all sit down. Invitation, indeed! As if you needed one! Ah, here is Eduardo."

The two men greeted each other by embracing and it was Eduardo who noticed the black band about Luis' sleeve, almost invisible against the fine black broadcloth of his jacket.

"Mourning? What has happened, my friend?"

"My father has died," Luis said simply. He crossed himself. "The day after you left Mexico." There were murmurs of sympathy, none the less necessary even though the elder Chavero had long been an invalid. Death could only have been considered a release to him and to those who cared for him.

In the interval that followed, Majella did not speak beyond simple courtesy, letting Cecilia and the men carry the burden of conversation. It seemed, Majella thought, as it had been in the garden at home in Mexico—careful people, saying all the expected and proper things. Many times in the past she had been restless in moving through the careful patterns laid out for her. Mama had cautioned her about the value of all the proper things. She watched Cecilia. Cecilia had never been restless within the bounds of all the proper things.

Now Cecilia, her voice just slightly brittle—or was that imagination?—was saying all the things required of the lady of the house. Who had accompanied Luis from Los Angeles? Had the men of his hired escort been sent to the back of the house for refreshment? How long did Luis think he could stay with them—a long time, she hoped winningly, as they would so enjoy visiting with him, and on and on and on. Majella murmured something now and then, and toyed with her bracelet, or one of Cecilia's fans she had picked up from the table. It was good to have something to hold on to. It was something to do, a momentary purpose in life. Having a little purpose, having something to do, kept madness at bay. She looked at Luis' elegant form, his rather gaunt aristocratic face, so set in lines of sadness. Poor Luis. What would Luis say if she spoke to him openly, honestly. The men were talking about the scarcity of water on the arid California plains. They were talking about thirsty cattle. Luis, she could say, I know about thirst. I know of water. You see, I carried the heavy bucket of water up through the rocks and soaring cliffs until I thought my arms would break. I took the jug to the well in the village, and I left it there half-filled for the old man to carry back. I forgot it. Because, you see, Joaquín was standing by the Indian house with his life's blood running out and nobody was helping him.

She stood up suddenly, dropping the fan to the floor. Consternation whipped through the room.

"Majella?" Luis' voice, full of concern, guilt, love.

"Majella!" Cecilia's voice, sharply warning.

"Majella, my dear." Eduardo's voice, firm and reassuring. Both he and Cecilia were warning her to say nothing, tell Luis nothing, wait for the brothers to arrive. They would decide then what was best for her. And Luis? What was Luis trying to tell her? That he still loved her? That his father was dead and he felt free of family obligation? It's too late, Luis, Majella was thinking. You see, you are too late. But all she said was, "I must ask that you excuse me for a while. I'm not feeling well. I shall lie down."

Then she waited, knowing to the least syllable what was coming, the murmuring concern, the reassurances, the little pattings from Cecilia's nervous hands. She endured it. Then she escaped at last.

Safe in her bedroom she had shut the door before she realized that the Indian servant was still there, having made the bed and tidied the room. The girl glanced at her covertly, then quickly lowered her eyes. She knew. And Majella knew she knew. They all must know, but Eduardo Obregón, their master, holding almost the power of life and death over them on his isolated estate, had wielded his power and sealed their lips.

"Have you finished here?" Majella asked, marveling at the quiet gentle tones of her own voice. "What is your name? Have I seen you before?"

"Lady, my name is Lucía. The Señora told me to attend you."

The Señora. That would be Cecilia. It sounded strange.

"Well, I need nothing now and I wish to lie down. Thank you." And she watched the girl go, her all-knowing Indian eyes cast modestly downward.

Two more long days were to pass before Miguel and Hernán were to arrive. During this time Eduardo—faithful, careful Eduardo—kept Luis occupied and entertained. He acquainted him with some of the complexities of running a California ranch, now diversified to include more than cattle alone. And he conveyed to him at some point that the Moreno brothers were expected. It became understood between them that Luis would await their arrival before he spoke of his reason for coming. It also became understood that Majella was slightly unwell, that too many social demands were not made of her at this time. If Luis chose to believe this was because of the broken betrothal, Eduardo did not enlighten him. Luis did his utmost to conform to Eduardo's wishes, but his reason for coming was obvious, and something he felt so deeply he could not hide. He was still very much in love with Majella.

Majella made an opportunity to speak with Eduardo alone—though that was difficult in Cecilia's home—during this interval.

"Eduardo, this is a very uneasy time for me." Before Eduardo there need be no pretense.

"I know," he answered quietly.

"My brothers—*what* do they know?"

"So far, they would only know of your abduction."

"So that when they come they will not know that I was—was rescued and brought back?"

"They will be overjoyed, Majella, that you are safe."

"And then," Majella said bitterly, "their joy will be dashed when they are told what has happened. They will want me dead, Eduardo. I don't want to see that on their faces. I don't want to see them at all until you have told them everything. Will you do that for me—you have already done so much." Her voice shook with emotion.

A look of compassion was in his eyes. "Yes, Majella. It shall be as you wish. You have suffered enough."

"Cecilia?" Majella said uncertainly.

"I shall speak with Cecilia."

Majella gave a shaky sigh. She wished, really, that she need never face her brothers. What a terrible thing to wish. She wondered, almost idly, what they would decide to do with her.

"Someone will have to tell Luis something," she said after a moment.

"Your brothers will decide what to tell Luis. There is no need for him to be told anything at all. I think your brothers may simply reject him and send him away. He half expects that now—considering his past conduct. Is there anything else troubling you, my dear?" So kind. So polite.

Majella could not look at him, and folded her hands—smooth now—in a sedate and graceful motion, rising from her chair.

"No, Eduardo. Thank you."

Is there anything else troubling you, my dear? The question echoed in her mind as she walked sedately from the room, swaying gently in the accepted manner as she had been taught to walk, so graceful, such elegant carriage. Everybody said so. There *is* something else, Eduardo. I listened to the men talk in the house in the village, and there is really no Headman in the village to take care of the people. Leon puts it off, avoids it. He will die before his time. He has lived in violence and he will die in violence. But perhaps Joaquín will be spared. And—how odd it is—but beneath the violence and raw passion of Joaquín there is great gentleness and wisdom. He could be the Headman—if he survives. I know this. And Eduardo, I wake in the night reaching for Joaquín. I am sick with longing for him. I am wicked and evil and I loathe myself.

133

Outside the room she turned abruptly and went into the small chapel to pray, to plead for help, for forgiveness of her wanton heart, for mercy. Before the altar with its daily fresh flowers and immaculate linen she knelt until her legs were numb, and her mind was numb. Then she rose stiffly, clinging to the rail, and told herself she felt better. She could face her brothers after they had been told. She would accept their decision, whatever it was. And sometime, years from now, she would no longer remember Joaquín's slow smile.

She spent most of that night reading and rereading her father's letter. She found some strength in his account of how brave and forthright her mother had been in the beginning—abandoning everything to run away with the Indian, Alessandro. What a stupendous love that must have been, to make her mother throw away everything to cling to it.

And the Indian, Alessandro, what of him? Majella closed her eyes but, despite her striving, she could call up nothing of Alessandro, who had been her father. He remained the shadow figure beside her mother, walking through the endless night. Faithful and loving he must have been, to walk through the night carrying his child. And those other shadowy figures—what did she feel of them? Of the bitter childless woman, Señora Ortegna, to whom Angus Phail had given the casket of jewels and the infant child. Of Angus Phail himself, the ship's captain. He also threw away everything for love. Was there a streak of madness, then, that only their wild love could cure? Like some unseen power inside them releasing lightning across the sky?

Finally, very tired, Majella folded once again the many pages of her father's letter. She would always think of Felipe Moreno as her father; that she could not help. She looked at its bulky folds in the dresser drawer. The letter was her burden, like a yoke about her neck, and she would never be free of it. Sleep. She would go to sleep now. Tomorrow. Surely by tomorrow, Miguel and Hernán would come. And perhaps if sleep were deep enough she need never awake.

The Moreno brothers arrived the next day.

She learned later that they had arrived exhausted, having commenced the journey to the rancho as soon as their boat docked in the harbor. She never learned what passed between them and Eduardo.

She and Cecilia and Luis had been out for a short ride and a small picnic lunch by a stream—it having been planned by Eduardo in case this was the day the Morenos would arrive. It was a somewhat elaborate picnic—trust Cecilia for that. Majella sat on a mossy stone and observed the white linen cloth being spread upon the ground by two Indian servants, and thought about peeling the bark from the sticks to make a spit for roasting the rabbits. She watched them put about the dishes of delicious food. She even ate some of it. It was remarkable how simple it was to avoid Luis' unhappy eyes, to avoid thinking very much at all about him, with Cecilia like a polite, watchful little duenna to protect her. It was only when the servants were gathering up the remains of the lunch that Luis managed to speak directly to her.

"Majella, my dearest love, you must know why I

am here. May I not speak to you before your brothers arrive? It is not as if we had just met." His voice was bleak, tinged with hopelessness, as if he sensed that she was somehow far removed from him and his cause already lost.

"Luis, I am still more Indian than white—have you forgotten that?"

He winced.

"I am sorry," she said wearily. "I should not have said that."

"You should say anything you wish. Whatever you say, I deserve it, and more. I was weak. But I shall never be weak again. It cost more than I can pay. The night my father died—and I grieve for him, for he was dear to me—I cut my ties to family and ancestors. The loss of you was too great a loss. I must—" He stopped, for Cecilia had noticed and come quickly over.

Ignoring Cecilia for the moment, Majella said, "Luis, my brothers will speak for me. Let it go until they come." She longed desperately to return to the house, to the sanctuary of her room, to shut the door there and hide.

But this was denied her.

They were riding into the yard, and the first servant who ran to meet them informed them, with an air of great self-importance, that the Señora's brothers from Mexico had arrived. As they dismounted, gave the horses in charge of the servant, and walked toward the house, Eduardo came out to meet them.

"Come in. Come in," he called with a great show of hospitality. Behind him came Miguel and Hernán. Majella's gaze flew in sudden panic to Miguel's face. It was a mask of dull pain. He

136

might have pretended only fatigue but Hernán, close behind him, pushed him aside and hurried white-faced to Majella. He caught her in his arms and gripped her close. She felt his thin young body shiver uncontrollably. He moaned something she did not understand, and Eduardo said again, "Come in. Inside. We shall have a glass of wine and then these good men will be allowed to rest." He was trying very hard to avoid a scene.

Somehow he and Cecilia got them all in. Hernán would not let Majella go, holding fast to her hand in a painful grip. He was shattered and could not hide it. She thought, *Oh, my little brother*, in love and anguish.

And it was Hernán who spoiled all of Eduardo's careful plans for keeping the secret in the family and not letting Luis know. Inside the main living room a servant was pouring out the wine into finely cut glasses and Hernán turned to Luis.

"And you—Luis Chavero—why do you grace us with your presence? What have we done to earn this honor!"

Luis, knowing nothing, was stunned at the outburst. And for once both Eduardo and Cecilia were too surprised to speak.

Hernán dropped Majella's hand and went to Luis.

"Did you come perhaps to ask for my sister in marriage again?" he snarled, his face ugly with hate. "Is she good enough for you now?"

"Hernán!" Miguel tried to catch his younger brother's arm, only to have it jerked away.

"Well, have you!" Hernán thrust his face close to Luis'. "And they haven't even told you, have they? They didn't tell you that Majella was ab-

137

ducted by renegade Indians! That when they found her she was a squaw in an Indian village. Did they tell you that, Chavero? That she had been violated and despoiled? Do you want my sister now? Do you?"

"*Hernán!*" Miguel, for the first time in his life, struck his brother in the face. Hernán buckled beneath the blow, seeming to sag, to collapse. Burying his face in his hands, his hunched body racked with strangled sobs.

Luis Chavero stood unmoving before them, stunned, silent. Even his lips were gray. After a long, dead, silent time he spoke.

"I came, yes, to ask again for Majella in marriage. I ask it now. Miguel?"

Everyone stared at him stupidly. Even Hernán lifted his tear-drenched face from his sheltering hands and stared at Luis as if he had lost his mind. It was Miguel who finally spoke.

"Luis, you do not know what you are saying," he said dully. "Please be good enough to leave us. We will forget that you spoke without thinking."

"I did not need to think," Luis said. "I meant what I said."

Eduardo came and placed his hands on Luis' shoulders. "You are distraught. It has been a shock. Her brothers and I have discussed this for two hours. Majella cannot continue living in society. We find only one solution—that Majella be quietly placed in a convent. Not," he was careful to add, "as a nun, of course. But in a lesser capacity. That is the only way out of this tragedy."

A convent, Majella thought. Yes, a solution. She looked carefully at Luis. It had been a kind gesture, born of love, shock, hysteria, disappointment. Poor Luis. He would rouse from his night-mare soon and regret bitterly his heedless offer.

Then Luis spoke again. The only thing that re-vealed his inner stress was the very distinctness with which he uttered the words.

"Before we discuss this any further, I suggest that the ladies excuse themselves. There is no need for Majella to be subjected to any more than she had already endured."

Like a puppet on a string, Cecilia grasped at this and came quickly to Majella.

"Come away, Majella. Let us go."

Majella was not allowed to escape, for as soon as they passed the door of Cecilia's small sitting room she pulled Majella inside and shut the door, leaning against it. She shut her eyes a moment.

"Do you suppose he will do it?" she whispered. "I cannot imagine a man doing that." She was taut with a strange excitement. She went about the room restlessly.

"Sit down, Majella. We'll just give them time to talk it over." She flicked invisible dust from a ta-ble. She twitched at a window curtain. She straightened a lampshade that was already straight. "Miguel shouldn't have said that—shouldn't have questioned the offer. He should have just accepted instantly. Instantly! Before Luis had the time to have any second thoughts. Mother of God, Majella!" She came to stand be-fore her sister. "Do you see what this means? If Luis will marry you then—then—everything will be all right."

Slowly Majella sat down, gazing up at her sister. Never had she seen Cecilia so deeply moved, so profoundly excited. And yet—something wasn't right. She groped for it. Resentment. That was it. Beneath the outward show of relief, Cecilia resented, and bitterly, that any decent man would be willing to marry her. A little sick, Majella turned away her face.

"Well, what's the matter with you!" Cecilia snapped. "You should fall on your knees and thank all the saints in heaven that he will have you—if he will, after he thinks about it."

"I don't want to marry Luis," Majella said steadily. "I think perhaps Eduardo's suggestion about a convent would be better."

"Majella, don't be an idiot. In the first place we—it would cost a fortune. Eduardo would insist on helping, of course. Why *not* this?"

Majella got up. "We could give the convent the Ortegna jewels. That wouldn't cost you anything since they are already mine."

"What are you going to do?"

"I'm going to the chapel." She had actually been about to retreat to the privacy of her room and didn't want to argue. Cecilia couldn't very well try to dissuade her from praying. "You just advised me to pray," she couldn't resist adding, and left as quickly as she could.

In the end she agreed to marry Luis. There was no way she could avoid it. Every one of them—even Hernán, when he regained his composure—was determined that she should and supported Luis.

Their attitude toward Luis Chavero now was a strange blend, and it took her several days of observing them to understand what it was. He was close to sainthood, on this they all agreed. He had solved their terrible dilemma with a few words

140

and his now inflexible determination to marry her despite her changed situation, and they felt deeply indebted to him for this. There was also an odd underlying of contempt for him that he should so demean himself.

Luis, always sensitive and perceptive, knew this. Majella sensed his reaching out to her for understanding, for love, and she could not give it. A thousand times a day she reminded herself what she owed him for his kindness, for his generosity, for his mercy. And his sacrifice—for it soon came out what he was giving up.

There was no question of their returning to Mexico. Without a murmur Luis relinquished his whole way of life that had been so important to him. Although his father was dead and his inheritance had come to him, his aunts and other relatives still remained. He was deeply attached to them. She heard snatches of conversation while the men smoked and drank of an evening on the patio.

"Spain is a possibility," Luis was saying in his pleasant, thoughtful way. "My people began in Spain. And I think Majella might enjoy living there for a time." He twisted the wine glass slowly between his lean fingers. He seemed to have become thinner, gaunter, as each day passed. "Then again, I have always longed to travel."

Majella moved her fan. That was not true, and she knew it.

"I think we shall consider possibly sojourning in other countries, here and there—see the world, as it were. Would you like that, Majella?"

"I am sure it would be very diverting," she murmured. She could see them in her mind, always

141

aliens, always sojourning in a strange land. The wealthy elegant Mexican couple, living their wandering, reclusive lives, never staying in one place long enough for the past to catch up with them. The mysterious Señor and Señora Chavero, late of Mexico, late of Spain, late of England, late of Switzerland, who would soon be leaving for a sojourn in Bavaria. And Luis, so deeply rooted, so entwined with family and bloodlines, slowly dying before her eyes. She felt sick. She had felt sick for several days. She felt short of breath now. The gardenias were cloyingly sweet. Her fan snapped shut and she excused herself. She could not marry Luis.

But how could she not? How could she escape them, defy them all, when they were only trying to help her. But she must!

Safe again in her bedroom she watched the Indian girl turn down the bed. They had fallen into an acquaintanceship.

"How is your husband feeling?" Majella asked, knowing the girl's husband had been thrown by a horse and hurt. He was recovering slowly in the Indian village situated on the rancho.

"He is better. He was out today. He is restless and longs to ride again."

"Perhaps he soon will," Majella murmured, taking off her necklace. She had not worn the garnets since her return. They lay in a small heap in the corner of her jewel box. She looked at them now and then, trying not to see them twined about Joaquín's brown wrist.

"He must," the girl commented, straightening the items on the table by the window. "Señor Eduardo pays more to those who ride for him. We will need more money. It has been some time since I last bled and I think a baby is coming."

Majella turned. "This will be your first child?"

"Yes, Señorita," the girl said, smiling contentedly. She gave the table cover a final pat and turned to go, leaving Majella staring at the closed door in slow dawning horror.

It has been some time since I last bled and I think a baby is coming. Majella stifled a sudden cry and clasped her shaking hands across her still flat stomach.

Joaquín had won. He had planted his seed in her body. He had said she would never be anybody else's woman. And now she would not be, could not be. Because she was going to have Joaquín's child. Not one of them—not even Luis—would be able to accept an Indian child.

Joaquín had won.

Chapter Nine

There was no possibility of sleep. Majella paced silently back and forth throughout the hours of the night, crossing and recrossing the pallid patch of moonlight that moved across the floor of her room. At dawn, drawn and haggard, she stood at her window, clutching her robe about her, and watched the night retreat, watched the sky turn from black, to gray, to streaks of wild angry pink. Joaquín was out there, somewhere, under the same flaming sky in his beloved far-off village. Then there came full light and another day to face.

With a shaky sigh she turned to find that the girl, Lucía, had opened the door and stood just inside. She was holding the pitcher of hot water to place on the washstand, and stared in astonishment at the unused bed.

"Come in, Lucía," Majella said courteously. "Close the door, please."

The girl obeyed, crossing the room to put down the pitcher. Small drifts of steam rose from the hot water, as the room still held the chilly night air.

"I could not sleep," Majella said. She wanted to talk to the girl, but wasn't quite sure how to begin. "Lucía, could you bring me some hot chocolate?" As the girl went for it, Majella sat down at the small table by the window. How did one approach gossiping with a servant? In fact, how did one even talk to one's family? She must tell them today. It would not be fair to let them continue with their plans. Luis must be released and sent back to Mexico. Her brothers—here her mind refused to function further, and she sat on in a kind of blank vacancy until Lucía came back with the chocolate.

What was Joaquín doing now, at this moment? This Indian girl might know of Joaquín, of his village. Her tired mind searched for a way to begin. There was a sudden scalding pain on her fingers and she quickly put down the chocolate cup.

"Ah, Señorita! You are burnt!" Lucía sprang forward, righting the tilted cup and dabbing at Majella's hand and wrist unhappily. "I am so sorry."

"Thank you. Never mind. I was careless." Majella bit back the rest of what she had been about to say. The girl would think she was insane. She had been about to say that Joaquín had taught her how to keep from being burned when she roasted the meat.

"Have the others gone down yet?" she asked, watching the girl fidget with the things on the table, mopping up spilled chocolate, almost tipping over the small jug of bright flowers.

"No, Lady, not yet. It is too early. Will you rest today? I could tell them—"

"No, thank you. I shall go down. You can help me dress if you will." Perhaps the kindest thing to do would be to talk with Luis first. An early riser, he was usually down in the patio by the time the others started down in the morning. She let Lucía select her clothing, knowing that the girl felt sorry for her, knowing that she wanted to help. She even paused going out the door for an added moment.

"Wait, Señorita. Let me put this flower in your hair." The girl plucked it from the jug, blotting the water off the stem. "It is yellow like the dress. There. That is fine. Just right." The girl stood back and surveyed her handiwork a moment. Majella smiled slightly going down the stairs. Had she ever been that young? That eager? Had her life ever been so simple that a flower matching a dress was cause for pleasure?

Luis was on the patio. Majella stood in the doorway looking at him for some time. He would be well out of it, well rid of her in whose body slept the child of another man.

"Luis?" She spoke softly, stepping into the patio.

"Majella." He got up quickly and came to her, and before she could speak he had caught her in his arms. "Oh, God—how beautiful—"

Before she could protest he had crushed her close and his mouth captured hers. There was an impression of desperation, of raw passion that she had never encountered in Luis before. He did not, perhaps could not, release her for some time. When he did, he pushed her away and walked a

146

few paces, putting the fountain between them. "I must be insane," he muttered. "Forgive me for taking such a liberty. Did I hurt you?"

"No. It doesn't matter. We have all been distressed," she said, her lips feeling numb from his bruising kiss. "Luis, I must talk to you—before the others come down."

He turned to look at her for an instant as one might look at an enemy, cautious, wary. Then the mask was back in place.

"If you are going to tell me you don't want to marry me, spare yourself the trouble, my dear. I am going to marry you, Majella. I must have you. Neither God nor the Devil can keep you from me now."

She sat down suddenly on the bench. There was something so implacable in his determination.

"Isn't that what you were going to say?" His voice was somewhat gentler. He came to stand before her, reaching out to touch her hair. "Don't fight me on this, Majella. You have been shocked, hurt. But life will be good to us yet. I'll make it all up to you. I'll make you forget."

"Luis, I cannot," she said, starting to rise. "Let me—"

"No. Say nothing. It is not your decision now. I have the permission of your brothers. Say no more. We know what is best for you."

She pushed his hand away and stood up. She was shaking.

"Listen to me. I am not a doll, a puppet. Nobody listens to me! You must listen!" She reached out and caught his arm. "Please. I cannot. *You* cannot."

147

"Nonsense! I will hear no more about it!" He spoke to her sharply, for the first time.

"You *listen!*" Violently, she cracked her fan across his face, her eyes suddenly blazing with rage. "*Listen* to me!"

He was stunned, and showed it, staring at her in disbelief. At that moment, Cecilia stepped through the door onto the patio, followed by Eduardo. Whatever greeting they had intended was lost.

Something seemed to explode inside Majella.

"Come here—all of you. Where are the boys? Miguel? Hernán?" She felt color flooding her face. Tell them all. All at once. Make them listen. Finish it. Now.

Appalled, confused, they hurried forward—Cecilia starting to remonstrate; Hernán coming through the door, stumbling slightly on the threshhold in his haste; Miguel close behind him.

"Our plans must be changed," Majella said, feeling detached, outside herself. "It was kind of Luis to propose marriage again. I am grateful. We all are. But we cannot marry. The situation has changed. I am— I have—" She faltered and then plunged on. "I have discovered that I am going to have a child." She watched them, saw the varying degrees of disbelief and horror at this stunning news. "We cannot expect Luis to welcome another man's child. So there can be no marriage with Luis."

No one said anything for a long time. They all stood like statues, not moving. All the strength went out of her and she sat down on the bench again. Slowly they came to life. She watched with

148

remote interest. Luis simply turned away and leaned upon the fountain, getting his sleeve wet. She wanted to tell Cecilia to close her mouth. She could not look at Miguel. She looked instead at her fan. There was a small split place in the silk.

Then, as they came alive, there began the long exhausting battle against them. Against them all. The relentless beating away at her defenses. Breakfast was forgotten. They must go inside to close themselves in Cecilia's small sitting room for utmost privacy, as if the servants did not know everything that was happening. They were frantic, desperate, and beneath and over all—deeply angry. Angry at the dilemma, the impasse, at her flat refusal to marry Luis now, at—they could hardly believe this—at her demand to somehow keep her child. Bitter, too, and filled with hate, at the renegades who had done this to them. And lastly, angry at the unwelcome unborn child sleeping inside her. Majella tried to face them down, her head pounding, her eyes smarting with held-back tears, arguing, pleading, bargaining to hold onto her child. *She could never give up her baby.* At some time during the long sleepless night just past, this determination had emerged. It would never change and she knew it. The angry voices battered at her numbed mind. Anger from everybody.

Anger from the gentle Miguel: "Majella, you are out of your mind!"

The calm Eduardo furious: "How long have you known this, my girl!"

Icy rage from Luis: "I shall certainly not permit you to keep an Indian child."

Outrage from young Hernán: "Convents are for orphans—you will leave the child there and forget it."

Cecilia, in a cold rage, always reminding them: "Keep your voices down." Then, still furious, blue eyes flashing, Cecilia turned on her. "I have never heard of anything so mad. You simply don't make sense. Come, I'll take you to your room. Let the men talk in peace!" She took hold of Majella none too gently and pulled her toward the door. "We simply cannot discuss this rationally with you protesting everything!"

Distractedly, Majella turned first to one then another. She met with a blank wall of resistance. Their solution had been in hand. Luis would have married her and taken her away. Now this was escaping them.

"Majella," Miguel said firmly, "we must do what is best for you. Because we love you. Please go to your room now."

She held back hysteria. They loved her. And they would smother her to death with their love and steal away her baby. Blindly, she stumbled after Cecilia and when they were upstairs Cecilia, white faced, taut, pushed her into her bedroom. Then the key turned in the lock. Majella couldn't believe it. How childish. Cecilia would be embarrassed about that later, but at the moment she wasn't thinking clearly. Oh, what did it matter. Dully, she lay down on her bed. Perhaps she could escape into sleep as she had before. She lay a long time, looking at the wall, looking at the ceiling, but sleep did not come. She thought instead with a sense of wonder of the baby she would have, and that she must—somehow—not let them take the child away from her.

The maid, Lucía, wide-eyed and nervous, brought up a tray of food in early afternoon and put it on the table by the window. Timidly she came to the bed, fingering the door key she held uneasily.

"Señorita, I am sorry you are sick. The Señora said you must stay here and rest. She says you must eat something."

"All right, Lucía. Just leave the tray. Thank you." So Cecilia had told the servants she was ill. Outwardly, of course, they must accept this. Pretend. She glanced up and her eyes met the servant girl's troubled gaze. She felt a sense of affinity with Lucía. Was this because they were both Indian? The idea made her ponder.

"What else do you wish, Señorita?"

"Nothing, thank you."

The girl reached over and patted her hand, lax upon the pillow. Sudden tears of gratitude stung Majella's eyes at the simple gesture.

"Thank you, Lucía."

"I must lock the door when I go, Señorita."

"That is all right, Lucía. I understand. It is better that I stay here and rest."

The girl's eyes were glistening with tears as she left.

Poor Cecilia, she could never fool the all-wise, all-seeing servants. They knew. Majella got up and ate some of the food. Cecilia was right in one respect; she should rest. They were downstairs making new plans for what was left of her life and she must somehow gather enough strength to hold steadfast against them. Sleep seemed out of the question; her mind would not be still. Continually, she groped for some answer.

The jewels. They could use them as an offering at the convent. The hateful, terrible box of jewels that had come into her life to break it apart and smash it. She had handled this badly. She should have spoken quietly to Miguel. She still might, after their present panic diminished. Just she and Miguel. She must convince him that she *preferred* to go into a convent—as a kitchen maid, if necessary—if marriage to Luis meant giving up her child. In a convent, an arrangement could be made to keep the child with her.

Oh, Joaquín, she thought in anguish. If she were in a convent, she would truly never see Joaquín again. He would be lost to her, for she would be sealed away bringing up her secret child. She went to the window and looked out into the brilliant sunlight. Eduardo's house was built in the Spanish design, with beautiful iron grillework protecting the windows that looked out over a portion of the roof of mellowed tile. She climbed up onto the wide adobe window ledge and clasped her slim hands about the twisted iron. It was strongly, solidly embedded into the thick walls. *Oh, Joaquín. Where are you? What are you doing?*

Hopeless, she sagged downward, the iron sliding through her hands. Joaquín still had a little money from the raid, stolen money, but money nonetheless. Had he recovered? Could he travel? Joaquín was strong, unbelievably strong. Suddenly she gripped the bars.

Joaquín! I carry your child in my body. Help

me! He had stood against them all for her. He had turned on his lifelong friend. And the old man, the grandfather, had let them stay. He was her friend. She could go back to the village. *If only she could get to Joaquín.* Instantly, the madness of this idea was evident. There was no possible way she could get out of this room at the moment, or off the rancho when she did leave the room, let alone cross the endless miles to the village. And should she by some miracle manage to do this, Eduardo, her brothers, Luis, all of them would come with all the armed men from the rancho and thunder into the village.

And Joaquín himself? Helpless in this. He was an Indian. There was no imaginable way he could walk boldly up to the door of Eduardo's house and demand his woman and his unborn child. No way at all. He could be shot on sight if he tried.

She sat a long time on the window ledge, until the hot brightness of the sun drove her to the other side of the room. A little later Lucía came in for the tray and to put fresh drinking water into the carafe.

"Lucía?" Majella spoke tentatively.

"Yes, Señorita?"

"Do you know what has happened to me?"

"Señorita. It is forbidden to speak of such things. Señor Eduardo—" Her voice fell to a whisper.

"I don't ask you to speak of it, Lucía. I just ask that you listen a moment."

"Señorita, it is forbidden—"

"I do not want to leave my baby in the convent, Lucía. I must keep my baby. Do you know the

153

Indian village where I was found? Do you know of it?"

"Señorita, please, I—"

"I need—I must—get a message to Joaquín Salazar. He is an Indian in the village. He lives in the house of the Headman."

"Señorita, there is no way. I would not dare."

"Not you, Lucía. But someone. Anyone. I will pay. You know that I can. You have seen my jewelry."

Lucía was hurriedly gathering up the things to take out the tray, her face averted.

"I just need to let him know—about the baby. About what is happening." She spoke more quickly as Lucía started out. "Salazar," she added desperately. "His name is Joaquín Salazar."

At the doorway Lucía stopped, her eyes huge with apprehension. She passed her tongue over her lips in a torment of indecision.

"I will pay you, Lucía. You may have anything of my jewels that you want," Majella urged. "Please."

"I want nothing, Señorita," the girl said nervously. "But," she paused for an agonizingly long time, "Joaquín Salazar, yes, I know him."

"Lucía. You do! You *know* Joaquín?" Majella was suddenly breathless.

"Yes, Señorita. It is known—all is known—among us despite how the poor señora wishes us not to know. He came—he comes to the rancho's Indian village, Joaquín Salazar. He limps, doesn't he?"

"Yes, yes," Majella gasped. "He was hurt. Shot. At his village when they came to bring me back here. Where? Where did you see him?"

"Here, Señorita. Here on the rancho. He comes

154

into the Indian village here, where the workers live."

"Oh, my God," Majella whispered. "If my brother-in-law—if my brothers found out—" Her blood ran cold at the danger Joaquín invited.

"He knows, Señorita. He does not stay long. He comes to a friend sometimes in the night, then he goes quickly by morning."

"Why, Lucía?"

"To ask. To find out. His friend tells him what we know, what we have heard."

"Lucía, tonight when he comes, tell him—have his friend tell him—" she halted, twisting her hands together in a frenzy of anxiety. Wait. Should she send him any word at all? Should she do this? Was it like signing Joaquín's death warrant? "Oh, Lucía, I don't know what to tell him."

"But it is not for us to say anyway, Señorita," the girl said, shaking her head. "His friend will know by now because of all the arguments in the house today. His friend will tell him this. We can do nothing to stop that. By tonight he will know— if he comes tonight. He does not come every night, Señorita. Will you please lie on the bed and rest, like the señora says? And, please, do not ever tell the señora I spoke of this. The señora—"

"All right. I understand," Majella said. She watched the girl go and then stood a moment staring at the closed door, listening to the key turn in the lock. She was filled, consumed with a deep excitement. He was here. On the ranch. At such a terrible risk. But how like him. But the *risk*! She suppressed a shudder. He must have been seen by several, by dozens, of the workers. Any one of them could decide to speak to the señor, who would promptly reach for his purse so heavy with gold. *Go, Joaquín. Go. Quickly.*

Cecilia tapped at her door in the early evening, turning the key as she did so. "Majella? Are you sleeping?" She came in to find Majella seated in a chair near the window.

"No, I am not sleeping. Why do you lock the door, Cecilia? Where could I go?"

Cecilia's fair face flamed. "I am sorry," she said, sounding embarrassed. "I suppose we were all excited. I—didn't want you disturbed. I saw that your bed hadn't been slept in either, and I wanted you to get some rest."

"Never mind. It doesn't matter."

"Would you like to come down for dinner?" Cecilia said somewhat stiffly. "We have finished with all the—unpleasant discussions. Please, Majella, dear. The boys would be so happy if you would come down."

"Please give them my excuses, Cecilia. Perhaps tomorrow I shall come down." So they had finished with the unpleasant discussions. A grim smile touched her mouth. They must have convinced one another all over again of what must be done and now felt sure that she would agree.

"Well, all right," Cecilia said uncertainly. "But I am sure Luis would feel—"

"Tomorrow, Cecilia." She spoke firmly. Cecilia colored again but, murmuring something soothing, she left. Majella took some small comfort in that. There was something to be said for being big sister—it did give one a certain advantage at times. At least she was free of them all for another evening. She could not possibly go down among them tonight, not with this wild excitement and fear

156

pounding away inside her. Where was Joaquín—right now? Lucía had said he did not come to his friend every night. Would he come tonight? Majella sat in the growing dusk and waited—she was not sure for what.

At dinner time Lucía brought another tray, but as there were several other servants in the hallway Majella could say nothing to her. Lucía put down the tray and left. Majella could not touch the food—she thought if she tried to eat she would choke. Sometimes when she could sit no longer she got up and walked about the room. Her door was not locked now; she could walk outside if she wished. Perversely, she stayed where she was; she did not want to encounter any of her family. She did not light a candle or a lamp, but waited on in the gathering darkness.

It was well after midnight when she heard the sound. A dog had barked several times an hour or so before. Now the small sound near the open window. As silently as a ghost in the moonlight Majella left the chair and went to the window. The moonlight bathed the curved red tiles of the roof with a pale glow.

He was here. Crouched on the roof in a shadow. She knew it. She put her hands between the iron grille, knowing they would be seen. There was another small sound. *Joaquín.* Her heart was pounding; a thousand images raced through her mind.

"I am here," she whispered. Still he said nothing, but in a moment she saw him, coming from the shadow, and in a moment his hands clasped hers. There was a flood of excitement at his touch.

Balancing easily, he moved close to the grille and pressed against it. Her lips touched his, clung.

157

She pressed closer, the iron bars cold against her face.

"Joaquín, it is dangerous for you to be here," she whispered.

"It is dangerous for me to be anywhere." There was the sound of a smile in his voice, and when the moonlight fell on his face it seemed more of a grimace. "I spoke to a friend in the village here."

"I know," she said, her voice barely audible because her sister and Eduardo slept in the next room. "Joaquín, what is that? Your hand is hurt. It's bleeding."

"It is nothing." He withdrew the hand and wiped it down the side of his shirt. "One of the dogs. I could not make friends with him."

"Let me bind it up."

"No." He tightened his clasp on her other hand. "There is not enough time. We must talk. The man from Mexico will take you away, won't he?"

"I don't know. That is what they want. But I—"

"I know about the child." His whisper, suddenly savage, cut in. "I heard today."

"About the baby," she said faintly. "You see—" She strained to see him more clearly, trying to read something in his shadowed face.

"Yes." There was something grim and forbidding in his face when it came full in the moonlight again. It might have been carved of stone. "I have heard that you promised to marry the man from Mexico and today you changed your mind?"

"I promised because there seemed no other choice. But now a choice has been made for me. He—would not let me keep the child. I cannot give it away to the sisters. I cannot, Joaquín."

"Why not?" His voice was somber. "The sisters

158

would be kind to it. It would have food and a place to sleep safely."

"I cannot!" In her desperation she raised her voice slightly and his hand, quick as a snake, came through the grille; he placed his fingers over her lips.

"Be silent, little Wood Dove." Unthinking, he spoke in his own tongue.

"I am sorry," she breathed against his hand. "Joaquín, what can we do? Can you take me back to the village?"

"You would go with me?" he asked, sounding uncertain.

"Yes," she said. "It is the only thing we can do. Isn't it? It would not be as it was. Things are different now. If I can convince my people that I want to go, that I must go—would you take me back with you?"

He was quiet a long time.

She watched him absent-mindedly wipe his injured hand against his shirt again, leaving another smear of blood darkly visible against the fabric. Then he slid his hand inside his shirt and withdrew a small twist of cloth. Something was inside it. A smile touched Majella's lips briefly. Another cloth bundle, this one very small. What had he brought?

"I do not believe your people would permit it," he said finally. His voice held generations of hopelessness.

"But I am going to talk to my brother, Miguel. Just Miguel. I am going to convince him. I *will*. They must let me go. If you can get permission for us to return to the village. Joaquín, ask the grandfather." She paused a moment and then added,

159

making herself say it. "Ask Leon. Beg him, if you have to. They must let us come."

His mouth twisted and he was shaking his head in denial. "Why must they? Must they, knowing that your people will come in and massacre everyone there? No. I will think of something else."

"But if I persuade my family—if they *let* me go—" She pressed closer against the bars, straining closer to him. He must not withdraw into remoteness. He must not retreat from her.

He shook his head again. "They will not," he said flatly. "Never."

"All right," she placated. "We will go someplace else then." Even as she said it she knew how hopeless it was. His friend Leon, against his own wishes and judgment, had let them return to the village rather than try to live outside it in the hostile other world.

He moved closer to the bars again, his face somber in the moonlight.

"Joaquín," she whispered, "it isn't just to keep the baby. I want to go with you. *I* want to." She was admitting it clearly and openly for the first time, and to them both, that she was no longer his unwilling captive, that to feel whole she must be with him. And of her own volition, her own desire. "I love you—I think of you constantly. You are my love and it will be forever." The old dream from her childhood came and went in her mind. That dark night. Her mother walking silently beside the tired man who was her father and whose face she never saw. She knew now that her mother would have walked to the end of the world beside that man. Gazing at Joaquín through the iron grille, she knew that it was happening all over again.

160

This was the man she would walk to the end of the earth with. There was no other way for her. It did not matter that their love had been born in violence and conflict. The love had been born. It lived now. It would go on. "We have a touch of madness, my mother and I," she said softly.

"What?" He didn't understand.

"You remember. When we talked in the night-time and I told you all about my mother and my real father—the one I cannot remember. And my mother's father—he had it too. We do not mind throwing away the whole world for our beloved. Will you mind having a woman who is a little mad?"

A reluctant smile curved his mouth. He leaned forward and they kissed again through the bars. Slow fire crept through her veins at the magic of his touch and she clung to him. He drew back finally, fingering the tiny twist of rag in his hand.

"All right. I will try to plan a way to take you away. It may take a while. Days. Maybe many days. I will do the best I can." He crouched down slightly, preparing to ease his way down the tile roof as silently as he had come. He thrust the tiny cloth packet through the bars and she took it without thinking. "If I do not come back—"

"Joaquín," she gasped, straining to see his face which was now turned slightly and hidden. "You *must* come back."

"If I cannot come back, I mean. You know, my love, no matter what I try, it could be that I will fail. You must understand that."

"You must not fail," she whispered urgently. He must not fail, not only because it would leave her to live out her life as a shell of nothingness, but also because she knew if he failed it would be because he was dead.

"If I fail," he persisted, "eat these."

"What?" she asked blankly. "I don't understand."

"In the cloth. When I learned about the child inside you, I went out and found these leaves for you. Child-killer leaves. They are fresh now. You must put them in the sun. Dry them. When they are dry, break them up and eat them. They will kill the child inside you before it is born."

"Joaquín," she gasped in horror. She flung the little bag from her, out onto the dark roof. "What are you saying! How did you even know such a thing!" She pushed her hands between the bars, grasping his shoulders. She felt him move and realized in a moment that he had not been able to suppress a brief, bitter laughter.

"You said in the village how few children there were, Majella. Didn't you even wonder why? There is no place now for the people—I mean my people, and the tribes die out because fewer are born. In the olden days—you should hear the grandfather tell of it. In old days the child being born brought joy. But no more. Better not to be born. So when a woman knows that a child has started she eats the leaves. Majella, listen to me." He waited a patient moment until she could bring her attention back to what he was saying.

"I will do my best. If I do not come back it will be because I cannot. But do not wait too long to eat the leaves. You must do it before the child moves inside you." He inched his way down the roof, groping for the tiny bag. When he had it he crept up again. One of the tiles creaked, making a small noise. He froze for a long moment. When he got to her window he thrust the twist of leaves between the bars again. When she could not take them, he dropped the packet inside on the ledge. She waited another moment, unable to touch the little twist of cloth.

"Joaquín?" She pressed against the bars, straining her eyes into the darkness, aching for his touch again. But he was gone. Numbly, she picked up the little bag and stared at it in horror.

Chapter Ten

Majella knew she could never use the leaves, but she could not bring herself to destroy them. Instead she placed them in the corner of the drawer near the garnet necklace and left them there, still in the grimy cloth wrapping. If Lucía saw them and knew what they were, she said nothing.

The next day she made an opportunity to talk with Miguel, steeling herself to face the anguish that came into his eyes every time he looked at her. Always serious and loyal, he felt now a heavy responsibility for what had happened, blaming himself. He as head of the Moreno family should have—somehow—not allowed any of this to happen. He felt a sense of personal failure, and felt it keenly. She knew that she dare not broach directly the idea of going away with Joaquín until she knew how he would receive it. She began cautiously.

"Miguel, sometimes I think it would have been

better if Eduardo had not searched and found me."

"Don't speak like that," Miguel said, coming to sit beside her. They were on the patio, speaking softly so no loitering servant would overhear. "This is much better. Luis' coming was a—a godsend. This way you can, my dear, find some measure of happiness. I know," he said, lifting her hand to his lips and kissing it gently, "you think not, but someday, when all this had faded—well, if not happiness, at least peace."

"But not now, Miguel," she persisted. "Luis cannot accept the baby and I—cannot give it up."

"But you have to give it up. There is no other way." He released her hand and there settled over his face a grimness that seemed out of place on one so young.

"But couldn't there be?" Majella asked. "Think a moment, Miguel. If Eduardo had not found me, if you had all thought me dead, I would have gone on living in the village."

"As an Indian squaw?" Miguel got up from the stone bench.

She caught his hand to hold him. "Miguel. You don't understand them. They are different. Indians are not bad people, only poor. Try to remember, Miguel, that Mama was half Indian. And the man who—the man became very kind to me. He is—" The look on her brother's face stopped her.

"He is an animal," Miguel said, his voice shaking. He jerked his hand away and looked down at her with the face of a stranger. This was not her beloved brother, kind, steady, soft-spoken, whom she, his older sister, could quell with a glance. He continued in his stranger's voice. "And if I ever see this carrion I will empty my pistol into him. He will have so many bullets in him that it will take two men to lift his body off the ground and throw it on the dungheap. Put this idea out of your mind, Majella. You are not rational. I think this has driven you out of your senses." He turned and left abruptly.

So, Joaquín was right. Her family would never support her in this. She sat there on the bench until the feeling of sick chill brought on by Miguel's words began to diminish. She had only Joaquín to depend on now. And Joaquín, though he would try his best among his limited choices, even Joaquín had agreed filled with hopelessness, saying he would try, and at the same time handing her the medicinal herbs with which to kill his unborn child.

Wait, she told herself, getting up from the bench to go inside. And the waiting was long and tedious during the long summer days and the warm summer nights, when she longed for Joaquín so intensely she wondered how she could stand it.

Majella now kept to herself as much as she could and still remain aware of what the family was doing and planning. There was a definite schism now, with them aligned against her, even Miguel. The old closeness and understanding was gone. They still loved her, of course, and frequently assured her of this, but she had become a stubborn problem to be dealt with. It was impossible to discuss the matter with them; their minds were made up. She knew when they were selecting the convent in which to place her for the period of her confinement. She knew when they settled more firmly on a specific one in Guadalajara. Luis was preparing to travel there to make the arrangements. All of this had taken several days.

Day after day, night after night, she waited, hoping for some word, some sign, from Joaquín. He had been right about her family, and since he had never counted on their permission, he would be planning another course. He would come. And soon. She kept telling herself this. How would he come? How would it happen? What should she prepare? She should be ready in case it had to be done quickly. Carefully, she put together certain garments, selecting sturdy ones to survive better in an Indian village than the elegant rooms of Eduardo's house, and garments that would wear well and last long, for she and Joaquín would be poor.

Now and then she wondered and worried about the Ortegna jewels. Her mother had wanted her to have them, and she had hated them and recoiled from them, but now she was undecided. In the brief look she had taken at them she had seen what seemed to be good stones, gems of value. At the same time she knew they would be difficult for an Indian to dispose of, and if they could be disposed of it would likely be for only a fraction of their value. She thought of Trinidad, selling the stolen articles for about a tenth of their worth and grateful to get it. Were there stores in Los Angeles that might buy them? What would happen if an Indian walked into a store in Los Angeles offering for sale a sapphire brooch? Instant suspicion? Arrest?

In any case, she had no idea where in the large Obregón house Cecilia had put them. She must ask Cecilia, make up some excuse. No, she dare not ask Cecilia and face that bright, searching gaze. If they suspected, even slightly, that there might be some alternative to their own plans it could prove to be the death of her beloved.

She spoke to Lucía about Joaquín, hoping she could trust the girl. "Does Joaquín come to see his friend in the village now?"

"No, Señorita. Not for many days."

What more could she say to Lucía? She had not wanted to burden the girl by telling her about Joaquín's visit to see her, and his promise to return and take her away with him. It might be tempting fate, and there was too much at stake.

It was maddening not to know what was happening, not to have anyone to talk to about it, not even knowing what she could do to help. It began to take its toll. She had to force herself to eat. She must not be frail and sick when he came. She choked the food down when she didn't want it—if not for her sake, then for the baby's. She sorted out again the small horde of things to take. She spent endless hours in the chapel on her knees.

The day after she felt the infant quicken to life within her, she finally destroyed the leaves. They were quite dry now, and she broke them into smaller and smaller pieces, and threw them to the wind.

The next night Joaquín came back; again, silently, secretly to her window. She woke from a sound sleep knowing he was there and got up, stumbling hastily out of bed, dragging the covers on the floor.

"Majella," he said her name soundlessly and thrust his hands between the bars to bury and tan-

-gle them a moment in her flowing hair. "Do you still want to go with me?"

"Yes. Oh, yes." Her heart was pounding. She could barely see him for there was little moonlight. "But I must tell you, my family—"

"I know about your family, Majella. They will not give you up. I did not think they would. Can you really leave them? Never to see them again? Back in the caves you dreamed of them; do you remember?"

Her breath caught in her throat. Never? Could she do it? Then remembering what Miguel had said, and the merciless fury in his voice, she said, "Yes, Joaquín. I can. I must."

He withdrew his hands. "All right. First, we will marry in the Christian manner. I have spoken with the Christian father in San Gabriel."

"But how could we do that? Won't they know who I am?"

"I told him you were an Indian girl and your last name is Moreno. There are many people named Moreno, and many are Indians using the name from the mission times. He will not think to question. He will only be glad we marry in the church. That is their way."

"How—is it arranged?" she asked, her whisper suddenly faint at the enormity of what she was doing.

Joaquín's hands came through the bars and drew her close as he could against the grille. "I cannot say what is in my heart—I have no way with words. But if you had changed your mind I would have died from it. Coming here tonight I promised myself that if you would not come with me I would go back to the grandfather's house, and lie down in my place, and turn my face to the wall and die, and it would be better so."

"I will come with you," she answered when she could. "I have thought of nothing else."

"All right. It will be in a few days. Four days from now I will come for you. Write out a letter to leave for your family."

"A letter?"

"Yes. Write to them that you are going away with me. *Away*. Not to the village. Make them know that."

"Joaquín, why?"

"Because I don't want your kinsmen riding into Leon's village. I don't want anyone killed because of us. Do not say anything about the father at San Gabriel. They would not think to go there. They would think to go to Los Angeles."

"All right," she whispered breathlessly. "Joaquín, it's almost dawn."

"I know. On the fourth night from now I will wait for you. I will be just inside the chapel. Come down from this room and go through the chapel."

"*Inside* the chapel!" A shudder went through her. Joaquín would be inside Eduardo's house.

"I can meet you outside," she protested.

He placed his fingers against her lips. "No, my love. The dogs outside would bark at you. They are all half-wild out there. Just come down through the chapel and we will walk out together. They know me now. It will be quiet, better that way."

"All right," she said faintly. "All right." Clinging to him through the grille she wondered if she could stand to wait another four days. When he

170

had gone she could not go back to bed. She was in a fever of excitement. Not going to the village. Then where? But it didn't matter. Joaquín would have thought of something. He would have planned something. And when Eduardo and her brothers stormed into the village again, she and Joaquín would not be there. The letter. That might help. She must be convincing. She must make them know that she went willingly. Perhaps they would not even look for her if they learned that, if she could make them believe it. But this was a forlorn hope and she knew it.

The next four days were an agony. She stayed as much by herself as possible for fear they might detect something in her eyes, in her manner, something of the feverish torment of emotions that gripped her. They were all mingled together—the excitement, a frantic relief and a sickening fear, sorrow at losing her family and always, underlying all these, the continual grinding hunger for Joaquín, the desperate need for him. Sometimes she longed in anguish to talk to her mother. For she too had had this streak of madness where her beloved was concerned—willingness to throw away everything to go with him.

When the long-awaited night finally came, Majella put on dark clothing and tied a dark scarf around her head. She propped the letter up on the dresser. It was well past midnight and she smiled as she stooped to pick up the two bundles she was to carry with her. Bundles again. The larger one was clothing, the smaller one the comb, toilet articles, and her garnet necklace. She had considered briefly about taking other pieces of jewelry, but had decided against it. Scarcely breathing, she crept down the stairs, not seeing anyone. The house lay cavernous and dark all about her. She went through the silent patio, and into the main living room, and through that into the small chapel that also opened onto the outside. The single candle flickered beneath the feet of the Virgin, making a small pool of light near the altar. The rest was darkness, the rail, the rows of benches, all darkness. There was total silence about her. Suddenly damp with fear, she went down between the benches toward where she knew the outside door was, going into the deeper shadows to do so.

Joaquín was not there.

She waited just inside the door, clasping the small bundle to her breast and holding the other one down by her side. There was a sound by the living room door and she melted back into the shadows, not breathing, praying that Joaquín would not choose this moment to enter.

It was Luis. He stepped into the chapel and knelt before the Virgin. Majella watched him, the sickness of abject fear stirring in her. How many other people lay wakeful in the house—angry, troubled. From the black shadows she watched Luis pray, the glimmer of his costly rosary sliding between his lean fingers. She felt guilty watching him in this private plea, and closed her eyes. If Luis wanted to pray in private, surely he was entitled to. Thankfully, his voice was so low that she could not hear what he was saying. She opened her eyes when he finished and watched as he rose, somewhat stiffly, as if he might already be old. With a terrible, maddening slowness he lighted a candle. Majella pressed herself deeper into the shadows, but the added light did not penetrate to where she was. She tried not to wonder what he prayed for—happiness in his marriage? Or perhaps forgiveness for wanting to marry an impure bride at all. *Go away, Luis. Go away.*

When he finally left the chapel she let out a shaky breath. She felt faint. She had been breathing to little and too shallowly. Oh, God, Mary, she must not faint. Then she felt Joaquín's hand sliding around her waist and she turned and pressed herself against him, having no idea how long he had been behind her.

He held her a moment longer and then moved toward the outside door. She followed, bringing her bundles. It gave her a strange and wild surge of intense happiness to do this. The spread of the outside yard was ghostly. She had no idea what time it was now, or how near the dawn was. Without any seeming hurry, they walked down the slope from the house. In a kind of cleft or shallow valley at some distance from the house was a clump of ancient twisted oak trees, spreading this way and that. They walked through the trees for a while before she heard the faint sound of horses.

Majella quickened her pace and caught up with Joaquín just as they reached them. There was someone else. She hesitated, straining to see in the darkness.

"Hurry up. It is almost dawn."

"Leon!" she gasped. "Joaquín," she caught his arm. "You didn't say Leon was here, too." The old fear of Leon had come crawling back and lay coiled inside her, making her hands go damp. Joaquín was surprised. He took the bundle from her and made as if to help her mount. "We have not

173

talked of anything yet," he said reasonably. "Here, let me help you up."

"Be quick about it," Leon said, his voice grim. Majella could feel the intensity of his sullen anger. He did not want to be here. He hated her still. He would never stop hating her. How had Joaquín managed to overcome his opposition? She mounted. She would never accustom herself to riding without a saddle. But she must. She grasped the reins firmly. Joaquín was mounted now. There was a moment of confusion and they were walking the horses slowly out of the trees. Joaquín had secured the bundles behind him on his own horse so she could concentrate on riding. When they reached the open terrain Leon kicked the sides of his mount and it sprang forward. She and Joaquín followed as closely as they could the pace he set them all.

The journey was exhausting. They rode well into daylight over the seemingly vacant, endless land. She knew that the land was not vacant; it was only that Leon avoided the settled areas. Then, at last, they stopped to wait, hiding in a sheltered glade near some water where they could fill the battered metal canteens. She tried not to think of what she was doing, of what kind of life she was undoubtedly going into, holding only to the thought that she would be with Joaquín—and that their child would be safe with them. She slid down from her horse, able by then to be grateful that they could stop and rest a while.

As she sat wearily down on a rock, Leon asked her a direct question, which he almost never did. "Did you bring any food?"

She looked up in consternation at his rough-hewn face beneath the drooping brim of an ancient felt hat. It was closed and sullen, his eyes opaque.

"No. There was no way to without arousing questions."

He gave a sigh of mingled disgust and contempt. She knew what he was thinking. That there was probably enough food in the house of Eduardo Obregón to feed their whole village and she had somehow managed not to get any of it.

Joaquín, his eyes troubled, slid his hands over Leon's broad shoulders. "We have dried beef, as you know, my friend. We can eat that. Let her alone. We don't know how it is in the Mexican's house. Maybe there was no way she could get any food."

Leon didn't answer, shrugging away Joaquín's hands. Majella realized for the first time that Leon's brooding anger now included Joaquín as well as herself.

They chewed tough strips of dried beef and drank water and lay down to rest. She wondered where they had got the dried beef; there had been no beef at all in the village. It had to be stolen, of course. Still tasting its saltiness in her mouth she could envision how it must have been. The strips of beef hanging like thick strings from racks under the hot sun near someone's house. And one of them, creeping forward slowly, silently, closer and closer to the racks. The racks were out in the open so there was nothing to hide a thieving Indian. Then the slow reaching up to take down one strip, two strips. Only silence in the smoldering glare of the California sun. Dare he reach for a third strip? Yes, one more. Now had he pushed his luck to the very limit? Still only silence; no shotgun blast from the silent window of the house to tear into his body.

What a terrible risk to take for a little food. She drank a little more water but the saltiness seemed to remain.

Leon was at some distance from them, the battered felt hat over his face. The deep peaceful silence of the woodland glade settled over them. Majella stretched her aching muscles and turned her gaze away from Leon.

They dressed so poorly, the men of the village. She would make some clothes for Joaquín. Shirt, trousers. She sewed well. She glanced over to him, stretching himself out on the ground a little distance from her, his heavily muscled shoulders moving beneath the thin worn cloth of his shirt. She felt a slow warmth steal up through her body, a yearning, a hunger so intense she had to reach out toward him. He saw the gesture instantly and his gaze locked with hers. He got up, pulling her to her feet.

"Come away," he said. "Come over here."

There was a subtle, but profound difference in Joaquín's lovemaking now, a sense of love, almost of cherishing, that underlay his passion.

"I almost lost you," he whispered again and again. "I almost lost you."

And her surrender to him now was also subtly different. There was so much more than the raw satisfying of the desperate need he aroused, more of a fulfillment of her deepest destiny. When their passion was spent and she lay in his arms she felt a deep, yearning tenderness. This was her love, and it would last forever. Loss of family, living in hardship for the rest of her life—this, what she had now, was worth all sacrifice. He gently smoothed her hair, plucking from it a small leaf that had become entangled. She drifted into deep and restful sleep, and did not awaken until almost dusk. Joaquín was sitting near her, his arms clasped about his bent knees. The sober look had returned.

"I wanted to see the wound on your leg," Majella said, sitting up. "I forgot. Is it all right now?"

"Yes."

"I also wanted to ask you—what about Leon? I was surprised that he was with you. Are we going back to the village?"

"No. Not the village, Majella. I told you, San Gabriel."

"Then why is Leon with us?"

"Because he did agree to let us ride there because of the distance, and because someone must return the horses. He said he would do that."

"But why does he help you at all, Joaquín? He doesn't want us to—"

Joaquín made a faint gesture of impatience, then tried to soften it by speaking kindly. "Because he is like my elder brother, Majella. He cannot refuse to help me even if his mind is set against what I do. Remember, in the cave, at the very beginning, when I offered to give up my share? He let me win at gambling instead, so I could keep my share and also have you. No, he hates what I am doing, but he is bound in his heart to help me do it if I must." It was said with an air of finality, as if he didn't want to say anything further. "We should eat something before we start riding again."

"When will we get to San Gabriel?" She got up, brushing twigs and leaves from her clothing.

"Before tomorrow night. The priest has agreed to marry us then."

She wanted to ask where they would go after that, but did not because it was clear he did not want to talk any more about it. His eyes, wary, uneasy, were on Leon, who came walking toward them with his easy grace, ducking his head beneath low branches. The battered hat was pulled down low on his forehead so she could not see all of his face. He was bringing some of the dried beef and a canteen of water.

At dusk the next day they stopped on the outskirts of the sleepy settlement of San Gabriel. They rested until later in the evening. They were not near any water and, without asking, Majella used some of the remaining water from a canteen to dampen a handkerchief to wipe the dust from her face. She paused, her hands motionless a moment, thinking of the contrast between this and what her marriage to Luis would have been. She wondered what they had all thought when they found the letter—better not to think of that. She hung the grimy handkerchief on a nearby bush to dry in the warm evening air.

Joaquín walked over to Leon, and the two men faced each other.

"Please come with me," Joaquín said softly. "Be with me at my marriage."

Leon pushed back his hat and looked into Joaquín's face for a long time without answering.

"No," he said finally. "You come with me. Forget this marriage. There is still time."

178

Majella felt a slow anger and it took all of her control to keep silent. How dared he?

"No," Joaquín said. "Don't say it, I beg you."

"You are a fool, Joaquín. If you do this you are no longer my brother." Leon's voice had that flat toneless sound she hated.

"Leon, you cannot say that—" Joaquín's voice broke, and he reached out to touch Leon. "I *must* do it."

Leon shrugged off the touch as he had before. "Then I do not know you." He went to where the horses were tethered and, without hurry, he mounted his, holding the reins of the other two.

In the final red glow of the setting sun she saw Joaquín's face twist in anguish. She walked over and stood beside him. Leon, mounted, was looking down at them. "I go back now," he said. "If the woman's kinsmen have ridden into the village killing, I will hunt you down, Joaquín, because you would have the woman, and it will be your fault. The woman will kill us all. Some day you will believe it." He waited a moment longer, and when Joaquín did not answer him, he kicked the sides of his horse lightly and rode away, the other two horses trailing behind him. Majella and Joaquín stood together on the road, looking after him until he was out of sight.

"Come. It is time to go to the priest," Joaquín said. The anguish was hidden now, but she knew it was still there. Silently, she walked beside him down the road. They were not challenged and walked slowly as both were tired. Majella caught glimpses now and then of small houses, mostly hidden behind trees and in the midst of straggled rows of corn. Majella was thankful that the Catholic Church was on the outskirts of the town so that they need not go through the business district.

The dim interior of the church was beautiful, and Majella's apprehension diminished as she knelt at the altar. They had waited a long time for the priest. He was very busy, the housekeeper told them, clearly hoping they would leave. The priest, when he arrived, seemed a kindly man, but impatient, because his mind was on other matters. He rushed through the service, scarcely waiting for their responses. He did not even glance closely at Majella. In a very short time they were outside and on the road again in the dark sleeping town. Majella, suppressing a slight shiver, folded the marriage paper and put it in her smaller bundle. She needed desperately to touch Joaquín and took hold of his hand.

"Where are we going? Shall we be living here? In this town?" She hoped that they would not.

"No. There is an Indian village a few miles away from the town. It is not an old village like ours. The people came here a few years ago when they were driven away from their old place."

They started down the road. "And they say we can stay in this village with them? How did you find it?"

He still held her hand now, as if to comfort and reassure. "You talked to me often about the white man who was your grandfather. The man named Phail, and his Indian woman. I looked for her family. I knew if you came with me, Leon would drive me from our village." He paused a moment and then went on without any change of tone. "I found those people—I mean, I found their old village. The land is owned by others now. Then I found the new place they had gone to and I spoke to your kinsman there."

"*My* kinsman!" Majella stopped in astonishment.

"The son of your grandmother, your Indian grandmother. She is dead, long dead, but one son remains. His brothers died when they lost their old village. He uses his stepfather's name—Phail. He is Alonso Phail. He is the Headman there. He said we could come and stay."

"My kinsman," she repeated in wonder, straining to see her husband's face in the darkness, realizing more than ever what it cost him to claim her. Perhaps he, with his deep, unbreakable bonds to clan and tribe, had given up more than she. So deep and strong were his bonds that when he must leave his own people he sought out hers. He must remain—had to remain—with his own kind. She moved close to him and he took her in his arms.

"Do not tremble, Majella. He was willing to take us in."

"Joaquín, wait a minute. He would be my uncle, wouldn't he? What kind of man is he, my uncle? Is he—"

Joaquín had released her and started walking again. "Come. Let us go. He said he was willing that we come."

Majella took a few quick steps to catch up, taking hold of his hand again. They walked on through the dark empty night to the strange village.

Chapter Eleven

The village—which was scarcely a village as it numbered less than twenty souls—was a haphazard scatter of a few dilapidated shacks. One of these empty shacks was a three-sided shed with no front. It had been at one time completely roofed with tulle thatch, but part of this was gone, having gradually been plucked off by the winds and blown away over a number of years. Some of the structures seemed very old. Majella wondered if perhaps her kinsman had stopped here because there already existed a few derelict sheds, long abandoned by others. It would have offered a beginning, at least, for them to build upon. She and Joaquín waited inside the open shed until dawn, when the village began to awaken.

The house of her uncle, Alonso Phail, was the largest one, but still only a single room. He lived there with just his wife, the rest of his family long gone. They were both elderly now. He himself opened the sagging door to admit them.

"Come," he said simply, and Majella felt her throat tighten that this unknown Indian kinsman would welcome them. He was a tall man, but slightly stooped, and when he spoke it was slowly, hesitating between the words. "Come and eat. This is my wife, Benicia." His manner was somehow genteel, which bespoke better days somewhere, of some sort of education. He turned and gestured toward the woman as they entered the small house. He told Benicia who they were, raising his voice slightly so she could hear him. She stood back timidly, a large barefoot woman in a shapeless cotton dress that had been print, but was now so faded that it was difficult to discern any pattern.

The house had several pieces of furniture, a table, some awkward, stiff chairs, very old and battered; two were repaired with twists of wire. Near the wall was a rough bedstead, obviously homemade. Instead of a mattress, crisscross rawhide thongs were there to support the sleepers a few inches off the hard-packed earthen floor. The walls were decorated with a crucifix and two faded picture postcards. One was a field of poppies and the other a tall square building in some strange faraway city.

They all ate steaming corn meal mush from an assortmet of chipped crockery bowls, which Benicia gathered up carefully when they had finished. She carried them outside. Majella rose and followed, offering to help. Her heart was filled with gratitude to these quiet, kindly people. Benicia, shyly at first, but with growing confidence, talked

183

to her. They used a combination of Spanish and whatever Majella knew of the dialect she had begun to learn in Joaquín's village.

Benicia took her around this village, awake now and beginning slowly to move into the day, speaking to people, telling her their names. The people had been expecting them and were interested and curious about her dark dress of fine cloth, about her husband who was in the house of the Headman, about their journey. Again, there were very few children here, and there was some headshaking when Majella referred to her unborn child. When she and Benicia returned to Alonso Phail's house, Majella's color was high and her eyes were shining with excitement. It did not matter that the tiny village was poor, and that the people were few and mostly twice their age. It did not matter that the ground was so arid that the cornfield patches were stunted and limp. It was a village. There was a waterwell in the center. And the people offered friendship.

Inside Alonso's house again, when she and Benicia brought back the clean bowls, Joaquín turned to her. "Your kinsman says we can use that house we were in this morning," he said. "He will help me put another wall on it before winter." Joaquín stood up, his eyes glowing. He was deeply excited. "He has already got enough rushes to fix the roof. And tar. He has a whole bucket of tar that he gave us."

Majella's heart quickened. Never had Joaquín looked so beautiful to her. They were going to be all right. They were safe.

They set to work immediately, with several of the more able people in the village helping. They

184

finished the roof that day, amid smoke and the acrid rank odor of boiling tar in the bucket. Before a week had passed, a rawhide bed had been built and part of the wall was done.

Majella knew that the bed was for her benefit. Joaquín was comfortable in the traditionally Indian surroundings of the grandfather's house, or in Alonso's, which was the more common haphazard blend of customs lingering from one's own ancestors, along with those of the Spaniards, Mexicans, and Americans.

She asked him once about this.

"Where did your people come from, Joaquín? In the beginning, were they just here? What were they called?"

"We came from the Mission San Luis Rey de Francia—we—my father's father and his father, worked for the Christian fathers there."

"No, before that. Before the Christian fathers came. In the beginning?"

He looked blank and shook his head. "I do not know. That is lost."

"Oh, surely not. The name? What was the tribe called?"

"That was too long ago. Time passes. No one remembers."

Majella had fallen into a sober silence. Somehow that did not seem right. Luis Chavero knew his beginnings from far, far back. Someone should remember about Joaquín's people. She felt dissatisfied about this, but said nothing more to Joaquín.

After much discussion with Alonso, Joaquín decided to use some of the small horde of money to buy enough flat boards to finish the house front.

He would also buy a table and two chairs, a blanket for winter, and a few other things Majella wanted for her new home. Joaquín, Alonso, and two other men from the village spent most of one day in town and returned with all the items. It did not matter that they were old and battered. They were sturdy and had cost little. And Joaquín thought he would find some work in the town from time to time. Two of the younger men in the village worked in town, one in the cantina and one for the livery stable. The latter said that sometimes the stable owner hired an extra man. Then the priest had remembered Joaquín and had spoken to him in the street.

"He asked me where I was living, and what I was doing," Joaquín told her.

"What did you say?" Majella asked eagerly, running her palm across the smooth, worn surface of the old table.

"I told him I was looking for work. He said he would pay me to keep the church yard clean." His eyes were gleaming.

"How much will he pay you?" Majella asked.

Both Joaquín and Alonso were surprised. The priest would pay what he chose. One did not ask. One took what was given. This dampened Majella's delight a little, but at least it was a beginning.

Pegs were put on the wall for hanging extra items of clothing and a shelf was built for dishes. And a lower, wider shelf was put up, which provided Majella a makeshift work table. On it she could chop onions and peppers, or grind the meal in the stone bowl. She had found herself unable to sit for long hours on the ground for this grinding, as the other women did.

"Perhaps you will become used to it," Benicia said as Majella got up from the ground again to stretch her legs and move about. "Or perhaps after the child is born," she added. But Majella felt she would always be more comfortable standing to grind. Their food was of small variety, but there seemed to be enough. There were several tiny patches of corn and some of melon, squash, and other vegetables. There was a milk goat that belonged to Alonso, but he was generous with any milk that Benicia did not drink. Benicia could eat little food but boiled corn meal, and drank goat's milk several times a day. Squirrel and rabbit were plentiful, and occasionally birds. Majella learned to use water with great frugality and, somehow, managed to keep the tiny house clean and cook the food.

She was making a new shirt for Joaquín as he had started to work every two weeks for the priest, Father Gaspar. The priest paid more than either Joaquín or Alonso had expected. Majella had had Joaquín purchase the cloth for the shirt. They had disagreed about this.

"I want to go," she had said. "I want to choose it myself."

"No, you stay in the village, my love. I will get it. Tell me what you want."

Argument had been useless, for Joaquín silenced her when he said, "Majella, there are some rough men in the town. I don't want them to see you." He stopped abruptly, his face darkening, and Majella knew, with a sinking heart, that Joaquín was not sure he could protect her. She said no more about it because she knew he would try, and they might pay too dearly for it.

187

They talked with Alonso often, with the quiet Benicia in the background. Alonso told Majella what he could remember of his stepfather, Angus Phail. He would tilt his head back and gaze thoughtfully up into the ceiling thatch of his house, saying slowly:

"A good man, but there was a wildness in him. He was kind to us children. He made my mother laugh."

"What was she like—your mother, my grandmother?" Majella would ask, leaning forward eagerly. And Alonso would smile and by and by he would reply, thinking all the while, remembering.

"Small, my mother was. A short, heavy woman. But strong. She could lift your grandfather up and put him on the bed when he was very drunk. She would never let him sleep on the floor. She used to be proud of how much he could drink before he fell down. She would say it was because he was white. No matter how much he drank he never hurt her. Never hurt us. Though he was in many ways a man of violence."

"And the baby?" Majella would say. "What can you remember of the baby girl?" Alonso would tell her of the beautiful fair-skinned baby girl that her grandfather would stare at for hours.

"One day he said that he would take the baby and give it away. My mother asked if it was because the baby was a girl. She did not give him any son of his own, and it shamed her."

"What did he say?"

"He said there was a different reason, but he must do it. And she said, 'Will you come back?' and he said he would."

Majella leaned back against Joaquín, smelling

188

the smoke from his pipe, and dreamt about her mother as a tiny, beautiful infant who was to be given away. How strangely God worked.

She told Alonso about her mother. He and Benicia never tired of listening to how the small infant girl had finally become a fine lady in Mexico. Sometimes she would clasp her hands over her growing belly and try to count up the time as best she could. A son? Would she give Joaquín a son? Would he be pleased?

In their own small house she tried to talk to Joaquín about it.

"Would you be disappointed if I gave you a daughter?" she asked, but she received a chilling response. He seemed to withdraw and close his personality against her.

"You should have used the leaves I brought," he said. He took her arms from about his neck and turned away.

Hurt and stricken, she crawled into bed and kept as near to the wall as she could, lying awake long after Joaquín was sleeping beside her. By morning he had forgotten, or seemed to have forgotten; one could never be sure with Joaquín. She did not speak to him again of the coming child for some time. Nor did he, although her belly continued to increase. She let out both her dresses. She took great care in this, because she knew she would take them in again after the child was born. She fretted for days before she asked about yardage for any baby clothes.

Again Joaquín's eyes became opaque and distant. "What clothes?" he asked. "I see no clothes on that child." They were standing in front of their house and he gestured to a naked toddler.

189

"They do not need clothes when they are young. Our child will be an Indian, Majella." Again, there seemed a deep reluctance to even talk about the coming child.

Troubled, she talked with Benicia.

"Ease your mind," Benicia counseled. "His heart will melt when he sees it. It is only that he fears for it, that is all." And Benicia helped her to make a back-cradle, so she could carry the baby about with her while she worked outside.

If Joaquín longed for his home village he never mentioned it. Now and then she awoke in the night to find him up and smoking by the doorway, and twice he spoke aloud to Leon in his sleep. She knew that he missed Leon acutely, missed talking with him, missed being silent with him when there was no need for speech between them.

He worked in the town on every possible chance. Once he had been allowed to clean the stable and the liveryman was pleased. He and another villager were hired to clear weeds, rubble and embedded stones from a plot of land a man wanted to plant. Señor Tippitt despised Indians. He was a hard-driving, frugal man and he worked them like beasts. Both men trudged home to the village each night so tired they could only fall asleep until just before dawn. The job lasted several days until the field was clear, and the amount Tippitt paid was so small that Majella seethed for days at their having been cheated.

"Take the money back," she said, clenching her hands. "Throw it in the dirt at his feet."

Joaquín stared at her as if she had lost her mind and then silently put the money into the small gourd they used for their funds.

Now and then she wondered how they all stood it—all these people. They lived in such abject poverty and with no hope of anything better.

Majella kept the small house clean and their few clothes neat and carefully mended. She was becoming a better cook. After making the shirt for Joaquín, she also made new trousers. She finished the back-cradle for the coming baby. But there seemed too little to do—there was too much idle time. She sometimes helped other women grind corn. She spent much time talking with Benicia and Alonso, but her fingers longed for the feel of fine silk thread for her exquisite embroidery. She longed for the taste of hot chocolate again. She longed for fresh flowers and music—there was no music at all in the village. Never by word or glance did she reveal these inner murmurs of discontent to Joaquín. She made a small centerpiece table cover out of cloth left from the shirt, and she gathered whatever wild flowers she could find to put in a gourd on the table, but always just before they ate because wild flowers drooped so quickly. And when she lay warm and drugged with love in Joaquín's arms at night she forgot all these things, content to lie there marveling and wondering how she could be so fortunate. It was at night that they talked to one another freely, openly, in gentle whispers and murmurs, often with sadness but sometimes with soft laughter. This was good, Majella thought in deep contentment at these times. Oh, this was good.

As nearly as Majella could calculate, she thought the baby would be born in two more months. She felt remarkably good, a bit clumsy perhaps, but never tired. It was midwinter and this was the first clear day after several days of rain. She was thinking how snug and firm the little house was when suddenly the baby moved rapidly. She was accustomed to this, for it was an active infant though yet unborn, and this never failed to fill her with wonder and joy. So restless was her baby today that she caught the shelf for support and started to laugh aloud in sheer delight. Alonso was by the half-open door and he had to call twice to get her attention.

"Majella?"

She hurried over and flung the door wide open.

"There is a friend here of Joaquín—Trinidad Méndez?" Alonso's voice and manner were uneasy. Benicia had told her that ever since they had been driven from their original village Alonso was always uncertain, and suspicious of any stranger who came.

Trinidad! Majella stood stunned and looked at the stocky figure of Trini, as he stood hat in hand, making a faint bowing motion.

"Joaquín is not here," she said uncertainly. "He is working in town today." Then remembering that this man was her husband's friend, she stepped back. "Please come in and wait for him. He will be back soon. It is almost dusk."

Alonso came in, too.

Diffidently, clearly ill at ease, Trinidad entered and sat down stiffly at the table as she indicated. Alonso seated himself on the other side.

"I came to see you both," Trinidad said, again with the little bowing motion toward her.

She held her lips firm against an impulse to smile—this was a different Trinidad from the si-

192

lent, somewhat surly man she had feared in the past.

"You must be hungry," she said. "I'll start the food. And she busied herself at this, leaving the two men to talk. She put wood chips into the small stove that Joaquín had made from a discarded metal drum and lifted down the kettle, listening to the men, wishing that Joaquín would come soon.

Trinidad was telling about his journey and how long it had taken him. "I stole a horse to ride most of the way," he said, and then added in a deferential tone to Alonso, who was Headman, "I let him go some miles from here, and walked the rest of the way."

Majella put down the kettle and went to Trinidad, able no longer to contain a burning uneasiness that had come into her mind. "Is everything all right in your village? Did my people come looking for me?"

"They came, yes, more than before. They searched the village."

"Did—anyone get hurt?" She made herself ask it.

"No. They were angry but they went away. Señor Obregón, your sister's husband, had many men this time. But they went away."

Relief flooded through Majella.

When Joaquín came, he fairly sprang into the house when he saw Trinidad, his face taut. He clamped his hand on Trinidad's shoulder and swung him around.

"What's wrong! Leon? Grandfather?"

"Nothing." Trinidad twisted away and stood up, a homely grin on his broad face. "Everything is good." He spread his arms and they embraced,

Joaquín gripping the shorter man tight for a long moment. He was overjoyed.

"Tell me!" He demanded. "Tell me everything!"

Trinidad, who could be talkative when he chose to be, poured out the news of their village. Alonso was included, hanging eagerly on every word, deeply interested in this distant village from which Joaquín had come.

Yes, Leon was well. Yes, Grandfather was well and lecturing anyone who would listen. No, they had not been on any raids for some time. Yes, rain had fallen there too. Yes, one old friend had died and it was better so, for his pain died with him.

He told Joaquín and Alonso, in more detail, about the visit of Majella's people and a large party of men. They had questioned both Leon and the grandfather, but Leon pretended stupidity and discouraged them. The grandfather had finally convinced them that neither Joaquín nor Majella was there and that nobody knew where they had gone. He invited them to search the whole village, which he knew they were going to do anyway. Yes, they had done that. Yes, the people had become frightened, for the Señor Obregón had brought many of his vaqueros, who were wild and restless men. But they finally left.

When it was time to eat Alonso went to bring chairs from his house and Benicia came back with him to help Majella. Two other men from the village here joined them to talk during the long meal. There was an air of great festivity in the little house.

"Wait," Trinidad exclaimed, after they had long finished. "I forgot the first reason for my coming. It is this." He reached inside his shirt and took out the crucifix that had hung on the wall in the grandfather's house. He handed it to Majella. In astonishment, Majella reached out and took it. It was a lovely one. Many times she had prayed in front of it while in the grandfather's house.

"Why?" Joaquín asked, half-laughing, half-touched. "Why did the old one do that?"

Trinidad laughed. "Who knows why the old man does things? You remember how much talk and argument there was when you said you would go and marry the woman at the church."

"I remember," Joaquín said drily.

"Well, when it was done and Leon came back, the old man decided to send a gift. He talked about it for days until Leon came to stay at my house for a while, just to get away from him."

Majella felt tears come to her eyes, remembering the grandfather. She clasped the crucifix close to herself for a moment.

"When you go back, you must tell him how grateful I am. Tell him I shall keep it as a treasure."

Trinidad nodded and went on. "First he said to give it to you, Joaquín. Then he changed his mind and said give it to your woman. He seemed very happy about it."

"Was Leon happy about it?" Joaquín asked.

Trinidad shrugged. "Who can tell with Leon? You are the only one who can read Leon's mind, my friend."

Joaquín did not reply, and looked somber for a moment.

Trinidad lingered in the village for several days. Majella knew with uneasiness that he asked Joaquín about joining in another raid, and she was flooded with relief when Joaquín refused. Late in the night, as they lay in bed together talking, he turned on his side to face her.

"Do not worry about me, Majella," he said softly, twining a lock of her hair around his finger.

"Worry? What do you mean?"

"I see the shadows in your eyes when Trini asked me about another raid. I traded my life there for my life with you. It is a bargain I made. I will never change from that now."

Majella couldn't speak, but turned and buried her face in his neck.

She wondered if he would ever regret it, but he seemed not to. He seemed, after Trinidad's visit, to settle more firmly into this village life. In addition to working as often as he could in the town, he spent long hours working in the village at anything it was suitable for a man to do. He worked in the corn patches. He cleared another small area of rocks and rubble so they could plant extra corn and vegetables. He helped Alonso with repairs to his roof. Alonso depended more and more upon Joaquín. He spoke to Majella about it.

"I am getting old to be Headman," he said one morning, watching Joaquín at some distance away. "A younger, stronger man is needed."

"You are not old, Uncle," she said, smiling. "You are a good Headman in the village. How did you come to choose this place?" she added.

He shrugged. "We were very tired. We tried to keep together. And we came to this place, with a few shelters already on it. There was no one here. It seemed to me that it was so dry that no one would come to want it."

Majella glanced up sharply. "Did you talk to

the Indian Agent about it? Did someone in the town say you could settle here?"

He seemed to shrink inside himself. "No, we did not speak to the Indian Agent. It is better not to speak to them. He came. Some time later—a year, I think. Since we were already here, and no one else seemed to want the land, he did not send us away."

Majella turned aside to hide any apprehension that she might show in her eyes. Later, she talked to Joaquín about it.

"Joaquín, we really have no right to be here. Uncle Alonso has no claim on this land."

"I know," Joaquín answered, looking off into the distance. "He has spoken to me about it. Some day we will be driven off—but who would want this place?" he asked. "That was why he chose it."

"But surely he should have talked to someone in the town, to some sort of authority—how do they handle things like that? Doesn't this land belong to someone?"

"No one knows who it belongs to. There is a disagreement in the courts. The American courts. It is still being decided."

"But our people did find water. They put in the well. That alone—"

Joaquín sighed. "Majella, do not steal tomorrow's grief. Let it come when it will."

"What we need is some land. I mean land that we own legally, that no one else can take away."

"Come inside. It is getting cold."

She followed him inside the house and shut the door, but she could not sleep that night for a long time. She was thinking of the Ortegna jewel box. The jewelry in it would buy them some land. They

197

would be safe. No one could take it away from them.

They quarrelled about it, briefly and sharply, in the morning.

"No!" Joaquín was enraged. He smashed his fist down on the table. "Never! Your people will come. Do you want them to destroy this village!"

"But they are *my* jewels, Joaquín: They have to give me what is mine. And we *are* married! There is nothing they can do about that!" Those jewels would be their salvation, their safe haven. She wanted them now as intensely as she had first hated them. She *must* get them.

"No!"

"They will give me what is mine! I will make them understand! It would be enough—"

"Be quiet!" He half rose from the table, his face suffused with fury at her persistence.

"Joaquín, I—"

His hand shot out and he hit her across the face. She was flung back onto the bed. Instinctively she curled her body, protecting the unborn infant. Joaquín stood over her.

"No, Majella," he said, more quietly now. "Do not speak of it again. Are you all right?"

She sat up shakily. "Yes. I'm all right," she said. That was the only time Joaquín had ever struck her since their dark beginnings in the caves.

"I have to go to town," he said after a while. "I won't be back until late. I am working for Señor Tippitt today."

"Oh, no," Majella moaned. Tippitt was the man who worked Joaquín so hard and paid him so little. "Please don't go."

"I must not refuse." He turned and left the little

house, and she lay huddled on the bed a long time, thinking resentfully, sullenly, of the wasted jewels that would provide enough money to make them all safe. When she got up to go about her duties, she felt lethargic and tired. Her head ached from Joaquín's blow.

That day, two white men rode into the village and took away Alonso's goat. Sometimes white men rode past the village, or came to it from town. Usually this was for legitimate reasons. This time they were looking for a missing goat and saw Alonso's, staked to graze at some distance from the houses. They rode in among the scattered shacks, demanding to see the Headman.

Majella went inside and shut the door. It was the inviolable custom for the women to hide indoors when strangers came. There were two of them and they did not dismount. Alonso came out of his house to talk to them. Majella strained to hear what was said, but could not. She knew in despair that Alonso knew only a few phrases of English, and hoped that the men spoke enough Spanish. She gathered from the gestures that they discussed the tethered goat, since they kept pointing to it. Alonso kept protesting in a respectful, almost servile manner. Anger was beating in her temples. Finally, one man dismounted and walked up the slope to the goat. He pulled up the stake. Grimly, he led the goat down and mounted his horse again, still holding the rope.

They were going to take the goat away!

Instantly, she rejected this. Benicia had to have the milk. She could eat almost nothing else without agonizing cramping and nausea. *Oh, please, God, don't let them take the goat.*

In mingled despair and anger, Majella flung open her door and went into the clearing. "What are you doing?" she cried in Spanish.

The men stopped in surprise.

"That is our goat! Leave the goat!" she commanded heedlessly, rushing clumsily forward and catching hold of the goat's rope. One of the men said something in angry astonishment. The other man shouted in outrage at her effrontery. He wheeled his horse around, jerking one foot from a stirrup. He kicked out at her. The impact of his boot sent her tumbling head over heels in the dust. Alonso, terrified, sprang forward and caught hold of her as she scrambled up. She was so enraged that she would have run after the men, but Alonso held her back, pleading with her. She could hear Benicia sobbing in fear just inside the door of their house.

When the men had gone with the goat, the other people gathered around her, chiding, admonishing, soothing her by turns, making sure she was all right and that the fall did not hurt her. She would not be soothed. She wanted to shout at them in fury. There were seven men in the village this day. There had been only two white men. She also knew that the village contained a motley assortment of weapons belonging to this man or that. Some were in good repair. They could have stopped the men. They could have! She was sure of it! Yet the men had cowered back, standing by while the goat was stolen in front of their eyes. She pushed at Alonso's hands, went into her house, and slammed the door.

Later, toward dusk, she went humbly back to Alonso's house to apologize. He had done the best he could. He took it kindly and held no anger toward her. Indeed, she wondered if Alonso was capable of anger. He talked to her quietly and she listened, sinking deeper and deeper into hopelessness as the evening progressed. Alonso had much experience in dealing with the Indian Agents, and with the other white men, as well as with the Mexicans. He explained that they must now forget about the goat. There was no possibility of appealing to the law about it. It was only recently that those people had added to their laws that an Indian could even testify against a white at all. Now it was written down in the law, but never practiced. For many years it had not even been legal for an Indian to give any testimony of any sort on any matter. Sobered and chastened, Majella sat for a long time in silence.

Who was to say, then, what bravery was, what wisdom was? How brave must a man be to sacrifice his pride to save, for a little while longer, the lives of those he cherished? Was there not wisdom in choosing the smaller of two evils? In giving up the goat, Alonso was inflicting hunger and pain on a sick wife and hating himself for it. In fighting to keep the goat he would have paid with his life, possibly his wife's also. And Joaquín, her beloved, what did he endure in the town? The priest was kind to him when he worked there. The man at the stables was not unkind. Some time, somehow, she had learned that the man Tippitt had a blacksnake whip but—so far—there had been no marks on Joaquín's body. So far. The burning anguish was that if the whip were ever used would Joaquín have the courage to endure it in silence and not fight back? A small chill ran through her.

201

Please, God, make Joaquín have that kind of courage, that kind of wisdom.

It became quite late and she knew dully that she had better go home and prepare something for Joaquín to eat when he got there. Tippitt begrudged any pause for eating and Joaquín often worked straight through the day without stopping, then arrived home exhausted and famished.

Finally, she got up and went to the door. She turned.

"Uncle Alonso, I wish—do you have to tell Joaquín what I did today?"

Her uncle looked at her in understanding. "I won't tell him, Majella," he said kindly. "But he will be told by a dozen others." He spread his hands hopelessly and she had to smile. She had shocked the whole village. They would never forget it. Or let Joaquín forget it.

Majella dished up Joaquín's food as soon as she heard him. Resignedly, she knew that at least two people had stopped to talk to him when he paused to wash his face and hands in the basin of water she had ready for him on the bench outside the door. She heard him speaking courteously to them. When he came in, the edges of his hair were wet and so was his shirt collar. He also looked deeply tired.

"Are you hungry?" she asked. "Everything is ready."

He sat down to eat.

"I suppose someone told you," she said when he had finished. She was lingering beside him, wanting to touch his hair, knowing she had embarrassed him before the villagers.

202

"Yes." He leaned back and regarded her thoughtfully. "Leon was right, as he always is. He said you were too unruly for me to handle."

"But the goat," she burst out. "What is Benicia going to do?"

"Forget the goat a while, Majella," he said in an oddly gentle voice. This surprised her for she had expected him to be angry. Perhaps he was simply too tired. "You took a great risk today. I have always told you to hide yourself when any strangers come. You disobeyed. Again. What if those men had wanted you? Think about that. No, don't turn away. Think about it."

She felt suddenly chilled.

"It isn't likely—as big as I am. I—look as if I am going to have the baby any minute."

"That is probably what saved you," Joaquín said, getting up. He took the crucifix from the wall. "I want you to swear on the crucifix that you will never do anything like that again."

Holding back the tears, she did as he asked, vowing to herself that she would *never* disobey him again. He was *right*. He had lived all his life as an Indian. She must abide by his decisions. *Always*. And she would *remember* that.

He took her in his arms and began to kiss her gently. She caressed his face and loved him so much that she ached with it. When he released her she clung to him, wanting to hold his attention.

"Are you tired? Was the work hard? Did Señor Tippitt pay you today or tell you to wait?"

"Yes and yes and yes, he paid." Joaquín smiled. Then suddenly he laughed, clapping his hand to his forehead. "I forgot. I brought you something."

"Me? What?" she demanded in a sudden surge of delight.

"This." He went outside a moment and came back with something small in one hand. She held out hers and he placed it in them.

It was a box of powdered chocolate. She was stunned.

"No! How did you know! Oh, Joaquín, I've longed for some chocolate. How could you do it! It's too costly! How much did you pay?"

He laughed again, taking off his shirt. "I know. I used almost all of the money Señor Tippitt paid me. But I often have tobacco. And I remembered that you wanted some chocolate. I sometimes hear you when you are telling Benicia about your life in Mexico. She loves to hear those stories. How in the afternoons you all drank hot chocolate from the china cups with violets painted on them. So I decided today that I could get you some chocolate from the American store."

She was staring entranced at the small box when Joaquín suddenly gave a shout of laughter and fell on the bed.

"What is the matter?" She started to laugh herself, not knowing why. "What are you laughing at! What is so funny?"

"Oh, Majella, don't you see?" He sat up, wiping his eyes. "The chocolate. I got you chocolate. But the goat is gone. There isn't any milk." And he started laughing again.

Majella put down the box and put her arms around him, laughing with him now. It was impossible not to join in. The laughter was contagious. Laughing together, they rocked back and forth.

Suddenly her body jerked convulsively. She pulled up sharply.

"Oh, Joaquín! It is time! Go get Benicia. It is time for the baby to come!"

Chapter Twelve

The baby was born in a few hours, but to Majella it seemed endless. When it was over, however, and her tiny son lay nestled in the crook of her arm the whole dark night slid away, not to be thought of again.

She knew a kind of glorious ecstasy that she had never known before. The whole world was beautiful. The sunrise through the open door was beautiful. The smell of tobacco from Joaquín's and Alonso's pipes was beautiful. Benicia, padding around the little house on her large bare feet, was beautiful.

She named the baby Mario. She had attempted to discuss names with Joaquín once but his disinterest had made her select the name alone. And this child, this beautiful infant, could not be named for any of her family, so she chose to call him after Mary. She tried desperately now to stay awake for the sheer simple joy of gazing into his

206

round, bland little face, but she drifted off and slept deeply for several hours.

When she was up and about again—very quickly, for she was in the best of health—the villagers made much of the new baby. Among a people with so few children any new one was a welcome diversion, although many thought her heedless to have had the baby at all. Several people who had always been polite, but not actually friendly, now found excuses to stop at Joaquín's house to pass the time of day. That the baby was quite dark, and appeared to be solely Indian and their own kind, made those who had been reticent now accept Majella more fully. This pleased her. As she laced Mario in the back-cradle she smiled ruefully. The fact that the two dresses she had brought with her were now worn and faded might also help to make it easy for her to lose herself among them. Some day—not right away, of course—she must think about some cotton cloth to make a new dress.

This brought her mind to more important expenditures that must be made first. They *must* do something about getting a goat. Benicia, always a large woman, was beginning to fail; lines were appearing in her broad face as she lost weight because of scanty food. Her garments hung loosely.

And little Mario? Majella frowned as she gazed searchingly at her baby, waiting apprehensively. She had waited long enough, she thought, to put him in the cradle, and had just got him laced in. But no. Again. She sighed. Often, as soon as he was laced in he vomited up the milk he had sucked so greedily from her breast. Patiently, she unlaced him and took him out. She had learned by now to leave the basin full of water. Sometimes she thought that Mario might be using more water than anyone else in the village—he was such a dirty little baby. After he was clean again she held him close in the thin sunlight by the door. *Oh, please, God, let him be well. Let him grow.* Benicia had said that if—when—they could get a goat, she thought he might not vomit goat's milk. They *must* get a goat.

Joaquín's attitude toward the baby saddened and puzzled her. He did take an interest in the infant, that she knew. She had watched him hold the baby on occasion. She had seen the brooding eyes resting on the baby for endless spaces of time. When little Mario was fretful and cried, he did not become annoyed. But this, of course, might simply be that it had always been the custom of the people to be indulgent with the little ones. Reprimands were rare, punishments almost nonexistent. These people—her people—seemed to have infinite patience where young children were concerned.

Joaquín had been right about the clothes; she enjoyed intensely seeing her baby's smooth brown skin and tiny body moving freely, and not smothered in layers of cloth with scratching lace constricting his tiny throat. She cradled the baby close, and stepped inside the house. Joaquín was home today and watched her somberly.

He got up from the table and came to stand before her, looking down at the baby's face, which was wrinkling up to start crying. For the first time, he commented on the baby of his own volition.

"I would like Leon to see the child while it still lives."

"What!" She didn't believe her hearing.

He looked at her with compassion. "Majella, it is not meant for us to have a child. You are too blinded by your love of him to see that he fails. Day by day. He does not keep his food. He does not grow. Please, do not set your heart too much on keeping him because he cannot stay."

"No!" She cried frantically, clutching the baby, making it wail out sharply in fright. "He is all right! He is fine! Don't you dare say he is not!" she blazed at Joaquín. "In a few days—in a few days—" Suddenly she started to cry uncontrollably. This was something she had refused to think about until Joaquín had made her think about it— that her baby might *not* thrive and grow strong. He was ailing. He was sickly. *Oh, dead God, don't take my baby.*

Joaquín reached over and took the baby from her, and she crumpled down on the bed, her body shaking, unable to stop crying once she had started. It was almost midday before she could regain full control of herself. When she did rise from her sodden weeping Joaquín was still holding Mario, with the old look of brooding in his eyes, but he was holding him so gently, and rocking him so slightly, that Mario had stopped crying and gone to sleep. Did that mean he loved the baby? Wearily, she pulled herself off the bed. Sometimes she had no real idea, as close as they were, what Joaquín thought or felt.

"Joaquín, we must take the baby to town then. Isn't there a doctor in the town?"

"Yes," he answered reluctantly.

"Then we must take him there," she said urgently. "If—if you won't let me come, then you can take him. Joaquín, please! You must. Do this for me, please."

"I cannot. He does not treat Indians."

She was aghast. "Then who *does*? Joaquín, who does? Where is the Indian Agent?" She went to him and gripped his shoulder, shaking him. "You said—you told me once—that your name was on the register at San Bernardino. How long would it take us to—I mean, take you to get there? You can take the baby there. They would get a doctor."

He gave her a level look and she knew that this line was hopeless.

"All right! All right," she said decisively, her voice still thick from weeping. "That settles it. We must have more money. I must—must—have my jewelry! I will—"

Joaquín stood up. "I told you, do not even speak of that again, Majella."

"But, Joaquín," she wailed in despair. "What are we to do?"

He looked down at the infant who had awakened again and gazed up at his father's face with the blank, faraway look of small babies. "I will take him over to Benicia for a while," Joaquín said thoughtfully. "She said yesterday that he might not vomit up boiled corn meal if it was very thin."

"Don't bother," she said sullenly. "I tried that yesterday." She turned away from him, angry, rebellious, wondering if she herself might somehow go from here to San Bernardino. Or perhaps the doctor in town would treat the baby if she took him. If she wore her better dress and the shoes she seldom wore now, preferring to save them. She would wear her garnet necklace. Her manner and speech were—but her manner and speech were Spanish. This would be an American doctor. But she must try, certainly. She at least knew the way to town from the village. She had come through the town on her wedding night. She knew the road. Angrily, rebelliously, she watched as Joaquín carefully laced the baby in the cradle.

"What about the priest?" she asked after a time, still watching him. "We must have Mario christened. And I must go with you for that because I am the baby's mother." She spoke with heavy sarcasm, which he appeared not to notice.

"I will speak with Father Gaspar when I go next to work for him, and see what he says," Joaquín said quietly, still looking down at the baby. He laid him on the chair and went to the door.

"Well, he will certainly christen an Indian baby—he married us, didn't he?" she said furiously, following him.

"Yes. But he may come here. He said once that he makes trips to the villages sometimes."

"No. Wait—" She bit back an angry comment. Joaquín turned and looked at her. His eyes looked tired. "Majella, I know what you are thinking. Stop thinking it. You are not going to town. If the breaker—if God wants to take the baby he will take him and there is nothing you can do to stop it." He left, not waiting for her to reply to this.

She stood there, seething with rage.

She would go to town herself. *She* would go to the priest. She would ask the *priest* to speak to the *doctor*. Surely the doctor would not refuse to look at the baby if the *priest* asked him to. She crushed down the sudden thought that the priest was Mexican and the doctor was American. There was much hate between these two peoples—but there were friendships too. Yes, yes. She had heard that there were some friendships, many friendships. She could take the chance. She must.

Grimly, she shut the door. How long would Joaquín stay with Alonso? Her eyes darted to where he kept his pipe. It was gone. There was nothing for the men to do today. Surely, he intended to visit a while with Alonso. They sometimes talked for hours together when there was nothing to do. It was only a few miles to town. She would take the risk. She must. The baby had not grown at all during all the days of his life. She could not let him die. If she lost him she would never be able to stand it; she would go mad.

She tied the dark scarf around her head and slid her arms through the cradle straps. She did it so carefully that Mario did not awaken.

With the scarf on, her head down, and in bare feet, she strove to look as much like an ordinary squaw as possible. Surely there would be no risk for a woman with a baby on her back. She would walk with her head down so that no one would really see her face. As an afterthought, she hid the garnet necklace between her breasts. If somehow she could persuade the priest to speak to the doctor and if somehow the priest convinced him he should look at an Indian baby, he might take the necklace in payment. Money would surely make a difference. If there were ever any such thing as a rich Indian in the world, he could buy whatever he wished—she was sure of this.

She must have that jewelry.

For a moment she longed so intensely for the ancient box of gems that she felt physically sick. Fool. She should have crept about the Obregón house and found it before she left. She should have asked, demanded, that Cecilia leave it in her room. She should have lied, pretended to want to wear them, pretended to love them—anything to have had them in her possession when she left.

Cautiously, she stepped outside and circled around the house. She would walk across the stubble of the corn patch and down the slope, the long way around to the road so that no one in the village could see her. She went carefully, avoiding the sharp stalks, her heartbeats almost choking her. *Oh, please, God, don't let Joaquín come.*

She got to the road and it was vacant in both directions. The sun was higher in the sky. Stepping quickly, she started toward the town. She was sure, quite sure, that she would remember where the church was. The dust was warm and soft beneath her bare feet. *Oh, Cecilia,* she thought, with a little gasp of laughter. What would Cecilia say if she could see her now? She was getting warm, too warm, but it didn't matter. Was the baby getting too much sun? Reaching back, she adjusted her head scarf so it covered the baby's face lightly. He was awake, but was not crying. He never cried when being carried around on her back. He seemed to like the motion. Had she gone a mile? Two miles? She blotted her face with the edge of her scarf. Still the road remained empty. If she saw anyone coming from the town, she would hang her head down and slow her pace to a plodding walk. She would hunch over her shoulders the way Benicia did. Meanwhile. . . .

She froze and shut her eyes against the glare. *Oh, dear God, please, not Joaquín.* But there was the steady pounding rhythm behind her of a runner. She whirled around.

Joaquín. There was no mistaking him.

Her first impulse was to start running, but instantly she realized that would be hopeless. Joaquín had run all his life and he was fast. She could never hope to outdistance those strong runner's legs.

All right. She would simply face him down. Convince him. If she could not convince him, defy him. She refused to consider the question of how she would do this. When he came up to her and stopped his face was grim.

"I am taking Mario to the priest," she said firmly.

"No. Come back to the village."

She started walking, her mouth suddenly gone dry.

He took hold of her and turned her around. "I will take you back to the village."

"No!" She struck out against him, trying to twist away from his grasp. The cradle started to slip and the baby suddenly wailed out his thin, angry cry. "No. Let me go. *I will go!*" Unmindful of the crying baby she struggled against her husband.

"Be quiet," he said grimly. "Let me take the baby." He tried to slide the cradle off her back and hold her at the same time.

"No!" She was shouting now. "Let me alone. I am going."

"Be careful. Do you want to drop him on the

214

road?" He handled her roughly and got the baby, sliding the cradle straps over one of his arms and clamping his other hand about her two wrists.

"Now, come to the village." He started back, pulling her along.

"No. No. No." She was crying, digging her heels in the roadway, sliding, stumbling, trying to keep from falling, and resisting, resisting, resisting wildly, tugging, twisting, trying frantically in a blind effort to escape his iron grip.

He stopped a moment.

"Please, Joaquín! Please!"

"Do you want me to drag you through the village?" His voice was cold, cutting. "How will you feel tomorrow with the other women? What will you say to them?"

She stopped struggling, falling to her knees in the dusty road. What was she doing? This man was her beloved. She had thrown away her whole family to be with him. Now she was hating him. If she could, she would dig her nails into his face and tear his flesh. Oh, dear God, it should not be this way. Somehow they had to buy some land. Far away. Where they would be safe. They must have money to pay a doctor. Money. They must have some money.

"Listen to me, Majella. I am taking you to the village. Do you want to go back like this or not?"

"Wait," she pleaded dully. "Give me a moment. I—I will walk back." Slowly she got up, wiping tears from her face with her scarf. Then she pulled it off. Let the sun beat on her head. Let her die of it.

He waited until she was ready, rocking the baby gently so that it would not cry.

"Put the baby on my back," she said tiredly. It was not suitable for a man to carry a cradle and she didn't want to anger him any more than she already had.

He did, speaking less grimly now. "I was going to town to speak to the priest when I saw you, Majella."

She refused to answer, trudging along beside him when he started back toward the village again. When they were again in their house, she took the baby off her back and laid him on the floor. He was sleeping again. He had really had nothing at all to eat today.

Joaquín stood by the door watching her.

"I will still go to see the priest."

"All right, go." She spoke sullenly.

"I am wondering what you will do while I am gone."

"Where could I go?" she burst out passionately. "The only possible place I could get to alone would be the town. There isn't even a horse—your beloved friend Leon saw to that."

"They were Leon's horses."

"They were *not*! Not *all*! You helped take them!"

He came to stand before her. "They were stolen horses. I was going to marry my woman before the priest in the church. You begged me to give up stealing. Many times. You remember. In the night times when we talked together?"

She had no answer for this. "What—are you going to tell him, tell Father Gaspar, about the baby?"

"I thought to ask about the christening, if he is

216

coming to the village soon. And speak about the doctor. That is useless, but I will do it."

"Why is it useless?" She sat down in one of the chairs, head down, still refusing to look at him.

"Because Father Gaspar will tell me to speak to the Indian Agent. Or, since he is a kind man, he may offer to do it for me if he has the time."

"What would you do then?"

"I will thank him and tell him not to trouble himself, that I will speak to the Indian Agent myself."

"Then will you do it?"

"No."

"Oh, Joaquín," she wailed.

"And I will tell you something else. If you try to leave the village while I am gone, Alonso will come after you. If you keep trying to leave, I will not trouble Alonso with it any more. I will tie you to the bed when I have to go to town to work, and I will leave the baby with Benicia." It was said simply, but there was in his voice that same toneless quality that she so hated in Leon's voice. Her gaze locked with his. He would do it too. And she knew without any shade of doubt that not one hand in the village would be lifted to help her.

She got up from the chair.

"What are you going to do?" he asked.

"I am going to make some thin boiled meal and try that again, see if the baby will keep it down. I will stay here until you get back." She made herself add the last part.

He turned and left.

Majella spent a dreary, hopeless day. The baby did not keep down the thin mush. She nursed him later. She thought—she tried to believe—that he didn't vomit it all again, not all surely.

Joaquín came back long after dark. She had his food ready. She heard him washing in the dark at the front of the house, and opened the door so that some light would reach him from the twisted rag which burned in the bowl of oil. That was something else they needed, a lamp. A smokeless lamp with a wick that could be neatly trimmed.

"Did you see Father Gaspar?" she asked as soon as he came in, not waiting until he ate.

"Yes. I had to wait a long time. He was busy."

"What did he say?"

"He was planning to come to the village. He said he likes to come about twice a year if he can."

"About the baby! What did he say about taking the baby to the American doctor?" she asked in exasperation.

"He asked me why I didn't go to the Indian Agent. He said the town doctor did not have the time to care for the Indians."

"And what did you—never mind! I don't want to know. We aren't going to the American doctor, are we?"

"No."

She sat down opposite him, feeling heavy and lifeless.

"Majella. I did get a goat. Benicia is sure he can drink goat's milk."

"You got a goat!" Her eyes, wide with sudden fright, flew to his.

"No. I did not steal it."

"How did you get it?" she breathed.

"Señor Clay at the livery stable has some goats. I asked him if he would sell me one."

"Joaquín! We don't have enough money!"

"I know. I told him what I had. He took that and said I could work for the rest."

"Oh, Joaquín!" Suddenly it seemed that goat's milk for the baby was the solution. The only solution, the wonderful, magic solution. Mario would love it. He must. He would thrive on it. He would grow strong and healthy.

"But I thought—you only work for Señor Clay once in a while. Your food is getting cold. How could you ever work enough to pay it out?"

"This is different, not in the stable."

"What is it?"

Joaquín started to eat. "He has a bad horse. He wants me to gentle him. I told him I could do it."

She watched him eat for a while, the strong movements of his jaw, a growing uneasiness in her mind. "Why doesn't he have another American do it? Or a Mexican?"

"Some have tried."

"You mean nobody could do it?" She was alarmed now.

"No one has yet."

"Can you? Would it be dangerous? Could you get hurt?"

He glanced up from his food, smiling with his mouth full. He swallowed. "Yes and yes and yes. There was never such a woman for asking all questions at once."

"You mean you could be thrown!"

He sat back, almost laughing now. "I have been thrown before. I did not die of it. I *can* gentle that horse for him. I *know* it. And he *did* give me the goat."

"You mean he gave it to you! Already! Before you—"

"Yes and yes and yes. I left it at Alonso's house."

"Oh, Joaquín, Joaquín!" Half-laughing, half-crying, she ran to him, embraced him, kissed him, and clung to him so that he could not eat.

"Let me finish. Let me eat." He protested, laughing at her. Then he pushed aside the food. "Never mind. I don't want any more—come here." He swung her up into his arms and strode to the bed.

Now that they had another goat, little Mario perversely started retaining Majella's own milk and didn't even need the goat's milk after all. Majella remembered with shame her anger against Joaquín, her standing in the road to town trying to defy him, shouting at him. She was humbly grateful that he never mentioned it once.

Nor, however, was he as overjoyed as she that the baby was finally eating well, that he seemed to grow before their eyes. He appeared totally indifferent to this.

He gentled the horse for Señor Clay, but it took him longer than he had thought it would. He had a number of bad falls and came limping down the road toward the village at night, sometimes as bruised as if he had been beaten with clubs.

There was also an underlying ugliness about it that Majella did not know about for several days. Joaquín did not mention it, but it was known in the village and one of the other women told her. An older woman, not very subtle, who was fiercely pleased that someone from their village seemed to be doing what none of the Whites or Mexicans could do with Señor Clay's crazy horse. When she told Majella, Majella got up without saying anything in response, picked up the cradle with Mario in it, and went into her house and shut the door. Stupid, stupid woman. Ignorant, dull. She hated that woman. Then she sagged against the door. How pointless to vent her anger against the poor simple-minded soul. But she felt sick and started to cry.

Joaquín's efforts to train Señor Clay's crazy horse had aroused a good deal of interest among the townspeople. They were taking a variety of bets on the outcome: On whether or not the crazy horse could really be broken, or on whether the crazy Indian trying to do it would be killed—and when. The man who had sold the horse as untrainable to Clay for a pittance was giving good odds that all Clay would have for his effort would be a dead Indian. There were different odds as to whether it would be by the end of the month or whether the Indian would last longer.

When Joaquín came home from town Majella asked him to give it up. She didn't know how he had managed at all today because his ribs were so sore.

"Give it up!" He was astonished.

"Yes. It is too dangerous." She pulled angrily at the lacings on little Mario's cradle and shook him slightly. "Why didn't you eat!" She demanded of the baby. "Why did you frighten me to death?" She looked up to see Joaquín smiling at her.

"He did not eat because he did not want to. He is unruly like his mother," Joaquín said. "But his father would eat. His father is hungry."

221

Majella smiled reluctantly and put the baby down so she could place Joaquín's food on the table.

"Anyway, it is finished. I rode that horse all over the stable yard today. He is going to be as gentle as a deer."

Majella went weak with relief.

"And he gave me this." Joaquín took a coin from his pocket and spun it on the table. It glittered warmly in the light of flame. "A five-dollar gold piece."

"But what about the goat?"

"That, too. Señor Clay is a good man."

Majella prayed before the crucifix for a long time after Joaquín was asleep, thanking Mary for the good things. Then, somewhat frantically, she sketched out a plan begging Mary's help. They must have some land of their own. And somehow Joaquín and Alonso and Benicia and the others would be there. They would have a field and a garden and fruit trees and goats and cows and chickens and houses. Nice houses. With oil lamps. And window curtains. When she became confused about the color of the curtains she knew she was simply too tired to go on and was falling asleep. She got up and crawled into bed beside her husband. She need not have harangued Mary so long. She only needed to have asked Mary for her own jewelry. And to have Miguel or Eduardo sell it, of course. No Indian could possibly dispose of anything like that. It always came down to that. Anyway, she was glad that Joaquín had gotten the goat for Benicia's sake.

And hot chocolate! Tomorrow she would make hot chocolate! There was quite a lot left.

Flooded with sudden bliss she nestled close to Joaquín and fell asleep.

Joaquín was getting more work in town. He was gaining a reputation as a 'good Indian.' Father Gaspar did come to the village. He said a mass and christened Mario. Alonso and Benicia became his godparents. Majella began to consider getting cloth for a new dress. The men put in the corn and seedlings sprang up.

Most important, the baby she had struggled so hard to keep was flourishing. Once he started eating, he seemed to grow daily. He was a bright, vigorous baby, already rebelling against the confines of his cradle. Any day—any day at all—he would finish with his crawling about and be up on his legs, walking. He was a solid, sturdy, robustly healthy baby now. He seemed to view the world around him with great joy and enthusiasm, and reached for everything he saw.

Majella watched her husband and baby together, and wondered constantly about Joaquín's feelings toward his little son. He was unfailingly gentle and patient with the baby's demands. Sometimes he laughed at his antics, at his stubborness and tenacity. Yet he had seemed quite willing for the baby to die in the beginning. She talked to Benicia about it, and Benicia only repeated what she had said before. *He only feared for Mario. The Indian life is one of difficulty.* Well, that was true, Majella conceded grimly.

Suddenly there was near panic in the village, for a party of Americans came very near with strange devices. A spindly tripod, tapes, and measures. They paced about, calling to one another in

223

strange codes and giving odd signals with their hands and arms. The women stayed indoors and the men gathered to watch them. Joaquín was not working in town that day and, since he knew more English than anyone else in the village, Alonso asked if he would go and speak to the men.

Majella's heart pounded so fast she could scarcely breathe, as he agreed to the request and walked carefully toward the party of Americans. She murmured a hasty prayer to Jesus, Mary, and Joseph to protect him, and watched while he waited respectfully, staying out of their way until someone spoke to him. Then he joined the group and talked to them. They seemed friendly enough. Someone even laughed. Joaquín gathered up the men's metal canteens and brought them back to fill them at the village well. Then he took them back. The men were thanking him. Then, before day's end, they packed up their strange implements and went away.

Joaquín explained that the men were surveyors. They were taking a measure of the land, marking out the boundaries. Title to the land was being argued over in the American courts, as they had heard. There was a dispute over the boundaries and until it was settled no one could be the legal owner.

"Who are the Americans fighting against?" Majella asked.

"They are fighting each other," Joaquín explained. "Americans do that the same as anyone else. Americans do not always agree with each other."

This was an interesting idea to Majella and she pondered it. Heretofore, she had thought of the

Americans as one single invincible group, acting and thinking as one.

Then her interest flagged. It didn't matter. It was all the same to the village. Whenever it was settled, no matter which side won, the village lost. They would all be told to move away. And where would they go?

"Joaquín," she said to him in the darkness that night, "where can we go when it is settled? And what about Alonso and Benicia and the others? Somehow we would—we would have to help Alonso. He helped us."

"Yes," Joaquín said somberly. "We would have to help them."

"If somehow I could make peace with my family—please, let me finish. I wouldn't ask for the jewelry. But if I could convince them to let us alone do you think that—" She hated to say it, but she had to: "Do you think that Leon would let us come back to his village?"

Joaquín moved restlessly. He got up from the bed and walked to the door and opened it. The cool night breeze rushed in and moonlight bathed his muscular body. Her eyes saw and passed over the scar on his thigh from the shooting in Leon's village. He had told her so many times not to waste anger on what had past.

"Have you changed your mind about asking for the jewelry?" he said.

At first she couldn't believe she had heard him right. Then, "No. Oh, no." She said it quickly, scrambling out of bed to go to him. "I still want to. I only stopped asking because you always said no. Do you mean that you don't care now?"

"I don't know. They will not let us stay here forever. Not even very much longer now, I suppose. I have to find another place, somewhere near a town where I could work. What were you planning to do with the money?" He was speaking slowly, thoughtfully, feeling his way. It was clear he had never really thought about it as a real possibility before.

Majella took a deep breath. She must go carefully. She must sound sensible. None of the long daydreams she had spun in her prayers about larger houses and oil lamps. She selected the basic sensible idea and presented it carefully: That they would be safe if they owned their own tract of land. Buy it—it would be legally their own, with papers under the American law to prove it. No one could take it away or drive them off. They would be safe. Mario would be safe.

Then she went into her belief that she could at last convince her family that the marriage, the child, this life were what were best for her. She had written and rewritten the letter a thousand times in her head. She felt sure—positive, in fact— that she could manage it. She would be dealing with Eduardo and Cecilia. Surely by now her brothers had gone back to Mexico.

"Let me think about it," he conceded after a long time. "I will talk about it with Alonso."

She knew—but didn't mention it—that he really wanted to talk to Leon.

"I don't understand you," she said, gazing up into his face in the moonlight. "Why, when the baby was sick, didn't you think like this so we could have done something for him?"

"I thought he would die."

"And you wouldn't help him?" That was what she simply could not understand.

"Would dying while an infant be so bad?" A faint smile touched his mouth.

"He is perfectly healthy now. And *now* you think about doing something for him."

"That *is* why, Majella. Because he *is* going to live. He is going to be as tough and strong as I am. He will live. He will not die. He will live until he is killed. That is a hard life." The words, she could not doubt, were heavy with sorrow and regret.

"Don't you even love him?" she asked, her voice suddenly thick with tears. It would break her heart if he could not love his son.

"Yes. I love him. I love him so much that all the times when he is punished my spirit will be in torment."

"He won't be," she promised wildly, twining her arms about him, clinging to him. "We won't let him be. We will think of some way. We will do something. Talk to Alonso about this. We will plan something."

He cradled her gently. "Come. We must go back to bed. We will talk about it tomorrow."

Chapter Thirteen

Cecilia could not stand it any more. She finished the prayer quickly and eased back, getting her knees off the pebbles and dried beans that she had placed carefully on the kneeler. She got up, her lips turning downward somewhat grimly. That was the point, after all. One sacrificed, one mortified the flesh, and then Mary, in her infinite mercy, might grant one's wish.

She went to the back of the empty chapel and sat down on the last bench so she could lean against the wall. Now, that was another small injustice. The least important workers on the ranch always sat back here, and they had the wall to lean against. Better people sat in front of them, without back support. The most important people of all, the ranchero and his wife, sat in front, without any back support either. She really would laugh if she had the heart for it. So many things were going wrong in her life, so many disappointments, so much tragedy.

And this haunting, terrible fear that she, whose desire for a child was so great she couldn't sleep nights, was being denied it. And Majella, poor Majella, had conceived her unwanted Indian baby so readily. And that child, seed of a renegade Indian, had finished Majella's life for her, had snuffed out the one chance she had for some sort of decent existence. Cecilia looked out the open door into the spreading yard, and wondered where Majella was, what she was doing now. What a tragedy to lose one's sister.

She was bitterly sorry that Eduardo and the others had not been able to find them. Somehow, given a little more time, she could have made Majella understand what was best. And Luis, poor Luis, had gone back to Mexico, still with hope. What a fool Luis was, really. He had even journeyed to that convent in Guadalajara and had talked to the Mother Superior. He had even—stupid Luis, it was too late—made tentative arrangements there, should Majella be found. He had written to them about it from Mexico. The Mother Superior was sympathetic. She had said that if Majella were found with her child, the child could still be left with them at the convent. The Mother Superior, a woman of infinite understanding, understood. She said that possibly Majella might love the child very much, even if it were an Indian child. She had assured Luis that a good home would be provided and some suitable instruction given it. And Luis, careful, tactful Luis, did not even mention how much he had paid for this understanding and assurance.

Well, it didn't matter. Majella was lost to them all now. Gone. Swallowed up among the countless Indian villages, unrecorded, undocumented. Unless she made her whereabouts known, only God Himself would be able to find her.

Cecilia closed her eyes and remembered the long ago, remembered the home in Mexico, when Mama and Papa were still living and they, the children, were little; remembered the laughter, the squabbles, the secrets shared, the surprises. Her lips curved. She had always loved Majella, even if Majella always had been the most favored. And now Majella, somewhere, even had a child when she herself could not have. *Oh, Blessed Mother, don't let me be barren.*

"Where did the lovely smile go?"

Her eyes flew open. Eduardo was before her.

She stood up, standing on tiptoe to kiss his cheek. "I was dreaming about the old days. At home, when I was young."

"When you were young?" He laughed. "And that was long ago, wasn't it?"

"Don't tease." She thrust her arm through his. They walked toward the front of the chapel. "Were you able to persuade the boys to stay a little longer?"

"Yes, but you know, my dear, they are restless." He shook his head sadly. "You must admit there is now no hope of ever finding your sister. They have realized it too. They grieve, but they want to go home. Miguel grows uneasy about leaving your father's affairs unsettled so many months."

"I know," she said somewhat sulkily. "But Eduardo—it may be years until I see them again. Years."

"Well, Miguel said they would linger for another month. So, you see, you have nothing to fret about for days."

Eduardo's heart grieved for the two Moreno men. Each was so different from the other, and each had accepted Majella's tragedy characteristically. Miguel, the sober, steady one, would sit for hours quietly brooding about it. Eduardo got the feeling that he had idolized his elder sister and would never recover from the blow of the terrible fate that had befallen her. The fact that she had willingly gone away with the Indian renegade had shaken the very foundation of his being. He seemed to put out of his mind entirely the fact that Majella's real father had been an Indian, and that his own mother had been of mixed parentage. Now Miguel, peaceable, almost placid by nature, held within himself a deep and consuming rage. Eduardo, whose prayers usually consisted of speaking the words required as quickly as he decently could, went alone to his small chapel sometimes. He would kneel at the altar, his mind fumbling for the correct thing to say, wishing with all his heart that Miguel could somehow—what?— recover? Surely *recover* wasn't the word he wanted. That Majella could be *restored* to her family, that things could be as they had been? No, common sense told him that was not possible. What then? *Help Miguel,* he finally pleaded. *Help them all.* He rose from his knees uneasily. That wasn't what he had wanted to say. He left the chapel with a vague sense of discontent.

He did not worry so much about Hernán. The rage was there, certainly, because of his sister's fate, but with Hernán, the temperamental, the

us." He waited a moment. "To us," he repeated.

"What are you getting at, Eduardo?" Really, sometimes Eduardo took forever to say something.

"She assumes that her brothers have gone back to Mexico, but it is clearly more than that. I think she knows that Miguel would still come for her and try to make her come back. She doesn't want that, Cecilia. She makes that plain."

"Well, what does she want? I don't understand."

"Read it for yourself, my dear." He handed it to her. "Stay where you are, I'll bring over the lamp."

"This paper," Cecilia said in surprise, taking the letter. "It is so cheap. It's not as good as parcel wrapping." With an expression of mingled distaste and uneasiness, Cecilia started to read her sister's familiar handwriting. It was like a letter from the grave. She tried to keep her hands steady. She should have known, been more careful while Majella was here. Majella was always so determined about what she wanted. And she was determined to keep that Indian baby. And why? There certainly couldn't be any pride or joy in carrying such a baby. Perhaps she had miscarried?

"Well, she had the baby and kept it, didn't she? She was determined about that." Her voice was grim. "Beautiful, yes, I can imagine how beautiful it is. How in the world could she think it beautiful? Oh, I see, like its father." She lifted her gaze from the letter. "Eduardo, did you see the one who was the father?" There was a dark fascination in thinking, really for the first time, about this baby's father. What was he like? Dark? Stupid? Savage? Oh, Majella, you should have died first.

"Yes, I think so. If he is the one I think he was. I saw a good many of them that day in their village when we found Majella. He was fairly good-looking for an Indian, you know—broad-faced, with a somewhat heavy mouth. But yes, I would say good-looking—the farthest thing you could imagine from Luis."

"I don't know that we should even mention him and Luis in the same breath." Cecilia made her voice cold, and went on reading. "Mother of God! Eduardo, she wants those jewels that Mama left her." How astounding! An Indian wearing jewels!

Eduardo gave an uncertain laugh. "Well, Cecilia, your mother did leave them to her. And, if I remember correctly, Majella offered to let you have any that you wanted, and you refused."

"Yes, I refused. I don't want any of them." She could not suppress a shiver. "They started everything. I hate them. Majella had hated them too. Now she has changed her mind. Why? Why should she have them now?"

Eduardo's voice was indulgent, cajoling. "They belong to her. She wants them. You don't. Then why in the name of reason don't you want her to have them?"

"I didn't say I didn't want her to have them," Cecilia said, continuing with the letter. "In the name of God, Eduardo, she doesn't ask for much, does she? She wants you—*you*, mind you—to go to all the trouble of disposing of them for her. And buying land. *Land*, Eduardo. What in—"

"Cecilia!" He was half-laughing, half-annoyed "I have never heard you swear before. What has got into you, girl?"

"I don't know." Hurriedly, fumbling, she folded

the letter. She wanted to cry but would not let herself. She thrust the letter at her husband. What ailed Majella—she had always been so considerate, so careful not to impose. Had she lost her wits entirely to think she could depend forever on her sister's husband? She knew, she certainly did know, that Eduardo had a big estate to manage, much to attend to, and that he had, most certainly, spent much time and money already on this terrible thing. She had simply lost her wits. She could not possibly realize what she was asking.

Eduardo took the letter, regarding her thoughtfully. "I am sorry this has distressed you. Compose yourself for a few minutes and then we will talk about it." He crossed the room and replaced the letter in the drawer, leaving Cecilia sitting stiffly on the window ledge, trying to sit still, unable to entirely. She smoothed her robe over her knees. Her shoulders twitched nervously. She alternately tightened and relaxed her lips. So Majella had had her baby.

He came over to stand before her, his hands deep in the pockets of his robe. "Majella is right about having someone else dispose of the jewels and make the land purchase. It is difficult enough for Mexicans to deal with the authorities now—an Indian doesn't have a chance."

"Well—what is the law? Is she Indian now? I mean, legally? Do Indians own anything? Like land?" Now, that was a ridiculous idea, as lazy and stupid as they were.

"Yes, they can have legal ownership, but—" he shook his head. "The way things are, the Indian would have to be—represented. Have help, advice.

236

Otherwise, I wouldn't take a wager on how much he would get from any transaction."

"Well, Eduardo, what are we talking about?" Cecilia asked, sounding distracted. "It isn't up to us anyhow. It is for Miguel to decide." Why did this terrible thing have to rise up to haunt them all again?

"Is it?" Eduardo was looking at her searchingly. "That is what I am in such a quandary about. I have worried at the idea all afternoon. So much is at stake again. There has been so much tragedy and heartbreak over this. I begin to think that Majella has offered the best solution. If only her letter had been delayed until next month."

"Eduardo, really, I have no idea what you are getting at." Cecilia said in exasperation.

"Think about it. Miguel and Hernán return to Mexico next month. If they had already gone, and Majella had written this letter asking me to do this, with her brothers in Mexico, I could have persuaded myself immediately that I should do as she wished. As it is, with Miguel and Hernán still here, would it be my right to do it? Or would it create a family disagreement that would never be healed? Is it my duty now to hand this letter over to Miguel? Can't you see my dilemma, my love?"

"Not entirely," she said somewhat tartly. "What difference would it make to Majella either way? Majella has what she wanted. She is keeping that baby," Cecilia said. Oh, God, all this was giving her a headache. And after she had spent the evening flirting with and enticing her husband, willing him to desire her again. That was never difficult, but it was such a delicate balance—one must

237

never appear wanton by granting too many favors. But if one wanted a baby. . . .

"What difference? You aren't thinking, Cecilia. I would go ahead, as she asks, dispose of the things, find some land, buy it, let Majella and her—family, I suppose—know about it. But if I just hand the letter over to Miguel, what will he do?"

Cecilia was staring at him intently. "He wouldn't do that," she said slowly after a moment. "I see what you mean."

"If she were my sister, I might not be able to be so detached either, so I understand his feeling."

"Miguel worships Majella. He always has. And— and—he wouldn't consider letting her go on with this."

"No, I'm afraid he wouldn't. He would want to gather a small army and ride into their village shooting, if I'm not very much mistaken."

"Would that be so bad?" Cecilia asked. "He would get rid of that renegade. He would get Majella out of that—oh, Eduardo, it must be terrible the way she lives. And he could take that Indian baby to Guadalajara and leave it. God bless Luis! Then Majella could have some decent kind of life. Luis said they would travel, and they would come back here sometimes. I would see Majella the way she used to be—beautiful, dressed in suitable gowns, the fine lady Papa always wanted her to be. Surely, Eduardo, surely she would come to her senses eventually."

"You've read the letter, Cecilia." He sounded tired. "I've wracked my poor brain over this. What is right? What should I do?"

"On the other hand," Cecilia said uncertainly, "if—if we do as she asks, she and her child, and all the other children she will probably have, will be buried on some grubby little plot of land somewhere. Can you imagine why she would want that? Can you?"

Eduardo went to sit on the edge of the high bed. He was partly in shadow and Cecilia could not see his face.

"Cecilia, Majella is your sister. This is your family. You know them all far better than I ever could. Will you let me pass this burden on to you? You decide. And tell me. And I will do what you think best."

Cecilia slid off the window ledge, her eyes enormous. "Yes," she said. "Let me think about it. And I will decide what is best."

Chapter Fourteen

The American from the livery stable in town, Señor Clay, came into the village with another American. They rumbled along the dusty road in a lopsided wagon used mainly for hauling feed. It was empty now, except for some odd tools rattling about in back.

The village women went inside the houses and the men gathered in the clearing to see what was wanted. A murmur went around the group that something might have happened to Andrés Orozco, the other villager who worked for Señor Clay.

Majella thought, and crossed herself instantly, that if something had happened to Andrés, Joaquín would work more at the stable and could get away from Señor Tippitt. What a wicked idea. She asked Mary for forgiveness and opened the door a crack to listen to what was said. She watched the

Americans get down from the wagon and speak to Alonso, after lifting their hands in greeting to Joaquín. Almost immediately they turned to Joaquín. She heard him invite them to the house. This surprised her. She knew he would not have suggested it. They must want to talk to him only, and in private. How odd.

Americans—in the house! She cast a quick glance around and everything seemed to be in order. What should she do? Certainly not what she would have done at home in Papa's house. A look of sadness touched her eyes. Don't step forward with hands extended, smiling, greeting, welcoming. She picked up Mario in his cradle and stood uncertainly by the table as the door opened. The Americans stepped inside, taking off their dusty hats and looking around the interior of the small house. They seemed to look as uncertain as she felt. Perhaps they had never been inside an Indian's house before. Señor Clay had been speaking a slow, but fairly good Spanish outside to Alonso and Joaquín and continued now, although she knew that he and Joaquín often spoke English together in the stable.

"It is very clean," Señor Clay said, turning to Joaquín, who stepped inside after them. "Looks very clean. And that is your little squaw?"

"Yes, Señor." Joaquín's face was blank. Señor Clay nodded, clearly uneasy. The other man said nothing, frowning constantly as if he had a headache.

"And that's your little son?" The American Clay stepped forward, peering into Mario's face. The baby stared unblinking into the unknown, craggy face, with its stubble of gray beard. Then Clay,

241

the amenities completed, turned from the baby and looked at Joaquín.

"You're a good Indian, Joaquín. I told you that before. I told Hagerman here that we could take your word. Isn't that right? If I ask you something, will you tell me the truth?"

Joaquín gave the briefest nod. "Yes, Señor."

"Are you expecting any trouble out here?"

"Trouble, Señor? No, Señor." Joaquín shook his head, and Majella became aware of the slow pounding of her heart. Joaquín wasn't going to mention the surveyors. It was just as well. That might not be what they wanted to know.

The other American said something to Clay in English and walked restlessly across the small house. He stood staring at Majella's work shelf, with the stone bowl, a squash, the box of chocolate, and an accumulation of cooking things.

"You are sure about that?" Clay asked, fingering his hat.

"I do not know of any trouble, Señor."

"What kind of trouble?" Majella asked—and could have bitten her tongue. This was not Papa's house. She must not speak out. She must not call attention to herself in front of these men. She must appear dull, stupid, lumpish, no more noticeable than the table, than the squash on the shelf. She felt her cheeks getting hot. The man by the shelf turned to look at her in mild surprise, and she was fearfully aware of how limp and thin the fabric of her dress had become with many washings, how it clung to the curves of her breasts. I am sorry, she thought, I am sorry, Joaquín.

Joaquín, who could stand motionless for hours if he wanted to, moved and brought their attention back to himself. "What kind of trouble do you mean, Señor?"

"That's what I don't know," Clay said uneasily "We don't want any trouble in the town, Joaquín. We've had it in the past, but things are settled now. A rider came into the stable this morning to leave his horse awhile, and I don't know. I just don't know. He told of talking to a large party of Mexicans. About twenty. Looking for an Indian village, this village. You see what I'm getting at?"

"Did they say why they want to find the village, Señor?" Joaquín asked, and Majella's palms went damp. Was it Eduardo? Men from his ranch? *Oh, God, let them come in peace.*

"No." Clay paused a long time, frowning. "Look, Joaquín, I like you. Always have. You are a good Indian. Clean. Tame. Those men were armed and I think this may be some kind of trouble for your village here. I have nothing against you Indians. You've never raised any hell in the town. You're peaceful. But you see, Joaquín, if trouble comes to your village—it's too close to the town. The fact is, some of the people are worried for fear it might cause trouble in town. Now we don't want that! We've had trouble with the Mexicans. We've had trouble with the Indians. But that's all past now. Things are peaceful, settled. I wish to God they would get this damned tract out of the courts and decide who owns it. Then you could all move on to some place else." He paused, clearly unhappy, and walked toward Majella again. He looked into the baby's face and touched his cheek with one finger. "Pretty little Indian baby," he said absent-mindedly. "I sent word to that Indian Agent, but he's fifty miles down south

243

at the Indian village there. No post office, no telegraph. I had to send Andrés with a note in the other wagon." He fell silent again. "But there is no guarantee that the Indian Agent will leave what he's doing there and come back here, is there? You know that agent?"

"Yes, Señor."

"You think he'll come back because I asked him to?"

"No, Señor."

"I thought not. Well—" He was slapping his dusty hat lightly against his leg, frowning at Joaquín. "Do you have any guns here in your village?"

"I never saw any guns. I have no guns, Señor."

"Jesus," Clay said softly. "Ducks on a pond."

"Señor?"

"Nothing. Joaquín, if the Mexicans ride through the town, the Sheriff has agreed he would ask them what they want. But if they don't, if they go around the long way, he just flatly refuses to ride out and bother them. He says we've had enough trouble with the Mexicans."

Suddenly little Mario made one of his crowing, delighted baby sounds. His piping baby voice startled them all. He wriggled vigorously a moment inside his lacings and then settled down with his black, unblinking stare at the American.

"Damn," Clay said. "Damn. Babies all sound alike, don't they?" He sighed deeply. "I don't know what else to do, Joaquín. What do you think will happen here?"

"Nobody can know, Señor." A near-smile touched Joaquín's mouth and disappeared immediately. "Perhaps nothing, Señor."

244

"You're a funny one. You wouldn't change expression if your insides were falling out, would you? Never know what you're thinking. No matter. But I wanted you to know in case—well, do you have any place to send your women and children?"

"Inside the houses, Señor."

Clay sighed. "Well, good luck with it, Joaquín. Maybe it is nothing. We'll hope for the best."

"Thank you for coming, Señor."

When they had gone, Majella put Mario down and flew into Joaquín's arms. "It's Eduardo. I know it. I know it."

Joaquín ran his hands lovingly over her back. "We did decide to send the letter, Majella. You were sure in your mind that he would answer."

"But with armed men? Twenty armed men? I'm afraid, Joaquín."

"No man of sense ever travels alone, Majella. You—of all people—you must know that. He would certainly come with a party from his rancho."

"Yes, that's true." But she was afraid.

There was no time for anything further because Alonso and two other men were at the door. They came inside. Alonso had brought his chairs so they could sit down around the table. They talked for a while. It was finally decided that Alonso, as Headman, would call all of the men together and talk to them. Majella, grinding meal slowly, her back to them, felt her heart aching for Alonso. He was old, as he often said. Old and tired, and sometimes confused about what to do. Carefully, and with great courtesy and patience, Joaquín let him know what he should tell the rest of the villagers. And her heart ached for Joaquín. If only she could talk to Eduardo about Joaquín—make him understand. Her hands became still over the stone bowl while her mind worried with an imaginary conversation. *I know you will understand, Eduardo. You are a kind and thoughtful man. My husband is not what he seems to you. He is a wise man, wise and good and gentle and loving. He speaks quite a lot of English with the Americans, yes, that surprises you doesn't it? And he has Spanish, very good Spanish, and his own tongue. He works very hard. The plants seem to grow under his hands, and he has a magic with all the animals. That is why we must have a place, you see. He is too good for this. There is no end to what he can do, so he must have something. Something where we can have a peaceful life. He must not spend his life shoveling manure out of the stable. Eduardo, my husband must not be wasted. It is so important that you understand. Please, please understand.*

They rode in during the late afternoon. There seemed more than twenty, there seemed to be an army. They came cantering their horses down the road in no special formation, just many, many armed men riding along. The first one Majella saw through the crack in the door was Hernán.

Her heart leaped. Her little brother, her darling. There was a swift, sweet memory of the laughter they had shared. She wanted to fling open the door and run to meet him.

They came into the clearing, almost filling it, the horses milling and snorting, leather squeaking. The vaqueros' serapes slung over their shoulders made the men look larger than they were. Rifles were in all saddle holsters, all pistols were at the men's hips. The seven or eight Indian men who waited on foot seemed pitifully defenseless. Majella's mouth felt dry with fear. She heard the demand to speak with the village Headman. With his slight bowing motion, Alonso stepped forward.

"I am the Headman." He was facing in her direction and she heard him clearly. He did not sound frightened or confused. He sounded simply polite. She felt a rush of pride, for she knew he must be sick with fear.

"What is your name?" Eduardo was speaking. Where was Miguel? If Hernán was still in California, then certainly Miguel was, too. Her eyes searched the group and then she saw him. He had lost some weight and his face was haggard. *Oh, Miguel, my dearest brother, it's all right. Everything is all right.*

"Alonso Phail."

"Phail! That is the name! This is the village!" It did not sound like Miguel—so harsh, so brusque. He kicked his horse and it pushed forward. "Where is my sister? Majella Moreno? I know she is here—where are you keeping her?"

Alonso hesitated and Joaquín stepped forward. *Oh, no, stay back, Joaquín.*

"Majella is in her house, Señor," he said.

Three guns came out of their holsters. Majella flung open the door and sprang out.

"Wait! Miguel! Hernán!" She picked up her skirt and ran headlong into the clearing. "Miguel! Hernán! It's all right! It's all right!" She managed to stop beside Joaquín, the Mexicans staring at her dumbfounded, trying to keep their horses under control, trying to hear what she said—not really believing what she said. "This is Joaquín, my husband," she was saying breathlessly. "You see? Our marriage paper? I have it, you see?" She caught hold of the pommel of Miguel's saddle and clung to it, thrusting the paper up at him. It seemed an age before he took it. Then he did not read it, but continued to stare down at her in disbelief, in anguish.

"You—you look like an Indian," he said finally, still holding the marriage paper. "You—haven't any shoes on."

"Miguel, please come into the house. Please. I want you to see my baby, your nephew. His name is Mario. Please come in." She had started to tremble visibly, and felt Joaquín's hand at her waist to steady her.

"Take your hands off her!" Hernán spurred his horse and came plunging at Joaquín, scattering several other riders and making the Indians scramble out of his way. Joaquín pushed Majella out of the way as Hernán's hand rose, lifting the coiled rawhide reata off the pommel. Using it coiled as a weapon, he brought it down on Joaquín.

If Joaquín had not turned his head quickly he would have caught the blow full in the face. As it was, his shoulders took the force and it knocked him to the ground. Eduardo, and a man Majella did not know, pushed their mounts forward, crowding Hernán back.

"Stop! Stop I tell you!" Eduardo commanded. "We don't want any difficulty here. We came to get Majella. Come! Miguel. Hernán. Both of you. Let us go into their house and talk about this. Majella—" He turned again toward her, still keeping his horse between Hernán and Joaquín, who was getting up from the ground. "Which is your house?"

"That one," she said, pointing a shaking hand. "Go. I—I will come in a moment." She faced Joaquín. "I am sorry," she said in his tongue. "I thought he was going to kill you, or I wouldn't have come out."

"My God, she's even speaking their language! It makes me sick. It makes me sick." Hernán dismounted and stood rigidly, staring at her. Eduardo took his arm and pulled him toward the house.

"Come," he said. "Come to the house."

The Indians waited a moment before following. Two or three of the other Mexicans dismounted, and then seemed uncertain what to do. There obviously was not room in the small house for all of them. They mounted again and the remaining group of horsemen seemed to mass closer together, waiting. There were low murmurs and comments passed among them.

"Are you all right?" Alonso was looking at Joaquín.

"It it nothing. I fear you will regret that you took us in, my friend," he said.

"Let me come with you into the house," Alonso offered, brushing aside Joaquín's comment.

Joaquín shook his head. "It is better not to, I think. There is no need. You have done enough."

"I want to." The strange stubbornness was unlike Alonso, usually so willing to follow Joaquín's suggestions. "It will be better with two of us. You cannot stand against them all."

"And you think the two of us could?" Joaquín

smiled briefly and turned away. He and Majella started toward the house. Alonso stubbornly followed along and Majella was relieved. This was worse, far worse, than she had anticipated.

When they entered, her brother Miguel was seated on one of the chairs. It looked so strange, Miguel seated at their table. The marriage certificate lay on the table before him. He was reading it, a look of vacant disbelief on his face.

"Majella," he muttered. "Why did you do this? How could you do this?" He seemed only half-aware that she had actually come into the house.

Joaquín stepped softly to the table, and waited a moment.

"Señor, may I speak to you?"

Miguel looked up, his eyes haunted. "You are the one? The father of the child? The one who married her?"

"Yes, Señor."

Miguel's haggard gaze turned to Majella. "In God's name, tell me you did this when you were mad with worry about your unborn child. Tell me you want to come home."

"I—don't want to come home," she said carefully. "I love you all dearly, but—this is my life now. There is my baby, my husband. Dear Miguel, you must remember that I am truly Indian. You must remember this. I have a family here. This is my life now. Please, try to understand."

Eduardo moved closer and placed his hand on Miguel's shoulder.

"Think about what she is saying, Miguel. She is married to this Indian. They were legally married and in the Church. Nothing can be done about it now."

Hernán spoke savagely. "She can become a widow!"

"Hernán!" There was heartbreak in Majella's voice.

Joaquín spoke again. "My wife would not have sent the letter to you, Señor, but we shall have to move from this village soon. She thought we could find another place where we could stay."

"Why would you move from this village?" Eduardo spoke stiffly. He was kindly and somewhat indulgent to many of the Indians working on his ranch, but this was different and he was ill at ease.

"This is only a settlement, Señor. Alonso Phail and his people have no claim to the land. Their own village was taken away from them. Now this land is in the American court. When it is settled the Americans will own it and the people here must move on to some other place."

This was something Eduardo understood at once. Somehow, if the land titles got into the courts the Americans always managed to get the land. He had not realized that Indians faced the same dilemmas about land ownership. He should have thought about it more, perhaps.

"I want you to see my baby," Majella said desperately, and she picked up Mario, laced into his cradle just before the men arrived so he wouldn't be crawling about underfoot. All three men stared at the baby, snug in his Indian coverings. Miguel closed his eyes.

"You must come home," he said. "I will take you home. You must forget all this."

"Forget!" she gasped. "Miguel, forget my son?

251

Forget my husband? You don't understand! You don't understand at all."

"Majella." Joaquín's voice was almost inaudible but there was a warning note in it.

Hernán moved restlessly, almost distractedly. "My God, I must get out of here. Let's go outside. We can't even breathe in this—in this—" He wrenched open the door and plunged out into the gathering dusk.

Miguel got up stiffly, looking uncertainly toward the door, and then followed his brother.

"Wait a moment," Eduardo said, going after them.

Majella put Mario down on the bed. This was all wrong. They must not leave—nothing was settled. And they certainly must not go like this, angry and bitter. Not her brothers. She hurried out after them, with Joaquín and Alonso following. Joaquín brushed by her and she felt a tautness in his body. *Oh, Joaquín, wait just a little longer. Be silent just a little longer.*

The mounted Mexicans waited, but some of the Indian men had gone back into their houses.

"Stand away from my sister!" Hernán shouted to Joaquín. His pistol was in his hand, aimed point-blank at Joaquín. Majella was rooted in horror. It was Alonso who could move. He lunged at Hernán, pushing him aside. The gun went off, the explosion blasting their eardrums, the shot going wild. But the sound of the shot shattered any possible peace. The Mexicans sprang into action, shooting at any remaining Indians they saw. Joaquín leaped for Hernán and wrested the gun out of his hand. He caught Majella and dived for the ground. Some return shooting started to come sporadically from a few of the houses as those Indians who had usable guns fired them at the crowd.

The half-light hindered the aim, making targets less visible. Crouching, Joaquín dragged Majella around the corner of the house.

"Stop! Stop! Stop!" Eduardo was shouting constantly, trying to be heard over the gunfire and sounding like a madman. The mounted Mexicans moved about quickly among the houses, shooting into doorways. There were screams, shouts, curses. "Stop! Stop this!" Eduardo shouted, his voice hoarse.

Finally, miraculously, it did stop. There came a strange, eerie silence. Someone had set a thatched roof afire and smoke curled lazily upward, slowly, very slowly, for there was no breeze. Then—perversely—the breeze freshened, pushing at the flames, making them dance. Almost immediately the neighboring roof ignited, and then the next.

"Oh, my God, what has happened here!" Eduardo hurried about, trying to assess the situation, issuing commands to his men. There were the mingled sounds of the thatch roofs crackling as the flames ate through them, the rattling moan of someone as he died, the milling horses. An Indian woman, out of sight, was crying loudly in an undulating death wail. Someone coughed from the smoke. Little Mario was screaming hysterically inside the house.

"Majella?" Joaquín's steady voice spoke in her ear.

She sat up shakily.

"Are you all right?" he asked.

"Yes." What had happened? She felt stunned, detached, outside it all.

"Majella. Get up slowly. Go to your brother."

"My brother?"

"The elder brother. The one you call Miguel. I think he is dead. There. On the ground."

She got up stiffly. She could not believe it. Hernán had seen Miguel at the same time, and a moment later Eduardo realized it, too. All three of them reached the body about the same time.

Hernán fell down on his knees and lifted Miguel partly off the ground, holding him close, rocking back and forth.

"My brother, my brother, my brother," he was moaning softly. Tears started rolling down his face.

Majella felt Eduardo's arm about her shoulders.

"My dear girl," he said unsteadily. "You must come home with us. Oh, dear God, that this should happen. You must come home."

"I cannot," she said. "I cannot."

Hernán raised his wet face, twisted with anguish.

"Please, Majella, please. You—are all I have now."

She could not bear it, and turned away. "Can you accept my husband, my baby?" she asked, unable to look at him.

"Oh, God, Majella. Don't ask that. Never. Never." He buried his face against his brother, gripping the body close, huddling there as if he would never move from that spot.

She felt Eduardo's touch again. "Are you hurt, Majella?"

She looked down and saw that the side of her dress had blood on it. She thought, *Cold water will wash that out,* and was appalled at herself. She raised her eyes to Eduardo's.

"No," she said, looking at the carnage, looking at her dead brother, knowing she had lost them all now. "I am not hurt."

"There are some things to do," Eduardo said, sounding apologetic. She stood like a statue, watching him do them, unable to help him as she knew she should. He got his men together. Miguel was wrapped in a serape and placed on a horse.

"We will make a litter," Eduardo explained to Majella, "after we are away from the village." Later he said, "I do not know what to tell you, my girl. I can't think yet. You will not come with us?"

"No."

"My God." He turned away, and she stood by the side of the house and watched the mounted party move out, leaving the village in ruins. She seemed unable to move and watched as Alonso came limping across the clearing. His progress was slow. He made a zigzag path, looking at fallen men, making sure they were dead. Three times he did this, over the sprawled bodies on the ground, before he came to her. It was almost dark now, but there was light from the slow flames in the tarry thatch. Both stood a moment, watching the door of Alonso's house. Its roof was afire now. Benicia plodded in and out of the burning house. She had spread a blanket on the ground at some distance. She was carrying out various things to save from the fire. She was going to make a bundle of them. Sometimes she bent over, as if with a cramp, and then straightened up again. Majella's eyes roved over the clearing, looking for the goat.

255

It was there at the end of its rope, pulling continually backward, but unable to uproot the stake. The goat had survived.

"Where is Joaquín?" Alonso asked.

She glanced back from where she had been. Joaquín was standing, leaning against the house, his head slightly back, eyes closed. His shirt and the side of his trousers were wet with blood. She darted to him.

"Joaquín. You're shot! You didn't tell me." She touched him, his arm, his shoulder, his face, with small frantic motions, not knowing what to do. *Not Joaquín. Nothing must happen to Joaquín.*

"It is not much, Majella." He shook his head.

"You have to stop the blood, Majella," Alonso said.

She nodded distractedly, stumbling to the door of the house. *Thank God it wasn't burning.* "Bring him in. Can you help him in?"

Alonso and Joaquín had almost reached the door when, over the sounds of the dying village, there came the sound of a horse and clattering rumble of a wagon for the second time that day. Majella held her hands on Joaquín and felt his body jerk with quick alarm. They all looked toward the road. Señor Clay's old wagon came in rattling to a stop, its partial cargo of tools sliding across the boards. The horse stood heaving between the shafts, shaking its head.

Clay had another American with him, a different one from before. He jumped down from the wagon and came stamping into the little house, calling something in English back to the other man.

"Joaquín?"

"Yes, Señor?"

Clay took off his hat and stood looking at Joaquín, who was still standing. He shook his grizzled head. "My God, I thought something like this was going to happen. I just knew it. Well, I won't bedevil you about what they wanted. I talked the doctor into coming with me—in case there was anybody left. I waited down the road during the shooting. I told him I'd pay him." Clay shook his head again, gazing at the seeping blood stains on Joaquín's clothes.

"I thought he did not treat Indians, Señor."

"He doesn't like to. Says he's had to treat too many of their victims in the old days." The doctor came in now, carrying a black satchel and a lighted lantern. He was an old man, and thin. His hair was white and hung in light wisps from beneath his black hat.

The American doctor! Majella stared at him, dumbfounded. How strange for him to be here, hating Indians as he did. He put his satchel on Majella's shelf and snapped it open, issuing his instructions in English. In response, Clay helped Joaquín stretch out on the floor.

The doctor's thin, blue-veined hands worked with skill. He commented softly from time to time in English, almost to himself. Joaquín's eyes were shut. Mario started to cry again. Joaquín opened his eyes.

"Majella, take him out of his cradle. He'll stop crying."

With numb fingers she did, not taking her eyes off Joaquín and the doctor. Mario stopped crying, wriggling his small body in an ecstasy of freedom. She held him with difficulty.

When the doctor had finished, he and the others helped Joaquín to the bed. The doctor shut his bag and went outside, making a comment as he went.

"He's going to look around—see if he can find anybody else who needs help, since he's here." Clay told Alonso.

There was a half-smile on Joaquín's mouth, and a brief answering smile on Clay's face. He shook his head about the doctor.

Joaquín spoke to Majella in his own tongue. "The doctor also says it isn't decent to let the baby expose his private parts like that." Majella's mouth tightened and she hugged Mario close.

Clay sat down gingerly on the side of the bed. He reached over and placed his hand on Joaquín's shoulder, patting him.

"How many were killed?" he asked.

"I don't know yet, Señor. Many. Most I think."

"Jesus, Joaquín. I meant Mexicans. Were any of the Mexicans killed?"

"Yes. One. They took him away."

"My God. You're smart enough to know what that means. Those men weren't peons. They looked like hidalgos. Landowners. They'll raise hell. Lie still. Does it hurt?"

"Some, Señor."

Mario was restless, struggling, reaching out toward his father. Majella kept turning him around to face herself. Joaquín spoke to her in his own tongue. "Don't turn the baby around. Let him see. He must start to learn."

"Well, that's bad." Clay was saying. "But the doctor said it isn't much of a wound."

"It isn't, Señor," Joaquín agreed.

258

"You lost some blood, though. Do you think you could travel by morning?"

"If I have to, Señor."

Alonso was looking intently at Clay. "We must go, Señor?"

"I'm afraid so. No other way. The people in town are worried. There is a lot of wild talk. Nobody wants any more trouble with the Mexicans, so—well—the Sheriff said that if any of them got killed, the village would have to be cleared out by noon tomorrow. If the men from town come out and find any Indians left—" He shrugged, his eyes troubled. He was still patting Joaquín's shoulder from time to time. "How do you feel?"

"Well enough, Señor."

"It isn't as if you could have stayed on anyhow. You see that, Joaquín. All of you would have to leave eventually anyhow."

"That is true, Señor."

"It's hard," Clay said soberly. "I know it's hard for you. But I can see the Sheriff's viewpoint too, in a way. He has to keep the peace. That's what they pay him for. He can't have Indians scattered all over the countryside when there are settlements of people. You understand that."

Joaquín shut his eyes and didn't answer. Clay appeared not to notice. Very carefully, Joaquín sat up. Majella could not speak; she just sat clutching the baby, watching Joaquín, wondering if she should help him.

"Are you sure you can get up, Joaquín?" Clay asked.

"Yes, Señor."

Clay got up from the edge of the bed and helped him. In a few moments Joaquín was standing. His eyes looked dreamy, as they did when he was about to fall asleep.

"Have you got any money, Joaquín?" Clay asked, frankly worried.

"Some, Señor."

"It's wrong," Clay muttered. "It's all wrong." He was taking a wallet out of his pocket as Joaquín walked slowly toward the door. Alonso followed along anxiously. They both stood silently at the door, looking out over the village. More of the roofs were burning and smoldering.

Clay said, "I guess they'll all burn up during the night. When the fire gets to the wood part it may go faster." He was standing behind them now. "Here, Joaquín, take this. You'll need it. And have your little woman get some water and clean off the blood."

"Yes, Señor." Joaquín took the money. "Thank you, Señor."

"Never mind. It is nothing."

"Señor Clay?"

"Yes?"

"Your wheelbarrow is in the wagon, Señor. Could we have it?"

"That old barrow? Yes, you can have it." Clay stepped past them and began to wrestle the wheelbarrow out of the back of the wagon. The doctor was now seated silently on the seat, waiting. They exchanged some comments in English. Clay had the wheelbarrow down now and wheeled it up to the doorway.

"He says he found one he could patch up. Said all that were left alive could travel tomorrow." Clay dropped the barrow down and stood looking at them, frowning. He shook his head sadly.

"Damn," he said. "*Damn*." Then he turned and got into his wagon, snapping the whip over the horse's head.

Majella came to stand near the door. Would she ever grasp it all? Nothing seemed real. They were being driven from the village and Joaquín was hurt, but there was no feeling of fear. Would fear come? Miguel was dead, and there was no grief. Would grief come? How could she feel no grief when Miguel was dead?

"Why did you want that wheelbarrow?" she asked.

He pointed across the clearing. "Benicia has too many things she wants to take. She can't possibly carry that bundle." They all stood watching Benicia at work with her bundle.

Now that the Americans had gone, a few villagers emerged and began to gather in the clearing. Some looked around with something like confusion. Others just stood there.

"You will want to speak to them," Joaquín said to Alonso.

It was difficult to tell with just the light from the slow fires, but there seemed to be six or seven people left. Were all the rest gone? All?

"What can I say to them?" Alonso asked, looking dully at what remained of his village. There was a child wailing somewhere.

"They will need to know what the people in the town have said. About moving away before noon." Joaquín was speaking very carefully. "Then, you will need to decide if you will all stay together again, the way you did before. Is that child alone now?"

"What child?" Alonso asked.

"The one who is crying. From behind that house I think." Joaquín pointed.

"Yes," Alonso answered. "He is alone now."

"Will you take him with you?"

"Yes. We will take him. You speak as if you will not come with us."

"I can't, my friend." He held up a blood-smeared hand as Alonso started to speak. "Your people will not want me. They will be fearful after what I have brought to this village."

Alonso saw the truth of this and it showed in his eyes. Then they filled with tears.

"But since I can't go with you, I can direct you to another village." Joaquín smiled. "When you finish talking to the people I will tell you how to go to my old village. When you get there, speak to Leon Troncoso and his grandfather. Ask them if you can stay there. I think they will let you, if I am not with you. I know the old man will take in the child who is alone now. He took me in."

"But you cannot go back?" Alonso said sadly.

"No."

Alonso, head bowed, went out the door and walked a few paces. Then he turned slowly and came back. "The goat?" he asked.

"Take the goat," Joaquín said.

Chapter Fifteen

They all left before dawn, skirting around through the low rolling hills the long way, to avoid going through the town. Almost immediately the path of Alonso's people diverged from theirs. The parting was brief, as the two men had talked the night before about the routes. Majella watched her uncle and Benicia trudge out of sight, the others trailing along behind them. The orphaned child walked beside the wheelbarrow, reaching out occasionally to hold to it.

"Come," Joaquín said. And Majella started walking, filled with a terrible feeling of emptiness. Sweat was already creeping down her temples, for the bundle on her back was heavier than she could have imagined. Joaquín carried the baby in the cradle, slung over his arm as it would not have been fitting for a man to carry it on his back. She kept going over in her mind the contents of the bundle because all night long there had been an underlying panic that she would forget some important item. Like the metronome on the piano in her father's house in Mexico, her mind rotated back and forth between two things. Was everything necessary in the bundle? Was Joaquín's wound bleeding under the bandage? She looked at it every chance she could get without letting him know. They walked until noon, and found a resting place in some underbrush. They were both tired, neither having had any sleep the night before. Joaquín crawled in and she heard him moving gently about, obscured by the hanging leafage. He came out in a little while and tossed away a couple of rocks and a small dead snake.

"Come in here. It is almost cool, and very smooth."

She went down on her knees, eased off the bundle, and crawled in under the sheltering bushes. She dragged in the cradle after her and settled down on the ground, brushing aside a few twigs. Dimly, she could hear Joaquín moving about outside for a few minutes, and the cracking of some branches. Her eyelids drooped.

He came crawling in slowly, carefully, because of his wound. "I covered up the bundle."

She was going to commend him for being so sensibly careful of the wound, but forgot it as soon as she thought of it. Fatigue seemed to be drugging her brain. What was she going to say to Joaquín? Well, it didn't matter. She could say it later.

"Don't let me go to sleep until I feed the baby," she said, and saw that Joaquín was unlacing him. She reached out her arms, and froze. There was a tiny seepage of blood showing on Joaquín's shirt. He saw her glance.

"I broke it open a little when I crawled in," he said. "Don't worry." His eyes were smiling. "He was a good doctor, even if he didn't want to do it. Nothing would get this bandage off but cutting it with a knife."

She looked at him, her eyes wide and troubled. "Joaquín, will you have a scar on your side?"

"A scar?"

"I don't want it to leave a scar," she said.

He lay back limply on the ground, and it was a moment before she realized he was laughing. "You mustn't make me laugh," he said. "It hurts." But the laughter lingered in his voice. "No, of all things, I must not have a scar on my side."

The baby crawled from Joaquín to her, and she picked him up and bared her breast. "Stop laughing, Joaquín, you'll make it bleed more." Despite herself, a smile tugged at her mouth. "Please reach down and roll up your shirt until it dries. And lie still."

He did as she asked, getting the shirt off the bandage. Better not to let blood get on the shirt where it could be seen by anyone they encountered. There was no point in raising questions. She would not dare use their small supply of drinking water for washing. It would have to wait until they came upon a stream.

She drowsed off several times while Mario nursed, regretting this intensely because she loved to watch him nurse. In watching him grow and change daily—sometimes it seemed almost hourly—she never failed to wonder how a woman could deliberately prevent such a miracle. It was simply beyond her. She smiled to herself. Staying awake was beyond her, too. It had been a long night and a long morning and she was exhausted.

A little later she was aware that Mario had finished and that Joaquín had taken him from her. Then with a grateful sigh, she sank slowly into sleep. When she awoke she was crying, lost in a foggy dark dream in which she searched wildly for Miguel and could not find him because of the darkness.

"Miguel!" she cried aloud, starting up into wakefulness. "Miguel!" She looked with dazed, frantic eyes around the leafy shelter in which they rested, straining to see. For a moment she did not realize where she was. Then yesterday's horror engulfed her. The grief that had not come when she had looked at her brother's dead body came now, rushing over her. The tears she could not shed yesterday now flowed. She sat hunched over, swaying from side to side, weeping for her dead, and it brought no comfort.

As she became accustomed to the semidark she realized vaguely that night had come, and that the only light they had was the dim moonlight, which filtered through the interlacing branches and leaves. Joaquín let her cry, patiently holding the now restless baby who was hungry again, and who sensed the wild grief that surrounded him. Uneasy and frightened, he struggled incessantly in his father's hands, doing his infant best to move toward his mother. Gradually, she became aware of her husband and son again and began trying to stem her tears. Eventually she succeeded.

"I'm sorry, Joaquín," she said dully, reaching for the baby.

"You need not be sorry," Joaquín said, handing her the baby. Mario grasped with a small grunt of victory and clung to her, pressing his small body close. "You owe this grief to your brother."

While she fed Mario again Joaquín crawled out of the shelter and was gone for a time. When he returned he had a canteen of water and some of the corncakes she had put into the bundle. They sat quietly eating and Mario, satisfied now, alternately drowsed and batted at some low hanging leaves above his head, trying to catch them.

With the cessation of her weeping the night sounds came to her, the whisper of occasional warm breezes stirring the leaves, the scittering sound of small night creatures, the far off barking of a coyote or wild dog. There was something oddly comforting about the sheltering night, the warmth of Mario's little body, the calm presence of her husband, obscured by the shadows. By-and-by she would ask him where they were going.

"Did I sleep a long time?"

"Yes. It is well into the night. Are you rested now?"

"Yes." She groped across the earth and found his hand, entwining her fingers with his, clinging to his strength.

"When will we be leaving here?" she asked after a time.

"Soon. Before dawn. Then I thought we would walk until the sun gets high again. There is another place some miles along that should have shelters."

"Where are we going?"

"I want to get to the caves. We can stay there for a while until this heals up and I can take off the bandages. I can leave you and Mario there and go down to the nearest settlement and learn anything I can about the trouble back at the village. I need to know if the Americans are going to do anything about it."

"We left the way they told us to. What else would they do?"

Joaquín shrugged. "I don't know. But it will be best to find out before we try to find some place to stay, to live."

The baby drowsed off again and she changed her position, still holding to Joaquín's hand, thinking sorrowfully of Alonso's pitiful attempt to create a village and what it had come to.

"Aren't the caves too near Leon's village?" she asked, uneasiness creeping into her voice.

"No. You remember how far it was when we left there to go to the village the first time."

"But after we get to the caves, what will we do? You aren't thinking—" She sat up suddenly. "You aren't thinking of going back to the village secretly and asking the grandfather to keep Mario, are you?"

His hand tightened on hers for a moment. "Not unless that was the only thing I could do. Making you agree to that would not be easy." Laughter ran through his voice. "You refused to give Mario up before he was born. It would be hard to make you do it now."

"I would never do it." She withdrew her hand.

Joaquín did not reply to this. She knew that he sat up, and was feeling the bandage carefully.

"Is everything all right?" she asked.

"Yes. He was a good doctor." He was moving about quietly.

268

"What are you doing?"

"Putting my shirt back on. We have to go soon."

"Is the blood still seeping?"

"No. Everything is dry and firm." In a moment, she knew he was reaching for the canteen to take another drink of water, which surprised her as they knew without discussing it that they must use the water sparingly.

"Are you thirsty?"

"No. I just wanted to swallow a little. My throat is sore. It is nothing."

She put the idea aside, refusing to consider it. Joaquín's strength was limitless.

"Joaquín, I am uneasy about going back to the caves. What if Leon and the others are there?"

"They won't be." He screwed the top back on the old canteen. "They may have to give up the raiding. It gets more dangerous. It is in Leon's mind that there must be four men together. He won't go with less than four. I am gone. Trinidad says that Pablo's family wants him to give it up. His heart is divided about it now. I don't think Leon and Trini would go alone. And, of course, the grandfather is always telling Leon to give it up."

"Does Leon ever do what the grandfather asks?" Majella asked, her voice somewhat acid.

"Sometimes he does. When we get to the caves, I would know by the signs below if anyone had gone up. If anyone had we would go somewhere else. There might be other places near there where we could go."

She tried to be reassured and put aside this worry too, but when it was time to move on, she left the shelter reluctantly. So they resumed the long wandering journey that would take them to the caves, the area she did not want to go back to. She told herself firmly that it was only because of her early hideous memories of it, and trudged along as Joaquín led.

Their progress seemed incredibly slow and beset with delays. The route was winding and round-about, as Joaquín tried to avoid settled areas. Joaquín's sore throat did not go away, but became worse. Within a few days he was coughing deep, retching, tearing coughs, which were exhausting but gave him no relief. Her concern about this was tinged with fear. He must not falter. He was their strength. Both she and Mario depended upon him. He must not become sick. Then she realized with shame that her fear was in turn tinged with anger that he had let himself become sick when they needed him so. He could not help it, she told herself with remorse; he had lost so much blood from the wound that his resistance was low. He had no reserve strength, then, to combat illness when it struck.

"Isn't there some herb, some plant, growing wild that will help that cough?" she asked when they stopped earlier than they would have because he had become increasingly exhausted. He knew a great deal about the Indian medicines. Why hadn't he found something that would help?

"I have been looking," he said, lowering himself to the ground and leaning against a crooked tree trunk. They had found a scrubby patch of trees in a gully. "There is water near here. I will go and find it. After a little while." He closed his eyes, his hands caressing the now grimy bandage about his body. The wound had bled from time to time from the incessant coughing, and might be hurting him. His face was gaunt.

Majella bit back a sharp comment that he had found the child-killer leaves quickly enough when he wanted to kill his son. No. That wasn't fair, she conceded grudgingly. She was only tired and irritable.

A little later he roused himself and left the gully with the near-empty canteens. He was gone so long that Majella's heart was thudding with apprehension. She spent a hideous two hours thinking of all the things that might have befallen him. When he came back, finally, with the canteens filled, she went weak with relief and sprang up to take them from his hands. When she touched his hands, however, she was shocked. They felt scorching hot. He had a raging fever.

"Lie down, Joaquín. Lie down and rest. I'll get you something to eat." She tried to keep the panic out of her voice.

"I need nothing. I'm not hungry." His voice sounded thick, and he eased himself down as if his bones ached. "I think I will sleep a while."

"I'll wet a cloth and wipe your face," she said, unmindful of using water from the canteens to do it.

"No. Please. The water is too far from here. I should have got closer. There was an easier way I found. Anyhow, I—" He paused, leaning against the tree with his eyes closed, and seemed to forget what he wanted to say.

"You what, Joaquín?" She stood hovering over him, gripping the canteens, sick with worry.

"What? Oh, I washed myself in the stream. It was so fresh and cold."

271

"Joaquín, you shouldn't have!" She bit back anything else. It was no good chiding him now. The damage, if any, had already been done. She hoped he hadn't got the bandage wet.

"It felt so good," he murmured. "Let me sleep a while."

Watching him with growing concern, she fed Mario, drank some water, and ate part of a round disk of cornmeal bread. He slept until nightfall. Then he awoke, ate a few bites of the bread, and drank some water, coughing every time he swallowed. Neither of them could sleep now, but sat under the trees speaking from time to time while Mario slept.

Once he spoke of the water, telling her in a somewhat dreamy voice that the ferns grew in abundance around it. "It is difficult to find the source," he said. "The water falls out of the stones in a hillside among the rocks and it's almost hidden."

"Perhaps we could go there tomorrow and wait there a few days until you are better," Majella suggested. She felt his face from time to time, hoping for an abatement of the fever. It did not lessen, but seemed to increase.

"No, we cannot. We must move on. I have had this same sickness twice before. It will grow worse before it goes away. We must get to the caves while I still have my wits. The fever does strange things to the spirit."

"You mean you might be out of your head?" she said, chilled by sudden wild apprehension.

"Yes. It is possible. You know, while I was at the water I was going to bring you some pretty

272

ferns, but when I got the canteens filled I forgot it."

"It doesn't matter. Thank you anyway." She brooded for a long time on what he had said about being sick. It was terrifying.

"Joaquín," she said after a while, wondering how she should say it, "when it is daylight again you must sketch out a little map for me—on how to get to the caves from here, so I can remember it." She wondered how she could speak so calmly. She knew almost nothing about this land, had little innate sense of direction, and would be traveling over totally unfamiliar terrain. There was no possibility that she could commit to memory a map sketched in the dust with a stick, and follow the memory of it accurately to the right destination. "Will you do that? I must know how to get there if you become too sick to guide us." There was an unformed prayer in her mind that he would refuse, because it wouldn't be necessary.

"All right," he said. "I will do that."

Her heart sank.

The next day she made a desperate effort to engrave the lines on her mind so she would never forget them. She did this also with the landmarks, the names of settlements or towns or roads that would be the milestones. When they started their journey again she silently recited them over and over, and realized at some point that the incessant repetition was not unlike telling her beads. Beneath the litany of directions was a constant underlying prayer that she would never need to use them, that Joaquín would not lose touch with reality because of the fever until they were safe in the caves. She touched him every chance she got, always wishing fervently that his fever would abate.

She lost count of the days and nights of walking. Twice they stopped at an Indian village. Each time they were given a welcome, and some food to replenish the diminishing supply in the bundle. People in each village knew of the massacre in their home village, so they were not offered permanent sanctuary and knew that the villagers were relieved when they continued their journey. During the last two days of the journey, Joaquín's mind was drifting in and out of reality from the fever. Majella would have stopped somewhere to rest and wait for the fever to break, but Joaquín remained obsessed even in his fever to reach the caves. She did not know he was losing touch with reality, until one day when she seemed to lose her own understanding of what he was saying. Then she realized—with sudden chilling of her spine—that he was talking to Leon. She realized at that same moment that they were going in the wrong direction, veering off the route they should have been taking. She stopped.

"Let us rest a moment," she said.

"Now? Rest?" he said vaguely. "We cannot rest here. There is no shelter. It is too open." It was. They had been crossing for some time a wide expanse of sandy waste, broken only by a few embedded rocks and dry, desert plant life. She put down her bundle.

"I must rest," she insisted.

Frowning, he stood there as she sank down onto the warm sandy earth. Surely, she thought, they could not be too far from the caves now. They were in just such sandy soil as this, with just such sparse vegetation and scattering of dull colored stones. Up. They should be going upward now. The caves were high among massive stone formations and cliffs. And for some miles around that area had been the barren downward slopes. She must be right: They had taken a wrong turn because for the last hour they had been walking downward. She looked up at Joaquín, seeing him gaunt and slightly stooping, sweat running off his face and neck. His mouth was slightly open in an effort to make it easier to breathe. She groped for one of the tepid canteens. His throat must be parched.

"Drink a little water," she said, wondering how to tell him they had lost their way. She must do it—somehow—in a way that would not belittle him. Spare him that.

With a terrible slowness he drank a few sips of water from the canteen and handed it back to her. She wondered how he could remain on his feet.

"This is not the right way," he said finally, looking around. And she was filled with relief. His mind, wherever it had been, had drifted back into clarity.

"Which way, then?" She got up as quickly as she could. He did not notice any strangeness at her sudden resurgence of energy. She picked up the bundle and they started walking in the upward direction. The land stretched out endlessly before them. There was no way they could avoid sleeping in an open, unsheltered place this night. When the sun became high they stopped. There were more rocks now. Majella had found a boulder larger than the surrounding stones and used a blanket to make a lean-to tent. They stayed under this makeshift shelter during the worst heat of the day. It was sweltering, but less dangerous than long exposure to the direct sun. She divided her time between Joaquín and Mario. Joaquín lay on his back, his eyes closed, rarely speaking. She could hear the rattle of his labored breathing. The baby, hot and miserable, itching and chafed, finally stopped crying in exhaustion and lay limply, staring vacantly through half-closed eyes. Now and then she put a few dribbles of water in her palm and stroked his hot, throbbing little face. Then she would turn and pour a little of the precious water between Joaquín's parted lips. He never failed to murmur his thanks.

Nightfall was heaven. Temperature in the desertlike region dropped quickly.

"Could you walk a while when it is cool like this?" Joaquín asked, perfectly lucid again.

"Yes," she said eagerly, sick with dread at the idea of moving her exhausted body. Nevertheless she got up, clutching at the still-warm rock to brace herself.

By dawn she recognized where they were. The sun rose flaming red over the towering cliffs ahead. She felt a surge of strength. The cliffs! Just ahead! They were almost safe. In just a little while, in just a few minutes, they would be inside the dim, cool caves.

But she had not counted on how deceiving distance was in the area and it was the following day, after toiling upward for hours, that they came upon the small group of pale-trunked trees, and the stream, and the pool.

The pool.

For the second time in her life, Majella momentarily lost her sanity at the sight of this pool. Leaving Joaquín, leaving Mario, she staggered toward it and fell upon her knees beside it, drinking from it, dashing water into her face, drenching herself. Then, dripping with the water, she guiltily got up and rushed toward Mario. The baby, overjoyed at the sight of water, had gotten up from where she had placed him and was staggering in a zigzag path toward the edge.

Walking! Mario had started to walk! She laughed sharply, suddenly, her heart pierced with a moment of total joy. Then Mario, suddenly frightened at what he was doing, collapsed onto the sand and started crawling again. At the edge of the water, he plunged in with a small shout of surprised delight at the sharp chill of the rushing stream. She rescued him and, clutching him close, turned to Joaquín.

"Joaquín, he's walking! Did you see?"

But Joaquín stared at her blankly, lost again in the hot, misty dream of his fever.

Majella tethered the baby in a shallow puddle and took Joaquín's hand. At her bidding he sat down at the edge of the pool, and she spent some time bathing his scorching hot skin. Again and again, she dipped a cloth into the pool and pressed the water out of it. Over his head. On his shoulders. On his torso, drenching the dirty encrusted bandage. Surely the wound beneath it had closed and healed by now. She finally stopped when her arms were totally numb. Surely she had lowered his fever now. Surely he must feel better.

She rested then, sitting beside Joaquín in the

dappled sun and shade of the long afternoon. She only moved once—to get Mario when he became drowsy in his puddle of water, and he did not object when she moved him. Holding the baby loosely, leaning against Joaquín, she drifted in and out of sleep.

At dusk she roused herself reluctantly. They must go on up to the caves before dark. She found by wasted and fatigue-slowed motions, and much fumbling and dropping of things, that she could manage to take the baby and to help Joaquín stay erect and walk. She placed their diminished bundle in an outcropping of rock and laced Mario into his cradle. The baby, sleeping in exhaustion now, did not resist too much. Shrugging the cradle onto her back, she put her arm around Joaquín. Together they started up the long, twisting incline that would eventually bring them to the caves.

How strange it all was, she thought, bemused. Once in her life her greatest desire had been to escape from those very caves. Now, for many days, her one overwhelming need had been to find them again.

It was a long, slow climb. She remembered without emotion the first time she had climbed it, struggling along behind Leon, her then-smooth hands gripping the handle of the heavy water bucket. Tomorrow she would bring that bucket down again to fill it.

Slowly, step by slow step, they reached the small vacant clearing in front of the main cave opening. It was almost dark. Think about the little things, she told herself. One thing at a time. Her eyes were almost shut. It was time to let go of Joaquín's left hand. She had found that the best way to keep him from stumbling and falling was to encircle his waist with her right arm and hold tightly. His left arm she kept around her shoulders, beneath the cradle top. This pulled the straps too tight for comfort, but it could not be helped. It let her grasp his left hand firmly with hers and helped to hold him steady. What now? She must let go of his hand for a moment and wipe the sweat from her eyes again. She did this, lifting her head slightly and widening her eyes in relief from the salty sweat. She looked at the blessed caves.

As her vision cleared she saw him. The figure of the man. With the red glow of firelight behind him, outlining his body.

"Leon!"

Slowly, he started walking toward them. She could not see his face clearly, as the light was behind him. But she heard his voice, low and sullen.

"I knew you would do it. I knew you would kill him. Here, give him to me."

Chapter Sixteen

Stiffly, she let Leon ease Joaquín away from her, and stood there, trying not to sway, as she watched Joaquín collapse into Leon's arms. Leon lifted him up clear of the ground and stood before her, holding Joaquín like a child. Mario, in his cradle on her back, voiced a sudden resentful cry. He was too big now for his cradle, and had struggled in it, now and then, on the toiling upward journey.

"Come inside," Leon said grudgingly. He turned to the caves, carrying Joaquín. She followed, slowly taking the cradle off her back.

Only Leon and Trinidad were there. Pablo apparently had not come with them, or had gone out on an errand. Trinidad nodded soberly to her as she came in. Seeing Mario writhing inside the cradle, Trinidad reached for him with a question in his eyes. Without a word, she handed the baby to him and followed Leon as he carried Joaquín into the backmost cave. She paused at the entrance of it.

"Bring the lantern, Trini," Leon ordered. She felt Trinidad behind her, still holding the baby, while the lantern played its pale flickering light over the stone room in which had occurred the events destined to change her life forever.

"I left our things down by the pool," Majella said.

Leon grunted in reply, carefully putting Joaquín down on the floor of the cave. Joaquín, whose mind was wandering again, stretched out his weakened body on the cool, dusty floor. He made a sound, something between a sigh and a sob, and appeared to drift into sleep. Leon went back into the front cave and returned with a blanket. Majella stood numbly by, watching as he spread it out neatly on the floor and then moved Joaquín onto it. Joaquín did not even wake up. He murmured something but they could not tell what it was.

"Joaquín is not dying, you know," Majella said firmly and clearly. "He is very strong. Now that he can rest a while he will be all right. It has been a long journey."

Both men looked at her, Trinidad with compassion and Leon with anger. "How long has he been like this?" Leon asked.

"I don't know. Several days. He—says he is getting better." She desperately wanted to lie down, to sink into sleep and never wake up. Dully she watched Trinidad, squatting down on the floor, unlacing Mario. He did not look at either of them, but concentrated on the baby. Majella knew that Trinidad's woman had been pregnant several

281

times, and each time had induced a miscarriage.

"He started to walk today," Majella said. "Down by the pool earlier. He took his first steps."

Trinidad had him out of the cradle now and Mario stretched and twisted, giving an exultant little shout of triumph. A smile split Trinidad's broad face.

Leon got up, walked over to where Trinidad was, and stood looking down at Mario. She could not tell from his face how he felt looking at this baby who should not exist, whose birth he had resented. Then he squatted down in front of Trinidad and held out his arms. Mario, always fascinated with new faces, was torn a moment between the two of them. Then, making up his mind, he staggered and plunged toward Leon. Leon caught him as he fell forward. Still without expression, Leon turned him around and gave a gentle push, sending him back to Trinidad. He stood up.

"What happened in your village, Majella?"

She had known it had to come. She tried to straighten up. She would not appear cowering before him. "The people in the town said we had to leave. My uncle had no claim on the land. They were just staying there."

"How did Joaquín become hurt? His body is bandaged."

"He was shot. It is not a bad wound. The American doctor treated it." Oh, God, if she could only lie down. Her legs quivered.

"Why was he shot? There was trouble in the village?"

"Yes."

"Your people again?"

"Yes. Most of the villagers were killed. My

brother was killed. Why don't you talk to Joaquín about it when he wakes? You can tell him again what a fool he was."

Leon looked at her for a moment. "I'll walk down and get your things," he said finally. "Sleep a while if you want to. We won't eat until later. We just got here a little while ago."

It took Majella a moment to realize that she was free to rest now. As he left she glanced about the cave in which she had committed her life to Joaquín's. What now? Was there anything else to do? Was everything taken care of? Joaquín was sleeping. Trinidad was taking care of Mario. Slowly, with her bones aching, she lay down beside Joaquín on the blanket. She wanted to reach over and feel his skin again because of the fever, but she could not summon the strength. She closed her eyes and plunged into sleep.

She awoke, a long time later, from a place next to the wall in the front cave. She was curled on her side, her head resting on her arm, which prickled with numbness. Gingerly, she moved and began stroking the arm until the prickling sensation ceased. She was profoundly reluctant to rouse herself. Mario was playing near her on the floor and Trinidad was busy over the firehole. There was no meat, but she smelled corn roasting and she lazily watched small puffs of steam, wondering if they had some potatoes underneath. Hunger, sharp and excruciating, attacked her and saliva started in her mouth. She sat up, twisting, trying to move the stiffness from her shoulders.

Trinidad looked up from what he was doing and smiled his homely smile.

"How is Joaquín?" she asked.

"The fever went away for a while and then came back. Leon is watching over him."

She struggled up. "Can I help you?"

"It is finished. We have only to wait a little while. Does he still drink your milk?" He indicated Mario. "You were asleep so I gave him a piece of cornmeal bread to chew on."

"Yes, he still takes my milk, but he eats almost everything else now, too. I have to mash it up for him." She walked over to the firehole and stood looking down at Trinidad. Somehow or other, during the passage of time, Trinidad had changed from her enemy to her friend. It was a good feeling. Life seemed to be a series of changes. She wanted to reach over and touch him, as she might have touched one of her brothers, but she did not.

"How did I get in here?"

"I brought you in." His tone sounded faintly apologetic. "Leon wanted you moved from beside Joaquín because he was trying to bathe his face and we couldn't wake you up. So I put you over by the other wall." He reached over and with a stick he turned over the husk-wrapped ears of corn. "Then later I moved you in here because I wanted to watch the baby and he kept crawling back to where you were."

"Thank you, Trinidad." She sat down beside the firehole. "We thought the caves would be empty. Joaquín wanted us to wait here until he could decide where to go. I was surprised to find you and Leon here. Didn't Pablo come?"

"No. A kinsman got him work from some Americans. It is better that way."

"Were you and Leon going to try to raid by yourselves?"

Trinidad shrugged, somberly watching Mario crawling over to them. "There was no one else that Leon trusted to go with us."

"Have you gone on any since Joaquín left?"

"No. But Leon thought we must do something. We have no money left."

"And you will try it now—just the two of you?"

He shrugged again. "I don't know. It is for Leon to say. He has not said."

Leon came through the front cave, a wet cloth in his hands. He walked through silently. He had a slow and graceful walk. He was like a very strong animal that rarely moved rapidly because its strength was so great that it knew it could move with instant power and speed when the need arose. He went outside and draped the wet rag over a tough, branch-laden cluster of dry weeds. Then he came back and squatted down near the fire-hole.

"Thank you for taking care of Joaquín, Leon," Majella said courteously. "How is he now?"

"About the same. He burns up or he freezes. His body has done this before, when he was younger. He does not escape it now as quickly as he did." He half-turned to watch Mario. The baby reached them and stood up. He caught hold of Leon's muscular shoulder for balance and stood there, clinging and swaying. He reached up and clutched the sagging brim of Leon's old felt hat. Silently, Leon took it off and handed it to him. Pleased, Mario embraced it, crushing it to his chest, and stood there clinging with the other hand to Leon, balancing himself precariously on his sturdy, but unstable legs.

"Leon?" Majella asked. "Will you let us stay

here until Joaquín is well again?" It was Joaquín's place to ask that, but since he was unable, she had to.

With his somber gaze on the baby, Leon answered her after a moment. "Until he gets well or dies, yes."

"Thank you," she answered.

She commenced another interval of life in the caves, spending her time nursing Joaquín and doing the women's work. She included these chores willingly, because either Leon or Trinidad could be counted upon to watch over Joaquín while she was busy thus, and Trinidad seemed quite pleased to take almost sole charge of Mario.

Joaquín, ravaged by sickness, raged with fever or shuddered with chills. She took off the coverings and bathed him with cool, wet cloths, or she piled the covers back on and tried to keep him warm. Slowly, carefully, she got some food into him whenever possible. She performed with love and dedication all the unlovely tasks of nursing the helplessly sick. With her heart aching she watched his fine body waste and diminish, leaving him gaunt and haggard. She watched as he struggled with all his will against the disease, fighting to hold on, one more day, one more night. In his lucid periods he held her hand and spoke to her in a croaking whisper.

Leon left by himself for three days and came back with some medicine.

"What is it? Where did you get it?" she asked, examining the bottle of dark fluid.

"I went into town. I got it from the store. It is for the coughing. It says on the side how much to give him. Joaquín said before that you can read."

"Not in English," she said, shaking her head. It was American medicine, and she was mistrustful of anything American. They both waited beside Joaquín until he woke up, and found that he could read enough English to understand it. They started giving him the medicine, carefully following the dosage stated. It seemed to help. It did give him long intervals of sleep undisturbed by wrenching spasms of coughing.

Mario loved his new life in the caves. His private world was full. He had a small empire of possessions: Gourds, large twigs, rocks too big to put in his mouth. He played for long intervals, amusing himself with great absorption. He appropriated a small broken basket that he sometimes wore on his head in imitation of Leon's hat. Both men treated him with the infinite patience and kindness their people displayed toward very young children. Trinidad played senseless, childish games with him for hours, seeming to enjoy them as much as Mario did. Mario frequently stole Leon's hat, and once he wet on it. Leon just laughed and shook his head.

Majella, hot with embarrassment, stammered an apology. "I'll wash it. Here, please, give it to me. I'm so sorry, Leon. I'm so sorry." She washed it with great care when she did the rest of the clothing in the pool, and dried it carefully in the sun, fitting it over a stone to give it back some shape.

Finally, Joaquín seemed to win against his sickness and started a slow, faltering recovery, a shadow of his former self. When he could speak without the interruption of the shattering cough, he and the men spent long hours in intermittent conversation. He talked to them of Alonso's village and all that had happened there. Alonso and his small group had not arrived at Leon's village by the time Leon and Trinidad had left for the caves, so no one knew what had happened to them. Joaquín regretted this, but briefly. With the fatalistic attitude of his people, he seemed to accept that either they would survive or they would not, and there was nothing to be done about it.

His progress was slow. He remained physically weak. Leon had to help him to walk outside in the sun because if he tried it alone his legs would collapse beneath him. His awkwardness the first time had unbalanced both of them and they went down on the floor together, laughing helplessly. Majella agreed with Leon that he should be out in the sun some part of each day, and it did seem to help. Even in the sun, though, he sometimes shivered and pulled the blanket about his shoulders. Majella grieved about this. She grieved for her brother, too, but never let herself cry in front of Joaquín. A man who chose to laugh at his own misfortune instead of weeping did not deserve to have someone else's sorrow thrust upon him. Her grief came and went, as grief does, like the wind. She would not think of Miguel for two or three days and then, suddenly, her memories would engulf her and the grief would sweep through her. She held this rigidly inside her until she could get away from the caves and down to the pool, to do her weeping there for what release it offered. Since she always bathed herself in the pool she knew the men expected her to be gone some time. So each time, she waited long enough so that her eyes would not be red and swollen when she returned.

Once Leon appeared while she was crying miserably, sick with longing for her dead brother. Amid her sobs she was struggling to put her clothing back on her still damp body. Then suddenly there was Leon, returning from an errand. She crossed her arms over her breasts and turned away from him, tugging her bodice together, pushing at the stubborn buttons.

"Why are you weeping, woman?" he asked, seeming disinterested in her half-dressed state.

"For my brother Miguel. He—was very dear to me." Her voice still held tears and she strove to keep it steady.

"You should have stayed with your own people. Your brother would not be dead if you had." His tone was unemotional, even though his words were merciless.

She whirled to face him, her eyes gleaming with anger through the tears. "And lose Joaquín? My baby? Never. I would not!"

He shrugged, squatting down beside the pool. "Then you shouldn't cry over your bargain." She refused to answer him. "I want to talk to you about Joaquín and Mario," he said then, and she turned back to face him, suddenly wary.

"You should talk to Joaquín," she said coldly. "I did."

"Then you have the answer to whatever question you asked. I will do what Joaquín says."

"He asks me to take him back into our village. I told him I would do it until he is well. After that—" He shrugged again. "But I want to ask you now—do you think your people will come to the village again?"

She stared at him. He was offering them a reprieve, and he did have a right to ask this.

"When they took away your brother's body, did they say they would come again to find you?"

She groped back to the hideous images of Alonso's village being massacred. She could not lie to him about it. She had the feeling he would know if she tried.

"I don't remember it too clearly," she said hopelessly. "I don't think so. There was—so much confusion. But it seemed to me that they would go that time—and forget about me. I had the feeling that I was—lost to them, that they were giving up. But I can't say that for sure, because I really don't know what they will do."

"At least you don't lie," Leon grunted. Then after a while he said, "What is the custom of your people? What did they do when they took your brother's body? Burn it? Bury it?"

"They—" Her throat ached with held-back tears. She would not cry in front of this man. "The custom is a burial service—ceremony. He will be—was buried."

"And that is the end of it? No ceremonies later?"

"That is the end of it, except for each person's private feelings. No other ceremonies." The end of Miguel, steady and good and at last so mistaken— and he had paid for it so dearly.

"Grief dies," Leon said. He was rubbing some leaves between his blunt fingers, slowly breaking them, crumbling them. "After the grief has gone away, would they try to come for you? Make you change your mind again? You have another brother."

"I don't know, Leon."

"Would you want to go back to them?" He held up his hand. "Think before you answer."

"I don't need to think. How could I go back? They have rejected Joaquín and my child."

He looked at her thoughtfully. "I mean alone. Just you."

She felt a welling up of exasperated anger. He never gave up! "No!" She glared at him.

A near-smile twitched his heavy mouth. He shook his head.

"Well, we will go back to the village for a while, until Joaquín is well again."

"When will we go?" She had a quick surge of eagerness—to see the grandfather again, to find out if Alonso and his group had found the village and had been taken in. And she held the firm conviction that Joaquín would mend faster if he could be back in his home place for a while.

"Soon. Trinidad and I will go out tomorrow. We have to get some money. Then we will go back."

Apprehension touched at the edge of her mind. "With only the two of you?"

"Well, Joaquín can't come—it has to be just the two of us."

"Isn't that dangerous?"

He stood up, not bothering to answer that.

She caught at his arm as he started up the slope. "We have a little money left," she offered. "Why don't you and Trinidad use that and—"

"Joaquín has already offered that. I said he should keep the money. We'll be back in a few days." He was walking away again. She hurried along behind him. Regardless of their mutual enmity, she had a profound confidence in this man's unfailing strength. She did not want him hurt, or worse yet, dead. "Leon, wait, please—"

He paused and turned to look at her. His gaze, insolent as always, swept over her with an unmistakable flicker of desire in their obsidion depths. She felt color flooding into her face. Her love for Joaquín was so complete that it had excluded any thought of other men. Now there came thudding into her mind the memory of her first meeting with this man. He had picked her up from a pile of saddles and ripped her clothing. He had wanted her then. He wanted her now.

"What?" he asked.

"I—I—forgot—" she said in confusion. "I mean—nothing. If you have to go, then you have to go. We'll just wait in the caves until you get back."

But he understood the reason for her sudden embarrassment and gave a slow smile. "Do not worry. I wouldn't touch Joaquín's woman." He regarded her silently for a long moment. "You still stand very straight," he commented, sounding somewhat pleased. "You aren't bent over yet from the hard work. I didn't think you could last." Then he turned and started walking slowly up the slope.

Leon and Trinidad were gone five days. When they came back they had some money, but no goods and no one's personal possessions. She did not ask where they had been, nor did she want to. She was only glad that there would be no interminable waiting period in the caves while they disposed of stolen property. She was filled with restlessness to get back to the village.

They had intended to start at dawn the next day, but Mario caused considerable delay. He rebelled with vigor and rage against being laced back into the cradle again. He had not been in it since they had arrived at the caves. Joaquín was still too weak to help, and laughed helplessly at her struggles with the angry baby.

"Well, don't put him in the cradle if he feels like that," he said placatingly.

"I have to!" she snapped. "He's too active for me to hold while I ride. And he is certainly too little to ride a horse by himself!" Grimly, she grasped at Mario as he got away from her again, and dragged him back.

Leon reached over and plucked him up, along with the cradle, starting to do what Majella had not been able to. Little Mario, utterly enraged at this, started flailing at Leon with his small fists. At the idea of the baby trying to fight him, Leon started to laugh and couldn't stop. Mario escaped and fled in a half-crawl to Trinidad, who seemed his only friend at the moment. The men finally decided that Mario should have his way, and that he would ride alternately with Leon or Trinidad.

"Don't ask me to carry him," Joaquín said good humoredly. "I'll be lucky if I can stay on the horse at all." He managed to struggle to a standing position and stood there, leaning against the wall and shaking with weakness.

Majella forgot her annoyance at Mario and turned her gaze, suddenly worried, to Joaquín—

293

thin, gaunt, haggard, his face heavily lined. *Please, God, take care of my husband. Take care of your son Joaquín.*

As they finally started the ride to the village, Mario forgot his anger through his exuberant joy in the ride. Once again his world was a fascinating place. He loved being held in Leon's arms. He loved the motion of the horse. He loved the flying mane.

Once again, they rode as far as the Mexican's house where they must leave the horses and walk the rest of the way into the village. It had been decided before that as Joaquín could not be expected to walk these miles, Leon and Trinidad would take turns carrying him on their backs. Mario, now pleasantly exhausted, was willing to be quietly carried by Majella.

They were all tired when they reached the village. Darkness was just falling and there was the smell of smoke and cooking. The clearing around the well was deserted, all villagers being in their houses. Slowly, they went through the entrance of the grandfather's house.

"Come! Come!" The old man said, scurrying around eagerly, making them all welcome, giving everybody directions. "Joaquín! My son. My son. All right, put him here. I made up his place days ago. Days ago. What has kept you? As soon as Alonso Phail and his people came to the village I started preparing!"

Relief flooded Majella. Alonso and Benicia had arrived safely! Their own return had not gone unnoticed and people began welcoming them back. Alonso, Benicia, and several people from that village, plus old friends of Joaquín's for this village.

They crowded into the grandfather's house, talking, questioning, laughing. In the confusion Majella gathered bits and pieces of information. She watched her baby being received with joy and knew that no matter what happened to Joaquín and herself, Mario had a firm place in the village.

Joaquín, usually open and friendly among his own people, remained almost totally silent as she made him comfortable on the bed spread out for him near the wall. She explained to the grandfather that the gunshot wound had healed without difficulty, but that he had fallen sick. The grandfather talked, mostly to her, and she realized that Joaquín did not speak because he could not, so deep was his emotion at being back in his home place. She watched his hand, bony now, grope its faltering way over the earthen floor, almost caressing it. His great eyes gleamed with tears. She had to touch him. *She had to*. She sat down beside him and reached out her hand. Divining her unspoken wish, he took her hand in his and they sat together, holding on to one another as the homecoming conversation eddied and swirled about them.

Food was prepared, and several of the people had brought food from their own houses. It was passed around so that all might eat. Eventually, the others began to leave until all were gone except Alonso and Benicia. Majella felt exhausted, but peaceably so, leaning against the wall, clasping Joaquín's hand. Her eyelids drooped from time to time, and a half-smile of contentment curved her lips.

Home. Home again.

Chapter Seventeen

Perhaps the journey from the caves to the village had been too exhausting for Joaquín. Now that he was for the moment safe in his home place, he seemed to lapse into a kind of half-world, drifting in and out of sleep, unable to make even the smallest effort in his own behalf.

People came to see him, old friends from his early years in the village. When he was awake, they talked with him. When he drowsed off in the middle of the visit, they waited patiently until he awakened again. No one, especially the grandfather, seemed concerned at the persistent weakness, the raspy breathing. Their manner seemed to say that Joaquín was tired, but when he was rested he would be up among them again. In the meantime, one did not trouble him to move if he did not wish to. It was a deep kindliness, and Majella was grateful to them.

She was able to spend most of her time caring

for him, as little Mario, surrounded with new friends, required little from her now. He stopped nursing entirely and her milk dried up. She regretted this briefly—that he was growing up, that he would soon pass through his babyhood and become a little boy.

She found time now and then to visit with Benicia. She and Alonso and the orphan boy as yet had no house. As most of the others from Alonso's village, they were camping out in an open space near the village. Majella knew that this distressed Benicia, although the older woman did not complain. She was accustomed to her own house, and missed it. Majella knew how often she undid her bundle of possessions and rearranged the contents before tying them all up again. Majella also observed how careful she was to keep it well sheltered. It was not the time of year for rain, but rain would eventually come, and Benicia lived in dread that it would come some night and that her two picture postcards might be damaged.

The grandfather had told Majella that her kinspeople could stay in his house, with their belongings, if their house wasn't built when the rains came. Majella made the offer to her uncle and it was accepted with gratitude, but in the meantime, they lived outside. Alonso and some of his friends had explored the area and found some building materials—some sheets of rusted corrugated metal, a torn tarpaulin that had been discarded or lost by someone, and a few other things. The also had acquired from a store in town some lumber from dismantled shipping crates. The storekeeper had sold these for a few coins, promising more later. They had already withdrawn the nails and straightened them for use in the building. They knew they must start soon because in this area, when the rains came they could be sudden, fierce, and drenching.

Benicia's goat had made the journey well and was thriving in the new location. Benicia, whose belief in goat's milk was absolute, insisted that Majella give some to Joaquín to help him regain his strength. Majella persuaded him to taste it. Joaquín was not fond even of the far blander cow's milk, on the rare occasions when he had tasted it, and the strong taste of the goat's milk nauseated him. He gagged and almost vomited. This brought on a frenzy of coughing which frightened everyone, as his coughing spells had nearly subsided.

Majella, not wanting to waste the milk that Benicia had given her, poured some in a gourd and gave it to Mario. He, like his father, disliked it instantly and simply hurled the gourd across the house and returned to what he had been doing. This reduced Joaquín and all the other men to helpless laughter, which made Joaquín cough again. Angrily, Majella cleared up the mess and took the rest of the milk back to Benicia with their thanks. They had long ago used up all the medicine in the bottle. Seated beside Benicia, she watched Leon helping Joaquín to come outside again so he could sit in the sunlight. She listened absently as Benicia told her again how much lumber they had in the stack, and watched Joaquín across the clearing. He was seated cross-legged, leaning against the house. His face was upturned to the sun and his eyes were closed. The healing sunlight gleamed on his gaunt countenance. Majella slowly shut out the sound of Benicia's voice and brooded upon her beautiful husband, so ravaged by this lingering weakness. He was better. Her common sense told her that. All the sleep, all the food. All the quiet safety and security of the village. These were the things that were—*Oh, dear God, how slowly*—healing him. She felt Benicia's large hand touch her gently, and turned her somber gaze to the older woman.

"He gets well, Majella," Benicia said kindly, "but it takes time, it goes slowly. Be patient, my child. Be grateful for what you have."

Majella smiled. She should try. She had her husband. She had her child. They were alive. Her terrible fatigue from the long journey was over. She felt well and active. And they had sanctuary here until Joaquín was completely well.

She wondered again, as she often did, if Leon would relent and let them stay on after Joaquín was well. Surely, as time went on, and their being here proved to be no danger to the village—surely he would let them. That was really what Joaquín wanted. And what Joaquín wanted, she wanted. Covertly she looked at Leon, squatting down near Joaquín, now and then saying something, or listening to some comment of Joaquín's. Sometimes they smiled. And Mario—God bless her unruly little child—seemed to have won his way into all their hearts. It would be odd if Mario, the child none of them had wanted, became the reason they might be allowed to stay.

Tonight, when everyone else was sleeping, she would pray again to Mary. *This is Joaquín's home, Mary. Please, help us to stay.* She would do this on her knees before the crucifix. She and the grandfather had put it back on the wall of his house where it had been so many years, but he made it clear that when she and Joaquín went away she must take it with her.

That night, after she had prayed, she lay long beside Joaquín, her mind seething in restlessness. She forced herself to lie still so she would not disturb him. Some of this restlessness, she realized, was only the result of her perpetual hunger for Joaquín's love. He had not looked at her with desire since the massacre in Alonso's village. During the long days and nights of the journey to the caves, weakened from loss of blood, and then from his sickness, he had not once reached out for her in the night, being intent only on their survival. If they had had money and a secure place of their own, they could have found a doctor to help him.

No! Better not to think like that! The last time she had tried to better their condition she had brought tragedy down on all their heads. The blood of those dead villagers was, in some terrible way, on her hands. It was a chilling thought. A shaft of moonlight was slanting through the outside opening. Frowning in the darkness, she held up her hands and looked at them broodingly. They appeared pale in the moonlight. Joaquín's hand reached up and captured them, startling her. He had awakened and she had not noticed.

"You fight long battles in the night, my Wood Dove," he murmured softly. "Don't. It is no use. Take what the day gives. Tomorrow will come when it is time."

She turned to face him, moving closer, taking a sharp painful delight in his unexpected caress.

"Joaquín, do you love me still?" she asked, tears in her voice.

"I will love you until I am dead. Do not fret, Majella. My sickness makes me weak. But when my strength returns, so will my manhood. You will plead for mercy." There was a smile in his voice, but she could not see his face.

"Oh, my love," she whispered. "I don't mean to worry you. I try to be a good wife. I try not to be fretful and unruly." She withdrew her hands from his grasp and, raising up on one elbow, stroked his hair back from his forehead.

"Are you making a vow not to be unruly again?" he asked after a moment. Something in his gentle tone stilled Majella's hand and it remained, poised motionlessly, against his thick hair. She knew him too well not to sense the hidden meaning to his question.

"What do you mean, Joaquín?"

"I mean you have been so occupied with what has happened—in Alonso's village, finding the caves, my sickness—that you have thought of little else. Have you counted up recently how many days since you last bled?"

Sudden, terrible knowledge rolled over her and she went rigid at Joaquín's side. He was right. She had not bled for weeks. She was going to have another baby. *No. No. No.* She rejected the idea with terror. Could she—dare she—bring another child into the world to share their precarious existence? Then, almost as soon as this thought formed, she was appalled, revolted by it. She would never kill her unborn child.

"Have you?" Joaquín's soft voice persisted.

"I— haven't, but—"

"It is true, isn't it? There is another child beginning now, isn't there?"

"Yes," she said dully.

A long silence stretched between them. He sensed when she was about to speak and placed his fingers across her lips. "No. Say nothing now. Think of it for another day before you speak of it again."

She welcomed a chance to remain silent for a few more hours. He did not want her to have another child—she knew this, and feeling cowardly she grasped the chance to put off contending with him. Oh, dear God, she didn't want to quarrel with Joaquín, her beloved. Not when he was sick. Suppressing a shiver she pressed herself against him, clung to him, and silently prayed for sleep. It came eventually, shallow and uneasy, so that in the morning she did not feel rested and arose to her work with reluctance, to go about her tasks with leaden hands.

"What troubles you, girl?" the grandfather asked her in the afternoon as she ground meal. She started guiltily, realizing he had been talking to her for a long time and she had not heard a word of it.

"I'm sorry—my mind wanders," she said in quick apology, staring down at the meal.

"It does not matter," the old man said, smiling. "I talk too much. Look. Even the child falls asleep." Mario had crawled up in his lap. He and the grandfather were great friends. The grandfather talked to him a great deal about good and evil and Jesus, the son of Mary. How much little Mario understood it would be impossible to say, but the old man's thoughts had helped to shape Joaquín, so she was quite content to let Mario learn what he could in this manner.

"There is something, Grandfather. You are wise. Perhaps you could help me."

The grandfather chuckled, sounding pleased, and shifted Mario to a slightly different position. Majella smiled gently. It might well be that his thin old legs were becoming numb beneath the weight of the sleeping child. She reached over and lifted him off and held him.

"My husband spoke to me last night. He will want me to do something I don't want to do. What should I do?"

"Does he speak with reason in what he will ask?"

"Oh, yes," she said, bitterness creeping into her voice. "He always speaks with reason."

"Then you must do what he will ask," the grandfather said, sounding faintly regretful. "You should not even question, isn't it so? Or—" he added, looking thoughtfully into the distance, "perhaps you might speak to the Virgin. You sometimes do. She might tell you where your duty lies."

"Yes," Majella said uncertainly. "I think I will do that." She placed Mario gently beside her on the earth and resumed her slow rhythmic motions. "Before Mario was born, Joaquín did not want me to have him. Did you know that?"

"No. But my thoughts tell me it would have been so. It is a question that always arises. You disobeyed him."

"I did." The rhythm became more forceful. The old man didn't comment on this but continued

303

gazing off into the distance. "Grandfather, you love Mario. Do you think I should not have a second child?"

"I think you must in the end obey your husband, Majella. You have not been long in our life. He has. Be guided by his wisdom."

"Listen to the grandfather," Leon said, and she turned quickly in surprise. She had not heard him approach. "He is a wise old man." He squatted down near her, his gaze fixed on her face. The level stare filled her with uneasiness. Her mouth tightened in anger that she hoped he did not see. She must not antagonize him. Too much rested on his good will. She refused to look at him, gazing with pretended absorption down into the bowl. They owed this man a great deal. She tried to hold the thought that he was Joaquín's best friend, almost his brother.

"Are you deciding what to do?" he prodded softly after a moment. "I told that fool Joaquín he would never tame you, and he hasn't."

She refused to respond to this.

"You will end by defying him in this, won't you?"

She pushed the bowl from her and looked him full in the face, her eyes snapping venom. "What would you like to do, Leon? Go get those leaves and force them down my throat?" She could feel heat flaming into her face.

"No," he said slowly, with a slight smile. "Unless Joaquín asked me to," he added, standing up.

She scrambled to her feet. "And you will go inside and talk to him about it now, won't you?" She was breathless with anger.

"No," Leon said. "That is between Joaquín and

his woman. But if he wants to talk to me I will listen. If he asks my advice I will give it. I think he will let you have your way—he is too indulgent with you. But—" he reached out and caught her arm as she turned to walk away, "but if he says you will eat the leaves, *you will do it*." He let her go and she hurried blindly away toward Alonso's camping place, and the comforting presence of Benicia.

But here, too, she met with disappointment. Benicia was dismayed at her news, and listened to the spate of angry words in silence, her unhappiness clearly showing in her wide, plain face. When Majella, breathless, stopped talking, Benicia shook her head dolefully.

"You must obey Joaquín. You have one child. Surely that is enough for any woman. Many women have none."

Majella stared at her, furious, appalled. She had counted on Benicia. "You had more than one child," she said.

"And they are all dead," Benicia replied. "Their lives were hard, full of punishments. I was greedy. Listen to your husband."

Such harsh words from Benicia sobered Majella, but she could not speak again to Joaquín about it that night. Nor the next. She could not meet his eyes, and she knew that he was observing her struggle, waiting, not pressing her.

She became distraught and flew at her tasks in a haphazard manner, hating them, hating the difficulty of their lives, hating the everlasting dirt with which she tried to cope. She seethed with discontent, spoke sharply to the grandfather, was blatantly rude to Leon. She lost her temper with

305

little Mario and shook him until his head bobbed; he wailed sharply in astonished fright. He was totally astounded by receiving such treatment from the loving hands of his mother. When she let him go he plunged after her, catching her legs, clinging there, crying desolately. She was filled with guilt. It was not diminished when Mario followed her about silently for the rest of the day like a chastened puppy.

One heavy and oppressive thought was that she did not really know how far along she was. If she did indeed do as Joaquín clearly wished, she must not wait too long. It was still more oppressive that she could feel the condemnation of the others, like a silent wall surrounding her.

Then young Pablo came to visit the village. He had gotten work in the town through the efforts of his kinsman and he was allowed to visit his village once each month. He worked for a man who owned a restaurant. He washed the dishes and kept the place clean, for which they gave him his food, lodging, and a little money.

Majella had never disliked young Pablo, but she had not especially liked him either. Now she seized upon his visit with almost hysterical excitement. Anything to take her mind off her difficulty.

He was welcomed as all homecoming villagers were. A dozen or more people trooped out to meet him—greeting him, talking to him, laughing with him. He came with gifts, of course. Most of his wages he had hoarded to give to his family, but he had spent a few precious coins on small presents. A large group gathered in the grandfather's house to talk and visit until far into the night. Pablo had many fine stories to tell of the happenings in the town, of his work. His employer had a long grape arbor out behind the restaurant and Pablo had brought some grapes with him, large, sweet, pale-green touched with rose shadows. They talked and listened and laughed and ate the grapes, and eventually, one by one, they began to depart. Majella had welcomed the distraction, busying herself for the guests to the point. of exhaustion, bringing, serving, taking away.

Finally, only Trinidad and Pablo remained. The boy, who had grown and filled out, looked around the circle smiling. "Like our old days," he said, reaching over and placing his hand on Joaquín's a moment. He seemed uneasy now.

Joaquín shook his head slightly. "Time passes." And an odd little silence fell. There was something about the emptiness of it that implied words unsaid and caught Majella's attention. She left what she was doing and came to sink down on the earthen floor nearby and listen. She had the sharp impression that Joaquín was going to say something important.

"Pablo," he said smiling. "I know you well. There is something you have not told us. Is it because I am sick? Don't worry. I have been sick before. I will be well again. Is that it?"

Pablo looked into Joaquín's gaunt face, his eyes clouding over. "Not only because you are sick, Joaquín."

"Then what?"

Leon made a restless movement and Majella had the sudden knowledge that he knew what Pablo was troubled about. "It is nothing," Leon said.

"I must tell Joaquín," Pablo said doggedly, not

able to look at Leon. Joaquín was sitting very straight, his eyes intent on Pablo.

"It is in the posters in town, and the people talk of it, the trouble at the village of Alonso Phail. They talk about the death of the Mexican, Miguel Moreno."

Majella's heart plummeted. "What about my brother's death!" She moved over next to Joaquín.

"They say," Pablo said painfully, "that it was Joaquín Salazar who shot him. There is—they offer a reward. A hundred dollars. The hunters are out looking for you, Joaquín." Pablo reached over and took Joaquín's hand in his. "You understand, Joaquín. I have to tell my family. It is too much danger when you are—are here. I have to tell my family. You understand?"

"I understand," Joaquín said. "You must tell your family."

"Leon said not to. He said it would be all right but—they are my family. I must."

"I understand, Pablo."

"I'm sorry. I will go now. I'm sorry." But he did not move, sitting hunched over, a look of brooding on his young face. "Joaquín, if they kill you I will not be able to stand it."

"Don't worry. We will go away soon. I feel stronger each day. By the time anyone comes here we will be gone."

Where? Majella's mind screamed silently. *Where will we go?*

"You will stay here until you are well," Leon said. "That is decided. If any man *tries* to make you go he will have to kill me first. Pablo. You listen to that. You tell your father that when you tell him there is a price on Joaquín's head."

"But Joaquín didn't do it!" Majella cried suddenly. She rose up on her knees, looking around the circle of men. "He didn't, Pablo! Leon, he didn't! The others were shooting. He made me get down on the ground. He dragged me around the side of our house. He was with me. He was protecting me with his body. That's why he was shot—don't you see?" She looked at first one face and then another, pleading for them to believe her, her face vivid from the light in the firehole. She heard Joaquín sigh, and knew he was reaching out a hand to pull her back.

Leon shook his head. "Majella, it makes no difference. He has been accused. The reward has been offered."

"But it would come out at the trial. I would testify—" Then she stopped. All the men were looking at her with varying degrees of compassion. Even Leon. And she knew with a welling of physical nausea that if they came to take Joaquín away, there would not be any trial. The wanted poster was his death sentence. She sank back, feeling weak. She kept looking from one to the other, her lips slightly parted because she seemed to be having trouble breathing. She crouched down beside her husband, not saying anything else, because she couldn't.

Pablo left shortly, miserable and torn between his regard for Joaquín and his loyalty to his family. Numbly, Majella went to their sleeping place and prepared for the night. There was total silence in the grandfather's house. She had wondered at the custom of Joaquín's and Leon's shared silence. Sometimes it was not necessary for them to speak. This was such a time.

When Joaquín came to bed, she waited until he was beside her and she placed her hands on his chest, caressing him gently. "Joaquín, I am sorry I caused you so much worry." She paused. Then she made herself say the words she had decided she would never say: "I will not have the child. I will attend to it tomorrow."

She felt a faint shiver go through his body. "There will be some pain, Majella. You will be sick a day, or two days."

"It doesn't matter." She laid her face against his chest and felt his arms go around her. Perhaps she could fall asleep listening to the heartbeat of her beloved. *Mary, if I give up my unborn baby, please make them spare Joaquín.*

The next day the whole village knew that Joaquín was wanted, that there was a price on him. The news spread like a plague among them. Majella felt it; it seemed to shimmer in the sunlit space around the well when she went to get the water, and in the sudden silences when she came among people murmuring together. It was in their glances. The friendship had changed to fear. There was in the eyes of friends a mingling of fear and rejection, and sorrow because of it. Everything was strangely and subtly changed. Joaquín was a danger in their midst.

Majella put down the water jar outside the door of the grandfather's house. Leon was just coming out.

"Leon?" She couldn't look at him.

"Yes."

"I have decided not to have this baby," she said stonily. "Do you know where—I could find—" She faltered, hating herself for it.

"Benicia has some. Grandfather gave them to her three days ago. She has dried them on the stack of lumber."

She looked up into his hard rugged face. He had known that she was beaten. They had all known it. They had simply waited, with their hopeless, infinite patience, until she knew it too.

"Thank you," she said.

He gave the briefest possible nod, and walked away.

She turned and, feeling as if she were made of stone, she walked across the clearing toward Benicia and the stack of boards.

Chapter Eighteen

There *was* pain.

Joaquín had said one day. Or two days. *Oh, please, God, only one day of this.* Cramping such as she had never known before. Like some cruel, iron hand inside her body, clutching, gripping, twisting, wrenching. . . .

Oh, dear *God!*

Then the slow cessation of it. And she, not really believing it would cease—had ceased, cautiously letting herself go limp, letting her sweat-dampened body rest awhile before it came again.

And there were other things to worry about. Try not to let Joaquín know how much she suffered, as it broke his heart and shamed him because of his helplessness. Feel sorry, too, for the grandfather because this was happening in his house, of which he was so proud. In times past, a village had a separate house where a woman went at various times to attend to womanly things in privacy. Now the old times had fallen away, and there was no longer a separate woman's house. Or she might have gone to stay with Benicia—if Benicia had any house at all.

Well, so be it. It must take place here. She stayed as close to the wall as possible, and tried not to make any sound of pain. Well, at least not to cry aloud. Softly. Softly. Hold it back. Hold it in. Don't let them hear and be sorry and shamed.

Then there was the other matter, the fear. The fear from outside, because of the danger Joaquín posed for them. Time and again there were murmurs and muttering. Loud voices were raised in the clearing. There were arguments, hastily cut off. Quickly quieted comments inside the house. Trinidad came in with his face bloody from fighting with the friend of a lifetime. He had fought for Joaquín. But inside the grandfather's house, sitting all hunched over, blotting blood from his swollen mouth, he talked to Leon, thinking she could not hear. But she did hear. Where her beloved was concerned she would hear a whisper a mile away.

"He is right," Trinidad muttered. "I denied it to his face, but Leon, he is right. It is only a matter of time. They will come here. And when they come and find that we have hidden him—"

"Be quiet," Leon said grimly.

Then something else—something to break the heart of a mother. Her small son was aware of the fear. Aware of danger. How could that be so? It came to her on the evening of that first day that Mario, not understanding at all, understood the fear and had the sense of wrongness. So now, like a small animal in danger, he could suddenly fall

313

silent, stay motionless, blend in somehow with his surroundings until the danger passed him by. Born of the ancient wisdom of the helpless, and her son had it. He was learning. Back in Alonso's village, the day of the massacre, Joaquín had lain wounded on the bed in their tiny house and had said, *"Let him see. He must learn."* Now Mario, the happy, friendly little child, was changed. He sat quietly and soberly inside the house, usually as close to his father's legs as he could get. Now and then he played silently in some corner, but would soon be back beside Joaquín. How could such a small child—scarcely more than a baby—sense their desperate situation? Majella blotted sweat from her face with shaking hands and waited for the next pain, watching her small son across the house. He *did* know. Some instinct bred into him, into their people, from generations of suffering, had made him know.

Finally, when she could bear no more, her blood came and with it freedom from having this unwanted baby. *"I'm sorry,"* she muttered, speaking senselessly as she cleaned up, speaking to the unborn, the never-to-be-born. *"Forgive me. Forgive me."* And even this must be hurried because of the urgency to get up, to clear away the mess. Despite the sickness, the weakness, she must *move*. She must *not* lie back and rest. Something was happening outside, which she must see. Not go out. Oh, surely not. But lurk just inside and—at least—see what was happening. She could hear it. She had been hearing it all morning. The clearing was full of villagers. They should not be in the clearing at this time of day, but in their houses, or going about all the things they did in the day, not

314

standing, glowering, grim and muttering, all the men together in the clearing.

With many pauses and much faltering, she did what she had to do and crept to the door to watch. Little Mario was there, too, almost hidden behind the water jug, his somber eyes fixed on the group in the clearing. So quiet he didn't even appear to be breathing. Joaquín stood just outside the house entrance. Thank God she could not see his face.

Leon and the grandfather stood before him, well into the clearing. It seemed that Leon had just come there, that he had been some place else. He paused there and stood, legs slightly apart, arms hanging relaxed at his sides, somewhat away from his body. He didn't seem to be moving his head, but she knew those small, all-seeing black eyes saw every man there. When he spoke he did not raise his voice at all, but they all heard him.

"You want a council about this? Is that why you are here?" He waited a moment. "Then, sit." He made a gesture.

The grandfather began it by immediately sitting down on the ground, his legs crossed, hands resting easily on his bony knees. It was a pose that spoke clearly to all the other men. It said, *My grandson, Leon, is the Headman of the village.* It said, *Listen to my grandson Leon.*

Joaquín remained standing where he was, and she realized he was not going to sit down as the others began to. Then she knew why. He was not part of the council in his home village any more. He was outside. And it was so because his friends of a lifetime were shutting him out—because they had to. It was a matter of survival.

She should weep for this, but no tears came.

Her eyes remained dry. She wondered how many
Indian women long dead or now alive or yet to be
knew this silent, inner, dry-eyed weeping, this silent grief, this hidden, bitter mourning for all they
lost and all they never had. She mourned for her
husband who stood rejected by his own. She
mourned for her child who sat instinctively quiet,
like a tiny hunted creature. She mourned for the
grandfather who was too old to be the Headman
any more. She mourned for Leon, who could
never be the Headman because his personal loyalties ran too deep. He could never think first of the
village and second of his friend. She mourned for
the people themselves because they had to choose
between surviving and casting out one of their
own, and then live with the shame and sorrow of
it.

One of the older men spoke. "Let Feliciano
speak. He was the Headman before. He always
spoke with wisdom."

"I gave it over to my son," the grandfather said,
sounding firm and resolute.

"Your son is dead," the man said.

"I gave it over to Leon, my grandson," the old
man shot back. "Listen to Leon." It sounded convincing despite the thin, rasping old voice.

The murmur died away and they waited for
Leon to speak.

Dear God, let him sound reasonable, Majella
thought. She remembered how he could sound so
reasonable and convincing when he argued for
something he wanted. Persuasive, relentlessly persistent.

He did well now, speaking quietly, with cour-

316

tesy and underlying force, appealing to their friendship with Joaquín, reminding them of the many raids on which Joaquín had gone with much danger to himself, and recalling how generous he had been with the proceeds. Some of the men agreed, nodding and murmuring from time to time, for they loved Joaquín dearly, respected him, had been friends with him since childhood. But in the end it came down to the one question Leon could not evade, although he tried: Was Joaquín's presence among them a danger to the village?

The answer—inescapably—was yes. The brutal fact they could not escape was that Joaquín's continued presence was a threat to them all. Pablo's father was the chief speaker for those who opposed Leon.

"It is not just the woman's family any more," he said stubbornly. "It is the Americans. They offer a reward. They have it on the poster. It is only a matter of time until someone comes here. And they will be angry that we hid him. They could kill us all."

Leon's patience snapped. "And I will kill you if you don't hide him."

There was a quick intake of breath from the men assembled, an invisible coalescing of their will against Leon. He had made a mistake, and he knew it instantly, sensing their withdrawal, but there was no way he could unspeak the words.

"You see what you drive me to?" he asked after a moment, speaking into a wall of silence. "You set me against my own people. This is very bitter for me—for us all. But that is the way it is. That is the

317

way I am. My spirit is such that if you give up Joaquín for them to kill, I would have to kill in return. I could not help myself."

"Let us hear Joaquín," Pablo's father persisted. And immediately a murmur swept the crowd. There was a sense of relief.

"Joaquín is sick. I speak for Joaquín," Leon said.

"No, Leon. Let me speak for myself." Joaquín went to stand beside his friend.

"There must be no bad blood among our people because of me," he said steadily. "Leon is my friend, my brother, and he wants only to protect me, but the village must not suffer because of this. You have said that my woman's family is no longer the danger. I will go, but let me leave my woman and son here safely a while—until I can find a place for us. Will you do that if I go?"

Majella gripped her hands over her mouth. She must not cry out. Must not protest aloud. Never! Never would she stay here and let him go alone. Never.

"Be quiet!" Leon said savagely. "Don't listen to him. He speaks from the fever." He turned to Joaquín again. "Go inside! You are still sick. Go inside! Lie down on your mat!" He grabbed Joaquín roughly and pushed him through the door of the house. Still weak, there was no chance that Joaquín could stand against Leon's strength. He fell back through the entrance opening, down into the house, and groveled about a moment on the earthen floor, trying to get up.

Majella caught his arm. "Wait," she implored. "Wait, please." He shook off her hands and went outside again.

Pablo's father now had the upper hand and pushed his advantage. "We must not quarrel among ourselves," he pleaded. "Joaquín is our friend since childhood. Joaquín can decide. His heart is steady and wise. He will do what is best for us all."

There was a rising murmur of agreement among the men and the beginning of movement. They were fearful and angry and wanted to put this painful thing behind them. Joaquín had said he would go. Trust Joaquín to do what was right. Men started rising to their feet.

"Wait," Pablo's father raised his voice. "Joaquín, think of this tonight. Let us meet again tomorrow and you tell us what you have decided. And we will talk among ourselves about letting the woman and child stay. Let us all meet again tomorrow."

It was a wise suggestion. They were glad to escape, to put off for another day this casting out of one of their own. A possible danger from the woman's family—and they had not come again, had they?—must surely be a lesser danger than from Joaquín with a price on his head. Let Joaquín go then, but let him leave the woman and child. Thus they placated their heavy, guilty hearts.

As the men left Leon turned and faced Joaquín. "You should not have done that, Joaquín," he said.

"You should not have," Joaquín returned, his eyes hard.

"Wait. Say no more." The grandfather struggled up from the ground and put his hands on Leon's arm, looking up at him. "Do not speak in anger—

either of you. Come. Come inside. Let us think about it."

Joaquín went back in as the old one had asked, but Leon turned and walked sullenly away from the house. Majella knew instinctively that he was humiliated because he had not been able to force the villagers to his will, and that he was sick with fear for his friend.

Without even glancing at Joaquín or the old man, she picked up the water jug and walked out of the house. She had no intention of stopping at the well. Watching Leon cross the clearing, she put the jar down near the well and followed him. He was heading straight for Pablo's house. Stubborn Leon. He never gave up.

"Leon?" She said his name without raising her voice but he heard her. "Please don't turn around. I want—to speak to you secretly."

Without pause Leon went steadily on, out beyond the rim of houses around the clearing. She followed him. Beyond the village was a rising of the ground, and beyond that a wide depression, sandy and strewn with rocks and coarse dry growth. When he knew they could not be seen from the village he stopped and turned, waiting for her.

Her legs were shaking from weakness and she sank down onto the warm sand. She had not realized how much of her strength had diminished during the hours of pain and the flooding out of her blood. She wiped a film of sweat from her face.

"What do you want?" Leon squatted down before her. "You should have stayed in the house.

320

You are still sick." His black, intent eyes were on her face.

"I will be all right in a little while," she said grimly.

"If you are worried about Joaquín, do not be. I won't let him go. As weak as he still is, he wouldn't last very long."

She sighed. "Leon, thank you for what you tried to do. But you cannot stand against the whole village. You can't kill them all."

He picked up some sand and let it run through his fingers.

"I won't have to," he said in his deadly calm voice. "One. Two at the most. They are rabbits. When they see Pablo's father dead on the ground at their feet they will do as I say. No man will want to be next, so they will give in. They will let Joaquín stay and hope for the best. Rabbits." His voice was contemptuous.

"Will they?" She was surprised at the hardness in her own voice. Mama had taught them to speak softly, gently, as befitted Papa's daughters. She closed her eyes. *That was long ago, Mama. Before I knew what I know now. Before I knew hunger. Before I knew fear for my beloved. Before I could wash out my child with my blood. Too long ago, Mama.*

"What do you mean?" His hand, holding the sand, was motionless.

"Think, Leon. How long could you keep the whole village under your will? There are forty or more men. You cannot watch them all, all the time. How soon will one slip away and go into the town? They will finally come to think that the only way to get rid of Joaquín will be to inform on him. Isn't that true? Then it is only a step further for them to think that if someone will be paid the money, why not someone in the village? Joaquín will die anyway. This village is poor—you have no idea how poor, Leon. Why shouldn't someone in the village have something from it?"

"You are speaking of your husband's life, woman," Leon said softly.

"I am telling you what the village men will be thinking. They can't help it, Leon. Don't hate them for it."

He sighed and looked off into the distance.

"Isn't it true? Isn't that what will come to them?"

"I suppose so," he admitted. "They will let you and Mario stay—Joaquín got that much out of them. I could go with Joaquín. Maybe we could—" He paused, looking at her again. "You are thinking of something else? Some other way?"

"Yes."

A half-smile twitched his mouth. "I always said you were not stupid. What is it?"

"Take me back to my people."

Astonishment flashed in his eyes a moment. "You said you would not go back to them. And what good would that do for Joaquín now?"

"I don't mean to stay there. I mean to see them. To speak to them—let them know what has happened. I—"

He stood up, casting the rest of the sand from his hand.

"You tried that, Majella. And your people would not listen to you. Alonso lost his whole village because of it."

"I don't mean that." She rose up on her knees, catching hold of his arm. "Listen. Hear me out."

"All right. I'll listen."

"Sit down," she said grimly. "It hurts my neck to look up."

Smiling a little, he sat down cross-legged on the sand, sending a lizard darting away. He reached over and flicked a red ant off her skirt.

"Leon, I think there is a chance they will listen now. My brother Miguel is dead. Hernán—he is the younger one. His angers are violent and soon over. I think—I think *now* he might listen to me. I think *now* I could convince them. And you know they have jewelry that is mine. They know—they must realize now—that I will never leave my husband and my child. I want to face them one more time, there in my sister's house, without twenty restless armed men milling around. You know, my brother-in-law is a peaceful man. He was not shooting in Alonso's village. He was trying to stop it."

"Yes. Alonso said that," Leon agreed.

"There, in the house, talking quietly to Eduardo and Hernán I can convince them. I *can*." She gripped her hands into fists and leaned on them, pushing them down into the sand.

"Convince them to do what, Majella?" Leon asked, almost gently.

"Make them let me have what is mine. We have to leave here—I know that. But with money we could go to Mexico. Joaquín would be safe there. It doesn't matter where we live—all we want is a place, some secure land, land that belongs to us. Don't you see? I can make them do it, Leon. *I know it.*"

323

"And you want me to take you to them."

"I could never get there by myself. You know that."

He nodded slowly. "What about Joaquín?" He sounded uneasy. "Joaquín would never permit—"

"I know that," she said desperately. "I—you would have to do it without his permission. You could do that, Leon. You *could*," she insisted. "Couldn't you?"

"Yes," he said slowly.

"The other men might help you in that. Might hold him here, if they thought it was a way of getting him out of the country. Away. Away and safe."

"No need," Leon said thoughtfully. "I can make him go to sleep. Put something in his food. He would sleep two, three days."

"You will take me there?" She felt breathless and light-headed.

He gave a brief silent laugh. "I said you would be the death of us. What happens if your kinsmen ride out to meet us shooting? How much good will I be to you dead on the ground?"

"They won't—don't you see? There won't be time. We just go there. Right up to the door without warning. No letter beforehand. They won't be expecting us. There won't be twenty armed men waiting. I will just walk into my sister's house. It all went wrong before. This time it won't. *I won't let it.* I will make them understand. I'll make them." Her words were chips of granite.

"I believe you might," he said finally, "now." It was an unspoken acknowledgment that he knew what it had cost her to deliberately induce the miscarriage of her pregnancy. And he knew that it had unalterably changed her. She had a swift insight into how he must have changed over the years of his life, slowly evolving until he was the man before her now—hard as stone and without ordinary compassion, so that he clung fanatically to those few loves he had. A man who had lived with—could never escape from—a deep anger, and it sickened his soul, was killing him slowly. She herself must not become like that. She must—somehow—stem the tide, salvage what was left while there was still time.

"Then you see," she went on urgently, "when I have the money I can get Joaquín away, safe to Mexico—"

"All right." Leon lifted his hand. "I called Joaquín a fool. But I'm a bigger one. I'll take you there."

"Oh, Leon!" Suddenly she melted. "Thank you. Thank you, Leon." She caught his hand between her own and pressed it to her face. "Thank you."

"Don't do that," he said roughly. He stood up, looking down at her. "Tonight? Could you travel tonight?"

"Yes?" Despite the sickness, the weakness, the wrenching blow she had dealt her body, she agreed. They must go as soon as possible!

They looked at each other silently. Enemies since the beginning and now strangely allied.

"Leon, what about the men of the village? They said they would talk again tomorrow. We'll never get there and back by then. Will they wait?"

He looked thoughtfully toward the houses. "I'll go and tell them—I'll go and ask them. I think they will if it is a chance for Joaquín. It only means giving a little more time."

She watched him go, moving with his slow, in-solent grace, hating the task, hating the men in the village for their fear. Mean, crafty, cruel Leon, whose rare loves ran too deep. Willing to risk his life for his friend. Was it because he was brave? Loyal? Or because he really didn't care very much whether he lived or died? She and Joaquín must not become like that.

It was a long time before she could force herself to get up. She felt weak. Sick. Her body was leaden. She could sit here a moment longer on the warm sand. Rest. Sleep. Die, perhaps.

No. Get up. Move. Now.

Chapter Nineteen

Cecilia was stunning in her mourning garments, a sober study in black and white, and not really aware of it. She sat silently in her chair, the lamp-glow casting just enough light to show the smooth black hair in the widow's peak on her pale forehead, the gray shadows beneath her closed eyes. She might remind one of a revered masterpiece painting, a dim brass plate beneath inscribed with the picture's name—*Lady in Sorrow*, perhaps.

Forgetting now that a lady sat erectly with her spine unsupported, Cecilia had leaned limply against the back of the chair. She had even shut her eyes—unforgivable conduct when her husband was talking to her.

I can't help it, she said silently in her mind. *My eyes hurt. Thy burn. They are tired. Too many tears. Too many tears*. It was almost time to go to bed anyway. Soon she could hide in the darkness, not pretend any more.

"May we smoke, my love?" Eduardo asked.

"Oh, yes, of course." She spoke without opening her eyes. "Please do. I love the aroma of your cigars." This was not true, but it was what one said. Let the men smoke if it eased them. It was little enough. This brought her thoughts to Hernán—and she was sorry, because it recommenced in her mind the continual worry over him. He was so strange these days, as if the light had gone out of him, leaving only grim darkness. It was in the laxness of his quick nervous hands, in the dull lackluster of his eyes. It was as if the death of Miguel had left an echo in Hernán. She had not realized before that her brothers had been so close because their differences had been so many. There was so much she had not realized. Well, Majella had always been the quick and clever sister.

It was because Hernán was alone.

The idea smote her mind and grief clutched anew at her throat. *No more tears, now.* But he *was*. Completely alone. Soon—or sometime—he would return home to Mexico. He had said so, many times. "I really must be going soon," he would say dully. "I really must go home. There is so much to do. The estate . . ." Then his voice would dwindle and die, the thought unfinished. Then soon—or sometime—when he left to return to Mexico he would be all alone there. Their parents so long gone now, and Majella, his beloved Majella, as good as dead. And she herself, married to Eduardo here in California. Poor Hernán. Poor little Hernán. So involved with his family, and now they had all gone and left him. She tried to hold off the thought, keep it at bay. Think of something else.

The men's cigar smoke began to drift about the room. It was chilly on the patio and they had stayed inside this evening. She tried to breathe shallowly because of the smoke. Why didn't they talk? They didn't even talk much any more in the evenings. It had all been said, so many times. She moved slightly in her chair.

"Does the smoke trouble you, my dear?" Eduardo asked in gentle concern.

"Not at all," she lied quickly. "Not in the least."

"We could go outside to finish, Cecilia. Shall we?" Hernán asked, seeming to rouse himself from his lethargy with an effort.

"No. No, please." She lifted a pale hand. She would have added something else but there seemed to be a disturbance outside. There was the sound of horses coming. Then, at the approach of visitors, the sudden activity of their people—soft thudding of bare feet running, a shouted question and answer—some of the dogs started to bark.

"Now, who in the world—" Eduardo muttered. He looked at the red glowing tip of this thin cigar, clearly wondering if he should put it out. Hernán looked at his brother-in-law impassively, not really interested, no matter who it might be. Cecilia didn't even open her eyes. One still had a few moments time. A servant would come.

"Yes?" Eduardo spoke, and Cecilia reluctantly opened her eyes and sat straighter. The servant had come.

"Some men, Señor. From Los Angeles."

The servant's noncommital tone and no mention of names or relationships told them these were strangers, probably foreigners—that is, not Mexicans. Not their own kind.

Eduardo got up and placed his cigar gently on an ashtray. This would take no time at all.

"I'll come with you," Hernán said as a matter of course.

The two men walked outside with the quiet reserved air of courtesy that could so quickly shift into insolent disdain if the need arose. In the half-darkness they waited as the party of riders, three mounted men, approached. They were walking their horses now, and well they should for the horses had been ridden fast and hard. They came to a milling, heaving stop in the yard before the house. Eduardo lifted an arm in greeting.

One, apparently the leader, took off his dusty hat. "Good evening," he said in English. "We are deputies from Los Angeles. You are Eduardo Obregón?"

Eduardo looked at the men blankly and replied in Spanish. "We do not speak English." He did speak some English, and understood more, but Hernán did not and he had no intention of embarrassing Hernán by shutting him out of what must be a casual exchange of comments.

There was a grunt of contempt and the man turned to another of the party. Lack of a common language was always a barrier between the Mexican and the American, each clinging stubbornly to his own.

"You are Eduardo Obregón?" The second man asked in Spanish.

"I am." Eduardo's tone was icy.

"We are sorry to trouble you, Señor, but we have been deputized by the authorities of Los Angeles. We are looking for the Indian, Joaquín Salazar, a—" He stopped, quickly groping for another word. "—a connection of yours. Is he here, Señor?"

"He is not."

"Do you know where we can find him, Señor?"

"The last I saw him, he was in his village down—"

"I know where the village is—was, Señor," the man interrupted. "The Indians had to clear out of there. The townspeople—"

"What do you mean?" Eduardo asked sharply. "Where did the Indians go? I mean, the women there. Where did they go?"

"They followed their men, of course. What else could they do?" the man snapped, his patience wearing thin.

"Well, what do you want of me?" Eduardo snapped back, his voice just as sharp. He would take no nonsense from them and he let his manner show it.

"We are hunting for Joaquín Salazar," the man replied, moderating his tone. "We thought we'd just ask here since you know him. If he's not here, and you know nothing of him—" he let the sentence trail off.

"Why do you hunt him?" Eduardo asked.

"Murder. He's wanted for killing a Mexican. Miguel Moreno. In that village."

There was a quick intake of breath from Hernán. Eduardo moved just enough to touch him, willing him to keep silent. But Hernán did not.

"I am Hernán Moreno. Miguel was my brother."

There was a swift exchange in English among the men. "Well, then," the one said in Spanish.

"He couldn't be here, could he?" He sounded embarrassed.

"One moment," Eduardo said, lifting a hand. "Who said Salazar killed Señor Moreno?"

"Everybody. The authorities. There is a poster out. A reward is offered. A dozen posses are out looking for him. We—somebody will find him. Tonight probably. Tomorrow at the latest."

"So much zeal when a Mexican is killed?" Eduardo asked.

The other missed his point and answered matter-of-factly. "Can't let the Indians start getting out of hand. First time this has happened for a long time. Got to stop it. Make an example."

"And on what do the authorities base their—" Eduardo was starting to protest, but Hernán spoke quickly, forestalling him.

"He is not here," he said sharply. "I suggest you look elsewhere."

It was unspeakably rude. Even while Eduardo understood that Hernán spoke from the depths of his anger and grief, it made Eduardo regret that the old days were gone. In the old days, any stranger on your land deserved your courtesy. Those days were no more.

They watched the three men ride off. Then Hernán turned to Eduardo. "Were you going to tell them he didn't do it?"

"Yes," Eduardo said. "Impulse, I suppose, since he didn't. He may be guilty of many things, Hernán, but he did not shoot Miguel."

"I know that," Hernán said. "It is one of the things that tears me to pieces—I don't know who *did*. There was so much shooting. The shot came out of nowhere—everywhere. It was all over in a second. Miguel was standing there. Then he wasn't. He was on the ground."

"Hernán, spare yourself, for God's sake."

"I can't." He shook his head. "Never mind. Let it be. I'm all right. Let's go inside."

"Hernán, a moment please. Doesn't it matter to you that it *wasn't* Salazar? Those men who just left—deputies or not—are killers. Others are out there. If they find him, they will kill him. No trial. Nothing like that. That's the way it is done here. He's as good as dead when they find him."

"Well, is that supposed to make me grieve?"

"But he's innocent, man." Eduardo was almost pleading. "And he's Majella's husband."

The two stared at each other in the increasing darkness, straining to read each other's faces. They were kinsmen, bound in the unbreakable ties of family, but on this they were at odds, and it pained them both.

"I am sorry if it offends you, Eduardo. You are my elder and my sister's husband, but the sooner that renegade is dead the better I will like it. I mean no disrespect to you in saying it."

Eduardo reached over to touch the other man briefly.

"It isn't a matter of disrespect, Hernán." His voice was husky. "It is that *he* is your sister's husband, too—Majella's husband. She loved him enough to—"

"Forgive me, Eduardo, but Majella is—not responsible any more. She is—deranged. Miguel said so." He shivered. "Let us go inside—it's getting cold out here. Cecilia will wonder." He waited politely for Eduardo to precede him.

Eduardo sighed, re-entering his house, knowing

that the quick ears of the servants had picked up the conversation, wondering where in the vast expanse of California Majella might be tonight, regretting that the old times had gone. These were harsh times, ugly times. Inside he paused, waiting for Hernán, and together they went to rejoin Cecilia.

She was standing listlessly by a small table.

"Who was it, dear?" she asked without interest.

"Some men from Los Angeles," Eduardo answered.

"Are they being taken care of?" She turned to look at them.

"No, we sent them away." Eduardo sounded apologetic. "We couldn't help them."

If this surprised Cecilia she did not reveal it in her smooth face. She wandered about the room, going vaguely in the direction of the large framed mirror before remembering that it was covered with black drapery, because of the mourning, so she wouldn't see her reflection in it. Her gaze passed absent-mindedly over the closed piano. No music either. It was still too soon. Not for many weeks. Proper respect was important. It was the very least—

"What did the men from Los Angeles want?" she asked, turning back to Eduardo. She sat down, and both men did also. These were the long days and the long nights of mourning. They would never end.

"They were looking for someone. A criminal," Hernán said. "They stopped to see if we knew anything about him."

"What an outlandish idea. Why would we

know—" Something in his tone made her suddenly wary. "Hernán, what sort of criminal? Are you holding something back?"

Eduardo sighed. "There were three deputies from Los Angeles. At least, they said they were deputies. They were looking for Joaquín Salazar—Majella's husband."

A visible tremor went through her.

"Now, please don't be upset, my dear. We sent them away."

"But why? What have they to do with him? With Majella?"

"He has been accused of—being responsible for Miguel's death."

She sucked in her breath. "Was he? Why didn't you tell me?"

"No. No, my dear." Eduardo went to her quickly. "It wasn't like that. It was as Hernán told you when we came back. We do not know whose shot it was—"

"But it is his fault," she said breathlessly. "He caused it. He caused it all to happen. Everything from the very beginning! It doesn't matter whether he actually—"

"That's what I thought!" Hernán said. "With my apologies to Eduardo, I cannot be detached and judicial about it. He is guilty whether he pulled the trigger or not."

"Well, in any case," Eduardo said calmly. "They have gone. They will either find him or they won't."

Cecilia stood up, sliding her arm through his. She was frowning slightly, her gaze puzzled. "If they are looking for him around here it means

335

they aren't where they were—in that village—any more. Why did they leave that village? Did the men say? Did they run away?"

"Yes, in a way. I was hoping you would not ask. There is no way you can help her," Eduardo said. "The townspeople made them go, it seems. I suppose because of the shooting."

"It couldn't have been much of a village left anyway," Hernán said. "Some of the houses were afire. It might have all burned away before night."

"But, Eduardo," Cecilia said uneasily. "That means Majella and—and that Indian, Salazar, had to find some place else to live. I wonder where. I don't like that. That worries me. Eduardo, at least in the little village—terrible as it must have been—she had a place. She had somewhere to live. And the baby. What about her baby? Was the baby all right when you men left the village?" She felt a rising sense of guilt because she had only just now remembered Majella's baby. Certainly, she should have thought of the baby before now. What kind of woman was she? What kind of mother would she make? Maybe that was why none of her prayers were answered.

Hernán spoke thoughtfully from the other side of the room. He had wandered over to a narrow window.

"He was hurt, you know. That renegade Indian of Majella's. He had blood all over him. Maybe he's already dead somewhere."

"Hernán!" Eduardo said in exasperation. "May I remind you that your sister has already been too deeply shocked by this series of tragedies?"

"I'm sorry. I spoke without thinking. I apologize."

"It doesn't matter," Cecilia said. "Nothing really shocks me any more." She went over to her younger brother, looking carefully up into his face. "Do you think he was badly hurt, Hernán?"

"I don't know." Hernán said hopelessly. "I had just realized—about Miguel. I don't even remember looking at Salazar. It's just that it stays somewhere in the back of my mind that he—was there. And he was bleeding. That is, there was blood on his clothing."

"I hope he's dead!" Cecilia said. Then, quickly, "No. I didn't mean that. That's a sin, isn't it? A mortal sin? I don't wish anyone dead. I don't know what I wish!" Restlessly, nervously, she turned away from her brother. "Now what is that! All that noise? Have those men come back?"

Both men noticed the noise now too.

"There was no reason for them to come back," Hernán said.

"Let's go and see." This time Eduardo rolled the glowing tip of his cigar in the ashtray. He frowned. "Where the devil are the servants?"

Leaving, both men moved quickly. Curious, Cecilia followed them silently, as far as the front doorway, where she stood well back in the shadows. The men would handle it. The lady of the house must not expose herself to the view of ruffians. It was quite dark now.

"Pedro? Raúl?" Eduardo called out to servants. "Where are you? Bring some torches! Lanterns! Bring some light here!"

At a little distance there was unseen activity,

people, questions and answers sounding unintelligible, muffled sounds from horses. Two torches appeared from opposite directions, casting pools of reddish light on the ground. They moved and danced over bushes and rocks and part of the house wall. A lantern was brought from another direction.

One of the servants ran up to them. Pedro.

"Two people came, Señor. Indians, Señor. We will send them away. Do not trouble yourself to stay out here in the cold."

"What Indians?" Eduardo's voice betrayed quick apprehension.

"A man and a woman, Señor. We will—"

"Wait a moment! I will look at them." Eduardo strode forward, aware that several more servants had arrived from various places, aware that Hernán was only a step behind him, aware that Sergio Vasca, one of his armed vaqueros, had suddenly appeared at the edge of the flaring light.

The Indians had dismounted. The man held the reins of the horses and the woman walked slowly toward him. Her face, drawn from exhaustion, was clearly in view a moment into the dancing light: Dirty, streaked with sweat, eyes wide and a little glazed.

"Majella?" he said softly in wonder. "Majella! My dear! Where in the world did you come from?" Quickly he went to her and took her in his arms. "My dear girl. My dear girl."

There was a swift dark shadow running up to them. Cecilia had caught the sound of her sister's name.

"Majella!" she cried. She rushed up to her sister, reached out to her, almost touched her. "Oh, Majella. You came back!" Then, sharply, she stiffened and recoiled. "*Majella*! In the name of Heaven!" It was a cry, a wail of angry disgust. "Our brother is dead. Couldn't you even manage to wear a decent black dress for proper mourning? Have you no heart!"

Chapter Twenty

Majella, suddenly aware of how she must look to the stricken gaze of her sister, took an awkward step backward, and bumped into Leon.

"Do you wish to go home?" he asked in their own tongue.

"No."

"Cecilia!" Eduardo never spoke sharply to his wife, but he did so now.

"I—I'm sorry," Cecilia stammered. "It is just that—that you look so—so—poor."

"I am poor," Majella answered. "I am also hungry and tired. I think if this were Mama's house she would invite us in."

"Oh, yes. Yes, please. Come in. Do come in. Eduardo?" Distractedly, Cecilia turned to her husband. "What—" She was obviously uncertain about the silent Indian standing just behind her sister.

Eduardo stepped forward and held out his hand. "Joaquín?"

"No," Majella answered. "Joaquín is sick. He is back at the village. This is Leon Troncoso—our friend. He brought me here so I could come safely."

"Thank you," Eduardo said. "That was very good of you. Please come in. My wife will send for some refreshment."

With just a shade of hesitation Leon extended his hand in response to Eduardo's gesture.

"Take care of their horses, Pedro," Eduardo said. The servant, eyes gleaming with curiosity, did so. The servants would have much to discuss this night.

"And this is my brother, Hernán," Majella said. Hernán bowed stiffly. He could not, or would not, speak, nor extend his hand.

Again Leon spoke to Majella in their language. "I will leave you with your family. I can go some place else. I'll wait."

"No." Leon must not fade back into the darkness, to beg something to eat from some Indian servant. Never. He deserved better than that. "Please come inside. It will be all right. We both need food." He gave the faintest shrug and followed along as they entered the house.

Inside her own home Cecilia's composure began to return. She sent a servant away with instructions to lay out a meal. Majella knew she was doing the best she could. They were indeed a strange-looking group, as they stood awkwardly together for a moment in the sitting room after the servant had scuttled away. The three Mexican aristocrats dressed in their elegant mourning clothing. The two Indians in worn and ragged odds and ends of clothing, not good enough for any of the servants here, and none too clean after the journey.

"Let us all sit down," Cecilia was saying valiantly. "Majella, my dearest, are you ill? You look so—" The only word she could think of was *haggard*, but she didn't want to say it.

"I have been ill," Majella said, sitting down slowly on one of the velvet chairs, thinking of the sickness of yesterday—or was it the day before? She couldn't remember really.

Feeling oddly detached from them all, she watched as both Eduardo and Hernán seated themselves. Leon's restless eyes flicked over the richly furnished room. Apparently he could not bring himself to use one of the gleaming velvet chairs, as he selected the wide ledge of a nearby window. She knew he was watching her. In his own way he had been very kind to her, and he was determined to bring her back to Joaquín ailve. Twice she had fainted on the journey here. Neither time had he permitted her to fall from her horse, so careful had been his watchfulness. He had insisted on stopping to sleep when she had wanted to push on.

"I am so sorry," Cecilia was saying. "Would you like to go to your room? To rest? Sleep?"

"No. No, thank you, Cecilia. We must talk first. I must explain why I came back after—after what has happened."

"Why did you, Majella?" Hernán spoke for the first time, his voice oddly soft and tentative, as if he could not quite believe what was happening here.

"I came back because you are—were—my family. And despite everything, all our differences, I trust you still. I must trust you. I cannot believe that you would abandon me."

"Did we abandon you, or did you abandon us?" Hernán asked.

"I could not accept the conditions you laid down for me. By then I had loves and loyalties I could not betray. A wife cannot abandon her husband. A mother cannot abandon her child. I am sorry I caused you such pain, but always and forever my first loyalty must now be for my husband and child—it doesn't mean I love you any the less." A slight shudder went through her. It was more difficult than she had thought it would be. There was a terrible aching emptiness because Miguel was not there. Hernán's face was a study in anguish.

Eduardo got up uneasily. "You shiver. Are you cold?"

"No, thank you. Let me go on. We have been allowed to stay in Leon's village—Leon has been good to us. Now we have to go. We have learned that Joaquín has been blamed for—for Miguel's death." She leaned forward, gripping the carved arms of the chair with tense, grimy fingers. "It isn't true. Eduardo? Hernán? You know it isn't true."

"Yes. Yes, my dear. We know," Eduardo said quickly.

"What I must have from you now—*must have*—are the jewels that Mama left me. That little chest—that awful little box of jewels—means the difference between life and death to us. I must have them because of my husband's safety. He has

343

been sick. He is recovering, but it is slow. Soon he can travel. Soon. We can't stay in the village any more because the others are afraid. So I—" She paused, her strength seeming to ebb.

"An abominable situation," Eduardo muttered. "Surely, something—"

"We couldn't even sell the jewels," Majella said. "Because we wouldn't dare. We are Indians."

Hernán got up jerkily from his chair. "Indians. I never thought—my sister—" He moved restlessly about the room. He suddenly turned to her, a touch of radiance in his face. "Majella, remember? Remember how it was at home? In the old days? With all of us—"

"But it isn't the old days any more," Majella said with infinite gentleness. "Hernán, it is today, and we must accept today when it comes. I am sorry—but my husband's life is at stake."

"Majella," Eduardo said kindly. "I should tell you that a posse of men was here just a little while before you arrived. They were looking for Joaquín."

"We know, Señor." Leon spoke remotely from the window ledge. He was partly in the shadow and his image was not clear. One saw the strong, outstretched legs and bare, callused feet; the ragged trousers, one leg shorter than the other; one hand that held a battered felt hat. "We hid from them and waited for them to go."

"My God," Eduardo said. He turned to Hernán. "Your sister has been leading a hellish life, Hernán. Are you listening well to what they say?" His voice was unsteady.

"Do you mean did I hear him say that Majella Moreno has to hide in the shadows with an Indian

344

because—yes, I heard." His voice shook. He turned his back to them. "I might just mention—meaning no disrespect since it is clear where your sympathies lie—that Majella Moreno might have been the wife of Luis Chavero, living in ease and peace and luxury. If my sister Majella hides from the law in the shadows, it is her choice."

Majella ignored this. She turned her desperate eyes to her sister. "Cecilia, you do have my jewelry here. Isn't that right? You said you intended to bring it back with us from Mexico."

"Yes. Yes, of course," Cecilia stammered. "I did, certainly. And it is yours, certainly. Mama said so. I—Eduardo?" She turned frantically to her husband again. "I'm sorry—I can't seem to think straight." She whirled to face Majella again. "Oh, Majella, dearest. Wouldn't you like to wash? I could lend you some clothes. I would love to—"

"Thank you, Cecilia. I know you mean to be kind. But let us discuss this matter first."

Eduardo put his arm around Cecilia's shoulders and patted her, but his eyes were on Hernán's back.

"Hernán?"

"Yes?"

"Will you do me the courtesy to turn around and face me when I talk to you?"

Slowly, Hernán turned. When he did they saw that his face was pallid and tears were coursing down his cheeks. "I hate this," he said through his teeth. "I hate this."

"The servants—" Cecilia said faintly, because one of them had entered the room, and stood uncertainly at the doorway, not knowing whether to come in or to leave.

345

"What is it, Manuel?" Eduardo asked calmly.

"Someone has come, Señor. An Indian, Señor."

There was a strange, rather long silence in the room. Then Leon rose from his place on the window ledge. He seemed poised, waiting.

"Who is it?" Eduardo asked. "Did he say his name?"

Sudden knowledge leapt into Majella's mind.

"Could it be Joaquín—my husband?" she asked, hardly realizing she spoke aloud. Even as she said the words she knew that—somehow—Joaquín had followed them, and was outside. "Bring him in, Manuel," she said.

The servant quickly withdrew and the silence fell among them again. Eventually it would end, and Joaquín would stand in the doorway. It was almost exactly as she thought it in her mind. Indeed, in a few moments he did stand there. The only difference was that he had Mario with him, and a small bundle.

He stood there unsteadily, for he had ridden long and was still weak from his illness, not to mention the drugs Leon had put in his food. Very, very slowly, he released his grasp on Mario and let his little son slide down the side of his body until he was on the floor. Wide-eyed and silent in this strange place, Mario pressed himself against his father's shaking leg. Then Joaquín relaxed his other arm and let the small bundle fall to the floor. He passed his tongue over his dry lips and looked at them with his great burning eyes, in his gaunt, sweating face. His long, black hair hung down damply onto his shoulders. He looked as if— any moment—he would collapse into a heap in the

346

doorway. His eyes found Leon, and he spoke to him in their language.

"You should not have done this, my friend."

"I had to. I am sorry." Despite Joaquín's obvious exhaustion and weakness, Leon's stance was wary, as if he half expected Joaquín to leap at him. "I am sorry," he repeated.

"Majella—is this—?" Eduardo murmured.

"Yes. This is my husband, Joaquín Salazar." Majella stood up. She wanted to go and stand beside him. She had the terrible fear that he would fall down and she knew this would humiliate him. Meanwhile, she was saying the correct words. "My sister, Cecilia—Señora Obregón. My brother, Hernán Moreno. My brother-in-law, Eduardo Obregón—you remember, from Alonso's village?" Some part of her mind wondered in dim astonishment at the tableau they must present to the servant who lurked in the doorway behind Joaquín.

Leon walked closer to the group, his eyes still on Joaquín.

"What happened? How did you come to be here?"

"I threw it up—that which you put in my food. When the sleep came, I knew it wasn't my sleep— so I made my body throw it up. Then I made the grandfather tell me where you had gone with my woman."

A near-smile touched Leon's mouth. "Let your woman alone, Joaquín. She's trying to save your life. She may do it."

Joaquín's burning gaze passed slowly over the people in the room. "We will go," he said in Spanish. "Come, Majella."

347

"Where will you go?" Cecilia asked, her voice quavering slightly. They were startled at this. No one had expected Cecilia to say anything.

"I am going. I will take my family—" Joaquín tried to answer. His legs started to buckle and he grasped the door frame for support .

"Sit down, man!" Eduardo pushed forward a chair. Joaquín sank into it.

"Jesus," Hernán whispered. "Look at the poor devil. He's almost dying on his feet. My God—" He turned away, wiping his face, shaking his head. "All right, Majella. I can't stand against this. Do whatever you want and we'll help you." His voice was muffled.

"You will help me?" She couldn't have heard right! She got up and took a faltering step toward Hernán.

"Yes. Anything you want."

"I want those jewels sold. I want the money. I want my husband safe in Mexico."

"All right. All right. Anything." Hernán's resistance had collapsed completely.

"Manuel!" Cecilia cried sharply to the servant. "Help him." The servant was quick and caught Joaquín as he sagged forward out of the chair.

Suddenly life flickered back into the group. They must all help the exhausted man, fighting against the remains of the drug he had been given, fighting against the long ride he had made. Somehow, milling about, all talking at once, they managed to get him down the hall into one of the lower-floor guest rooms.

Joaquín stretched out on the bed, his eyes dreamy and drooping shut. At some point during their progress to the room a servant had said that a late supper had been laid out in the dining room. When it was clear that Joaquín was all right and they could leave him, they all did except for Majella. She lingered a few minutes. Alone with him, she leaned over the bed and took one of his hands in hers.

"It is all right, beloved. They will help us at last. You will be safe. We will be safe. You understand that? And don't be angry with Leon for bringing me here—he was thinking of you."

He was looking up at her, his eyes not quite focused. She couldn't be sure he understood, but she felt a slight compulsive tightening of his fingers. Then his eyes closed as he gave up the long struggle to stay awake. She listened a slow moment to his even breathing and then got up and left the room. She held out a hand to Mario, but he climbed up on the bed. He would stay with his father, a small watcher.

She slipped quietly into an empty chair before Eduardo and Hernán had a chance to rise, and reached out an unsteady hand for the delicate crystal wineglass. She sipped the wine slowly. In a few minutes, perhaps, she would eat something. She had been so famished for so long, it seemed, on the long ride from the village. Leon was eating—thank God, he would at least get a good meal out of this. She would ask Joaquín about giving him some money, but Leon was such a strange man—she understood him so little that she would not offer it herself. Leave it to Joaquín, who knew his friend. She sat there, silently observing them. What a strange sight they all made at Cecilia's lovely table. Such a thing had never happened before and she knew, with understanding, and without bitterness, that it might never happen again.

Leon and Eduardo were seated directly opposite each other. Twice Eduardo made some cordial comment to his strange Indian guest, and Leon replied with a glint of humor. How odd it all was. The two men were similar in many ways—both strong, quiet men whose loyalties ran too deep for comfort. Similar men but from different worlds. What would Eduardo have been today if he had been born an Indian? Or Leon if he had been born a Mexican aristocrat?

She tried now to eat, but the acute hunger of the journey seemed to have passed. Accustomed to never wasting food, she made herself chew and swallow a little of the tender venison. She did better with some vegetables and fruit. She tried a bite of preserved pear, but the sweetness made her throat ache—she had not eaten sugary foods for a long time.

Little tremors moved through her body from time to time. Somehow or other the sense of security she had anticipated had not come. Where was the joy she had expected? Where was the elation? She had lived too long with fear and dread. She looked again at Leon, eating for the first time in his life at a table spread with white linen—what a story he would have to tell the grandfather. She had an impulse to smile but it did not reach her lips. She was still too tense. But it was all true. She had beaten down her family's resistance. They would help her dispose of the jewels, help them get to Mexico. Joaquín was safe. *Safe.* They could buy a bit of land there far away from any of the cities. Joaquín's wisdom and kindness and strength being passed on to Mario and—if God permitted now—their later children. It would be good and simple—her throat tightened. She wanted suddenly to pray.

Then the sounds came, alien and ugly in the peaceful scene. Someone else was out front. Many, it sounded like. The sounds of horses, voices raised in challenge, anger, the pounding of bare feet running, the opening and slamming of the big front door. Protests. A scuffle.

All three men were on their feet. Eduardo and Hernán clearly angry at the disturbance. Leon, silent, wary, ready for anything.

A servant tumbled into the dining room.

"Señor!" He staggered frantically toward Eduardo. "A posse! Many men. Many. They demand—"

He didn't get to finish. There were sounds of more struggle in the front hall. In quick, quiet rage Eduardo strode out of the dining room. Hernán was at his heels. Leon came to Majella. Together they moved with silent Indian tread to the hallway door to see what was happening.

"What is the meaning of this!"

Several men, roughly dressed, dusty from long riding, milled about in the hall. Among them were the three who had stopped earlier. At the icy, arrogant rage in Eduardo's voice, some hats were taken off and a brief silence fell.

"Answer me!" Eduardo snapped. "How dare you force your way into my home!"

There was a growl from the intruders, a shuffling of boots against the flooring. One of them stepped forward.

351

"We are looking for the Indian, Joaquín Salazar."

"You were here before," Eduardo said grimly. "I told you then he was not here. Now leave! Go! At once!"

"Señor." The man also spoke harshly, wasting no courtesy on this Mexican, rich though he might be. "We've since been told that an Indian man and woman came here—to this house. Where are they? That was Joaquín Salazar and his squaw—*wasn't it!*"

Majella felt, rather than heard, the swift intake of breath from Leon. He moved closer to her. She knew he was thinking the same thing she was. Someone on the rancho had informed. One of Eduardo's servants had seen the two of them come in, had recognized her, had thought the Indian with her was Joaquín. The servant had known of the posses roaming the countryside. They could follow the reasoning—*someone* would turn Joaquín in—*someone* would be paid. Joaquín was going to die anyway so—

She crossed herself quickly, shrinking back against Leon. *Oh, God, dont let Joaquín hear and awaken. Don't let Joaquín come out and reveal himself. Keep him hidden, God. Protect your son, Joaquín.*

She turned to face Leon, and a shudder of near-panic went through her body. He took hold of her, gripping her arms.

"Don't," he whispered. "Be silent." She could barely hear him. She looked up into his broad face, into the small black eyes with God-only-knew-what memories and with strange wisdom behind their gleaming surface. "You have won,"

352

he went on almost soundlessly. "Be patient now. You have won a chance for Joaquín and yourself, so wait."

The men in the hall pushed forward.

"Señor! We demand that you turn over Joaquín Salazar!"

"He is not here!" Eduardo shouted, but he was being pushed back. "Manuel! Pedro! Get some of the men!" He meant armed men and they knew it. They could get them but it would take time, precious minutes, to find them.

Raúl, another servant, darted up behind Eduardo, holding a pistol in his hand.

"Stop right there!" One of the intruders leveled a rifle at him and Raúl stopped, looking sick.

"Drop it!" The man lifted the barrel of the gun slightly higher. In another moment Raúl's blood would splatter the hallway.

"Drop the gun, Raúl," Eduardo said. The servant obeyed.

"Do you deny that Indian is here?" the man demanded.

"Yes! I deny it! Now get out!"

"Stand back! We'll search the house. If he's not here then we'll go. If he's here—we'll take him. And there is nothing you can do about it. He's wanted. Now get back!"

Majella went sick. They were heading for the dining room, attracted by the pool of light that fell through the doorway into the hall. They were coming in here.

"Go!" She whispered frantically to Leon. "Run while you still have a chance. They won't do anything to me. It's Joaquín—" Then she stopped. The sense of what they had said was penetrating her mind. They would search the house. Find Joaquín.

It was too late, anyway, for the men surged into the dining room, pushing Eduardo and Hernán along with them, and the servant, Raúl.

"Well." The crowd shuffled to a stop as Leon and Majella moved out of their way. The men peered over one another's shoulders, looking at the two Indians. "What have we here? Señor, are you going to tell us this is not Joaquín Salazar?"

Leon stepped forward in his slow, insolent grace as Majella watched him in disbelief—horror—grief.

"I am Joaquín Salazar," he said.

"By God, I knew it!" The man said exultantly. He swung his rifle, hitting Leon on the side of the head. Leon staggered, but did not fall down.

"No!" All eyes in the room turned to Cecilia, who still stood at the table. Slim, beautiful, her face chalky, her eyes blazing blue fire at this invasion of her home. "*That* is not Joaquín Salazar! Let him *alone*! He is our—our—our *dinner guest*!"

Even in the outrage and terror of the moment Majella felt a swift sense of sympathy, of pity—poor little Cecilia, never quite—

"All right," the man snarled. "Is he, or isn't he?" He turned to the trembling servant, Raúl. "Who is this Indian?" he demanded.

Raúl tried twice to answer and could not.

"The squaw—ask the squaw." This was muttered from several men. The leader turned to Majella. She was sick. She wanted to hunch herself over and creep silently away. Leon said a brusque word to her in their own language. It was one of the words meaning "Stand up," the one meaning "like a tree, with majesty."

"Well, what about it? We'll find out anyway. Save yourself some trouble!" He lifted his hand to strike her. Hernán lunged forward, both arms outstretched, to protect his sister. Another of the intruders lifted and swung his heavy rifle, bringing the butt end of it down with a sickening blow across Hernán's arms. Hernán buckled, falling forward, a sound of gagging in his throat. He staggered a few steps and straightened up slowly, both arms hanging limp.

Oh, dear God, they had hurt Hernán. Time seemed to stand still.

Majella looked at them all, saw them all too clearly, it seemed. A small muscle in Eduardo's cheek quivered spasmodically. Hernán looked as if he might vomit. On Cecilia's face was a look of dawning horror. A small stream of blood ran down from Leon's ear. The side of his face was swelling.

"I am Joaquín Salazar," he repeated deliberately. His gaze locked for a moment with Majella's. He was giving her Joaquín's life. They both knew it. Accepted it. And he was doing it the way he always did things—with grace and insolence. He wouldn't even lift his hand to wipe the blood from the side of his face. He wouldn't give them the satisfaction.

Leon would die.

Or Joaquín would die.

Oh, God, don't make me do this. Even as she thought the words she walked forward, with quiet dignity, holding her back very straight—a little tribute to Leon—and stood in front of him. She

355

looked up into his implacable face. And she lied. Trading Leon's life for Joaquín's.

"Yes, this is Joaquín Salazar, my husband." Then in their own tongue she added, for Leon, "Forgive me."

Triumphant, the men were closing in. She would never know if Leon answered her. Being Leon, he might have or he might not have. They grasped him and started dragging him toward the hall.

She sprang after them. She couldn't stop herself. "Wait!" she screamed. "Wait! I—want to tell him something! I want to speak to him!" She stumbled and fell, and staggered to her feet. She followed them into the hall, pushing aside Eduardo's restraining hands. "Please! Oh, please!"

As they took him out the big front door she caught a glimpse of Leon's face, saw the familiar twist of his mouth, half-smile, half-grimace. One never knew which.

"Let him go." Eduardo caught her, pulled her back, held her as the door slammed shut. "Let him go, girl. It was—what he wanted. It was his decision."

She stopped struggling against Eduardo. She wasn't thinking of Eduardo, hardly aware of him. She was listening intently to the sounds from beyond the heavy door. The muffled shouts, curses, the horses. The men mounting up. Riding away. Taking Leon. He wouldn't make it easy for them.

Then they were gone. Joaquín was safe. Joaquín's magic fingers would work the soil around the corn seedlings. And he would do it in their village. In the home place. Leon had given them that. He had paid their way back to the village.

356

"Are you—all right?" Eduardo could hardly speak.

"Yes," Majella said. "Thank you, Eduardo." Then it seemed she must explain to him. "We will not have to run away to Mexico now, you see. We can go back to Joaquín's village."

"Yes," he said brokenly. "Whatever you want."

Gently, she disengaged his hands and moved away from him.

"Where are you going, Majella?"

"I am going to my husband," she said. "I want to wait beside him until he is awake. I want to tell him about Leon."

"Oh, God, do you have to, Majella? The man was his friend."

"Yes." Nothing in the simple answer could tell them of the terrible grief Joaquín would know at the loss of his friend who loved him better than life. And these people did not know of the deep enduring strength in Joaquín that would make him walk on through it. "I have to tell him we are going back to the village. We have to take care of the grandfather. Joaquín has to work in the field."

Majella started down the hall, her ragged dress swinging about her bare ankles, moving like a queen. Almost as if speaking to herself, she added softly, "We are going home."

Epilogue

Majella shucked the dry outside husks from the newly picked corn. She enjoyed this task. It revealed the inner, still-moist husks of palest yellow-green. She ran her fingers pleasantly over the cool ridged surface, and plucked off some strands of creamy corn silk. Then she laid the ears in neat rows in the wooden crate. This was the last box.

Los Angeles was growing—there were many more stores and shops there now. Every other day Trinidad drove the village wagon into the pueblo, loaded with village produce for the two stores they supplied on a regular basis. Majella looked up and smiled at the two women who were helping her prepare this load. Even so, she still regretted the loss of Benicia, who had died in her sleep several years ago, as quietly and gently as she had lived. Benicia's large, gentle hands had had a wisdom of their own in working with the vegetables. She had learned much from Benicia. They had, however, salvaged something from this loss. Alonso moved into the grandfather's house and as the two found much to discuss in their ancient years, neither was lonely.

Mario darted in under the shed and Majella looked up. Mario, at thirteen, was big for his age but withal as quick as a fawn. "A wagon is coming. Some American settlers, Father thinks. Is the corn ready—Trinidad says they might want to buy something. He says bring some out by the road."

"Yes, it is ready. Take this box along," Majella said, pushing back a damp strand of hair and watching his strong young shoulders as he lifted the crate easily and almost ran from the shed. She wished he would pay more attention to his lessons, perhaps, but she could never fault his willingness to do his share of the work. From the beginning Mario had been the child with a wellspring of inner happiness that showed in his sunny disposition and ready friendliness.

There were a total of seven children in the village now—three of their own—and Majella taught them all. She had to smile at herself, remembering her early expectations that Mario would surpass all the others, only to learn to her aggravation that Trinidad's little girl seemed the smartest of the lot.

The villagers had been pleased at her willingness to teach all the children to read and write, and there had been a surge of enthusiasm for learning. On the advice of the grandfather, several adults asked Joaquín to teach them English. Since it was the Americans' land now, the grandfather reasoned, it behooved them to learn to talk in the American manner. He pointed out that when it had been the Mission Fathers' land they had all learned to talk in Spanish. His logic was unanswerable and several adults, including Majella, were now comfortable in English. It had been a good idea. Two of the men had gotten town jobs because of it and it helped Trinidad in the produce dealings.

"They might like some grapes—it's such a hot day," one of the women suggested.

"Yes, they might." Majella glanced up, but Mario was out of sight over the rise. "I'll take them," she said, and picked up a shallow crate. Joaquín had put in the grapes soon after they had moved back to the village. Pablo had brought the shoots from his employer's grape arbor in Los Angeles. The vines had been bearing now for several years.

She walked through the village, which never failed to give her a sense of pride. Joaquín, as Headman, had a kindly, pleasant forcefulness that made the other men do their best, it seemed. Somehow, with Joaquín to turn to, life was no longer such a fearsome journey for them.

Eduardo, with substantial financial aid from Hernán and the Moreno estate, had not only secured the village's title to the land, but also had acquired an adjacent tract, which permitted the truck-farming venture. The village was comfortably self-sustaining. There was now a sense of order, a steady, purposeful busyness. Repairs were made as needed on the dwellings. Several new houses had been built, including their own, as well as the big, airy produce shed.

As she walked up over the top of the rise she saw that two wagons had stopped at the side of the road. There was a never-ending flow of incoming settlers. The Americans had gotten down from the wagons to walk about and stretch their legs. Majella put down the crate of grapes near the other crates that Trinidad had arranged at the roadside. The American women were picking out what they wanted, glancing at her curiously. She heard some of their comments. They were indeed more settlers, and had bought some land sight-unseen farther on. Where did they all come from? How many were there? There seemed no end to them. Perhaps someday they would fill up the whole country—it seemed hard to believe, but Joaquín expected it. It did not trouble him and he said, as he always did, "Don't borrow tomorrow's grief—enjoy the day."

Without betraying that she understood them, Majella started back toward the village. She heard the men thanking Joaquín for giving them directions, and they asked his name. One said he was keeping a journal—now, that was a good idea, to keep a journal. If one had the time.

"My name is Feliciano Troncoso," Joaquín said, using his present name. Cordially, he sent the people on their way.

Majella never did really understand the almost mystic preoccupation her people had with their names, but accepted simply that for them names had a special significance. There had been much thoughtful discussion about it when they had returned to the village. Joaquín, deep in his grief for Leon, had not taken much part in it. But he could not, the men decided, continue with the name of Joaquín Salazar because Leon had taken it with him to his death. Nor did they think it safe for him to take Leon's name. Leon, of the dark and angry heart, might have left many debts and obligations unknown to them that Joaquín might be called upon to pay. So it was decided that the grandfather would give over his own name to Joaquín. Trading or giving one's name was not unknown among their people, if the reasons warranted it. "And I won't need it much longer," the old one said quite sensibly. Joaquín had been Feliciano Troncoso from that day. Except that, in her own heart, Majella would always think of him as Joaquín.

The grandfather, no stranger to grief in his long years, withstood the blow of Leon's death in his own way. When told, he simply sat down on the ground and curled over into a small bony heap, totally silent. Majella wanted to help him into the house, but Joaquín shook his head. "Let him be," he said. "When he wants to go in, he will." This was true, for sometime during the night they heard him creep in, making sounds like a small creature who did not see well in the dark. He was silent and did not eat for several days, staying on his mat under his blanket. Then one morning they awoke to see him sitting by the firehole, kindling the blaze. Majella pushed off the blanket and went quickly to him. "Are you all right, Grandfather?" He seemed more fragile and emaciated than ever. "Yes. I have said good-bye to Leon." And from that day he was his old self.

Although Joaquín had his own house, he and Majella still spent time talking with the grandfather in the long twilight evenings after the work was done. This was almost ritual, for he had been reminding them for several years that he did not have much time left and they should visit with him while they could. Tonight, the children played a rowdy game in the failing daylight in the clearing. Majella sat contentedly near Joaquín, only half listening to the men's talk.

There was easy laughter now and then—the grandfather was telling again the now-familiar story of how he had awakened himself laughing in the nighttime because of his name being given to Joaquín. This had been before Joaquín's house had been built and they had still been living with him. The old man had awakened them in the deep of night with his cackling laughter. Wheezy with mirth, he had told them of his dream. He had long ago forgotten that when he had been born the authorities had written it down. Now, since he had given his name over to Joaquín, nothing else would be written down about it on the records until it came the time for Joaquín to die, many years away. So when the final entry was made, it would look to the authorities as if Feliciano Troncoso had lived years and years beyond his rightful time of dying.

"Let them puzzle it over," the old man said gleefully. "Let them wonder. Wonder is good for the soul."

As many times as she had heard the story, Majella laughed because the grandfather's manner of telling it was so droll. She glanced over to her husband, hoping he would laugh, too. Joaquín had moved steadily through his grief, and had come to terms with his sorrow with his own special dignity, but his times of solitude were deeper, and his laughter rare.

Aware of her, as always, he felt her gaze and

turned to look at her. Then he reached over and took her hand. She was suddenly breathless, knowing—in just a moment—she would see that which she always cherished, Joaquín's slow smile.

MORE
BEST-SELLING FICTION
FROM PINNACLE

More Bestselling Fiction from Pinnacle

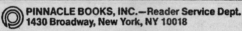